'Nostalgia-time dedicated to famous ghosts of the silver screen'

The Observer

'This book pulsates with superlatives, "wild conjunctions" of mating, liquor in "giant tumblers", the city "the hottest piece of real estate in the Orient" – all those within ten pages'

The Times

'A different and most enjoyable read'

The Sunday Telegraph

'A good keep-you-with-it yarn'

Irish Times

'A splendid action-pack'

The Citizen – Gloucester

'A breath-taking book of the highest category'

Liverpool Daily Post

'It's got everything ... Atmosphere as strong as old socks. A delight'

The Scotsman

About the author

John Gardner was educated in Berkshire and at St John's College, Cambridge. He has had many fascinating occupations and was variously a Royal Marine officer, a stage magician, theatre critic, reviewer and journalist.

The Creator of the Moriarty Journals and the Boysie Oakes series, John Gardner has written his latest novel in the wake of the hugely successful thrillers, *The Nostradamus Traitor*, *The Garden of Weapons* and *The Quiet Dogs*, and his three James Bond adventure stories, *Licence Renewed*, *For Special Services* and *Icebreaker*.

Flamingo

John Gardner

CORONET BOOKS
Hodder and Stoughton

Copyright © 1983 by John Gardner

First published in Great Britain
1983 by Hodder and Stoughton Ltd

Coronet edition 1985

British Library C.I.P.

Gardner, John, *1926–*
    Flamingo.
    I. Title
    823'.914[F]   PR6057.A629

ISBN 0–340–36026–7

Printed and bound in Great Britain for
Hodder and Stoughton Paperbacks, a
division of Hodder and Stoughton Ltd.,
Mill Road, Dunton Green, Sevenoaks,
Kent (Editorial Office: 47 Bedford
Square, London, WC1 3DP) by
Richard Clay (The Chaucer Press) Ltd.,
Bungay, Suffolk

All hope, promise and illusion lay ahead.
SHANGHAI . . . the Paris of the Orient!
SHANGHAI . . . the Home of the Homeless!
SHANGHAI . . . the Haven of Undesirables!
SHANGHAI . . . The PARADISE OF ADVENTURERS!

Shanghai, The Paradise of Adventurers, G. E. Millar
(Pseudonym: Diplomat. Pub., circa 1939)

AUTHOR'S NOTE

I have to thank my old friend Simon Wood, who searched libraries and bookshops, to come up with a most impressive list of titles, providing me with the historical and social background for this piece of fiction.

Also I must thank the Regent Cinema, Wantage, where this book really began, in the late 1930s and early '40s.

During those years I usually attended this place of 'worship' at least three times a week: for those were the heady days of double features, and three changes of programme a week (Mondays, Thursdays and a 'special' on Saturday mornings). The films I most enjoyed, and saw time and again, were those glorious black and white adventures, set in the Orient or thereabouts, peopled by soldiers of fortune or heroes with dark secret backgrounds, wily villains, gruff mystery men, a comic sidekick and at least one wonderful woman.

Since then, I have always wanted to write an adventure story set along the lines of those movies. So, with respect, the following pages are for, or in memory of –

. . . Mr. Humphrey Bogart; Miss Lauren Bacall; Miss Lizabeth Scott; Mr. Peter Lorre; Mr. Sidney Greenstreet; Mr. Akim Tamiroff; Mr. Mischa Auer; Mr. S. Z. (Cuddles) Sakall and Mr. Hoagy Carmichael. Together with a cast of thousands.

PROLOGUE

In 1588, when invasion by the Spanish Armada was immi-
nent, the people of England organised a chain of warning
beacons which, if the invasion had occurred, could have
sent news of it from one end of the country to the other.
In 1940 there was a similar plan, to be activated if the
threatened Nazi invasion should come: in that case the bells
of every church in the land would have been rung.

Such related and elementary lines of communication had
been set up over three centuries apart even though, in the
years between, Marconi had invented the radio; Alexander
Graham Bell the telephone; and, more important still, Sam
Morse had created a simple telegraph system. It would seem
therefore that, when the chips are down, people distrust
technological advances: they prefer to rely on their eyes and
ears to warn them of impending danger.

Nevertheless, before the end of the 1920s, for the ordin-
ary, day-to-day conduct of life the telegraph and cable
business was the most used method of long-distance communication throughout the world. Messages were trans-
mitted and received on a piece of equipment which looked
no more sophisticated than a slightly complicated type-
writer. The message tapped on to a keyboard at one end was
turned into electric impulses which were sent by land-line,
radio, or by undersea cable. Over certain routes the signals
had to go by all three methods, but at the other end a similar
machine automatically decoded the messages, clicking
them out in their original typewritten form. The technique
was almost as rapid and efficient as it is today.

By the year 1931, when this story begins, cables crossed
and recrossed the world in their thousands. Between July
and August of that year many hundreds were sent and
received in the great international port of Shanghai. One
such arrived for a certain elderly Chinese gentleman from

one Vincent Maes in Miami, requesting a meeting and reservations to be made at the Cathay Hotel in Shanghai for Mr. Maes, his brother, and two associates. The reservations were to be for the twenty-fourth of August, and for an indefinite period thereafter.

Already, for a man called Harry Byrd, danger impended. But, in the absence of warning beacons or church bells, he was unaware of it.

At the beginning of August there was a further cable, sent from the Telegraph Office at 8 Rue Gluck – behind the Place de l'Opéra in Paris – to the manager of the Cathay Hotel, reserving a room, also for an indefinite period and also starting on the twenty-fourth of August. That particular cable travelled via the Great Northern Telegraph Company, which had a traffic office high up in the large building complex known as Sassoon House, the bulk of which was Shanghai's most exclusive hotel: the Cathay. The cable was signed by a Mr. Waldo Bingham.

Danger, therefore, for Harry Byrd. But also, had he known it, a possible saviour.

A couple of days before the twenty-fourth of August, a radiogram came into the office of the Peninsular and Oriental Steam Navigation Company on Canton Road. It was a routine message from the company's liner SS *Empress of Asia*, the purser checking that accommodation had been reserved for passengers staying over in Shanghai on the ship's arrival, which was scheduled for the twenty-fourth. Among the several passengers listed for rooms at the Cathay were the names K. Morrow and T. Geddes.

For Harry Byrd: danger, a possible saviour, and now more danger, but of a different kind; emotional danger; danger to the fragile structure of the new identity that he had built up painstakingly, piece by piece. And still, unhelped by eyes or ears, he was unaware of it.

On the evening of the twenty-third of August the assistant manager of the Cathay Hotel would almost certainly have looked through the many arrivals listed to check in on the following day. He might have noticed that among these were a number of passengers for the SS *Empress of Asia*, but the names Morrow and Geddes would inevitably have meant little to him. As would Waldo Bingham, due in by train from Peking. As also would Vincent Maes and his party, arriving by plane.

Seven people – among many – came into the Cathay Hotel on Monday, 24 August, 1931: Vincent Maes, his brother, and their two colleagues; Waldo Bingham; also passengers Morrow and Geddes. Although the lives of some of them had already crossed, not one was to know that their lives would cross again, there in Shanghai. But they all arrived on the same day, and went to the same place. Coincidence? Yes, but where would an adventure be without that long arm that hovers between luck and fate?

BOOK ONE

The Flamingo

— (1)

In the Chinese calendar late August is known as *chu-shu* – the Stopping of Heat. Harry Byrd reflected that someone should make a drastic revision of the colourful Chinese climatic timetable, for the sun and humidity were as fierce now as they had been from *hsaio-shu*: The Slight Heat, in early July. The heat showed no sign of abating.

As so often happened, the city seemed to be pausing for a moment in the pearly moist atmosphere of mid-afternoon. It was a phenomenon of Shanghai: this time when, even if only for a few brief minutes, the place appeared to take a deep breath; when the eternal racket of the streets became less intense, and the constant sound of music from the shops and daytime cafés seemed to quieten.

It usually occurred just before the linen-suited taipans came down from their offices to take rickshaws, or big motors, back to their wives (often via their mistresses), or to the jaded bonhomie of bachelor apartments.

Harry Byrd awakened at this time of lull on the afternoon of Monday, 24 August, 1931. Only muted sounds floated up from the street, while from above him came the gentle, grinding slap-slap from the slowly turning fan on the bedroom ceiling. Reaching for cigarettes and his gold lighter, he thought – not for the first time – that he would have to get the bloody fan fixed.

The lighter flared in the gloom and he dragged smoke back through his teeth. The dry paper of the cigarette attached itself to his moistened lip, tearing the skin as he prised the white tube from its accustomed place. His little yelp of pain made Jeannie Chin stir beside him.

Dabbing irritably at the blood and exposed flesh, Byrd stretched back on his pillow and made shushing sounds in Jeannie's general direction. Far away, he could hear the buzzing of an airplane. Probably one of the China National

Aviation Corporation's new tri-motor German machines – the ones that looked as though they were made of corrugated iron – on its final turn over the city, inbound from Nanking, Peking or Canton.

He was also aware of a sudden eruption of hooting from the direction of the Bund, the great modern waterfront business area, and remembered that the *Empress of Asia* was due to dock that afternoon. Byrd smiled to himself, for the arrival of a big liner usually meant that the café downstairs would not have a spare table for a few nights. He had an arrangement with the head porter at the Cathay Hotel, and the Flamingo Café was on the porter's recommended list.

Unwinding an arm from behind his head, Byrd looked at his watch, tilting it to see the hands pointing exactly to four o'clock. He and Jeannie Chin had got to bed around six that morning: asleep by seven thirty. Eight hours was enough for anyone. Beside him, Jeannie moved again and moaned, her naked thigh touching his, starting ripples of pleasure around his loins, the area – he smiled again at the thought – which Chinese girls artlessly called 'middle-piecee'.

Turning his body, Byrd looked at her: long black hair spread over the pillow, the large oval eyelids closed without a flicker in dreamless sleep. Beautiful she certainly was at twenty-three years old; it was a shame that, with her mode of life and diet, Jeannie would be as fat as a little pig by the time she reached her early thirties. There were droplets of sweat, like a glittering rash, showing high on her forehead. Even in the half-light of the bedroom her complexion appeared more sallow than ever, and he could already see large pores in her facial skin.

He sucked more smoke in through his teeth and smiled again; this time at the girl's vulnerability in sleep. She had been an unexpected find, like most of his staff. A year ago now, after the explosive row with Molly Chow over the girls' bar chits. Molly had worked for Byrd from the start, supervising the girls: she had been educated by the Jesuits, but they apparently had failed miserably to teach her even the rudiments of honesty.

The girls, like all Shanghai café hostesses, got a percen-

tage on the amount of drinks bought by their partners –
particularly on the champagne, purchased at astronomical
prices. It is the same the whole world over, and always will
be.

For quite some time now Byrd had known somebody
was fiddling the girls' bar chits, and that only one of two
people could be responsible – Max the diminutive barman,
or Molly. It was certainly not Max, so Byrd set a small
entrapment for the girl and came up with irrefutable evidence. The last thing he wanted was to lose Molly; she was
too good with the other girls; so he got her into the office
one evening and presented her with the facts, and paperwork, simply as a friendly warning; whereupon, however,
Molly lost her temper and told him that no white bastard,
who rooked his customers anyway, was going to call her a
thief. With that she was off – goodbye for ever, and no
decent senior girl to oversee the hostesses, except perhaps
the Russian beauty, Arina Verislovskaya; but she was unpredictable, with a will and a life of her own.

About an hour after Molly had flounced out, Jeannie
Chin flounced in, all paint and powder and slit skirt, with a
young taipan in tow – a new American resident who had not
been in the city for more than a week. The taipan became
very drunk, insulted Jeannie and then spoke to Harry Byrd
as if he were a coolie.

Byrd personally threw him out, instructing Max never to
serve the young man again. The American taipan, like
everyone else, had to learn that it took time for bad be-
haviour to be accepted in Shanghai – unless you were just
passing through and did not know better. With residents
acceptance took time – except, of course, for Harry Byrd
himself, who was his own law, and had ridden the devil into
the city three years ago, breaking all the rules of protocol.

Within a week of his arrival he had bought and paid in
cash for the property which stood at the point where
Nanking Road turned mysteriously into Bubbling Well
Road; had designers and workmen installed three days later;
and opened the Flamingo Café the following month with
everything in order, including his own six-roomed apart-

ment – 'above the shop' as he liked to say.

Three years, a lot of nerve, even more luck, chance meetings and a nose for bribing the right people, had put Harry Byrd among the top bracket of Shanghai café owners. He felt that he had a right to be pleased with such progress.

Later, when he had a chance to look back on that hot afternoon, he was to doubt if he would have felt so happy with his lot had he known that both the airplane and the ship, heard in the distance, were coincidentally bringing his past irrevocably into the present. While the train just coming into Shanghai South Station, inaudible, of course, from the dim bedroom, was bringing with it yet a third coincidence.

Jeannie stirred again, and he propped himself up on one elbow, preparing to kiss her. She had shared his bed since the night he kicked the young taipan out of the café: by the following evening, even though she had not been educated by the Jesuits, which Byrd considered a distinct advantage, she was working for him as senior girl.

Since her sixteenth birthday, Jeannie Chin's education had been undertaken in the ballrooms and cafés of Shanghai. Byrd knew nothing of her family, except that she had once mentioned her brother had been a Communist – whether lost or gone underground since the General-issimo's purge, she did not say. She had come up river from Woosung to make her fortune, and basically Jeannie was a peasant village girl, thinly varnished by Shanghai café sophistication, and therefore far more dependable than any Molly Chow.

He began to kiss her awake.

A loud knocking at the outer door of the apartment put an end to any further delights, and with a resigned and good-humoured sigh, Byrd climbed from the bed, wrapping a silk robe around his nakedness.

He picked up the small automatic from the bedside table, placing it in the pocket of his robe, fingers curled around the butt. He always kept a weapon within reach – carrying a pistol wherever he went. Shadows from his past held no active terror for him now, but he remained alert, conscious that, to stay alive, he had to keep one eye always on his own back.

In the main living room, stale with last night's cigarette smoke, the drapes were still drawn, and he dragged one set back as he crossed towards the door, letting the dusty sunlight into the room.

The knocking became more urgent.

He kept the chain on the door, so first viewed the Chinese boy through a crack of about four inches. The boy was taller than average for his race: muscular and elegant, clad in loose trousers and an exquisite purple jacket of diaphanous Canton silk. Below his sleek cap of black hair the boy's face was serious, as if his mission were a concern of life or death.

Even had Byrd failed to recognise the boy, he would not have been misled by the expensive clothing. Canton silk, as all old Shanghai hands knew, covered a directory of sins, for it soaked up sweat without leaving a trace. The boy was a servant, even though he might like to pass himself off, to inexperienced taipans or tourists, as someone rather more important.

"Lee Yung?" Byrd stated the boy's name like a query, as though uncertain of his identity.

Lee Yung gave a small bow and then arrogantly placed a hand on the door, as if to push it from the chain. "Master say pay you talkee chop-chop." He almost certainly spoke better than the pidgin English he now affected, but having learned discretion from his master – the well-nicknamed 'Billion Dollar' Foo Tang – he would never use it to carry messages to someone like Harry Byrd.

Byrd did not react, simply asking curtly which way Lee Yung had 'come topside'.

There were two ways of getting to the apartment above the café: from the street door in Bubbling Well Road, or through the Flamingo itself, and Lee Yung immediately said he had 'come streetside'. Clearly he knew what was expected. It would have been outrageous for the Chinese boy to have walked through the café at any time, unless specifically invited.

Byrd nodded. "So your master wants me at his house chop-chop?"

The Chinese grinned. "He say you catchee one piece rickshaw chop-chop." The grin betrayed that he knew an insult was buried, as in a shallow grave, within the message. Possibly it comforted him for having been obliged to come in streetside.

Slowly Byrd unlatched the chain and leaned out, placing his fingers lightly on the boy's silk jacket, just below the neck. When he spoke, there was no anger in his voice – the words almost whispered in the slow American drawl which was as much of a trademark as his eternal cigarette.

"The day you, or your master, finds me catchee one piece rickshaw chop-chop on your say-so will be the day the Hong Kong-Shanghai Lions get off their stone asses and claw you to death." He gave Lee Yung a slight push, closing the door swiftly, and hearing the clear sound of spittle hitting the woodwork on the far side.

In Shanghai the big stone lions, sentinels outside the Hong Kong & Shanghai Bank on the Bund, were constantly touched and petted for good luck. Byrd laughed and turned back into the room.

In the bedroom, Jeannie looked bleary but was at least on her feet. As ever, her naked body gave Byrd a regiment of sensations. She seldom failed to rouse him sexually. On a cold day, he often thought you could warm your hands a foot from her flesh. Clothed or not, Jeannie radiated physicality. She had the longest legs he had ever seen on a Chinese girl: long, sensual, enticing. When fully dressed, Jeannie gave the illusion that her legs went on for ever: particularly when she wore the white evening gown, her normal uniform in the café. Now, without clothes, and the morning scent of sleep still musky on her, she presented the eternal challenge.

"Trouble?" she asked without looking at him, brushin her hair. During the year with Byrd her English had much improved. She had even developed some of the slight nasality of Harry Byrd's East Coast drawl, but she still had problems with the letter *r*.

"'Billion Dollar' Tang wants me. His boy Yung tells me chop-chop."

"So you go chop-chop like good taipan," she laughed.

"I go slow chop-chop." He crossed to her, cupping her breasts from behind.

Nobody in Byrd's situation would disregard an invitation, however phrased, from Foo Tang. The wealthy Chinese held too much power. Also Byrd could never forget that his own success in Shanghai was largely due to this underworld manipulator who lived in style among the fashionable and wealthy of the lush Jessfield Park area. Yet, however urgent Foo Tang's summons, the sight and smell and touch of Jeannie Chin was an unfought temptation to go chop-chop slowly.

Their love-making was always passionate, tinged at times with cheerful lewdness, for she was without inhibition, unlike so many of the Western women he had known who took their pleasures, he often thought, as though a prelude to execution. With Jeannie he could laugh and catch her sense of fun, both at the passion and the joy; for they giggled a lot, and were noisy – particularly Jeannie: to a point which sometimes caused him anxiety, lest the staff in the café below should think he was ill-treating her.

"You won't leave me, Harry. Not for tai-tai woman. Please," she whispered, and he lied to her as ever. No, he would not leave her. No, he would always be with her. Though he knew all too well that he did not love the girl, he was not a man to use women lightly, and he could only calm his conscience by the hope that she also knew he lied, but for the best, the gentlest of reasons.

They lay in each other's arms for some time, Jeannie whispering words, half Chinese and half English, proclaiming her devotion. "Foo Tang waiting," she finally whispered, disengaging herself; getting from the bed to run his bath.

He lit another cigarette, slowly got up and went to the wall telephone which connected with the café, cranking the handle to alert Max in the bar. Normally the little Mexican acted as his chauffeur, but he would be busy now with

Herman and Casimir, setting up things for the evening and night rush. The café would be safer if he left Max to keep an eye on things, getting one of the senior boys to drive him.

He spoke for about thirty seconds, telling Max to give the keys either to Koo or Hang, who could both handle the shining black Delage coupé with adequate skill. Jessfield Park, he told Max: ready in twenty minutes, glancing through the window across the now struggling and crowded thoroughfare to make sure the motor was in its usual place. He paid four street children to keep an eye on the car, and they did more than that: the impressive Delage always appeared to gleam like a mirror even in the dustiest summer.

He bathed and shaved quickly, catching sight of himself, full-length, in the mirror, thinking briefly that his body looked in good shape for a man of his age; while the leathery face appeared to be more interesting than the one he vaguely remembered when he left America three years before, exiled for ever from a life which diminished in memory so that, now, there were times when he could scarcely connect his present self with the man he had been.

As he wiped lather from his face, so half-recalled dreams of the past flooded through his thoughts: childhood in Britain, the move to America, the house on the hill and knowledge that his father held power as an accountant of great repute; playboy at Harvard; the Great War; the Air Corps; longing to be where the action was and never getting there; playboy again and final capitulation: joining the old man's firm; then the desire for action again, leading to unease, then terror, and the events which caused his present exile. The present was not so bad; it was the past which locked in the nightmares.

Jeannie came in to rub him dry with fresh towels and help him dress – the silk shirt, open-necked, blue contrasting with the light grey shantung suit and soft moccasins made for him by Hwa Foong in Carter Street. Putting on his jacket, he came out into the main room, now full of light, the curtains drawn back and windows down to let in what small breeze found its way up the funnel of the street.

As Jeannie handed him his wallet, lighter and cigarette case, Byrd cranked the wall phone, telling Max he would be down in a minute.

The gold link was undone on his right shirt cuff, and he stood at one of the tall windows, looking down and across the street while Jeannie struggled to fix it – playfully slapping his wrist, telling him to hold still.

He saw Hang, short and on the heavy side, crossing the road towards the parked Delage, swinging the keys in his right hand, strutting a little as if proclaiming to the world that he was on an important errand.

For a moment, Hang was obscured by a passing tram, clanking down into Nanking Road, jammed full; laughing Chinese hanging on to the platform. The tram passed: Hang opened the door of the Delage, climbing in as Byrd began to turn away.

The flash came a split second before the blast, so that Byrd had time to push Jeannie on to the floor just as the whole building shook with the explosion. The windows were open, so did not shatter, and Byrd's head was up again quickly.

Thick black smoke clouded upwards, swirling in constant motion, changing patterns and shapes. A section of the car's roof appeared to hang motionless, almost level with Byrd's window, before lazily turning to start its fall, while the rear section of the car cartwheeled backwards. With the unpredictability of explosions, the front of the Delage remained intact, oddly tilted on its front wheels, as the rear, splintered, ripped and shattered, continued to slide back along the kerb.

People had been lifted, rolled and hurled around the street and there was broken glass scattered about. Byrd had a vivid sight of two young Chinese, almost stripped of their clothes, laughing hysterically with fear.

Then the gas tank went up, sending a sheet of flame over the street, enveloping a lone rickshaw, its puller and passenger already blown clear; mercifully, for the flimsy vehicle went up in a crackle of flames, its wood and bamboo collapsing like a badly built bonfire.

Byrd tried to take in the extent of the damage: people still screaming, others moving, picking themselves up; nobody lying in that sinister stillness which indicated death or serious injury. He saw an old woman, huddled on the kerb, her black loose trousers frayed and burned by the fire from the gasoline, body rocking to and fro as she wailed in pain.

Hang staggered, dazed, from the untouched front section of the car; already Max, and some of the other boys, were running from the café to help him. Any minute now, Byrd knew, both the Shanghai Municipal Police and the French Police would arrive – probably both fire brigades as well, their co-operation being gratuitously zealous along the boundaries between the International and French Settlements.

He lit another cigarette and looked at Jeannie, who stood bundled up at his shoulder, white-faced and shaking with shock.

"Guess it's going to be a bad evening," he said aloud. Then, almost to himself, "This is where Harry Byrd catchee one piece rickshaw chop-chop."

二 (2)

A little earlier, the big Junkers tri-motor Byrd had heard on waking taxied in over the dusty field which was Shanghai's aerodrome, coming to a stop beside the straggle of huts that served police, customs officials and the major lines which used the field – the China National Aviation Company, Pacific American Airways and the Eurasia Aviation Company.

The Junkers had flown in from Canton with a few Chinese businessmen, several American and English tourists, three diplomatic officers and a party of four men who were now nearing the end of a long business trip, bringing them – by train, ship and air – from Miami, via San Francisco, the British Crown Colony of Hong Kong, and Canton, where they had completed certain business arrangements before leaving for Shanghai.

Their passports were in order, showing them to be Vincent Maes and his brother, Valentine, both travelling on American documents; a Dr. Carlo Zuchestra, clearly of Italian extraction, who also carried an American passport; and a very large, bull-headed man called Boris Oblosky, of mixed Russian-American parentage, whose lengthy criminal record in the United States had obliged the Maes brothers to use much guile in obtaining a passport for him. The problem was compounded by Oblosky himself, who, although immensely strong of body, was signally short on intellect. He could neither write nor read, yet, paradoxically, was fascinated by books and, as a child, had been entranced when a kindly teacher had read to her class from Baroness Orczy's classic adventure, *The Scarlet Pimpernel*. From that time onwards, Boris preferred people he liked to call him 'Percy' – after the book's aristocratic hero, Sir Percy Blakeney. His great strength and unpredictable nature had caused much grief and misunderstanding during the journey, both to the Maes brothers and the Italian, Dr. Zuchestra, whose papers described him as a dealer in fine art and who did indeed deal in fine art – the fine art of weapons.

The four men quickly cleared the aerodrome formalities and were shown to a limousine, awaiting them with the compliments of the Cathay Hotel's management.

As the Junkers tri-motor touched down at the aerodrome, so the train from Harpin (or Haerhpin, depending on which way the English clerks were spelling it that day, orthography not always being their strong point) via Peking, steamed into South Central Station.

For the bulk of the passengers, this was the last leg of a twelve-day journey, starting on the Trans-Siberian from Moscow. For others, like the Englishman Waldo Bingham, it had been longer, for he had come the full distance from Paris: two full weeks overland. And he had arrived in Paris only a month before that, after making the considerably shorter journey from London.

Waldo Bingham was a well-seasoned traveller, but this did not stop him being hot, tired and more than usually choleric.

A tall man, Bingham carried far too much weight. His jowls hung down like those of a bulldog, while a large belly stretched shirt, trousers and belt to their outer limits – a physique which did not lend itself to travelling in hot climates. Inclined to drink more than was good for him at the best of times, Waldo Bingham perspired like a soaking sponge, feeling like a man fully clothed in a steam bath as he clambered down from his first-class compartment to be reunited with his luggage – a vast studded white cabin trunk and four suitcases – which appeared to be the cause of great squabbling among a handful of porters.

Waldo Bingham allowed his spleen to pour out on these hapless individuals, calling them the offspring of mangy dogs who fornicated with monkeys, and other choice phrases which suggested that they were illegitimate, lazy heathen who consorted with their sisters: regularly. He even summoned up enough energy to kick one of them. But eventually decisions were made, and the porters came to some agreement. The luggage was borne away, with Waldo lumbering in its wake, still sweating and trying to cool himself with a leaf-shaped fan made from bamboo and parchment.

Steam hissed from the train's engine, spreading like a pungent ground mist; smoke and grime added to the un-savoury smells of human bodies, while a constant babble of voices, proclaiming every emotional permutation in several different languages, combined to make the railway station as near to hell as Waldo Bingham ever wanted to get.

Finally, the luggage was loaded into two rickshaws while Bingham haggled a price with their owners; the financial details concluded, he climbed into a third and the little procession set off at a trot, weaving its way through the crowded late afternoon streets, towards the Bund and the Cathay Hotel.

Once there, Bingham looked forward to a leisurely bath and a change of clothes, followed by several well-iced tall glasses of gin, lime and soda, before setting out for the Flamingo Café where he would call upon Harry Byrd.

The explosion in Byrd's Delage, outside the Flamingo Café, was actually heard by two passengers from the SS *Empress of Asia* – Kate Morrow, newspaper reporter, and her photographer fiancé, Tom Geddes.

At the time, they were aboard the launch which had started ferrying passengers across the two miles of water, between the anchored liner and the Bund, almost as soon as the ship was secured.

Kate was taking in the panorama of the Bund: the imposing waterfront, a bizarre contrast with the ugly, ramshackle skyline which flanked it, and the dirty soupy river in which the glaring white liner rode imposingly between steel-grey naval vessels and grimy freighters.

Sampans juggled around them, and larger junks slalomed in and out between the crowded shipping. The breeze, as they chugged inland, was a relief from the oppressive heat; just as the opulence of the Bund – with its wide frontage, greenery, statues and massive white buildings – was a welcome relief from the rickety rubble of villages and ugly shoreline they had viewed coming in from the mouth of the Yangtze and up the Whangpo River: the gateway to Shanghai.

In comparison with the scenery they had passed, the Bund was undeniably majestic: Greek columns; high, almost top-heavy, gables; white domes. Geddes, standing at Kate Morrow's elbow, constantly referring to a guide book, pointed out the imposing turrets of the Custom House, the Hong Kong-Shanghai Bank, the North China Herald Building and the Cathay Hotel itself. Then he went for'ard, balancing himself against the side of the launch to photograph their rapid approach to the landing stage.

From inland came the muffled boom as Byrd's beloved Delage joined the eternal scrap-heap.

"For God's sake, what was that?" Kate turned sharply,

her face contorting with alarm; there had been much talk on the ship about the delicate situation between China and Japan, Shanghai's vulnerability, and the Communist activity which had plagued the city for years. "They're not shooting at us, are they?" she called towards Geddes.

He laughed, looking back at her as a cloud of spray leaped up from the bows, dipping in the wash of a passing junk. "They're most probably firing a salute of welcome for America's best-known woman reporter and her photographer," he shouted back.

Kate relaxed again, scanning the horizon to see if she could make out where the noise had come from: senses alert, eyes taking in everything, brain already recording detail that would be committed to paper as soon as they reached the Cathay Hotel.

The series of feature articles on the world's great cities, illustrated with Tom's photographs, was already more than enhancing her impressive reputation back home. The assignment was taking a whole year and she was determined to make her report on Shanghai – last in the series – outstandingly the best of the lot; for ambitious Kate Morrow had come a long way in the past three years – from odd-job girl reporter on a city daily to leading features' writer for the nation's second largest circulation illustrated magazine.

Geddes was first off the launch, bracing himself on the landing stage to take pictures of the passengers stepping ashore; paying particular attention to his fiancée, hoping that his photograph of her arrival in Shanghai would be worth a whole page in the following January's edition.

He framed her in the viewfinder as she reached out to take the steadying hand of one of the ship's officers, pressing the shutter as the beaming official pulled her up – one foot on the stage, the other in mid-air, her short blonde hair blowing all ways at once as the breeze gave a sudden quick eddy, and the white pleated skirt whipped around her calves; the slightly large mouth opened in a gasping, breathless smile, eyes bright with excitement. It was how Geddes wanted to capture her on film, for it was Kate's pleasure in discovering each new experience which made her writing so fresh, alive and vigorous. Having not yet reached the stage of cynicism, Kate was one of those newspaperwomen happily bestowed with the power to transmit her own delights and excitement through her written words.

Yet another part of Harry Byrd's past – perhaps the most important part – had arrived in Shanghai.

三　(3)

Foo Tang was a small man, painfully thin, with a face like a skull. This death-head appearance, however, was very much at odds with his manner and energy. 'Billion Dollar' Tang radiated activity; made complex decisions in the time it took a normal man to open an envelope; was invariably right in his judgements of people, and subject to moods which were legend.

Some said that, like the mandarins of old, Tang was capable of presenting you with a priceless piece of jade from his substantial collection one minute, and having your throat slit the next. It was rumoured that he had actually done this to a man who had not shown proper respect towards the beautiful tropical birds which Tang kept and loved almost as much as his jade.

The villas and large houses around Jessfield Park were owned only by the wealthy – the seventy-thousand-dollar-a-year taipans had the smaller places: after that you stopped counting.

Harry Byrd arrived at Foo Tang's ornate walled mansion a little after six o'clock. An armed guard unlocked the large gates, giving access to a shrub-lined drive, and Byrd was met at the house door by a white-coated boy who led him through the richly furnished rooms, then out again, across lawns to the aviary.

The aviary was divided into several sections, all surrounded by fine mesh and glass: the bulk of these entirely closed in, full of tropical plants and trees – an electric and steam device keeping the enclosed area at a regular dripping-hot jungle temperature. Off this sprouted smaller enclosed spaces for very rare birds needing different climatic conditions, the whole culminating in a section open to the sky, to which the more tame birds would return each night. The aviary gave Harry Byrd the creeps; silent one moment, alive with bird calls and sudden rushes of wings the next.

Foo Tang spent much time in his aviary, and at the moment of Byrd's arrival was talking to an extraordinarily docile quetzal which sat facing him at head level, claws wrapped around a branch, its long green tail hanging down almost as far as Tang's waist.

The quetzal regarded Harry Byrd for a moment, then turned its somewhat bewildered attention back to Foo Tang with his cooing words. Foo Tang, when he finally spoke to Byrd, did so without taking his eyes off the quetzal.

"Ah, Mr. Harry Byrd. At last I've captured you for my aviary. I had expected to see you before this." He chuckled at his own little play on words, and Harry Byrd forced his lips to spread in the semblance of a smile. Foo Tang would have to work on his repartee – the joke about Byrd in the aviary was his regular remark whenever they met.

"Someone took exception to my automobile." Byrd reached for his cigarettes, remembered Tang's rule about no smoking in the aviary, so took out a handkerchief and mopped his brow instead. "They blew most of it away, and nearly killed one of my best boys."

"You are one pretty green boy," Tang said to the quetzal.

At the far end of the aviary a group of macaws began to squabble, and a large cockatoo flapped noisily towards them, its wings brushing Byrd's shoulder as it went. The quetzal remained on its perch.

"Regrettable about your motor car. I hear about it. You could have been inside."

Byrd said that he presumed whoever boobytrapped the

vehicle had probably intended him to be inside.

"And who would do that to you, Harry?" The Chinese finally turned his attention from the quetzal, making a small motion with his hand towards the far door of the aviary.

They moved off.

"Well, it certainly wasn't a Chinese wedding party. Perhaps your enemies are mine also. Perhaps someone saw Lee Yung bring your message. Who can tell?"

Tang nodded as if this was a brilliant piece of deduction. "It is true I have enemies. What the police say about this unfortunate incident?"

Byrd said that he had not waited to find out.

"Considerate of you." They reached the door. Water dropped from the leaves above them like fine rain. "Considerate of you to put me before your motor car."

"It crossed my mind that the explosion could have been you trying to tell me something."

Outside, the air was fractionally more fresh than inside the aviary, but when Tang turned towards him, Byrd realised that he had gone a shade too far. The smile on the death-head had turned to a look of grim displeasure.

"I would do that to you, Harry Byrd? I would try to take your life? You speak like a girl, without thought or logic. Am I not your friend? Your partner?"

Byrd acknowledged that Tang took a quarter of the café's income each month. Income, he stressed, not profit. "Small beer for you, Mr. Tang. Just about keep your birds in seed for a week."

"Some of my birds are predators, Harry. They do not need seed. Anyway, my friend, I am a businessman. I do not part lightly with income."

They crossed the immaculate lawns, avoiding the sprinklers, then up weathered stone steps leading to a paved walk running the length of the house. Foo Tang gestured towards a low set of French windows – a small movement, Tang was not expansive in his body language – and, as if by some occult command, another white-coated boy opened the windows from within. As Byrd stepped back to let the Chinese enter first, he turned and caught a glimpse of Lee

Yung hovering near the aviary door. That Lee Yung was one of Tang's most trusted killers he was in no doubt. The boy, it was plain even from this distance, looked upon Byrd as an animal looks hungrily on prospective prey.

"Besides," Foo Tang continued, "I am *not* at the top of my profession. There are others far more powerful than I. Possibly the destruction of your car was a warning from one of them. Possibly they will come in the night and ask you to make an arrangement with them. I hope you would not do that."

There was no apparent menace in his voice, but Byrd was aware that any rival who attempted to ease himself into Tang's territory would quickly find himself in grave trouble. Tang was being modest. Probably he was not quite at the top of his ladder in Shanghai, but he was certainly on one of its highest rungs.

Tea awaited them, inside the cool reception room (*Or do you care for something stronger*? but Tang did not mean it). He silently watched the boy pour dishes of weak, scented brew and withdraw, before he spoke again.

"It is regrettable about your motor, Harry Byrd. Perhaps, if you do me one time small favour it will be restored to you."

"That which is dead cannot be restored." Byrd was pleased with the phrase; a parody of the eternal proverbs which littered polite Chinese conversation.

Tang was not without humour, smiling and nodding. "But the living refresh themselves through the lives of the dead. Maybe it can be replaced."

"A favour?" Byrd sipped his tea. The scent of it somehow reminded him of Jeannie Chin and he saw them together, only a short time ago, on the bed. . .

"It is granted?" Tang interrupted his thoughts.

"Tell me the favour first; then I'll see what can be done. How many teeth'll it cost me to begin with?"

Tang nodded again. "No teeth. The price of a little food, maybe. A bottle of wine or liquor." He paused. "The use of your most private room for an hour."

When you passed through the Flamingo Café and

climbed the stairs leading to Byrd's private apartment, you had to go through a small passageway. To the right was the room which Byrd used as an office. There was a two-way mirror in the wall, giving him a view of the whole café, below, at a glance. On the left side of the passage stood another room, always kept in good order and used for private parties, or assignations (the furniture included a bed). Like Byrd's apartment, these rooms could be reached from the street stairs as well as through the café.

"You protect me well, Mr. Tang," Harry took a moment or two – pausing to think. "That is well known, and I am grateful. However, I must be as careful as yourself. I'd need to be advised on who wishes to use the private room, and for what purpose."

"Is it enough to say that I shall be present?"

Tang himself: the thought jolted, for the matter concerned had to be one of great delicacy. Tang's kind of meeting would normally take place in his office on the Bund, or here, at the villa in Jessfield Park. Clearly the Chinese wanted neutral ground away from prying eyes, so Byrd said of course it was enough if Mr. Tang was to be there.

"Good. I shall bring the admirable Lee Yung and two boys. My people can take in food and drink from your own boys. I want the meeting private and undisturbed."

Byrd said it was enough; it was good; and asked when Tang required the room.

"Tonight. Aroun' eleven o'clock. The men I am to meet have only just arrive Shanghai."

Byrd pretended he did not care when they had arrived, or even who they were. He was naturally curious, but it did not do to show too much interest. Then, for no apparent reason, Tang volunteered the information.

"These men I meet tonight come from your own country. They are American."

"Yes?"

"I doubt you know them. You ever hear of a Mr. Maes? Two Mr. Maes? Brothers?"

Harry Byrd's stomach contracted and he suddenly felt

35

very hot, as though air had been extracted from the room, leaving it dry and stifling. Thoughts and pictures rushed through his head, ending with a sense of deathly fear which stretched out to his nerve ends. He did manage to stumble out a negative: No, he had never heard of any brothers called Maes.

"I think they gangster. You would not know." Tang did not seem to have noticed any change in Byrd who felt his face drain of blood, and saw too that his hands were trembling.

He reached for his cigarettes, giving Tang a questioning raise of the eyebrows. The Chinese nodded assent.

Byrd said, no, he would not know; no, he would not have come across any brothers called Maes, particularly if they were gangsters. But he could see them clearly in his head: Valentine – stocky, with sulky good looks and curly hair; Vincent – the more intelligent, well groomed, sharp, patient. "The only gangsters I've ever met've been here in Shanghai," he murmured, lighting the cigarette.

"Come now, Harry Byrd. I know of no gangster, here in this beautiful city." Tang had the wit to smile as he said it.

Byrd tried to remove the cigarette from his lips, dragging a pull of smoke, but it stuck, his fingers running the length, taking the glowing end with them. Little red ashes scattered over Tang's costly carpet, burning Byrd's first and second fingers as they went so that he swore extensively.

Tang made a movement suggesting the slight damage to his property was nothing; and Byrd pulled himself together, saying that all would be ready for Tang that night at eleven.

"Will you be all coming together: arriving at the same time?"

"I shall arrive before them. They will come from the Cathay. I shall see to it that they have precise instructions on how to reach the café, and which door they must use."

They spoke for a little longer: polite conversation, and when he left, walking quickly down the driveway, Byrd felt that a knife – despatched if not by Lee Yung then by one of the Maes brothers – might part his shoulder-blades at any moment.

The armed guard was still at the main gate, as was the rickshaw boy who had been told to wait. Harry Byrd hated rickshaws. On first arriving in the East he was told that he would soon get used to that method of transport, and recognise the fact that the Chinese coolie was made by God to act as a human machine for his superiors. Never having been able to accept this convenient supposition, Byrd avoided, whenever possible, being pulled by another human creature running barefoot between shafts. Now however, although he watched the moving sweating shoulders of the rickshaw puller and was conscious of the thump of feet and rattle of wheels, his mind remained centred on other more immediately important things.

The sky had fallen in and, as Chicken-Licken, he would have to go and find the king.

Was there a direct connection between the arrival of the Maes brothers and the bombing of his car? They had come during the late afternoon – *The men I am to meet have only just arrive Shanghai* – so if there was a link, the situation was not merely potentially dangerous: it meant they already had people working in Shanghai, and Byrd's goose was not just cooked but burned to a frazzle.

On the other hand, if the Maes brothers had nothing to do with the car, there was still a chance for him – if he could just keep his head down. Of one thing there was no doubt: if they found him, recognised him, Vincent and Valentine Maes would take him apart, one bone at a time, and feed him into the China Sea.

People like the Maes brothers did not take kindly to men who gave evidence against their colleagues, particularly if that evidence resulted in those same colleagues being put away for a long time. Nor would they have forgotten their own narrow escape, or the fact that the whole world – their world anyway – knew that Harry Byrd (though the name had been different) had done the biggest deal of all time with the Feds: an arrangement which also technically should have included putting the Maes brothers out of circulation for a considerable period. After all, Byrd's own story had been published coast to coast. They must also be aware that there was a convenient (for Byrd) discrepancy in the financial figures given in evidence. There were many reasons the Maes brothers would not rejoice in a face-to-face meeting with Harry Byrd.

His mind turned to Cat. By now, three years had turned any thought of her into a dull ache, replacing the searing pain at the start. Like all old wounds it had almost healed, causing him only a small amount of discomfort, when he heard a particular kind of laugh, or a song. . . His recent interview in Tang's aviary recalled the time he had taken Cat to a zoo somewhere, and they had stood by a cage trying to make a parrot talk. "Do you think the paper would buy an interview with a parrot?" she had said, and he realised she was serious: always full of crazy ideas to push her work. "You're like a cat worrying a mouse when it comes to stories for your damned paper," he'd laughed. It was after that he began to call her Cat. . .

They had removed most of the wrecked Delage from Bubbling Well Road, leaving only a few pieces in the gutter, and a blackened smudge where the rear had blown. At right angles to this there was a smear of oily dirt to mark the explosion of the gas tank. The bits and pieces had gone, but there was a uniformed police inspector waiting just inside the café entrance. A pair of Sikh coppers stood near him, and another by Byrd's apartment entrance.

The inspector looked familiar to Byrd. He also looked unpleasant.

四 (4)

The inspector from the Municipal Police was English; the worst kind: pompous, going to seed in the climate, fattening around the middle, with skin flaccid in texture, most apparent around the cheeks of his pale, puffy face. Once inside the café he introduced himself as Fisher, and Byrd immediately knew why he had looked familiar.

'Pearly' Fisher was notorious for taking squeeze and then not honouring his word. They said he was a good copper, but several quite influential people had tried to get his name off the membership of the Shanghai Club, and he was certainly not tolerated in the American Club.

"You're Byrd," he began. "Heard about you. Have to speak." When he spoke his thick lips moved like the mouth of a netted orangutan.

Behind the policeman's back, Casimir, the Maître d', made discreet signals indicating that he also wished to talk. Casimir was said to be still wanted for a clever piece of forgery back in his native Hungary, and always showed signs of anxiety when the police were about.

"Sure." Byrd took out his cigarettes and did not offer one to Fisher. "Just give me a minute with my Maître d' here, then come up to the office. The barman, Max, will show you the way. Have a drink while you're waiting. On the house."

"I've already been waiting, Byrd. This is serious. I want to talk now."

"Have a drink: the policeman's lot is not a happy one." Byrd motioned to Casimir to follow him, pushed past Fisher and walked the length of the café fast, without looking back; then up the curving stairs to the passage and his office.

"Mr. Harry, there's been a man. Keep calling you on the

phone. He's coming eight o'clock and want to see you very bad." Casimir hovered, just inside the door.

"What man? For God's sake, come in, Casim, and close the door."

Casimir obeyed. "Says his name's Bingham. Waldo Bingham. Keeps calling all the time. Says it's important. You know this Waldo?"

"And he's arriving at eight?"

"Eight o'clock. You know him, Mr. Harry?"

Byrd said, truthfully, that he had never heard of Waldo Bingham, but he would be in the office at eight – it was already after seven thirty – and Casimir should give the usual signal, or get Max to call so that he could look Bingham over when he arrived. Then he quickly gave precise instructions regarding the visit of Foo Tang and the Americans at eleven.

Casimir looked worried. "We are much full up tonight, Mr. Harry. Twelve people have reserved from the Cathay alone. The boys will have work in abundance. Too much in abundance. I don't know if we can give time. . . Phew!" He caressed his fat little cheeks.

"Where in hell d'you get words like abundance, Casim?" Smiling, Byrd walked over to the desk and dosed himself with a shot of Teachers. There was not much to smile about, but Casimir's occasional lapses into elaborate English always amused him.

"It is not a good word? Who says it not a good word? The boys have work in abundance: it means they have work enough, and then you have arrange special private party tonight. What do you think I am, Mr. Harry? Magician? Bloody illusionist. . . ?" He lapsed into a grumble, reverting to his native language.

"Casim," Byrd raised a placating hand. "I didn't arrange the private party. You have to thank 'Billion Dollar' Tang for that; and I have no intention of offending Uncle Tang. The last time I heard of someone offending him, they ended up on meat skewers."

Casimir stopped growling and nodded slowly. At this moment the door opened and Inspector 'Pearly' Fisher barged into the room: "Byrd, I've been waiting a long time –"

"You often walk into offices without knocking?" Byrd did not look up.

"All the time. Part of the job. Now let's get on with the talking. Enough time wasted."

Byrd nodded to Casimir and the tubby Hungarian left with a shrug. There was no point in delaying matters; the sooner Fisher was off the premises the better. The policeman, all bluster, irritation and puffing of lips, pulled a chair up to the desk, scraping the legs across the carpet.

"You planning to sit down without being asked, as well?" Byrd had to talk with the man, but there was no need to suffer brash discourtesy without fighting back.

Fisher said he sat where he pleased.

"Never seen you sitting in the American Club. Not even on the steps."

The policeman opened his mouth to speak, but Byrd cut in again. "Some bastard turned my motor into scrap, Inspector. Your job's to find out why and how – right? How far've you got?"

"Very droll," Fisher began. "Your motor explodes in a crowded street – God knows how we avoided fatalities; it's a miracle that we've only got walking wounded. The fire services of both French and International Settlements are tied up for over an hour. I'm pulled off another case: several other police officers with me. What do we find? We find that the owner of the vehicle – you, Byrd – has calmly walked away."

"I was late for an appointment."

"Anyone I know, or did she work in Blood Alley?"

Byrd could do without the cheap laughing-copper routine. "You want to talk to me, Fisher, okay. We either do it quick, here, or I drop by your office tomorrow. Like you, I got work to do."

Fisher rocked back calmly in his chair, taking his time, not even a twitch in his eyebrows. From the café below they could hear Herman starting his first stint at the piano: the heavy bass beginning a slow intro, then the right hand coming in with the melody, twinkling and sliding around: 'What Is This Thing Called Love?'

At last the policeman asked, slowly: "You made a lot of enemies since you arrived here?"

"I said I've got work to do."

"Don't worry, we'll get it over fast. I don't want to stay here any longer than I can help. Not even to drink a Chefoo beer. I don't really care about your motor car, Byrd, but it's my job, as you rightly say. I have to make a report."

"Pop a paper bag, then, Pearly. Put in a note I said so."

Fisher puffed impatiently, drumming on the desk. "I have to interview the injured party, whether I like it or not. I do not like it. Enemies, Byrd?"

"None I know of."

"Friends then. People you pay to keep the trouble away." He managed a macabre smile.

"I've never worked like that," Byrd lied.

"No? What about Uncle Tang? 'Billion Dollar' Tang?"

"What about him?"

"I've read your file. More than once. Fascinating."

Byrd willed himself from shifting in his chair, or showing any sign of concern.

"My men keep their eyes open," Fisher continued. "You left to see Tang immediately after the explosion."

Byrd said, of course: it was a business appointment. He had been preparing to go when the Delage exploded.

"You have mutual business interests, you and Tang?"

"Tropical birds. I'm thinking of going into the export market with him."

Fisher's eyes indicated that he was not convinced. "I said your file was fascinating. As I recall it, you arrived here in Shanghai during the autumn of '28. You were loaded – I believe that's the American expression. Yet you found it necessary to take Tang in as a business partner. We're talking about this place now – the Flamingo."

"Where I come from, it's better to do business with somebody else's money."

Fisher gave a long sigh. "And where I come from, it is well known that Tang's not good at investing his own cash.

42

When you bring Tang into partnership it is Tang who takes the money *out*. But you've done well since you've been in this city, Byrd. Too well. You mix with bad company." He gave what passed for a thin smile. "What would you say if I put this explosion down to a gangster vendetta and closed the Flamingo for a month or so? Public danger. Bombs in cars are not a good advertisement."

Byrd did not think Fisher had enough muscle to close the Flamingo, but he did not say so. Wisely, he kept silent.

"So you've no idea who might want to tie your motor around a king-sized firecracker?"

"No idea." It was the bald truth – unless Tang was doing some psychological softening up, or the Maes brothers were on to him, and he was certainly not going to mention them.

The inspector nodded. He was very sorry about the car, he said, but did not sound sincere, adding that there were no obvious leads, and he had grave doubts whether they would ever nail anybody. "Unless they have another go and blow this whole place to kingdom come – an advent which I, for one, would welcome. I suppose you know your file has a 'hands-off' stamp on it? I don't like people getting that sort of preference. It sometimes means they're important; but it's usually a case of efficient corruption. You look clean, Byrd, but I've always had my doubts about you. Now, after your exploding motor, I'm certain."

There was a further ten minutes of questions and answers; then Fisher left. Byrd sat at the two-way mirror watching him go, threading his way through the tables, now starting to fill with the early-evening drinkers. They would stay for a while, then the dinner bookings would start arriving at around nine. The joint would not really start jumping until quite late.

As Fisher crossed the long room, Herman switched tunes neatly, moving into 'I'll See You Again', leaning back at the piano and grinning up at the invisible window.

A couple of minutes later, Jeannie Chin came in, dressed to kill somebody – though not Byrd, if her actions were anything to go by. She crossed the small room, perched

43

herself on his knee and began absent-mindedly to nibble his ear, whispering that she was frightened since the explosion. Soon, however, she came to the real purpose of her visit, cursing the girls: two had failed to turn up for work, and Arina looked as though she had not slept for a week.

Only a few minutes before, as he was watching Fisher leave, Byrd had spotted Arina at the bar, talking to a middle-aged taipan. He thought the Russian girl looked as stunning as ever and put Jeannie's remarks down to pique. Jeannie always felt threatened by Arina, who claimed aristocratic Russian heritage – but half the Russian girls in Shanghai claimed that. The other half stuck to helping out in kitchens.

He patted Jeannie's bottom, asking her what she had against Arina, squinting through the window, down into the bar, to see if the girl was still egging the taipan to have another drink. She was there: balanced in a beautiful shallow S-shape, almost pressing her large breasts into the man's face. He did not stand a chance.

"I think Arina put bomb in your motor," Jeannie pouted.

Byrd grinned.

"Russians are known to make trouble," she went on lamely.

Enough, he told her. "Get out there and make sure the girls are circulating. Out." He meant the girls should be sorting the punters, sifting the wheat from the chaff: the wheat being those with money to spend, and the chaff those penny-pinchers who should be sent packing, one way or another.

He still had to look over the previous night's books, but it was too late for that now – almost eight o'clock, and time for the mysterious Mr. Waldo Bingham. There were many other things that had to be done before eleven when Tang would arrive with the Maes brothers and he would have to go invisible. At least, if he fixed the private room, he would get some inkling of whether or not the brothers Maes had fingered him. Now he had to change for the evening, and make his customary round of the café: check with Descales that the kitchen was in order; look in on the gaming room,

44

and attend to any other small items that might crop up.

He cranked the interconnecting phone and asked to speak with Casimir, telling him that if Bingham arrived he was to be given a drink and kept happy. In the meantime, he was off to change. All Casimir said was that they were "getting more full by the minute". Byrd murmured something about having an abundance of customers, and cradled the earpiece.

He carefully locked the office door, glanced into the private room opposite, and went along the passage to his own apartment.

He felt the presence the moment he opened the door, and, in a reflex movement, had the gun out of its hip holster – too late. Someone small and smelling of sweat launched himself at him, knocking the gun to the floor, twisting his arm and throwing him face downwards on to the carpet.

His forehead hit the ground: a great jarring, breathtaking, thump which seemed to fuse high-voltage lightning inside his brain. He tried to roll in the direction he knew the gun had gone; but, even though his eyes were open, he could not see. Stirring in the back of his mind was the momentary panic that he had gone blind; then his fingers touched the barrel, only to lose it again as something – a heel? – ground into his wrist.

五 (5)

Byrd felt the pain, excruciating in both wrist and head, but still struggled, slowly, as in a nightmare where his limbs were hampered by invisible molasses. Then the mist suddenly cleared; he was aware of the gun, a long way off on the carpet, viewing it as through the wrong end of a telescope. Then pain again, as something crashed into his ribs: a foot – he could see it, dirty and unshod, being drawn back for a further blow; he even recognised that the skin and flesh on the foot was very hard; a foot which had probably never been protected by sandal or shoe since birth.

He tried to roll away, tensing for the blow, but it did not come. From far away he could hear a voice: gruff, as if its owner's larynx was filled with powdered glass. The voice was speaking alternately in English and another language – not Chinese, he would have recognised that. The English he could recognise: things like, "Child of a Death Adder . . . yellow Nip . . . Scum of a black pond. . ." Interspersed with these ripe insults came the foreign words, rapped out and obviously commanding.

Byrd shook his head, hoisting himself into a sitting position. Backing away from him was a small Japanese, behind whom was the door and a tall, extraordinarily fat man with a revolver clutched in his pudgy right hand.

This latter had his bulk propped heaving against the doorjamb, as though out of breath, or condition, or both. He had pushed his broad-brimmed cream hat on to the back of his head, and the linen suit he wore hung around his frame like a damp sheet. Dark alert eyes peered from the bulldog face, and the muzzle of his revolver did not waver, pointing directly at the back of the ragged thin shirt which just covered the Japanese thug's muscular torso.

"Mr. Harry Byrd?" queried the large man.

Byrd nodded, his head still swimming from its hard contact with the floor. Climbing on to his hands and knees, he raised himself, staggered slightly, then straightened and swayed across to where his gun lay.

"Waldo Bingham," said the large man. "Glad to make your acquaintance; I took the liberty of entering your premises via the rear door. A happy chance, it would seem."

The Japanese started to turn, but Mr. Waldo Bingham's growl turned into a rapid flow of what Byrd now clearly recognised as Japanese – surprised at himself for his own slow thinking. The assailant stopped as though turned to stone.

"Little fellow jumped you in your own quarters, eh?"

Bingham growled. Byrd nodded and said yes, that was the way of it.

"Off his own territory, isn't he? Bloody ronin by the look of him. Shoshi hoodlum: Black Dragon I shouldn't wonder. Usually stay to the north as I recall. Only the more respectable business people find their way down here."

Byrd said he thought they did, his voice sounding hollow in his own ears. A ronin was synonymous with hooligan; Shoshi an underworld society, of which the Black Dragon was probably the most extensive and powerful among the Japanese community which centred itself near the Hongkew area, to the north of the city.

Bingham came forward and shot another stream of Japanese at the little thug, who threw a few words back over his shoulder at the fat man.

"Asked him what he was doin' in your rooms." The revolver was now pressed into the ronin's back. "Says he was here on orders: told me it was none of my business. We did have an appointment for eight o'clock, didn't we?"

"Yes, I'd just come to get dressed."

"Ah, then I suspect we should do something about the Nipponese fella, and after that get on with our talk."

Bewildered, Byrd stared at Waldo Bingham, his unlikely saviour, and then at the Japanese, whose glower was far from inscrutable. Finally, still dizzy and a little sick, he stumbled over to the communicating phone and cranked down to Max for Che and Koo to be sent upstairs. Max sounded worried: "You okay, boss? You not hurt?"

"Bump on the head from a Japanese gentleman, Max, that's all: just get the boys up here chop-chop." He cradled the phone and turned back to Waldo Bingham. "I shall have to call the police."

"Ah." Bingham did not sound happy. "Is that absolutely necessary?"

Byrd told him about the earlier incident. "They might be connected, and I'm in for a lot of trouble if we just dump the Nip somewhere quiet."

Bingham nodded wisely, the revolver still pressed very professionally into the Japanese's lumbar region. "You must do as you see fit, but I would prefer to be elsewhere when your friends from the Municipal Police Force arrive."

"You got problems, friend?"

"Not the kind that you are probably thinking about, Mr. Byrd. But I consider it best if we do not bandy my presence around. Don't want to tell the whole world. Which is why, incidentally, I've made so sure this Nip fella shouldn't see me."

Che and Koo appeared behind the large Bingham, who backed discreetly from the room, and Byrd instructed them to tie up the Japanese and tuck him away somewhere safe. "Like in that pantry off the kitchens. It's empty and hot down there. But tie him up good; I'm saving him for the police."

The ronin did not seem to like the idea, but Che had brought some cord with him, and under the lethal eye of Byrd's own gun, there was no option. The boys trussed him like a chicken and carried him away, as if lugging a carcass of meat. As they were leaving, Jeannie Chin fluttered in, looking flushed. Max had told her what had happened, she said. She fussed and stroked Byrd's cheek and head, making a great show of affection.

Byrd did not care to admit to her that he now had a raging headache, and a great deal of pain around the right eye. His head had been angled to the right when he struck the floor, and he had vague worries at the back of his mind about concussion, or even damage to the optic nerve; but he gently assured Jeannie that he was okay, telling her to get back to work. She left reluctantly, giving Waldo Bingham, who had returned by now, a look of marked mistrust.

Byrd went over to the main telephone and called Municipal Police Headquarters. Inspector Fisher was out, but they could get a radio message to him; he should be at the café within fifteen minutes.

"Just in time for me to change and tuck you away somewhere safe." He eyed Bingham's large revolver, which made his own .25 Pieper automatic look like a child's toy.

Bingham weighed the big weapon in his hand, as though

he was thinking about finding a good place to hide it. "Sorry about the cannon," turning it over, then sticking it into the hip pocket of his voluminous trousers. "Standard issue, you know; they haven't got out of the habit. The good old Webley MK.IV Service: wonderful if you've got the big leather holster, lanyard and all that. Good for leading men over the top; not so good for my kind of work. Tends towards bulk – like myself. It has its uses, however. . . You say there's somewhere for me to hide away while your bobbies are tramping around?"

Byrd said he would not let them near the bedroom, but that he would have to use it first, to change and wash up. "I haven't said thank you, yet; guess you saved my life coming up the back stairs like that."

"Think nothing of it. You will doubtless repay." The heavy jowls quivered. "But I'll tell you about that when the police have left us in peace."

In the bathroom, dousing his face with cold water, Byrd reflected that the already-eventful evening was likely to turn into an even more formidable night. He took to the large Mr. Bingham, though as yet he could not figure the man's part in the scheme of things.

He washed and sprinkled cologne over his skin, rubbing it in, taking just over ten minutes to change into the black trousers, shirt, silk tie and white tuxedo – his evening uniform for the café.

Checking his pockets and the automatic, Byrd finally emerged from the bedroom to find Waldo Bingham settled, his bulk overflowing one of the bamboo chairs, a glass of Teachers – to which he had helped himself – wrapped in one big paw.

"Sorry, I guess I should've thought about offering you a drink before. . ." Byrd's apology was cut short by the grinding bell of the wall phone: Max tipping him off that Fisher was on his way through the café with a posse of four uniformed men at his heels.

As quickly as his weight would allow, Bingham was hoisted from the chair and bundled into the bedroom, which Byrd locked before peeking into the mirror. One glance was enough; he had looked bad enough in the bathroom, now in this light he appeared to have been in a major accident.

He reached the door just in time to meet Fisher, who seemed to be followed by a small sea of uniforms. The policeman's eyes scanned the room, as though trying to catch sight of something he could finger as incriminating.

Byrd had to go through his version of the attack twice – explaining Waldo Bingham for the official story as one of his own men, and adding that they had the Jap in a sweatbox off the kitchens which were directly under that end of the café.

"Bloody ronin," Fisher grunted. "Bloody Black Dragon, put me money on it. Sounds like something from old E. Phillips Oppenheim. But don't be misled, Byrd, they're getting cheeky; coming out of their own ground. Always had the banks and businesses down this end, of course, but they kept the strong-arm stuff away. Now they're making a play for some of the action; probably thought you were a soft touch. Anyway, we'll take this joker off, grill him to a turn; got a couple of good Nip-speaking interrogators. Let you know what they come up with." He grinned. "Glad to see he hurt you a bit. Do you good to get knocked about, Byrd."

Two constables were despatched to pick up the ronin, and Byrd asked if they would all please leave by the side door. "Gives the place a bad name, police tramping in and out: frightens the customers."

Fisher said the prices probably frightened them more, repeating that he would be in touch. It sounded more of a threat than a promise.

Within minutes of their departure, Byrd sat in his office, the door secure and the vast Waldo Bingham, now visibly sweating, on the other side of the desk. Things appeared normal in the café below, and Byrd now waited for Bingham to talk first; long ago he had learned that it was better to let others speak when you were unsure of what was required from you.

Bingham opened cautiously, "Your name was suggested to me by friends."

Byrd wanted to know in what connection, and Bingham indicated that it was a delicate, sensitive, matter. "You have to take me rather on trust, but the friends I speak of suggested to my superiors that you are a man with a past; though a man who might not be averse to working for a good cause."

"Your superiors, Mr. Bingham?"

He said to call him Waldo, but Byrd did not respond with an invitation to use his Christian name: the fact that someone had suggested he was endowed with a 'past' was not the best news of the day.

"Who are your superiors, then, Waldo?"

Bingham managed to look sheepish. "You are an American," he stated the obvious. "I presume you have an American passport, so I cannot appeal to you on grounds of King and Country, and all that sort of chauvinistic rot. I gather, though, that you have become attached to Shanghai: that your future is invested here."

Byrd gave the hint of a nod.

Bingham sighed heavily, his great belly rising and falling, as though life had become too much for him. Then: "I gather that it is possible your livelihood is now being threatened by a Japanese criminal society. I mean it doesn't take a great mind to deduce that after the recent events."

"Could be."

"Then you must realise that Shanghai itself is threatened by the Japanese. Not just the criminal societies, but by the Japanese nation as a whole."

Byrd spent most of his time running the Flamingo as efficiently as possible, steering clear of trouble from the teeming underworld by allowing Foo Tang to take care of that side of things for him; but he knew the fears, the talk, and the facts: the political wrangling, and the constant anxiety of many Shanghailanders – the Communist agitations, and the worry that Japan had her sights set on Manchuria. Shanghai had always lived near to trouble. Had not Chiang Kai-shek arrived in the city, only four years ago, to be welcomed by a Communist People's Army, which had seized all key points? Before that there had been grave incidents between Japanese businesses and the Chinese Communist workers. Japanese business was still tolerated on the Bund, and even in Nanking and Bubbling Well Roads; though Japanese criminals found it more difficult.

Chiang Kai-shek had quickly turned his coat, and the Communist Party was now outlawed; so the Japanese watched the whole situation with great interest. Overall, Byrd preferred to think of it in biblical terms – 'Sufficient unto the day is the evil thereof.'

"It's a threat not to be taken lightly," Bingham growled. "They'll come. One day they'll come, and the day approaches. It's always later than you think. To be frank, if I had a business here I would be thinking of getting out. You could lose the lot to the Japs." He paused, wrinkling the fat brow. "Or the Communists, of course: whichever is the more nimble."

"The Japanese wouldn't dare do anything within the International and French Settlements." Byrd stopped abruptly, realising that Bingham had side-tracked him. "Your superiors, Waldo?"

The big man sighed again. "Ah yes. My superiors. They are in London, my lords and masters. For my sins they have sent me on a small recruiting drive." He allowed his face to lift into a broad smile, then spread his hands wide; almost a gesture of apology. "I look like a bulldog, maybe; but not a Bulldog Drummond. You will find it hard to believe, Mr. Byrd, but I represent His Majesty's. . ." he coughed, ". . . His Majesty's Secret Service. In plain terms, I am a spy. I have come here to implore you to join our ignoble ranks."

There should be a classic response, Byrd thought. "You been a spy long, Waldo?" was all he could manage, lighting another cigarette with a show of bored worldly wisdom.

"Since the war. Army, of course. They shifted me around, and I've spent a lot of time on this beat: the Orient; Mystic East, all that sort of thing. Speak a bit of the lingo: spot of Mandarin, few dialects, enough Jap to get me a drink or a woman – which I don't need so often these days: the bulk, you know," he patted his stomach. "I get by."

"You got by with our visitor."

"Oh well, usual commands. Know a bit of obscenity. Threats: they come in handy. Feel like joining the old firm?"

Byrd could not get it straight in his head: unable to think properly, finding it hard to believe the proposition that was being put to him.

"Why me?"

"You're in a trade which automatically picks up pieces of local information. You overhear things. I gather you're not afraid of a little danger."

"You gather wrong, Waldo." He adopted a poker face. "I don't know what these friends told your superiors, but they didn't get it right." He closed his eyes, wincing against a stab of pain in his head. "What did they say? What did they tell?" Behind his closed lids, in the blackness, he wondered how much had been said in private and how much committed to paper. He could work out the logic of it if he thought hard – the British going to the US secret people who then went to the Feds (*We've got this guy in Shanghai who might be good for some pressure. We have a hold. . .*).

"They said that you had once performed a great service at risk to yourself. High risk."

That was true, the high risk bit. "It wasn't courage,

Waldo. It was a question of fear and survival. They give you any details?"

"Dear boy, nobody in this business provides details for the poor bloody man in the field." He shifted his elephantine bulk. "China is split and divided. Communists plot everywhere – even in this café of yours, I have no doubt; and one day the Generalissimo Chiang Kai-shek will have to face them head on. In the meantime, the Japanese rattle their swords and prepare to move in. They're like jackals waiting for the lone antelope. Not bad that, eh? The lone antelope of Shanghai?" He paused, pleased with himself. "I need someone here who will pass on tidbits: Japanese moves – military and criminal. Today, for instance, I've learned much: that the criminal element are also brandishing their weapons. At least think about it. You come highly recommended."

"I can get you . . . ?"

"At the Cathay, with all the smart people. Where else does one stay in Shanghai? Perhaps tomorrow evening I shall dine here and we can talk again. At least sleep on it." The elephant finally got to its feet, taking a couple of lumbering paces towards the door.

Byrd started to say he really did not think he would be of much use, but Waldo Bingham held up his hand. "You've already been useful. Think about it. There's a little – a very little – spending money in it, and if the situation alters, as I'm certain it will, you'll need every red cent." He chuckled, "Red cent, that's good. Talk tomorrow, Harry Byrd."

Byrd heard the man's footsteps, very light for someone of that build, pass along the passage. He glanced down into the café, thinking it had been a long time since he had felt less like work; but work certainly had to be done. First, the private room for Tang's meeting with the Maes brothers. At least he would be able to listen in to the conversation, which might possibly yield a tidbit for himself – and even for Waldo Bingham.

He had three telephones on the office desk: one with an external line; the interconnecting phone, with its old crank handle, which operated on the same circuit as the one in the apartment, and linked the whole café; while the third was a direct internal line to the private room. Byrd had made sure of this when originally instructing the builders; with private rooms you never knew what might happen.

He took the earpiece from its cradle and placed it on the desk, then walked the few steps to the door, and across the passage to the other room. The instrument there hung on the wall, low down near the bed – discreetly placed in a corner, with a folding screen nearby for the sake of the exceptionally modest. Taking the earpiece from its hook, Byrd wedged a small, specially shaped piece of wood under the claw rest, then replaced the earpiece. The telephone was now live and directly open to its twin in Byrd's office. He had used the device before, found it efficient, and knew that Foo Tang was unaware of it. As far as one could rely on him being unaware of anything.

Casimir had already prepared the room – chairs placed around a table in the centre; bottles of liquor and glasses arranged on a smaller table, together with linen, cutlery, bowls and chopsticks, so that any of the visitors' gastronomic whims could be dealt with. As a final thoughtful touch, Byrd put a key into the lock on the inside of the door.

The pain in his head had localised above the right eye, which was still giving him trouble, and the spectre of blindness, or even partial sight, nagged at the back of his mind. There had been a man in his childhood, a tall skeleton of a man, blind and led around by a small girl. He had been terrified of the blind man, just as he had been frightened by the pirate Blind Pew when first reading *Treasure Island*. Loss of sight had always been a nightmare for him.

He was closing the door when the unmistakable sound of a footfall on the street stairs – at the far end of the passage – made him turn, hand going automatically to the pistol at his hip.

The tread was heavy, and whoever was coming up the stairs made no attempt to disguise his presence. Byrd saw a shadow fall across the point where the passage divided, from the short landing leading off the stairs to the door of his private apartment. He blinked – conscious that the right eye took longer than the left to get back into focus – and in that brief moment the shadow became substance.

The man was the size of the Frankenstein monster, as played by Boris Karloff in the movie which had only recently reached Shanghai, having just been released from Hollywood. Byrd had taken Jeannie Chin to see it at the Cathay. She had been terrified.

This one was big, but did not have a bolt sticking through his neck; and the face, while ugly, appeared friendly.

"Boris," Byrd breathed aloud before he could stop himself. He was not referring to Karloff, but to this other Boris – the one standing at the end of the passage: a man whom he had seen before though never met, either socially or professionally, and had never wanted to.

Boris Oblosky was instantly recognisable however, and Byrd could only hope that the legendary simple-mindedness of this huge, bull-headed man could be put to good account. At the same time, he prayed that Boris was not on an errand for his masters, for if he was, it would not be an errand of mercy. . .

But Boris smiled a very friendly smile. "Hi!" His mouth opened in a broken-toothed gape. "I was sent to look the joint over."

"Yeah?" Byrd heard the quiver in his own voice.

Boris advanced, pushing a huge ham-like hand in front of him. "You can call me Percy," he said. "Only my friends call me Percy."

Aliases yet, thought Byrd, wincing as the handshake crushed his fingers. "Hi ya, Percy. Who sent you to look the joint over?"

"My bosses sent me. Vincent and Valentine. We all got a meet here later. They said I should look and make sure there were no gunsels around. We got a meet here with a Chink. Said I should see the owner. I forget his name: Flamingo or something."

"He had to go out, Percy," Byrd said quickly. Clearly he had not been recognised. If he could keep it that way he might still live. "But the man told me all about it. You're meeting Mr. Tang here at eleven. You want to see the room? Very private." He gestured towards the door.

"Sure, I better take a look. Vincent and Valentine're awful particular about me doin' what they tell me. I get into some terrible scrapes with 'em for not doin' things right."

"There you go," Byrd opened the door. "That's the room. Very private. Even a key so you can lock yourselves in. Nobody'll disturb you. You can tell your friends that."

"Sure," his eyes alighted on the bed. "You got girls here? You know what I mean?" He giggled: a series of little hyphenated chuckles.

"Well, Percy. . ."

"Chink girls? I like Chink girls. Had one of my own once. She left. Wanda: her name was Wanda. I loved my Wanda. Really loved her: you know what I mean? I would never hurt a girl. You got girls?"

"Tell you what, Percy. When your meeting's over, you ask one of the Chinese boys. . ."

"I don't like boys. Only girls."

"You ask one of the Chinese boys to let you have a word with Mr. Casimir. Mr. Casimir sees to the girls. You remember that?"

"Mr. Casimir," the giant repeated slowly, with a smile. Then he said it again, as though burning it into his mind. "Mr. Ca-si-mir."

"Good. He'll probably be able to fix you up." The way to a simple-minded killer was not through his stomach, Byrd felt. The passkey lay well below the navel.

"Will he get me one like my Wanda?"

"He'll try." Polly Sing would take care of Boris. She liked them big and stupid, so it could pay dividends.

"Okay. The room looks okay." Boris nodded, then again displayed an unnecessary number of ruined teeth. "Mr. Ca-si-mir. Okay." He started to amble away up the passage. As he got to the end, he turned. "If he finds me one like my Wanda, he can call me Percy as well."

Byrd went back into his office, took another shot of Teachers, then left, carefully locking the door behind him. Suddenly life seemed to be one long crisis. He still felt groggy: head aching and the eye throbbing right behind the

57

iris. Maybe he needed medical attention, but there was too much to be done: too many holes to be plugged. Maybe tomorrow he would see a doctor; now it was time to have a look around the café. He headed towards the curving staircase.

The Flamingo Café was basically an oblong room, very wide so that Byrd had been able to line the two longest walls, which stretched back from the street, with recessed arches. The middle arch on the right, as he came down from his office, was deeper than the others and formed the large bar. Max, his little Mexican barman, was already doing brisk business, providing for customers and dealing with the waiters bringing orders from the tables.

Max's complexion and the pencil-line moustache would have typed him as a Mexican sidekick in any Hollywood movie. He worked on this flamboyant appearance, and about a year before, Byrd had taken some snapshots of him in a braided bolero jacket, elaborate boots and a sombrero. The result made the Mexican look decidedly evil and an enlargement of one of these pictures now hung behind the bar to discourage aggressive patrons.

In fact this picture was entirely unnecessary, as were the boots with built-up heels that Max wore to make up for his diminutive stature, since he enjoyed a well-deserved reputation as a man it was unwise to tangle with. Brilliantly good at his job as a bartender, he was equally fast with his fists, feet or a knife, having picked up the art of survival tending bar in some of the most glamorous – and violent – cities of the world. His present employment at the Flamingo dated back to the opening of the café, and was the direct result of coming to Harry Byrd's assistance only a week after the latter had arrived in Shanghai: a dark night, a back alley and a pair of Chinese hoods who had caught Byrd off-guard. Both of the Chinese had ended up in hospital. Max ended up as Byrd's barman, chauffeur and occasional bodyguard.

The other archways were white, their interiors blazing with coloured murals, executed by a local Chinese artist, depicting flamingoes and other large birds. The bulk of the room was filled with tables, immaculate with white linen, glistening cutlery and glasses.

You entered from the street, into a long, but narrow, foyer, where Casimir could usually be found – allocating tables, smoothly greeting old customers and making new ones welcome. From the foyer there were four steps down into the main room: the tables stretching almost the full length towards Byrd's end, finishing in a crescent dance floor. The stairs, down which Byrd now walked, finished almost on this floor itself and, across the long expanse of tables, he glimpsed Casimir bustling around the foyer. To his immediate right, again almost on the dance floor, Herman – known to most people in the trade as Herman the German – sat at the baby grand piano which had been imported specially from Berlin.

Each evening, Herman went through hours of a constantly changing repertoire: popular songs, swing, jazz and romantic ballads, which he often sang in a soft, very English, accent not unlike that of the popular British composer, Noel Coward, who had noted the fact during his visit to Shanghai a couple of years before. This last oddity always amazed Byrd, for Herman's normal speaking voice was thick and guttural. He even looked aggressively Teutonic, complete with blond hair and a long scar slicing down the right cheek – the result of a knife fight in Puerto Rico and nothing to do with either student duelling or the Great War, which he had avoided by conveniently being otherwise engaged in the Orient during the European conflagration.

Behind the rear wall of the café, down which Byrd's stairs curved, lay the holy of holies where most of the profits were made: another oblong room with two fan-tan games, a roulette table and, usually, at least one game of chemmy in progress. The croupiers and dealers were all girls, normally working under the eye of a senior boy, trained personally by Byrd. These girls had nothing to do with the come-on girls in the café itself, overseen by Jeannie Chin. These latter girls were there simply to get lonely male customers to buy more drinks, or linger in the gaming room. Byrd did not worry about, or profit by, any arrangements the girls cared to make outside their normal working hours.

The kitchens, directly below the gaming room, were in sole charge of Descales, French by birth, international by adoption having seen service in the best hotels – from Paris to Rome, the Adriatic to the Côte d'Azur. The Flamingo put great score by its food, advertising it as being both the best and most cosmopolitan in the city – the menu catering for English, French, Italian, Chinese and Indian cuisine. People were rarely disappointed.

Byrd paused for a moment to acknowledge Herman, who had shifted key adroitly, going into one of his favourite tunes – 'Time On My Hands'. He looked up.

"You vas heving trouble, Herry?"

"A couple of small problems."

"You hed a boomp on der head, ja? Mex tol' me."

"Yeah."

"You vantta vatch det. You vanna vatch det pig Fisher as vell. He makes plenty trouble, det von."

Byrd promised he would watch Fisher, and wandered into the gaming room, which had not yet become active, with only a few clients in. There were one or two, however: a girl of around thirty playing the Black Jack table for small stakes. Military wife, probably: she had that look about her – waiting for husband or lover. The Chinese girl running the table dealt the cards with quick skill, executing neat and fast riffle shuffles after every fourth hand, and pushing the cards forward for the player to cut. They did not use a box and there was no shill at the table to bring in further stimulation. One of the bar girls would be sent in later if the action was slow.

A couple of very obvious sailors, in civilian clothes – probably stewards from the *Empress of Asia* – played at one of the fan-tan tables, more interested in the girl operating the game than the betting itself; though the money they pushed over was reasonable. The girl was tall with long, beautifully manicured hands which moved like those of a magician as she rattled the beans under the bowl, took the bets and then flicked her little black wand with great accuracy, spinning away four beans at a time from the pile until the last set was left under the bowl.

As Byrd watched, the last set on this game turned out to be three, and both the sailors had their bets on two. The fan-tan girl swept their cash into the till with the same dexterity as she had counted out the beans.

"Everything okay, Mr. Harry?" Hwa, one of Byrd's most highly trained boys, stood by his side. He was dressed like Byrd, only with a black jacket instead of the white tux: in charge of the gaming room for the night.

Byrd said yes, and asked a few fast questions regarding the state of the bank that evening – the float and reserve. Silently he cursed himself for not yet having checked the previous night's books, for he liked to keep up to date with every aspect of the café's affairs. But Hwa's answers were all fast and confident.

"Foreign money?" Byrd snapped, crisply but not unpleasantly.

Hwa knew his stuff again – to the last cent and shilling of American dollars and British sterling, which they always kept on hand together with a few roubles and francs. Finally, Byrd queried whether he was satisfied with the croupiers and cashier on duty with him.

Hwa grinned and nodded. "Flamingo girls best in town. You know that, Mr. Harry."

"Just like to keep it that way." Byrd answered the grin, and slowly left the room to complete his rounds.

Down in the steaming kitchens he found the rotund French chef belabouring a Chinese cook with a large sieve, and tongue-lashing everyone in sight.

"Things okay, Des?" Byrd dodged the swinging sieve.

Descales paused in mid-flow, "*Oui*, everything fine and normal, Monsieur 'Arry. You wish to take a peep?"

Byrd said that was why he had come. Descales grumbled at the Chinese who had been the cause of his wrath, and made a sweeping regal gesture, as though giving his boss permission to examine everything in sight, glaring as if daring Byrd to find fault with anything.

As they walked around the kitchens – occasionally stopping to test-taste a dish, or look at the state of some cooking in progress – Byrd kept up a non-stop series of questions: the price of vegetables that day in the market (Descales played the various vegetable and meat markets of Shanghai as a dedicated broker played the stock market), the price of meat, their current supplies, future trends? Reserves?

Like Hwa in the gaming rooms, Descales had facts at his fingertips.

Byrd showed no sign of his pleasure at the efficient way the culinary side of the operation was being run – lifting a lid from one of the soup vats and putting out a hand for a ladle to sample it. The soup was one of ten on the current menu: a Chinese water-chestnut which Byrd swilled approvingly around his mouth to savour the distinctive flavour before swallowing.

At the large swing doors, he paused to glance through the night's menu, as he always did, noting that, among the dishes recommended by the chef, there was Lemon Chicken and Ginger Beef, for those who wanted Chinese cooking; Steak and Kidney Pudding and Rare Roastbeef from the trolley for the British palate; Hamburger Flamingo, especially for the American patrons; Duck Pâté, and *Poulet à la Comtoise* for the French; Beef and Lamb curries, and a dozen other tempting items which included Shanghai specialities like Squirrel Fish, Red-Braised Hand of Pork with Crystal Sugar, and *Chiao Yen P'ai Ku* – Salt and Pepper Spareribs.

Byrd gave a final nodding 'okay', and Descales went back to his work, sliding neatly from his broken English into hysterical French to tell the under-chefs, cooks and assistants that they were lazy and not fit to cook for swine.

Harry Byrd shrugged and smiled. Yes, everything was normal, screaming chaos in the kitchens. With luck he might even get through an evening during which Descales did not actually resign, or bring one of the other chefs up to the office to demand his instant dismissal.

At the bar, Max gave him a questioning look. Byrd returned it with an almost imperceptible nod, to let him know that he was all right. At the same time he made a mental note to speak with Max later about the bar stocks, and Casimir about the wine cellar.

The girls were around him in a flash: Jeannie immediately hanging on his arm in a proprietary manner. Arina leaned across and spoke in her low, heavy accent: "How about you giving me a chance sometime, Mr. Harry? I can do things these slant girls don't know have been invented yet."

Jeannie eventually calmed down enough to ask after his head. He said he had known his head when it had felt better, but he would be okay and wanted to talk with Polly Sing. Jeannie reacted with her normal petulance, but eventually stamped off, sending Polly over to him. He had a special for her later, Byrd said, adding that it would pay well.

Polly was a delicate, small girl – deceptive physical attributes, since she was known among her sisterhood at the Flamingo as a tigress. It was said that she had dealt with, and satisfied, a gigantic alcoholic English sailor, a Russian wrestler and three fighting drunk American marines in one evening alone. Even for her, however, Boris Oblosky – Percy – would be a challenge.

Byrd briefed her, and then went over to put Casimir in the picture: about Boris and various other aspects of the evening ahead.

In particular, Casimir would have to do without Koo, one of his most trusted boys, together with a younger waiter, because Byrd would need them upstairs – particularly Koo, who would be required as a look-out to warn Byrd when he should go invisible, with his ear pressed against the telephone connection to the private room.

Casimir was difficult, but finally accepted the situation and gave in, though with ill grace. Byrd re-threaded his way through the tables and was half-way up the curving staircase when he suddenly realised his headache and the vision problem in his right eye were getting worse.

He made it to the office and slumped into his chair, head thumping and a fine red screen of pain behind the eye. He also felt sudden nausea which made him close both eyes and lean back, trying to reach through the pain to check and make sure that all the evening's possible eventualities had been covered.

When Koo arrived for his orders, Byrd pulled himself together, giving the boy details of how he wanted the meeting handled in the private room. Then, locking the door, he gave himself another shot of Teachers and stretched back in the chair.

Slowly he drifted into a floating sleep, enveloped in a merciful cloud of unknowing. The next thing he heard was a steady tapping at the door.

He felt better: only a dull pain in the head and a little muzziness of vision. It was ten forty-five. Out of habit he glanced down into the café through the mirror, to see that it was getting more crowded by the minute. Crossing to the door, taking stock that his physical condition was much improved, he spoke softly, establishing that Koo was on the other side before he opened up.

The boy gave a flustered little bow. "Mr. Tang motor all just arrive. He coming topside, chop-chop."

If Tang be here, he thought, the Maes brothers cannot be far behind. As if on cue, the Maes brothers were alive in his head – the naked light bulb and the man with his hands crushed, screaming.

七 (7)

Byrd nodded his mental picture of the Maes brothers away, already aware of the shuffling sound coming from the stairs. A moment later, Foo Tang appeared: his death-head set above rich, brocaded silk robes, an ornate round cap sitting neatly on the skull. He was flanked by Lee Yung and another Chinese heavy. Koo stood ready near the door to the private room, while Byrd's other waiter remained stationed by the exit leading to the stairs and café.

"Welcome." Byrd bowed in greeting. "Everything's

ready, just as you wanted." He motioned towards the private room, and Koo sprang forward to open the door.

Tang nodded his own two men inside, but turned towards Byrd's office. "A word for your most private ear, Harry Byrd."

Byrd closed the door on them and put his back against the desk to mask the connecting phone which stood there with the earpiece removed. "I've done as you asked. My boys'll provide you with anything you need, and you won't be disturbed."

"I am most glad to hear it. However, I understand you have had a visit since we last met."

"Several: the police, a muscle man from the friends you're about to meet. . ."

"Ah!" It sounded as though Tang did not know of Boris' look-around. "So, our Americans are also being careful."

"Very. This guy was almost as big as General Chow, and looks like he can pack a matching punch." General Chow's statue – that of a particularly massive warrior – had stood guard over the temple at the North Gate of the walled Chinese city since the twelfth century.

Tang said that General Chow held no fears for him, so he doubted if the American version could frighten him. "As for the visit, I was speaking of the attack made on you. You look bruised about the head, and it has come to my attention that a Japanese ronin was sent to give you trouble. That is correct?"

"First my motor, then me. Yea, Tang, a lousy little ronin jumped me. I handed him over to the police."

Foo Tang inclined his head, tight-lipped. He was not used to being called Tang so abruptly, but he did not labour his displeasure and went on to say that he understood it was the Municipal Police who had the Japanese. "The unpleasant, drunken Inspector Fisher, yes? You should have called me, Harry. I would have dealt with this little Black Dragon." He brought his hands together in a vicious slap, as though destroying a mosquito.

"I had Fisher on my back because of the explosion. There was no option but to hand the Nip over to him. Was he really Black Dragon? I've not had that confirmed yet; not by the police anyway."

Tang remarked that the Japanese Shoshi were very active. "I am told it was Black Dragon who exploded your machine; when that failed, they sent a man to damage you. I already warned you that rivals may come in the night and ask you to do business with them."

"But Black Dragon are Japanese. They never try any rough stuff around this end of the city. Sure, there's violence in the north: but here?"

Tang smiled: almost a trace of pity crossing his lips. "You cannot speak of the ocean to a well frog, or of ice to a summer insect. You, Harry Byrd, like so many, can only see what you wish to see, or what you desire to see. To you, Shanghai is a great and powerful city: a place of wealth where money is always present. You cannot, my summer Byrd, see the winter of Shanghai's destiny. The Japanese desire much of our land, and all of our wealth. Certainly the International Settlements here are a bulwark, but even they can crumble. Where politicians and military men plan, so the Shoshi act. The Black Dragon people are crawling from their territories around Hongkew. They will try to make a foothold of violence here, in the centre of Shanghai, so that when their armies come, they will already have power. These are the men to be wary of, for they will come again. They do not fear death, like the Western man: they have not finished with you or your Flamingo Café." He placed a hand on Byrd's shoulder. "Any more trouble, then you call me. I shall watch out, for we are not going to let them spread their fire and slime in our land."

Byrd gave a quick nod. For the second time that evening he had heard of the Japanese threat to China; and particularly Shanghai. The man Bingham's fears had not worried him, but when Foo Tang began to take threats from the Japanese underworld seriously then maybe it was time to be anxious. He could not deny the wrecked Delage, nor his aching head and the pain in his eye.

It was better to have Tang as an ally, and he told the Chinese that he would call upon him if needed; in the meantime all was ready for the meeting: food, drink, boys to serve them, and even a lock on the door. "You'll not be disturbed," he repeated. "All I ask is to be left out. I don't even want to know that a meeting took place here tonight. I met your friends' emissary, and if he's anything to go by, then contact with these guys is bad joss."

"You are not invited, Harry Byrd. I would consider it an impertinence if you even suggested to anyone that I have been here to meet these Maes people."

"You haven't been near the place." Byrd went to the door. Foo Tang bowed his thanks and passed out into the passage, crossing to the private room. Lee Yung stood outside – waiting, Byrd presumed, for their guests to arrive. Koo, nearby, gave him a reassuring look, as if to communicate that his instructions would be carried out to the letter.

Back in his office with the door locked, Byrd quietly lit another cigarette and picked up the earpiece of the connecting phone. He could hear quite clearly: Tang speaking in a normally pitched voice to the other Chinese. He spoke fast enough and in Mandarin, so Byrd only got about one word in fifty; not enough to make any sense.

Presently there was more noise in the passage, indicating that the Maes' party was not attempting to disguise its arrival. He could hear conversation outside the door as well as via the telephone, so that it sounded like feedback and caused him to place his right hand over one ear, pressing the telephone earpiece hard into the other. The first clear words he heard were those of Vincent Maes. "Mr. Foo Tang? It's good to meet you; we've come a long way for this."

Involuntarily, Byrd shivered. It was more than three years since he had actually heard the man speak, but the smooth accent and penetrating quality of the voice was unmistakable. Vincent Maes could have been standing by his shoulder now, introducing his brother. Although Valentine's voice did not betoken the same commanding presence as Vincent's, it was memorable in a more directly sinister way. Then Vincent said, "Mr. Tang, I'd like you to meet our expert: the good Dr. Carlo Zuchestra." There was a murmuring, and Vincent Maes continued, "Dr. Zuchestra has spent most of his life in the study and collection of armaments. As a young man he worked for the great Beretta family. He –"

"I have already familiarised myself with Dr. Zuchestra's personal history, since you first approached me, Mr. Maes."

"Sure, sure." Vincent Maes sounded far from sure, but he was still in command. Byrd smiled to himself and wondered if the Maes boys imagined they were dealing with some illiterate Chinese hood.

Tang spoke again. "Gentlemen, you are here, in this place, as my guests. Before we discuss any business perhaps you would care for some refreshment." There was a general muttering, the sound of bottles, glasses and plates through which only the odd word escaped into the earpiece. At length it was obvious that the attendants had withdrawn. The sound of the key turning in the lock was distinct.

Sitting hunched over the phone, Byrd was conscious of his own pounding head, the ache spreading in tight waves down the back of his neck. He had reason to be tense, he told himself, with the Maes brothers only a few steps away in the next room.

There was a scraping of chairs; then silence, as though each of the participants was waiting for one of the others to begin. Tang, as usual, remained silent. He would always wait for others to start speaking when it concerned business. Byrd had once heard him quote some old Chinese philosopher – *A dog is not considered good because of its barking, and a man is not considered clever because of his ability to talk.* The wily Tang would sit all evening in silence if need be.

Eventually it was the less conversational of the Maes brothers who began. "Guess we should start talking turkey then, Mr. Tang," said Valentine.

"Okay, okay. . ." Vincent cut in, as though worried that his brother might go too far. "Mr. Tang knows the outline of our proposition. That's more or less agreed, Mr. Tang? Yes?"

"So you have said in our correspondence, Mr. Maes. I have merely expressed interest."

"Okay." Valentine had an edge to his voice which teetered on the brink of irritation. "Okay, so we get down to cases. The theory's sound enough, yeah?"

"I have always thought the barter system an excellent way of doing business." Byrd could almost see the smile on Tang's impassive death-head. "The problem is that, over the years, the westerners who have bitten into my country have bartered with only their own profit in mind."

"We're square enough, Mr. Tang. It'll be a fair deal; an equal deal. We end up with what we want; you finish up with what you need."

There was a long silence before Tang spoke again. The telephone connection was so clear that Byrd could hear a match flare: Vincent lighting a cigarette. He remembered that it was always Vincent who smoked, never his brother.

"Your words interest me, Mr. Maes." Byrd recognised the soft tone as one of Tang's danger signals. "What you *want*; what I *need*. To be fair we should both get what we want *and* need."

"Sure, Mr. Tang, you're playing with words now."

"I think not. To be precise is a virtue. Only a rogue misreports."

"Well now. . ." from Valentine. "Just a moment, Mr. Tang . . ."

"Mr. Tang's right, Val. Want and need are two different things." Straining to catch everything, Byrd thought he detected a hardening in Vincent Maes' voice.

Tang said nothing: the pause seemed to go on for ever. Byrd had to cover the mouthpiece of his phone because the sound of Herman's piano, starting to roll into 'Chinatown', was percolating up into the office. Herman always swung 'Chinatown' loudly when the tourists were in.

Finally, from Vincent: "So let's try to figure out who *needs* what, and who *wants* what. Okay, Mr. Tang?"

"Whatever you wish. I am open to bargaining. I have to warn you, though, that it is not always possible for people

69

to have either what they need or want. This is a hard fact of life."

"Okay." The irritation was now all too apparent in Vincent Maes' tone. Byrd had heard him at the negotiating table before, and knew that if he wanted something badly he usually got it. One way or another. "We want – we *need* – opium. We want and need it for our operations in America. It's a commodity that calls for shrewd investment. I make no bones about it, Mr. Tang, we can realise high profits with opium in the States. It's big business that's going to get bigger all the time." He cleared his throat, a signal Byrd knew well. A trump card was about to hit the table. "We, personally, have no real problem. There is no difficulty in getting the amounts of opium we need. I'm figuring on a large shipment out of this trip. Early next year we expect to take something like one million pounds of opium into the States. That's around five hundred short tons. A lot of dreams, Mr. Tang."

Tang said it was indeed a lot of opium. More than he could handle.

"That's why we're approaching several sources: why we're cutting you in, Mr. Tang. Came to you especially because of your high reputation. Our contacts, who you probably know well, in Canton, have already done their deal. We're paying them in money. In turn, they're bringing the stuff through Hong Kong. We plan to bring a ship in here first before picking up the Hong Kong consignment. But with you we trade, Mr. Tang – goods for goods: not cash. Am I right?"

"It is what you have offered. On my part, I have expressed my interest."

"Okay." Vincent Maes was speeding up his rate of words, as if he had passed on to safer ground. "I'll level with you, Mr. Tang. We already have half of the opium we need: five hundred thousand pounds of the stuff. We've put down half the price and there's a pick-up date arranged in Hong Kong. We're asking you to secure the other five hundred thousand pounds, weight, ready for delivery to our ship, here in Shanghai, around the end of the year. . ."

"Beginning of next," Valentine corrected him.

Vincent acknowledged his error. Originally they had planned it for December – now it would be January, he said; around mid-January. Was it possible to get that much opium ready for shipment by then?

Tang said that all things were possible, but it was not altogether up to him. There was one man he would have to deal with – the man who controlled the opium trade in Shanghai. However, if the payment was right . . .

"I don't think you'll quibble about the payment, because it's what *you* want, and need." Byrd could almost see him smiling, the perpetual Miami tan making the skin crease heavily around the eyes.

Again, Tang was playing the waiting game. You could have counted a hundred before Vincent Maes was pushed into speaking again. The silence teetered nervously: a sudden focus down to the group gathered in the room around the table, as if the whole world had shrunk to that one place.

"In the current situation, Mr. Tang, you need arms and ammunition."

"Correction, Mr. Maes. It would be helpful for my people to be supplied with good, *modern* arms and ammunition."

Maes said he could guarantee it. "Only a fool could close his eyes to China's precarious situation. I am no politician, Mr. Tang, but they'll come, won't they? They want Manchuria, and when they take it they'll want Shanghai and the rest of China."

"Unless they are stopped."

"Sure. With Chiang Kai-shek's badly trained troops and their ancient weapons? Or Shanghai's Volunteer Corps: clerks and businessmen playing tin soldiers?"

"Good modern weapons would be an inducement, Mr. Maes. Also I have to agree with you: the sooner the better. A man whose leg has been cut off does not value a present of shoes."

"You mean, what are we offering?"

"Precisely."

Vincent Maes handed the ball to Dr. Zuchestra. Byrd

could not even picture him, and found the accent difficult to follow as the Italian was obviously seated at the end of the table furthest from the telephone.

The gist got through, however, and, if it was all for real, Tang would be mad to turn it down. Nine hundred brand new Lee Enfield rifles, together with a large amount of .303 ammunition; six Italian Revelli light machine-guns, plus five hundred thousand rounds; one hundred factory-cleared Smith & Wesson revolvers with shells; five hundred Mills grenades, and – the prize of the lot – fifty Thompson sub-machine-guns with a large quantity of loaded ammunition drums.

After Zuchestra had finished reading off his list, Tang began to question him in detail: an interrogation on the quality of the weapons and other associated matters. Byrd was impressed at the knowledge displayed by the Chinese. It was as though he had just taken a most comprehensive series of lectures on modern armaments – which was a definite possibility for one like Foo Tang.

"A generous offer, gentlemen," Tang said at last. "If left to me I would be inclined to accept it at once – subject to certain matters of scrutiny before we make the exchange. However. . ." He explained once more that, with such a large amount of opium, he could not be expected to arrange everything. "As you know, I do not have the monopoly here. The man of whom I spoke is most powerful. He is also a very private gentleman; but I think I may be able to arrange a financial deal which will suit our mutual pockets."

Maes asked if they could take it that they had a deal in principle, and Tang said, probably. "You say January?" he asked.

Maes repeated that it would be around mid-January. Once Tang gave his word, they would set things in motion and have the arms and explosives moved down to San Francisco. It would all take time, but the ship would come straight to Shanghai for the exchange – weapons for opium – before going on to Hong Kong to pick up the rest of the consignment.

"You will have to return to America to make these arrangements?"

"One of us, only," Maes told him. It would be less conspicuous if they did it that way.

"And that one – yourself or your brother, I presume – would return to Shanghai with the ship?"

Naturally. The ship concerned was waiting. A freighter, the *Bel Canto*, registered in Paraguay – a matter of convenience.

The conversation lapsed into pleasantries and arrangements for Tang to make contact with the Americans – *within two days* – at the Cathay. They all had one more drink to toast their plans, and finally the meeting began to break up.

Byrd heard Boris, who must have been standing near to the bed and telephone, telling Koo that he could call him Percy and that some guy had told him to see "Mr. Ca-si-mir". Valentine Maes, overhearing this, told Boris to behave himself; Vincent laughed, while Tang held a quiet discussion with Zuchestra about the relative merits of the revolver and the automatic pistol.

Byrd put the earpiece quietly on to the desk and slumped back in his chair, contemplating the sickening fact that at least one of the Maes brothers was going to be in Shanghai for some time to come: until January – five months. Big though the city was, with its various Settlements and the old Chinese walled city, it was unlikely that a man in Byrd's situation could avoid coming face to face with whichever brother stayed behind.

They all appeared to have moved into the passage, outside his door, heading towards the rear stairs. It seemed safe enough for him to replace the earpiece on the claw arm of the telephone without anyone being near enough to hear the tell-tale click at the other end. He did it gently, then picked up the interhouse phone, cranking down to Max, asking him to put Polly Sing on the line.

"Jeannie want talk with you," the girl said as soon as she came on. He might have known it. Jeannie was acquiring eyes and ears in the back of her head; suspicions grew from small seeds of nothing.

Byrd said okay, but first he wanted to tell Polly that the special was on his way down. "Get him loaded, Polly, and, as a favour, you can use the private room tonight. Tell Mr. Casimir I said to get it tidied up." Casimir would love that.

She hardly had time to tell him okay before Jeannie Chin was on – "What you want talk with Polly for, Harry? Polly a lazy cow."

"Polly's looking after a client for me, honey, and you know it. In the private room, right? Now you behave yourself or I'll spank that little yellow ass of yours."

"You promise, Harry?" and she was gone with a happy laugh, not even bothering to ask about the condition of his head.

Byrd closed his eyes tightly, trying to put events into perspective: aware that everything was getting very much out of control. It shouldn't happen like this – his car bombed; the most dangerous Japanese criminal society in Shanghai after him; a request, which he could hardly credit, to join forces with the British Secret Service; deadly shadows from his past appearing to plan a deal with his own gangster partner – guns for opium – and, if either of them recognised him, being only too happy to kill. Probably slowly. On top of which, the rogue ronin had left him consciously uneasy about his personal physical condition. Enough was enough. He only needed bad trouble in the café tonight, and the day would be complete.

On the credit side, he had a small piece of information for the Englishman, Bingham, who would be interested to hear of the proposed deal between Tang and the Maes brothers. It might even help get them off his back. That would be dealing with two things at once: Tang's hold over him, and the eternal business of always having to look over his shoulder in case the Maes brothers appeared – as they had now done – on the horizon.

Glancing down from his private viewpoint, Byrd scanned the tables below. He recognised one or two regulars: the bar was crowded, a large number of tourists having arrived, mainly seated towards the front where they could best take in Herman's performance. Three couples were actually dancing; the massive Boris stood on the steps, at the entrance, talking to Casimir who appeared to be making wild signals in the direction of Polly Sing, temporarily with a British sailor at the bar.

Byrd cranked Max, telling him to get Polly over to Casimir – fast. He was not going to have Boris taking another customer apart in full view of the tourists.

He turned away to replace the receiver, then instantly turned back again, not really believing what he had glimpsed at the moment of looking away: certain it was simply some freak ghost image in his brain. He hunched forward, staring down from the mirror; his guts contracting, then sinking with a nauseating lurch. At first sight he could not credit it; especially on top of everything else that had happened. Yet the more he stared, the more it became obvious that this was no hallucination.

Below him, Casimir was leading Cat through the tables towards a floor-side seat. Cat. His Cat, from what seemed a million years ago. This was Cat in the flesh, and not the fantasy figure his imagination had lived with, on and off, since leaving America. Certainly she was more polished now: more sure of herself, as she turned to speak with her companion – a slim, angular, sandy-haired young man – but still his Cat, throwing her head back in a laughing gesture he had seen a thousand times.

He felt his brow crease, and even that brought pain, as his mind wrestled with the situation. Not only was it impossible for Cat to be here, in the Flamingo, but also it was very dangerous. Yet it was no ghost; no mistake: her walk, the toss of her head, the way she smoothed her skirt, as Casimir fussed around the couple.

Byrd lit a cigarette, and saw that his hands were trembling. Below him, Herman was playing 'Ain't She Sweet?'. He took a long drag at the smoke, thought to himself that – in the end – Cat had been about as sweet as sour cream, then tore his lip on the cigarette paper again.

His hands still shook as he reached for the Teachers, pouring a dose, and knocking it straight back. He had felt bad enough before. Now that Cat had turned up – a wraith from the past – Harry Byrd felt more shot-up than ever. Yet he remained realistic enough to know unpleasantness could not be avoided for ever. In a way he had always known it.

Bingham's proposition; the possible threats from the Black Dragon; the definite threat from the Maes brothers; and the complicated difficulties with Tang, would all have to be faced. He also had to face Cat. The good, bad, holy and unholy always returned – if not in nightmares, then, eventually, in the flesh. A cliché, Cat would say, but all debts in this life were redeemable.

Straightening his tie, Byrd faced the mirror, smoothing his straight dark hair, crushing out the cigarette and taking a fresh one to light as he paused on the stairs: a routine that rarely changed.

A final glance through the window – a few couples dancing; Herman switching again, this time into the slow, smoochie stuff: 'Melancholy Baby', 'What Is This Thing Called Love?', 'Blue Moon'. Boris stood at the bar, laughing, one great arm thrown across little Polly Sing's shoulders, the free hand curled like a bunch of bananas, around a glass. The waiters skipped between the tables, doing impossible feats of balancing with trays of food and drink. Casimir looked half-demented because there was a largish crowd forming above the steps, in the foyer, while a thin layer of smoke hung, like an evening haze, over the whole scene.

Just as he was about to leave, Byrd saw 'Pearly' Fisher, in a lightweight crumpled and stained suit, push his way through the crowd and whisper to Casimir. The Maître d' had to give him preference, that was unavoidable. He led Fisher to a single table away from the bar, signalling to a waiter as he went, his face openly betraying the dislike he felt for people like Fisher.

Okay, thought Byrd, forget overbearing corrupt coppers like Fisher; forget the head and the eye; forget Cat down there, looking into the young guy's eyes as though they were set in diamonds; forget the whole damned lot; just go out and do your job: run the best café in the whole of Shanghai.

八 (8)

He carefully locked the door and headed down towards the café, even managing to look calm – the usual unruffled image of one of Shanghai's top café owners – as he paused on the stairs, quickly scanning the room below. It was like an actor making an important entrance. Hadn't Shakespeare said something about that – one man in his life playing many parts? Okay.

Herman changed key, rolling into 'Let's Do It' – a private joke which had turned into a kind of personal signature tune, played each night when Harry Byrd came down the curving staircase at around this time.

Birds do it,
Bees do it,
Even educated fleas do it. . .

Slowly, he began to make his way through the tables, acknowledging Herman, and a few of the regulars he had not seen earlier. At the bar he gestured for Max to come over, and the little Mexican whispered to his Chinese assistant, giving him instructions so that drink-serving time would not be lost.

"Didn't ask you earlier," Byrd leaned over the bar, his face unfathomable, very professional. He had his job to do, and he wanted to be seen doing it. "What's the booze situation? We okay for the rest of the week?"

Max said they were getting a bit short on gin, but the next order was due in the morning.

"Thought you usually took delivery on Monday?"

Max told him they normally did. "There's been some trouble at the warehouse." It would be okay: by tomorrow night stocks would be up to their usual quota. Byrd asked if the girls were behaving themselves. Max nodded and gave a sly smile. "There's a ship in, boss, they'll be making plenty of squeeze on the side tonight."

As he turned away, heading towards Casimir, Byrd saw 'Pearly' Fisher trying to catch his eye. But he was not going to be distracted at the moment, either by Fisher or by the mysterious arrival of Cat. The general running of the café came first. On his way across the room, Byrd stopped at several more tables to ask if everything was to the customer's satisfaction, or pass a few words with people he recognised.

Fisher was still signalling, but Byrd paused, stopping one of the Chinese waiters to examine the dishes the boy carried on his loaded tray. Excellent – an order of Fried and Braised Carp, garnished with onions and ginger (the menu stated, correctly, that a famous Soochow chef first served this dish to the Emperor Ch'ien-lung when he visited the area south of the Yangtze); together with a huge watermelon filled with kumquats, mandarins, grapes, lychees, pears, peaches and apples. Byrd smiled, and patted the boy on his way before continuing towards Casimir, who by now had settled Cat and her companion and was out in the foyer, apologising profusely to three parties of English visitors forced to wait for tables.

Byrd added his weight of charm, telling them they would not have to stand around much longer. Then he led Casimir to one side.

"Tables fifteen and twelve – over there, Casim. Crew members from the *Empress*, they've been sitting around drinking Chefoo beer half the evening. We can't afford it."

"Those are big men, Mr. Harry. We want no trouble. If I tell them to move on, they squash me like a wheat flour ball. What do you think I am? A karate master?"

"You're a tactful and diplomatic Maître d', Cas. But I do

see your point. I'll have a word. You coping?"

Casimir lifted his hands to his pudgy face, emitting one of his characteristic 'pheews', then shrugged – "I need more assistants. Monday night only, and we still have not enough tables, not enough waiters, not enough space. You have to expand, Mr. Harry. This café get more popular all the time. . ."

Byrd let him run on until he finally admitted that he could just manage. Then he sent Casimir back, smiling, to his patient customers.

Fisher could not be avoided for much longer, as the signals were getting more difficult to ignore. Passing him on the way to the adjacent tables twelve and fifteen, Byrd slung a "With you in a minute, Pearly," in his general direction.

A group of large seamen, smartly – if a little loudly – turned out, sat drinking beer at the two tables: just as they had been doing since Byrd first looked in earlier that evening.

"Sorry, boys." Byrd spread his arms wide and gave them his biggest smile. "I need the tables for people who want dinner. 'Fraid I'll have to move you on."

"Like hell," one of the largest men began.

"Yes, like hell, if that's necessary." Byrd did not let the smile fade, but inclined his head in the direction of 'Pearly' Fisher's table. "There's one senior cop sitting over there, and I've got enough bouncers around to have you out, and hurt, very fast."

Two of the men rose from their chairs, spoiling for a fight. "However," Byrd held up a pacifying hand, "if you vacate the tables and go over to the bar, there'll be a couple of rounds on the house."

That made a difference. Slowly the men began to rise, casting glances at the bar. It was a tactical victory and Byrd gave Max the high-sign, then circled the group with his hand, indicating that they were to be given a couple of free rounds. He also made another sign which told Max that they were to be eased out quietly when they had consumed the quota. Byrd then nodded towards Casimir, who hastily bowed to his waiting customers and started to lead them towards the now vacant tables.

"What you drinking, Byrd?" Fisher asked, as a man will speak to an unloved dog who has to be watered.

"Not in office hours, Pearly. You developed a nervous tic, or did you want to talk?" He pulled a chair up to the policeman's table.

"Thought you should know we put the sweat on that ronin who jumped you. They meant business, Byrd. Hope you realise that. Out to kill."

"He talked?"

"Not really. Enough though. They don't have to pour it all out in words of one syllable, you know. Hint here; word there. Piece it all together. He's Shoshi. Black Dragon, and they're after you, Byrd. Little beggars have you, and your café, on their list. Right at the top." He leaned forward so that it looked like a casual exchange; but his eyes still glittered unpleasantly.

One of the boys brought a large pink gin – Fisher's third, though he did not even acknowledge the service. The boy turned an enquiring look towards Byrd, who lazily nodded him away with a smile.

"If the Shoshi want you," Fisher continued, "they can have you as far as I'm concerned. You should know that, Byrd. Do my duty and no more. Places like this're breeding ground for vermin."

Byrd stayed casual. "You reckon things'd be easier to control if the Black Dragon boys moved in?"

"Much easier. If they moved in, we'd have an excuse to close them down."

Byrd stubbed out his cigarette, reaching immediately for another. "And the big-time Shoshi would just sit around on their tails and do nothing? Come on, Pearly, the rich would get richer, the poor poorer, and the graft graftier." He wanted to say a lot more, but managed to curb his tongue. The last thing he needed was a public showdown with Fisher. He knew, only too well, that coppers like Fisher made their paltry pickings from the streets and small-time chancers. They did not give a damn how places like the

Flamingo were run. Their beef was with the fact that they were not big enough in the league to take any of the real action from this place, or the Canidrome Ballroom, or the Venus, or any of the top cafés. Fisher would be as happy as Larry if he had the muscle to take squeeze from people like Harry Byrd.

Fisher knocked his gin back in one gulp, letting the glass come down heavily on the table. "You know what I don't like?" he asked.

"Tell me."

"I don't like half-baked little adventurers who home in on Shanghai to make a few quick bucks by running glorified gin palaces and bordellos like this. In particular I don't like your kind, Byrd. The kind with some sort of pull from way back; the kind who have a 'hands-off' stamp on their file. What is your pull, Byrd? Rich uncle Senator back in the States?"

Pull? If only he knew, thought Byrd. His only pull was liable to whisk him into the sea, neatly clad in size fifty-two lead boots.

"I have no rich uncles, nor any idea why my police file carries what you call a 'hands-off' stamp. Sure, Pearly, I'm an adventurer. I just wanted out of my own back yard. Come to that, why did *you* leave England, home and beauty?"

Fisher opened his mouth, then appeared to think better of it, so Byrd went on talking. "I ended up here and got lucky. It could just have easily been Hong Kong or Macau, where I might have become a cop, drinking too much, bullying the locals, taking squeeze. But I'm here, and I'm straight."

Fisher grinned. "Straight as a coil. Have you one day, Byrd. Have you on toast."

"Have a drink on the house in the meantime, Pearly; and thanks for the warning about the Black Dragon. Must get my St. George suit out of the closet. Watch how you go."

He left the table, knowing that he had trodden a dangerous line. But better to humour Fisher than go for a short, easy victory.

He walked away intent on looking in at the gaming room

once more – anything to delay facing Cat. Glancing at his watch he thought there was just enough time to do that and get back into the main room for Arina's spot. Arina did three songs, two shows a night: another reason for Jeannie Chin's jealousy. Jeannie had a singing voice only marginally more tuneful than a laryngitic Peking duck, while Arina was very good, in a throaty, sexy way: especially when she did the sultry numbers.

He had not, however, kept his mind on where Cat was sitting.

She caught him off guard. "Hallo, Harry," reaching up and touching his sleeve as he passed. She was alone now. "I saw you come down."

"And I saw you arrive. You made quite an entrance." Byrd drew smoke in quickly through his teeth. She was wearing a sleek silk evening gown which clung to her in a way which made him wonder if she wore anything underneath it. Her shoulders were bare and tanned a smooth brown like her face. Sun and health radiated from her. "You had a guy with you."

"Yes," she gave a nervous laugh. "*You* had a whole café with you."

It was all very matter-of-fact, with no real smiles. They stared at one another as though trying to expunge old memories, searching their faces for some trace of the people they had once been. Each of them saw a different reel of film running through the screen in their brains: laughter, tears, places, times, rooms, beds, streets, parks: on and on until Byrd broke the gaze and looked pointedly at the empty chair at the table.

"Tom Geddes," she explained. "My photographer. One of your boys headed him in the direction of some gambling. You remember how I am about that. It's the one thing Tom and I disagree on."

"Lucky Tom. As I remember it. . ." He stopped. It was no time to start talking about the past: not yet anyway. "You staying in Shanghai or just passing through?" He hesitated, then moved closer. "Ah . . . if your friend comes back, the name's Byrd now. Harry Byrd. That's Byrd with a *y*." For a second he was lost in her large brown eyes. At first sight he thought there was a new hardness about them. Maybe he simply imagined it, but they appeared to soften as he looked at her.

"Here for a few weeks, Harry. Staying at the Cathay Hotel."

"Assignment?" Of course: stupid question. The guy was her photographer.

"Yes" – world weary – "an assignment. Series on the great cities of the world. Tom's photographs: my words. *View Magazine*."

"The big time, huh?" He was aware of *View*'s circulation. With its international market, who wasn't? "You got what you wanted, then?" He did not mean to sound harsh or bitter, but he knew it came out that way.

"Do we ever? Really get what we want, I mean."

"Elusive. You walk into my place by accident?" – A flash picture in his mind: pouring rain, and men being led from the Statler Hotel, in the city back home, by police, at gun point. Cat was at the wheel of the car, and the windshield wipers did not appear to be doing their job, trying vainly to slough the torrent from the screen.

The hardness in her eyes had completely gone now as she looked back up at him: the old brimming look. *The eyes with the chocolate centres*, he used to call them. Her voice was only just controlled, quiet and sincere: "I didn't know you were here, Harry, if that's what you mean. I've always made a point of not knowing. It's okay, though; I won't come back if you'd rather . . ."

"It's a free city. Free world. You're entitled."

"I'm sorry. Look, please sit down." She swallowed and looked away. "I can't tell you how good it is to see you after so long."

So long? Three years? "You always did have resilience. Personally, I find the reopening of near fatal wounds a difficult business."

"Harry," as though pleading.

Herman went into 'Dance Little Lady'. It was almost time for Arina's spot, and he should really be in the gaming room by now; but he pulled up the empty chair and sat. *Darling Harry, I love you. Never doubt that. I guess I'll always love you . . . but I have to tell you straight . . . I'm not coming with you as we planned. . .* She had written that, three years ago. He knew the letter by heart, and still had it, locked away upstairs.

"I mean it," she said. "It *is* wonderful to see you again. I didn't expect. . ." Then her eyes widened, like someone coming across a particular horror. "Oh Christ. You've not forgiven me, have you? You've not forgotten. . ."

"You ask a lot, Cat. Or do I have to revert to Kate? Or Miss Morrow? You ask too much. It's a shock, that's all. Don't worry about it. But it's also hell's inconvenient for both of us. There are old chums in town that you wouldn't want to meet. Our old friends the Maes brothers." Her brow creased, and as Byrd said it he saw her, in his mind, standing in his apartment on that unforgettable night, long ago now, with the rain lashing at the windows, while he sat and shakily told her of the terrors and insoluble problems. She had been very calm, said she knew the one way he could get out, told him of the dangers, but swore she would help him, stand by him and be with him. *I love you too much, Harry. I'll see it through, then we'll be together. I promise you that.*

Back at the table, here and now, she stammered out that she was sorry. She had realised, very quickly after it happened, how much she must have hurt him; that she could never cause pain like that to anybody ever again. But she thought by now he would have come to terms with her decision: understood it.

"I understand – understood – understand all your reasons," he said quickly. "All of them. It's just getting used to seeing you again. Understanding isn't forgiving, and I was just really starting to live with it. You bring things back that I'd rather forget." Herman flourished the final bars of 'Dance Little Lady'. "And things I'd like to remember."

"Harry, before we go any further, there's something you should know. I'm. . ."

She failed to complete the sentence, because Herman

began his introduction for Arina – *The Flamingo's own tame Russian princess: Arina Verislovskaya.*

The lights dimmed, and the big spot circled round to the piano, with Herman softly playing the lead-in as Arina strode, rather than walked, to her position, applause scattering the room. Then she began: a lingering, haunting melody which Herman had written to words concocted by the pair of them – about lost love, and loneliness, and the hope of some future time together: trite if you just repeated the words, but poignant when sung to Herman's arrangement. It was the kind of song with which lovers and ex-lovers identified, and cried over, cursing fate or folly, whichever seemed appropriate.

As Arina reached the end, Byrd, lighting another cigarette, glanced across the table, perplexed to see tears in Cat's eyes. So he might not have got over the pain, but his emotions were bitter: wormwood and gall, he thought. She wept, however, and he did not understand tears in one who had been so ruthless, cutting open his heart with the blunt knife of words on paper – too cowardly even to do it face to face.

The husky quality of Arina's voice made her a particularly seductive singer as far as the male patrons were concerned. The girls always got their best propositions after Arina had done her stint, and now she began another sad ballad – the usual thing, about love turned sour – then ended her performance with an upbeat version of 'I'll See You Again', in duet with Herman.

This time, the whole room rose in applause as the lights came up. Big Boris was at the bar with Polly, clapping his hands above his head; Jeannie Chin looked contemptuous, glancing constantly in Byrd's direction: he would have green-eye trouble with her tonight.

"I'll see you again," Cat muttered. "I always knew I would, Harry. But I didn't think it would be quite like this."

Out of the corner of his eye, Byrd saw that Max had left his post at the bar and was hurrying out to the table. Byrd looked, blank-eyed, at Cat. "Where's that old hard-boiled

girl reporter I used to know?" Even to him it sounded nasty.
"You weren't emotional when you took a powder on me,
Cat. Cool, calm, collected, calculated – as the clichés have
it. But you don't like clichés, so why let a couple of corny
love songs throw you?"

Red circles of anger rose to her cheeks and she was about
to reply when Max reached the table, bending over to speak
quietly in Byrd's ear.

"Message from Hwa, on duty in the gaming room, boss.
He wants to see you. Small problem, I think." Max sprinkled his conversation with 'I thinks', unintentionally turning
himself into even more of a Hollywood Mexican, since they
always came out as 'I theenk'.

Byrd nodded, excused himself from Cat with "See you
later", and walked quickly towards the doors which took
him down the few steps into the gaming room.

Hwa was sitting behind the girl cashier, in a small wired
cage, set on a dais slightly above the tables so there was an
uninterrupted view across the entire room.

Standing outside the cage, the slim, sandy-haired young
man, who had come in with Cat, drummed his fingers and
tapped a foot impatiently. For a moment, Byrd could not
think of the guy's name: the throbbing had returned to his
head and eye – steady, pounding, the eye feeling as though
red hot pins had been inserted behind the pupil. The guy's
name? Dennis? Something like that. Tom Geddes. *My
photographer*.

Hwa saw Byrd, unlocked the cage and stepped out, down
the small stairs to the floor.

"Gentleman here wish to change diamonds for gambling." He gave Byrd a look which said they could probably
make on the deal.

Geddes edged up. "You the boss?" He had the abrupt
manner of a stranger trying to impress, lording it in a
foreign country; or a man who was putting on a show
because things were not quite right. It was not possible to
make a snap decision. Byrd had much experience in sizing
up credit – experience which went back a long way. Gently,
he told himself, play it gently. Just because he's with Cat,

don't let your emotions run away. Don't get suckered either.

He acknowledged that he was the owner, repeating his name twice to make sure that Geddes got it.

Geddes did not offer his own name. "I've run out of ready cash," he spoke quickly, smoothly, sure of his ground. "Thought your place would probably do me a good deal on some stones I have here." He opened his hand to show four glinting, nicely cut diamonds on a small square of black velvet.

Byrd hardly glanced at them. "How much is he down?" turning his head towards Mu – the girl on duty behind the cage.

"He cash in five hundred dollar." She made it sound flat and unimpressive: a girl used to dealing with more substantial sums.

"Go down all the way," added Hwa without any sign of contempt. He knew better than that.

"We'll take your personal cheque, Mr. Geddes." Byrd looked him in the eyes. "Your cheque'll be good here. Anyone from *View Magazine*. . ."

"I didn't tell you. . ." Geddes began. It was the first indication: a minute change of tone. Something was bugging Mr. Geddes. It was plain enough to Byrd, and to Hwa if Byrd read the tiny twitch in the eyes correctly. The Chinese face looked impassive unless you learned to read the signals.

"You didn't have to tell me. I'm an old friend of Kate Morrow's. Not wise to leave a beautiful lady out there alone, Mr. Geddes. Not good manners in Shanghai, either. But if you want to go on playing the tables, we'll take your cheque."

Geddes put a hand gently on Byrd's shoulder, but the café owner dislodged it with a quick shrug. He loathed being touched by men, apart from a civilised handshake.

"I have a private word?" Geddes looked him in the eyes.

"Sure."

Hwa vanished from their side, as though reacting to a silent order.

"The diamonds are my travelling reserve. Better than cheques or cash. I figured on selling them here anyway. Perhaps you'd care to do the deal. You must know the right people: where you'd get the right price."

Byrd thought for a moment, then asked Geddes if he would care to come to the office. "I can take a proper look there and, maybe, we can figure something out. I'll have to take a percentage, of course."

"Okay." The thought of Byrd taking a percentage did not seem to worry him.

Once back in the main room, Geddes excused himself – "Just a quick word with Kate" – and Byrd nodded towards the curving stairs, telling the photographer how to get to the office.

His head and eye were both still giving him some pain, and Byrd was very aware of it by the time he unlocked the office door, going straight over to the two-way mirror and glancing down. Geddes leaned over Cat, talking to her, while she, in turn, was trying to persuade him of something – to cut out the gambling, Byrd guessed. She was unsuccessful – Geddes was putting on a lot of charm. Byrd knew the type; he could turn it on or off, entice birds from trees and then ensnare them. He found himself disliking Geddes the more he observed him; but if the diamonds were good stones, well . . . money was money.

Geddes crossed towards the stairs, and Byrd drew the curtains over the mirror; it was not his policy to let strangers know that he could oversee the action.

Geddes only gave a perfunctory knock, walking straight in, allowing Byrd just enough time to get behind the desk, indicate a chair, and switch on the desk lamp.

"Okay, Byrd, what you reckon?" Geddes spread out the piece of velvet in front of him displaying the four stones.

Byrd moved the lamp closer to the velvet, picking up each stone in turn, holding them between finger and thumb, using the black velvet as a backing, but not lifting them to the light. He did not possess a glass, but they looked good to the naked eye: even one naked eye. If they were genuine they could realise, perhaps, four to five thousand dollars.

"You trust me?"

"You're an old friend of Kate."

"I'll have to get them valued. All I can promise is I'll find an honest dealer. Ten per cent to me. An honest dealer, here, will have to make a reasonable profit. Say twenty per cent. You'll have to lose around thirty per cent on the true commercial value."

Geddes still did not appear to be concerned. "The diamonds are my reserve. I expected to make a loss, but if I tried to do the job myself I'd probably end up by being cheated out of fifty per cent."

Byrd said he would try to have a definite figure for him by around six that evening – it was now past midnight – and if he would like to call, personally or by phone, the whole business could be completed within an hour or so. "In the meantime, I'll lock them away in my personal safe. Better than a bank. Unless you want to stay with them. I'll give you credit in the café though; say a grand – gaming room and the main room. You want a receipt?"

Geddes said yes, and that he would call personally at six, waiting and watching carefully as Byrd locked the stones away and wrote the receipt.

"Take my advice," Byrd said, disguising the natural dislike for the man, which welled up almost as violently as the pain in his head. "Don't leave Ca . . . Kate alone for long in this city. Apart from the bad manners. . ."

"Okay, okay," Geddes raised a conciliatory hand. "Okay. She's not happy with my gambling, but you can't let women rule your life. I'll watch what you say: one thing though, I'd be obliged if you didn't mention this little business – the diamonds – to my fiancée."

Byrd was puzzled for a moment, almost opening his mouth to ask, "What fiancée?" – then realised that Geddes was talking about Cat. He felt the breath go from his lungs.

It must have been apparent on his face, for Geddes was grinning at him. "You didn't know? Yeah, I'm the lucky guy. We got engaged on this trip. Paris. Over dinner at Maxim's, would you believe?"

Byrd managed something about congratulations, and said he would see Geddes around six.

After the photographer left, he drew back the curtain and looked down into the café. He did not see the many people dining and drinking, nor the waiters and girls going about their work; did not even hear Herman at the piano. All he saw was Cat, sitting waiting for Geddes at the table. All he remembered was what they had meant to each other a few years ago. A lifetime ago.

九 (9)

Byrd's eyes narrowed. He felt like some stupid teenage boy thwarted by a fickle high-school girl. It was not the axe in his head or the needle in his eye, but what he could see: Geddes crossing the floor to take his seat at the table opposite Cat. She smiled, and the man stretched over, cupping her hand in both of his. It was a mannerism: he had shaken Byrd's hand with both of his. Engaged. Cat, engaged. Geddes would marry her.

Cat rose: they were preparing to leave; Geddes spoke to the waiter and then to Casimir – obviously saying he had credit. Casimir would take his word for it without checking; in Shanghai there was unlimited credit if your face fitted: anyway, they were at the Cathay and easily contactable. Byrd again shied away, both mentally and physically, as he saw Geddes slide an arm gently around Cat's waist.

He would go down and have a chat at the bar with Max, Byrd thought. Solitary drinking was hell. The customers were thinning out anyway, and he did not feel well enough to catch up on the paperwork. He craned forward to see the bar. Jeannie, hands on hips, was giving instructions to one of her girls, her lips spraying out the dialect almost viciously, head back and the small breasts curving aggressively against her white silk evening gown.

In spite of everything, Byrd wanted her. In an unconscious shift he realised that it was Cat he really wanted. Maybe it had always been Cat – with all the girls in all the beds in all the rooms he had shared during the past three years.

He was in the passage, locking the door, when he heard Boris coming up the stairs with Polly Sing – the Chinese girl's tinkling giggle counterpointing Boris' heavy slow speech.

Polly appeared at the stairs' door first, giving a little mock-modest gasp on seeing Byrd, then hurrying past, hands crossed over her breasts as though she was naked, into the private room, still giggling like a set of glass bells Byrd remembered from a Christmas tree as a child.

"Hi there," Boris lumbered drunkenly into the passage, his smile as wide and unsavoury as before. "I saw Mr. Ca-si-mir like you said" – proud of having remembered his lesson. "She's great: just like my Wanda, only she's called Polly."

"That's fine, Percy."

"Come, come, chop-chop, Percy," Polly insisted, high-pitched, from the room.

"Real cute." Boris gave another huge grin. "Thanks a million, buddy."

"Any time, Percy," and Byrd nearly let it go at that. Boris was almost at the private-room door, when he asked: "You have a good meeting, Percy? With your friends?"

Boris stopped, his face radiant. "Yeah, it was great. My friends're very pleased. They done a deal."

"Good."

"Yeah, they done a deal," he dropped his voice, "with some dumb Chink. He's giving them a lot of the dream stuff. They're giving him guns." He began to laugh, like a large child with a secret joke he has to tell. "What the Chink don't know is the guns're no good. All spiked surplus stuff." The grin disappeared and a tiny cloud of concern crossed his face. "Hey, ya won't tell anybody, will ya?"

"Of course not, Percy. Not my business; I won't tell a soul." It was doubtful if Boris would even remember talking. He appeared to be very drunk – and equally horny, for when Polly Sing called again he edged quickly towards the door.

"Hey, I'll have to go. I got the hots; you know what I mean?"

"Go ahead, Percy." He almost added – *Be my guest*.

So Vincent and Valentine were planning to cross Foo Tang. People had to be really early risers to manage that, and the information made Byrd much happier. He should have guessed the Maes brothers would be incapable of playing it straight. Now he had the edge on several people – Tang himself, the Maes brothers, maybe the large Waldo Bingham too.

Byrd surveyed the possibilities as he descended the stairs. Maybe it would be wise to do a direct deal with Vincent and Valentine. Buy his own survival by arranging for certain information to go to Tang should he die. Then he realised the false logic. Tang would be the better evil, because he was there permanently and his methods of retribution were as final and silent as those of Vincent and Valentine. Going to Tang would wipe the Maes duet from his personal map for good and all.

Time enough tomorrow, he thought, walking towards the bar and Jeannie.

If he was hoping for a little affection he was disappointed. "Who the fuck's the little light-haired tai-tai you make the goose eyes at, you bas'ard?" she greeted him.

"She's not a tai-tai, Jeannie. She's an old friend from America."

"Ol' frien'? It look like ol' frien'. Too much ol' frien'. I see the way you look at her and she look you." Jeannie's English suffered when she felt threatened.

"Old, old friend, Jeannie. Going to marry the man she was with tonight."

"When marry make difference you, Harry? I saw. I saw way you–she looked."

"Come and have a drink, baby. Then I'll take you to bed and show you who's my number-one girl." This appeared to appease her, at least for the time being, and she allowed herself to be led to the bar. "I'm not feeling so great," Byrd said to Max. "Give us something that'll remove all pain."

"This do it, I think." Max poured them large drinks made to his own specifications and pushed the glasses over the counter.

Byrd talked to some of the regular bar flies, met a couple of visiting tourists, danced with Jeannie – who gradually regained her usual good humour – and had a few more drinks.

They got to bed around five. Early, but after all it was a Monday, and even with a new ship in Mondays were usually early nights. The drink had no bad effects, and they made love twice: both wild conjunctions which ended slowly; great tenderness in the aftermath of passion. Then sleep came.

He did not feel the hands grab at his feet, nor hear Jeannie's first scream. He heard the second piercing shriek, felt himself being yanked forward, and his bones judder as his back hit the floor. The lights were on, and he was lying naked on the ground at the foot of the bed. There was time to glance around and see Jeannie, eyes dilated with fear, as a sallow Japanese held a knife to her throat. Then Byrd felt more pain as a foot connected with his ribs.

As well as the Japanese with the knife, there were three others in the room: two more ronin, dressed in loose karate trousers and shirts – dressed, literally, to kill – and a short, dapper Oriental, immaculate from his linen suit to the hand-made suede shoes on his feet. He stood near the closed door and was the first to speak.

"Good morning, Mr. Byrd. We have come to do business with you."

Harry Byrd had no doubt about the kind of business, or that the small man was a ranking member of the Black Dragon.

His head began to hurt again, and focus appeared to have gone completely from his right eye.

"What kind of business?" Automatic speech. Drills bored into Byrd's head and eye, while now there was an additional focus of pain from the last kick, and the heavy landing on his back.

The smooth little Japanese gentleman contorted his features into a humourless smile. "Your car was damaged yesterday, Mr. Byrd."

"You know . . . it." The last word hardly came out at all because of another fierce kick in the ribs. There were shards of broken glass lancing inside his lungs. Jeannie began to scream again, and the ronin with the knife muttered something in fractured Chinese which made her stop abruptly.

"So" – the Shoshi executive was not smiling now. "Your car was meant to do you harm. Unfortunately you escaped. You also escaped the retribution Mosiko was supposed to mete out to you. Him you turned over to the police. Not good, Mr. Byrd; not good at all."

"What're you hoping to gain?" It was not he who was speaking: the words seemed to come from a great distance.

"The organisation which I represent has sent me to say we intend to take over the ownership and running of this café. It seems obvious to us that you are unlikely to agree readily to such a measure."

"Too right. You're Black Dragon Shoshi." Taking a breath was like sucking in a packet of iron filings. "But you don't need to fight me, whatever your name is. Go talk to Foo Tang."

"It seems best to the organisation I represent, that we dispose of you before talking with respected Mr. Foo Tang. We can then present him with what the French call a *fait accompli*."

"A bi-lingual gangster." The bravado was hollow, but it was all he had.

The Japanese gave a small laugh. "Mr. Byrd, I am from an educated family. School in England, followed by reading Modern Languages at the University of Oxford. I speak eight tongues."

"Is that a record? You should get in touch with Ripley." Ripley's 'Believe It Or Not' syndicated column was a regular feature of the *North-China Daily News*.

"I am pleased you can face your fate so humorously; but we have not much time. First it is necessary that we have your keys, your private papers, and your signature on a routine legal document."

"Like hell."

"Yes, like hell, Mr. Byrd. Pain is a great persuader."

He nodded towards one of the ronin who did something with his foot, deep in the lower part of Byrd's stomach. After Jeannie, now it was his turn to scream. He had no alternative. The sound was animal, and quite involuntary.

It brought help – in the most unexpected form. As the scream began to take its downward curve, so the bedroom door seemed to splinter, and buckle inwards. A huge, half-naked figure appeared through the shattered wood, standing among the wreckage for a moment, shaking its head and taking in the situation.

"Hey, what ya doin' to my friend?" Boris spoke slowly, but moved with a speed born of survival in the seamier streets of big cities. The ham hands clamped around the smooth little Japanese man's neck, one above the other, and moved apart. It was like an infant wilfully trying to tear a doll in pieces, and the small man was lifted off his feet, making noises indicating that he was choking and having his neck broken at one and the same time.

For Byrd there was a sudden flash of hope in the middle of the turmoil and pain. He shouted – "Boris . . . Percy . . . look to Jeannie. . ." He could have saved the agony in his lungs. However slow-witted Boris might be, he was an instinctive fighter. Jeannie had began to scream again, which probably meant the ronin on the bed was about to perform with the knife, and the smooth Japanese, legs kicking like some demented clockwork toy, went flying through the air, propelled by one great movement of Boris' arms and shoulders. His aim was as accurate as a sharpshooter: the Japanese pitched and yawed, then straightened out so that his head connected with that of the ronin. The knife flew from the ronin's hand, and the pair of them dropped limply on to the bed. From there they rolled on to the floor.

The remaining couple of ronin had by now turned their attention from Byrd. They both lunged out at this sudden, large and unexpected attacker, assuming positions which Byrd associated with the ancient Japanese martial arts. For a second he wondered how Boris would deal with a pair of men obviously experienced in the most deadly of fighting techniques.

Boris apparently knew little of such subtleties, however, and was therefore in no way worried by them. His arms came out wide – giving the illusion of almost telescopic lengthening; the hands grasping the ronin, one around each neck. The larger of the two brought the edge of his hand down in a classic chopping blow, catching Boris' forearm as he reached forward. The force of delivery should have been enough to smash a four-inch plank, but Boris did not even wince. He simply went on with what he was doing – lifting the pair clear off the ground, just as he had done with their leader. This time, though, Byrd thought he was showing off, doing the trick with one hand for each.

The ronin (plural) dangled at the ends of the thick arms, making Boris look like a macabre caricature of Justice, complete with scales but without the blindfold.

He then moved quickly again, bringing his arms together, an action which caused the pair of thugs to come heavily into contact with one another in an unpleasant crunch of flesh and bone. Boris opened his hands and there were two more piles of rubbish on the carpet.

Boris looked around him with a smile of pleasure. "I hope they didn't hurt you too bad."

Byrd swallowed hard. Instinctively he grabbed his pyjamas from the chair. Far off, he heard Jeannie having hysterics.

"Could I have a cigarette?" he asked, through the waves of nausea and agony; adding that they were on the bedside table.

"Sure," Boris lumbered over. "I did right, yes?"

Polly Sing appeared in the doorway, dressed only in her

flimsy panties, arms modestly crossed over her breasts. Jeannie immediately recovered from her hysterics and let fly with a mouthful of Chinese invective, which obviously meant that Polly should get the hell out and put some clothes on. She fled, and Max appeared in her place.

"Boss, I'm sorry. You need help? What happen? You have trouble, I think."

"Right, Max. You win the plaster dog and the necklace. Luckily our house guest was on hand." He took a deep breath. Mercifully the broken glass appeared to be dissolving.

Max looked around the room at the tangled bodies; then at Boris with unconcealed awe. "He did all this?"

"The lot." Byrd allowed Max to help him into a sitting position on the bed, and Boris lit his cigarette.

"I did it good, yes?" from Boris.

"I think you kill some of them." Max did not disguise his alarm. "You want a doctor, boss?"

He probably needed a doctor, but the main concern at this point was to see how much permanent damage had been inflicted on the Japanese intruders. A doctor might mean the police, and the police could only bring more trouble. Besides, if Boris was brought into the open, the Maes brothers would soon follow.

Max went to the injured, one by one, like a looter on a battlefield. "The man in the good suit is dead," he announced. "Also the other one – by the bed. These two," he indicated the last pair of ronin, "won't wake up for a long time."

"We get rid of them?"

"Sure, boss. Nobody here'll speak of it. Anyway I see that only a couple of people know. We load 'em into the garbage truck and dump 'em somewhere, I think. Where you want us to dump 'em?"

"Take them back where they came from."

"Where they come from, boss?"

"They're Nips, aren't they?"

Max chuckled. "You want I take them to Tokyo?"

Byrd sighed. "Take 'em to Hongkew. That's where they all live, isn't it?"

"Leave it to me, boss. You get out the way now, and I fix it. Okay?"

He disappeared, brushing past Polly Sing, who had put on a minimum of clothing and was hanging on to Boris' arm, giving it an occasional tug.

"Come back to room now, Percy. We just making one time good loving when all go wrong."

Byrd drew in smoke, order and sense returning to his mind.

"Polly, I'm sorry, but I think Percy should go. I don't know how to thank you, Percy, but you shouldn't stick around here. Too dangerous."

"No need to thank me. You're my friend. I didn't mean to kill those guys. Was it bad mistake?"

Byrd said that Boris had saved their lives. "But the police might not understand that. It would be best for you to disappear. I shouldn't mention it to your bosses either. They might get cross."

Boris nodded slowly, trying to look wise. "Sure, they get awful mad if I do things wrong. Sure I won't say anything." His face brightened. "Maybe it would be okay if I came back to see Polly tonight."

"Why don't you think about that, Percy?"

Max returned with a sleepy-eyed Koo, and the pair started to remove the human debris. The giant Boris sidled out of the room with Polly, and Byrd was able to give some attention to Jeannie, who had been sitting up in bed all this time: white, tear-stained, but beginning to reassume her normal poise.

"You look terrible, Harry. You look – how you say? – beat up."

"They beat me up. Yesterday; and then today. They also beat up my beautiful motor. How d'you expect me to look, Jeannie? Like I just came out of a fucking health farm?"

"Come, lie down. It still not twelve o'clock noon time."

"Jesus." Not yet midday. "It's still the middle of the

98

night. There must be easier ways. . ." He thought about what he should do next. Tang would have to be told, if only to protect their so-called partnership. He also had to get a valuation on the diamonds for Geddes before six o'clock, and it would not be a bad idea to put in some kind of report to Waldo Bingham. That would mean stopping by at the Cathay – untamed Indian country now that the Maes brothers were in residence there.

Max and Koo were removing the last corpse: the small, spruce, well-educated Black Dragon executive. Byrd said he needed a note taking to Foo Tang, and would Max send someone, perhaps Woo, up in about five minutes. "Then I'll come back and sleep," he told Jeannie, dragging his aching body through to the main room, flopping into a chair at the small writing table, gathering his thoughts.

Woo arrived and was kept waiting for almost ten minutes while Byrd composed the note to Foo Tang. For simplicity's sake he left out the participation of Boris – Tang would probably discover it anyway, and that bridge could be crossed then. It was hardly important. Neither did he mention the proposed double-dealing of the Maes brothers. There would be a time for everything, he thought, the phrase bringing his childhood vividly into his mind. *To every thing there is a season, and a time to every purpose under heaven: A time to be born, and a time to die*: that was one of his father's favourite biblical quotations – and he had a lot of them. The old man, with his stiff collars and manner: the complete accountant; professional, respected, with the house on the hill and Mama, beautiful and always laughing. Christ, if they were alive now, they would not be laughing at their errant baby boy.

He gave Woo the letter, and detailed instructions that he was to put it personally into Foo Tang's hands at the house in Jessfield Park. As he slogged back into the bedroom, he thought that it would be in fact surprising if Foo Tang did not already know it all. Foo Tang's information was second to none in this city.

Jeannie was asleep again, so he set the alarm for three forty-five and tried to switch himself into sleep, but it was a long time before he succeeded; then only a few minutes, it seemed, before the alarm rang.

What sleep he managed to get must have done some good, because his head felt clear and the eye was almost back to normal. But, when he moved, there was intense stiffness and discomfort around his belly, back and ribs.

Jeannie still slept, the scent of last night's gin hanging around her, mixed with the sweet smell of her perfume. Sleep for her was total oblivion, and it would not have surprised Byrd if she had managed to remain unconscious throughout the visit from the Black Dragon emissaries. It took him three cigarettes before he could move enough to crawl out of bed, and a long time to get from the bedroom to bathroom, so bruised and solid were his muscles.

They eased after a hot soak, and, by the time he was dried and shaved, Byrd found he could move with only a constant soreness. Uncomfortable, but not unbearable.

He was dressed in shirt and trousers when the knock came at the outer door. Going through the usual routine with the pistol, Byrd opened up a crack and Lee Yung, Tang's head thug, leaned against the jamb. This, Byrd thought, was where he had come in. But this time Lee Yung said nothing: just handed a note through the space between door and chain, then departed without even a glower.

The note was short:

Harry Byrd,
I have put men on the café to watch and protect our mutual interests. News reaches me, and will doubtless soon reach all quarters of Shanghai, that a most noteworthy Black Dragon leader has been brutally murdered. We must expect trouble. You will neither see nor recognise my men, but they will be there. You must take great care. In the meantime, if you look from your window you will find a small repayment for the service you performed for me last night.
May your Gods and mine protect us both,
Foo Tang.

Looking from the window, Byrd saw that, in the space where he used to park his treasured motor, there now stood a brand new, shining scarlet Delage. How Tang had conjured up a new model so rapidly would probably remain a mystery for ever.

He cranked down to the bar. It was time to deal with Geddes' diamonds. Max was there and sounded cheerful, for he had also seen the car, but was less happy when Byrd said he was going out in it.

"You want a bodyguard, I think."

Byrd said yes, he thought that was a good idea if his barman could spare an hour. He then left a note for Jeannie, who would not be overjoyed at waking to find him gone.

The café looked strange, deserted and silent at four thirty in the afternoon, with all the life and noise going on in the streets outside. The boys worked silently, cleaning and setting up for the night's work. Max was waiting, and Byrd had already collected the diamonds from the safe.

Outside, the street was thick with rickshaws, trams, motors, jostling crowds, street traders sing-songing their wares, or calling attention by clapping pieces of wood together. The air was heavy and the sky like lead; the smells were of sweat and wood smoke with a hint of rotting fish. Byrd did not even attempt to look for Foo Tang's watchmen.

They were just about to step across the road when, with a blasting of its horn, a black police car hurtled through the traffic, squealing to a dramatic halt in front of them.

✝ (10)

"Going out, Byrd?" asked 'Pearly' Fisher, climbing from the police car, the beer gut sagging below the puffed-out chest. He looked pleased with himself. Too pleased with himself.

"We've all got our work to do." Byrd felt for his cigarettes – a nervous reaction. Fisher made him twitch.

The policeman's smile widened. He reeked of gin. "You had trouble with the Shoshi yesterday, right? Bloody Black Dragon?"

"That's what everyone tells me."

"Not been foolish enough to try any reprisals, have you?"

Byrd did not have time to ask why he asked. Fisher held up an early edition of the tabloid-sized *Evening Post and Mercury*. Ladow's Casanova Café was advertising on the front page; also the Palais Café on Avenue Edward VII. A photograph of the *Empress of Asia* dominated the bottom centre, with a piece about celebrities who had arrived on her. There was also a story released by the City Government: the distinguished soldier, General Wu Te-chen, was to take up his appointment as Mayor of Greater Shanghai on 1 January next year. Normally this would have been the lead story, but under the flowery imprint of the *Post & Mercury* banner headlines screamed – Japanese Gangster and Bodyguard Murdered.

"So?" Byrd took the paper, scanning the story which was terse and mainly factual. The dead man was a Mr. Awa Katachi, and the photograph showed clearly that he was the man whom Boris had hurled across the room. Early that afternoon, Mr. Katachi had been discovered beaten to death, in an alley off the Hongkew area. The corpse of his bodyguard was found nearby. Mr. Katachi, the paper went on, was a well-known businessman thought to have close ties with the feared Japanese underworld society known as the Black Dragon. Some sources claimed he was among the top three leaders of that society, and the police feared a Japanese gang war.

"*Do* you fear a Japanese gang war?" Byrd asked.

"Not my province, but I would not like to be in the shoes of anyone who had had recent dealings with that gentleman. One of your nastier specimens actually. Educated fellow. Knew a lot of angles. Just my job, Byrd, but I have to ask you if you've seen him recently? Had any dealings with him?"

"You know about my dealings with the Japs. Only the one you hauled off yesterday. I didn't even glimpse the mad bombers who did the car."

Fisher looked across at the Delage. "Got it patched up pretty chop-chop, didn't you?"

"I have my contacts. That all, Pearly? I'm a little busy."

The copper grinned again. "You sure you haven't seen the late lamented Awa Katachi? Just for the record; for when they find you tied to the bottom of a sampan. That's one of the Shoshi idiosyncrasies. They take you out for a swim tied to the bottom of a sampan. Tied with nails through your hands and feet as a rule."

"For the record, Pearly. No." Byrd started to turn away. "This paper accurate? Was Katachi their number three man?"

"So it is written in the book of judgements."

"Who are numbers one and two?"

"Very meaty gentlemen, Byrd. The old puppet-master trick – not unlike your mate Foo Tang. Pull the strings. Say jump and a hundred ronin jump: say shit and the same hundred have diarrhoea in your general direction. Katachi operated outside his nice house up in Hongkew Park. He did things. The other two sit quietly in their nice houses and give the orders. Mr. Takahome and Mr. Hitchimata." He shook his head sadly. "Our people know all about them. So do the French. Very difficult to drive the old stake through their hearts, though. Nobody there to give evidence when the time comes. If the Black Dragon's been breathing fire in your direction, Byrd, it'll be those two who'll be twitching its tail. Beware the scaly monster."

"I think," Max said slowly after Fisher drove away, "that we should be very careful. Where we goin', boss?"

Byrd felt the little packet of diamonds in his pocket and told him to head towards the Chinese city. He would direct Max from there.

The keys were in the Delage, and Max made a great show of screwing up his face, as if expecting an explosion as he switched on and pressed the starter. The motor took up a pleasant throbbing roar, and within minutes they were edging dangerously into the crowded, undisciplined throng which all but blocked the street – Max sounding the horn relentlessly to urge coolies, rickshaws and ambling pedestrians out of the way.

Slowly they negotiated Nanking Road – past Kelly and Walsh, the American Bookshop, Whiteway and Laidlaw, The Chocolate Box, all crammed between shops with more traditional Chinese signboards. A brass band – Chinese style – blasted its timeless tooting from one shop. Advertising was an on-the-spot, off-key, art here.

Byrd gave Max the name of a street you would not find on any map of Shanghai – like so many of the Chinese streets within the walled city – Beat Dog; Stealing Hen; Iron Street. They were going to Chessboard Street; to a small apartment over a baker's shop. There, Byrd knew, lived a man who had worked for Tuck Chang, the famous jewellers on Broadway – Broadway, Shanghai – until, armed with experience, he had started his own small and secretive business: much of it dealing in illegal stones.

"Where precisely did you dump 'em?" Byrd asked as they cleared a path through the crowds.

"Who, boss? Dump who?" Narrowly missing a pair of Chinese girls, dressed identically in blue, sharing a rickshaw – one perched precariously on the other's lap. One of the girls reminded Byrd of Jeannie; the blue pyjamas simultaneously brought Cat to mind. The first time they had ever gone away together on a weekend, Cat brought along some new blue pyjamas. They were left unworn.

"That's the right answer, Max," he stared straight ahead.

"But you can tell *me*. Where'd you dump Katachi and his hoods?"

"Oh, them. Well, we took 'em up towards Hongkew, but I thought it'd be nicer to leave them on the good side of the tracks. I think we did right, yes? Not to go to the crowded Jap area? We left them near the Golf Club."

Byrd chuckled. "Then someone moved them."

"Of course. Nobody's going to leave corpses lying around near the Golf Club."

Byrd still chuckled. The greater part of the Hongkew area was what the British taipans called 'select' – the Broadway Mansions, the Russian Consulate, General Hospital, and the beloved Golf Club. Hongkew meant 'Mouth of the Rainbow'. The rainbow came to a verminous end in the adjacent area – Hongkew Market and its attendant sprawl which had become mainly Japanese. A nasty, tough section of the city.

Max was shrewd enough to have put the bodies where they would automatically be moved – either by locals or by the pair of ronin whom Boris had put to sleep on a temporary basis; though it was far more likely that the class-conscious local residents had ordered the corpses removed. The injured ronin would only have enough strength to crawl away and lick their wounds.

"Mr. Takahome and Mr. Hitchimata," Byrd said, thinking aloud.

"Very bad joss, those two." Max smoothly directed the Delage between a pair of rickshaws and an old man pulling a wooden cart by a piece of rope looped around his shoulders. "Perhaps they saw to it that Mr. Katachi and his man were taken."

Byrd said, maybe, but he thought not. If the Black Dragon leaders had done it, Katachi and friend would have turned up on the doorstep of the Flamingo Café.

Fisher had said, "Beware the scaly monster", intimating that he would not like to be in the shoes of anyone even remotely connected with Katachi's demise. Byrd was not happy about being in his own shoes; he did not need to visit the Temple of the Queen of Heaven to know that the Flamingo and Harry Byrd would be high on the Black Dragon hit list – the Temple being the dwelling place of the gods Liu Tsiang Ching and Ching Tsiang Ching: the former credited with the ability to see anything up to within three hundred and thirty-three miles of Shanghai; the latter believed to have the power of hearing over the same distance.

Max stayed with the Delage in Chessboard Street while Byrd went in search of his freelance jewel expert, whom he found in the clean and tidy pair of rooms tucked away above the baker's shop. The stairs to the rooms were narrow, creaking, and as dry as bleached bones.

They went through the usual polite ceremonies, and tea was brought by a plump unattractive girl who was inclined to linger, but was quickly banished to some cubbyhole at the rear of the rooms. The place smelled of the bread from downstairs, a hot, yeasty redolence mingling with the slightly sticky-sweet aroma of incense, which burned before a small shrine to the household gods in a corner of the room.

Byrd knew that Sun Yang, the jeweller, would be honest with him. In the past three years he had done business with the man some five times. On the first occasion the Chinese had tried to gyp Byrd; but happily the American knew the true value of the ice he handled. A word to Foo Tang, and Sun Yang had not stepped out of line since.

After the tea and exchange of pleasantries, the stones were laid out on their small piece of velvet in front of Sun Yang, who took his time: glass screwed into his eye, each stone examined with shakings of the head, tutting noises, and the occasional sharp intake of breath. In the end, Byrd had to ask bluntly about the real value. Sun Yang, who appeared to have a perpetual smile lingering among the wispy grey hairs of his beard, still tried to prevaricate, but under pressure admitted the true worth of the stones to be, as Byrd had guessed, around five thousand dollars.

"If my friend wishes to sell these stones, will you buy?"

Again the smile and a shrug. "I buy, but my own poverty must be appeased." Sun Yang had worked for Tuck Chang, and, therefore, picked up much about dealing with foreigners; he had also acquired an odd vocabulary. Like all good hagglers he claimed poverty, so Byrd asked what he was prepared to pay in hard cash.

The old man held up four bony fingers. "Four thousand dollar, folding cash. You will take now?"

Byrd said, no, he was doing this for a friend and must

check back; if he returned later that evening, would Sun Yang still pay four?

The Chinese nodded and said that this price would only hold for today. Tomorrow he might not be able to pay as much. His family was large and scattered, there were many mouths to feed, he was responsible for much – wringing every ounce from the ritual bargaining. Byrd said he would either return or send a message. It took another five minutes before he could politely leave.

Back in the car, Byrd did some fast and easy mental arithmetic. He would offer Geddes three and a half grand. Five hundred dollars seemed a reasonable commission – particularly as the remainder would almost certainly end up across the Flamingo's gaming tables. He told Max to head back to the café, but to drop him at the corner of Nanking Road on the way, as he had to stop off at the Cathay. He would make his way home on foot afterwards.

"Alone?" Max sounded concerned.

"It's only a short way."

"I think I take the car back, then come and meet you, yes?"

Byrd agreed. Max could walk back and wait in the opulent foyer of the Cathay Hotel. Already he had made his mind up about who should get what information. Foo Tang had pledged that he was taking care of Byrd and the Flamingo, but you could never tell with a man like Tang. If the pressures became really hot, he might just be tempted to form some kind of an alliance with the Japanese Black Dragon. Byrd had no illusions about his own usefulness to Foo Tang. If the Chinese could get a similar financial deal from the Japs, Harry Byrd's future would worry him about as much as that of a mosquito. He would keep the Maes brothers' doublecross as his own ace in the hole: to be played if the going got rough. He knew enough about arms and ammunition to make more than a shrewd guess about the kind of stuff Dr. Zuchestra had stashed away, ready to lay on Tang.

Back in the old days he personally knew of a case where someone had provided a marked man with a spiked tommy-gun. The whole of the hammer, bolt and outer casing had blown back at the first squeeze of the trigger, most of it exploding upwards, almost decapitating the guy.

Waldo Bingham, on the other hand, was an unknown quantity, but he would try him out – give him a rundown of the events since they had met; tell him about the Black Dragon threat, with its increased pressures, and possibly provide him with a taste of the Maes-Tang deal – name of the ship, rough time of delivery and exchange. Not all the details, but enough.

Big Ching, the great clock on the Custom House, chimed five as Byrd stepped from the car into the thick heat and noise at the corner of Nanking Road. He staggered slightly, his muscles stiffened from sitting in the car. The heat seemed to have started his head off again as though a small vice had been clamped around the temples. He shook his head and squeezed his eyes: on cue the needles darted in and out of the right eye. He would have to see some trustworthy doctor within the next few hours, for this had gone on long enough.

In the late afternoon hustle and noise, Byrd suddenly felt sick and very much alone as he watched Max steer the Delage away up Nanking Road. It should take the barman about five or six minutes to get to the intersection, where Nanking Road turned into Bubbling Well. Another five would see Max back, on foot, at Sassoon House – the correct name for the white, luxurious and modern building which bore the legend 'Cathay Hotel' above its three-arched glass doors.

The rattle and clank of two trams heading up Nanking Road temporarily overrode the other cacophonies; they also had the effect of bringing Cat back into his head: her face lazily turning and smiling in a series of flash pictures, all associated with times they had spent together, the trams passing in the road outside.

Almost physically, Byrd banished her from his mind and set off, dodging the traffic, rickshaws and smart gleaming automobiles alike, to cross the wide road. Suddenly he hoped very much that Tang really did have someone watching out for him as well as the Flamingo; for he was seized with an uncanny knowledge that, whatever Tang's men were doing, at least one of Mr. Takahome's or Mr. Hitchimata's men was very close. Crossing towards the Cathay felt like walking over a piece of ground marked out with traps and spring knives. Once on the far side he paused for a second to look back, as though trying to spot a watcher. But that was impossible in the crowd. He could see down the Bund and over the road towards the river and the statue of Sir Harry Parkes – one-time Envoy Extraordinary and Minister Plenipotentiary to Japan and China. Harry Parkes would not have had this trouble crossing the road. Byrd was dithering and knew it; loitering on the sidewalk and scanning faces, his stomach turning over as he spotted a pair of well-dressed Japanese gentlemen in an automobile parked right in front of the hotel. There was a bunch of Chinese coolies, chattering like monkeys, leaping from the back of a truck, just ahead of the Japanese car – road workers about to undertake some repairs. A pair of very young girls with an older woman paused to gape at them, grinning golden smiles.

He could watch people – in Chinese and European dress, traders, runners, tourists, business people – all the afternoon and not know if any were for or against him; out for his life, or there to protect him, or simply about their own business.

Byrd took a deep breath, hoped in hell that neither of the Maes boys were lounging in the lobby, and pushed his way cautiously through the middle of the three entrance doors. The lobby was crowded, but he saw no sign either of them or of the friendly Boris.

Waldo Bingham had said that he would probably dine at the Flamingo that night, and had also suggested that Byrd should telephone the Cathay. But Byrd was not going to leave the matter to chance. Beard Bingham in his den, he said, inside his head, as his feet touched the highly polished marble of the Cathay Hotel's lobby.

Yes, they had a Mr. Waldo Bingham staying at the hotel,

the solemn young Chinese girl at Reception told him. They would ring his room. Who should they announce? Byrd was tempted to say Bulldog Drummond, Richard Hannay or the Lone Wolf. "Harry Byrd," he told the girl, cravenly, taking out his cigarettes, lighting up and slowly turning at the same time to survey the entire lobby. By the time his eyes were back, looking across the reception desk, he realised that he was safe. The lobby was so crowded that you would have to look hard to recognise your own sister at two paces.

The solemn girl returned. Yes, Mr. Bingham was expecting him. Would he go up? Room 204.

Waldo Bingham looked rested and in good spirits, coming to the door draped in a crumpled floral-patterned bathrobe, and sporting an elegant black cigarette holder which did not go with his style, bulk or face.

"You came in person, then, Mr. Byrd. Enter. It's good to see you. Can I offer refreshment?"

Byrd said that he would have a Teachers if there was any, discovering immediately that Mr Bingham was a man of taste and had a well-stocked drinks' trolley in his room; also that his drinks reflected the expansive manner and size of their dispenser.

"So?" Bingham began when they were settled with giant tumblers of liquor. "I hope you bring me good tidings. Your decision."

Byrd told him that he was willing to help in any way the Englishman thought possible, and he was now in little doubt that the Shoshi society of the Black Dragon was making a determined attempt to take over the Flamingo. He did not go into any details, other than the fact that they had paid him another visit.

Bingham nodded. "A place like the Flamingo would make a good base of operations for them in the business area."

"They've already got businesses. At least the respectable ones have – banks, commercial houses."

"As you say, the respectable ones," Bingham grunted. "They undoubtedly want somewhere with good exits and entrances, so that their less respectable hooligans can move with safety."

"And after the Flamingo? They'll try others?"

"Difficult to tell. They're obviously intent on taking over certain business ventures within the International and French Settlements, so they'll be well prepared when their armies arrive. There is another matter. . ."

Byrd waited. Bingham seemed to be wrestling heavily with his own conscience. "The Black Dragon," he said eventually, "is thought of mainly, by police and public alike, as a criminal organisation. In truth it's more than that."

Byrd frowned and Bingham continued. "When I talk of the police, I mean, of course, the rank and file. The *authorities* are aware of the facts." He paused and took a large swallow of his drink. "You must have noticed that the Black Dragon people often, quite literally, get away with murder. They may finance their own criminal endeavours, but their other activities – well, that's another matter."

"You mean it's Black Dragon people who are mixed up in the political agitation." Byrd winced suddenly at another twinge of pain, agonising for a second in his eye.

"Putting it mildly. Putting it factually, the Black Dragon Society is, without any doubt, the secret overseas agency of the Japanese War Office. They hold great power; they're not just one of your little secret criminal societies with odd rituals. They operate at many levels, and are most effective." Bingham went on to outline the structure of the Black Dragon Society as he saw it. They were a cross, he suggested, between the old and honourable Japanese societies and the gangsters of Chicago. Their ranks contained priests, politicians, men of business and commerce, highly qualified people. The membership also included the lowest dregs of Japanese criminal society.

As far as military intelligence was concerned, members of the Black Dragon could be found sprawled right across China, living secret lives, suitably disguised as traders, merchants, even peasant farmers. They were, he again stressed, a mixture: criminals, experts in military and police affairs, men trained in the techniques of sabotage, fanatics who would kill to order and then rip their bellies open in public if commanded to do so. The Black Dragon contained men who would act as strike breakers, or strike originators; organise public riots, assassinations and political unrest. They also fed back military and commercial information directly to Tokyo.

"You must realise, Byrd, that at this moment Shanghai is the hottest piece of real estate in the Orient. The Black Dragon are here for a purpose, and so well organised that they could produce a kind of secret terrorist army quick as kiss your ass. If attack comes, or public unrest grows to chaotic proportions, you might even see them taking over the police. They're damned well organised."

Byrd had understood nothing of this before. Waldo Bingham continued to open the American's eyes to the truth about this dangerous organisation. The Black Dragon had, at its heart, political, nationalistic and religious ideals, and received strong backing from Japan itself. They also possessed the power to act as both agents and criminals.

"It's difficult to decide whether their attempted take-over of the Flamingo is a criminal or an intelligence move. Their bulk funds certainly come directly from the Japanese Army, and they take particular orders from their own people in the Japanese Consulate."

"So the gangsters are spies."

Waldo Bingham sighed with his whole body. "And the spies are gangsters. I was hoping they would leave you alone a little longer. It was going to be my suggestion that you played with them."

"You mean played ball with them?"

"Only an idea. Come to some arrangement – in all innocence, of course. Go along with them. The Flamingo would need a figurehead. You would offer to stay on. The pickings for you would be high. And for me also."

It was impossible: 'Billion Dollar' Tang would never allow it. Byrd knew that, and he told Bingham so with some fervour. The big man took the news placidly. "If it cannot be done, then it cannot. I know all about Mr. Foo

Tang. So you have him to deal with as well as the Japanese. I fear for your safety, Mr. Byrd."

"If you know all about Foo Tang, then you'll also know that anybody setting up my kind of business in this city needs the backing of a man like Foo Tang. He was the last thing I wanted when I opened up the Flamingo, but the man's a necessary evil. Wouldn't have lasted a day without him." Byrd gave a wry smile. "You fear for my safety? What about me? One of the big Japanese boys is lying dead, and I've got a suspicion they want my neck for it."

Bingham nodded. "Katachi?"

"Of course, Katachi."

"And is your neck deserved by them?"

Boris hurling Katachi across the room; Jeannie's shrieks. "Not really. Indirectly."

Bingham grunted, "Accessory before the fact, eh? And after?"

"I pass."

Waldo Bingham remained silent for a long time. Then: "You have serious problems, Mr. Byrd. If you wish to resign from our little arrangement. . ."

"Fair-weather friends." Byrd did not feel like being sharp and amusing, but he smiled as he spoke. Then he asked Bingham if he had ever heard of some American syndicate hoods called Maes. Bingham nodded and began to rattle off a series of statistics which not only made Byrd forget the pain once more building in his head and eye, but produced grave suspicion about how much Bingham knew of his own past.

"What of the despicable Maes brothers?" Bingham asked finally.

Byrd did not give him the full tale: only the juicy morsels; the swapping of weapons for opium; the rough-date – mid-January; and the ship's name and country of origin, *Bel Canto*; Paraguay.

Bingham's grunt turned into a heavy chuckle. "I'd lay money on a double-cross, and I wouldn't like to bet on who would cross whom. They'll probably both try it. Carnage, Harry Byrd. A little more carnage if I place the word in the right ears. Is it possible. . ." he began to muse, " . . . Is it possible that you, in turn, could cut Mr. Foo Tang in on some arrangement with the Nipponese? Explain the subtleties of the situation? I see the play going like this. . ." He started to outline what seemed to Byrd a highly impractical scheme involving the Black Dragon Society taking over the running of the Flamingo, with Foo Tang's knowledge. There were even promises. He could speak to Foo Tang about the involvement of the British Foreign Service, in an undercover manner; suggesting that they would supply special protection, and even arms, if the Flamingo was set up as a Japanese base of operations, from which they could successfully 'steal' information. Bingham kept saying it would be "Worth its weight in gold."

With great misgivings, Byrd eventually promised he'd think about it. And when he left Room 204 he automatically checked his wallet, pistol and the diamonds, wondering if this precaution was a reflection on the company he now seemed to be keeping.

In the lobby, despite his caution, he bumped straight into Cat, trim in a beige silk suit. The crowd had thinned out, and he also spotted Max, looking nervous, sitting near the entrance.

"Harry," Cat seemed agitated.

Byrd said hallo and, unwilling to linger in possible Maes country, was prepared to walk straight on, but she grabbed at his arm.

"I've been trying to get you at your café for the last half-hour, Harry. I have to see you: talk to you. It's important."

It was almost twenty minutes to six. Geddes would be at the café by six and, if he took Waldo Bingham seriously, he should get in touch with Foo Tang pretty soon. "I don't have a great deal of time –"

"Old times' sake won't mean much, Harry. But this is desperate. Tom's out. Can you come to my room for a few minutes?"

Her room, back in the city all those years ago, came vividly into his head: the great drapes (*pond green*, he used to call them), the brass bedstead which she always kept polished; a copy of Renoir's *The Luncheon of the Boating Party* – a bad copy with the colours all too bright: he used to make jokes about the people in the picture and they would work out who was going to make whom, and how many bottles lay empty under the table.

"Okay." He stood in the elevator, almost imagining for a brief wink of time that they were going back to that room of memory – that apartment – and not to an hotel room, like all hotel rooms: places where you waited, or slept, or had lovers.

She looked as though she had been crying, and they had hardly got inside the door when she flung herself into his arms, sobbing. Her hair smelled of the damp heat, but he still detected the old odour which he used to call champagne and strawberries – even though it wasn't really that.

"Cat, what the hell. . ." he began.

She sniffed, and he pushed her away to arms' length. They were real tears; streaming. He had long learned about the wiles of women's tears. If the nose went red, they were real. Cat's nose was crimson. She sniffed again.

"Harry, I think I've made a terrible mistake about Tom. It's not just seeing you again," she added quickly. "Not that only, though. I . . . I . . ."

"What's the real problem?" Byrd kept his voice hard.

"I think Tom's crooked."

"Geddes? He's a gambler. None of them is always clean as your ma's laundry."

She took a deep breath, wiping her eyes with the back of her hands, like a small child. "I need your help, Harry. He talked with you last night. I think he's a thief."

"He's your future husband. Better find out now rather than later."

"Please." She rested a hand on his cheek for a second. It was damp with her tears. "The magazine put me in charge of the trip – finances and all. He didn't like that. As a reserve – in case of real currency problems – they gave me some diamonds to be sold in emergency. They've gone, Harry. Stolen. He's the only one who could have taken them. The only one who knew."

The small package of diamonds suddenly weighed very heavily in Byrd's pocket. Only once, in that distant past shared life, had he seen Cat in a state as disintegrated as this. He placed his hands on her shoulders, gently pushing her backwards, manoeuvring her into a chair.

"You're absolutely certain your friend Geddes was the only one who could have lifted the stones?"

She sniffed, "Yes," nodding slowly.

"How many?"

"Four."

"Value?"

"My editor reckoned around five grand." Her face was still watery around the eyes, in that dilapidated condition which overtakes pretty women when they are distraught.

"Proof?"

She fumbled for a handkerchief. "Proof of ownership? That I had them? What?"

Byrd said proof that she had them in her keeping on behalf of the magazine. She delved further into her bag, extracting a notecase from which she eventually produced a typewritten document listing sums of money payable on bankers' draft in certain cities, travellers' cheques and, at the end, details of four diamonds placed in the safe keeping *of the above-mentioned Kathleen Ann Morrow, to be sold only in emergency, civil disturbance, extreme currency fluctuation, war, the closing of banking establishments etc. The above-named Kathleen Ann Morrow is to return these precious stones, or authorised copies of bills of sale, to this office on completion of assignment. Loss or theft of the stones will be covered only by Miss Morrow's personal insurance and upon her own recognisance.*

"They insured?"

"What do you think, Harry? It would have cost me a fortune."

"You didn't think of putting them in hotel safes?"

She turned her head away. "I sewed them into the straps on a spare brassiere. It would've meant turning the whole room around to find them; emptying cases, drawers, everything. Nothing else was disturbed. Whoever got them, cut them out and substituted pebbles. His sewing isn't good: that's how I found out. He's been losing money the whole trip. I'm always having to advance cash. Then I put my foot down. He's a nice guy, Harry, but money's his weak point." It was an almost accusing look. "We all have our weak points." Eyes brimming again, head nodding as if to signify that she knew what her own had been.

"You really want him, Cat? Really, for good and all? Forsaking all others, in sickness and in health, all that kind of thing?"

The silence stretched back into their mutual past, and when she spoke it was a whisper. "I thought so. For about a month or so, I thought so. Now. . ." The sentence unfinished; then the characteristic shrug, one shoulder after the other.

Byrd withdrew the packet of diamonds and put them into her hands.

"But. . . ?"

"He was trying to get me to sell them. Leave him to me, Cat. I'll fix him. You still want him around while you finish up here, or shall I send him packing? No sweat either way."

She clutched the small packet of diamonds to her as a woman will clutch a baby. Her tears were drying and she spoke very calmly. "Send him back to me. I'll do whatever's to be done."

Max still waited downstairs, more watchful than ever, like a dog alert to danger. Nobody else who mattered was in the foyer.

"You okay, boss?" Max's eyes flicked to and fro, looking behind Byrd's shoulder and then glancing back, out into the street. He lowered his voice: "I think Mr. Foo Tang want to see you. He's outside in his big car. Bulletproof, I think."

Byrd raised his eyes to the wide glass doors. The long, distinctive bright blue, sedate Hotchkiss Chantilly – large enough to seat seven people – stood directly outside the hotel. Other traffic crammed around it; the *cognoscenti* giving it wide berth, the more foolish pressing their horns only to receive hard glares from the driver and Lee Yung, who sat next to him in the front. Blinds were drawn over the rear windows, and Byrd had little doubt that Max was correct. Tang would be quietly waiting in the rear.

He told Max that he was to go straight back to the café, if Tang indeed wanted him. "He can bring me back. We all know how much extra weight's built into that tank of his. He carries more armour than old King Arthur. I reckon I'll be safe."

Max was unhappy. He did not like it when Byrd went off in the company of Foo Tang, mainly because of the un-savoury reputation of Lee Yung and other members of Tang's entourage. He hovered near his chief as they emerged into the cacophony of the street, then stepped back a couple of paces as one of the car doors opened, and Lee Yung placed himself between the car and Byrd.

"My master wish speak with you. In back of car, please," a hand reaching out to the rear door.

Byrd nodded, and eased Max away with another head movement. The Mexican retreated, reluctance showing in his dragging heels. Through the open car door, in the darkness of the Hotchkiss interior, Byrd now dimly saw the figure of Foo Tang, upright, face forward, blank and impenetrable.

He ducked his head, stepped into the motor and heard the door slam behind him. Foo Tang offered no explanation, ordering the driver to move off before Lee Yung was even back in his seat.

"You are making a special visit to the Cathay Hotel, Harry Byrd?" The tone was distinctly unfriendly.

"I've been known to go there from time to time."

"You have my protection. You have received my gift?"

Byrd used some flowery phrases about the gift being more valuable than the rendered service, and went on to say how much he appreciated the new Delage. "You taking me home?" he added.

Foo Tang nodded. "Eventually. I feel we should talk. My men have told me of your movements. A visit to a well-known dealer in diamonds, followed by a talk with some Englishman registered as Waldo Bingham. I wondered if the two events were linked."

"How linked?"

"Perhaps you were disposing of some assets. Diamonds are always good for cash. Then a visit to Mr. Bingham, who is known to have contacts with the British Foreign Office. A British passport, Harry Byrd? A quick sell-out to the Japanese gentlemen; a realising of all your assets, and a disappearing trick?"

Byrd wondered why he had not thought of that himself. It would have been an easy way out. Leave Shanghai and take unobtrusive residence in, say, Cheltenham. Unfortunately, as he knew only too well, the Black Dragon people were not offering ready money for the Flamingo as a going concern. He laughed aloud. "You are a suspicious man, Mr. Tang."

"There is a Persian saying which is difficult to translate in my tongue. It goes – 'Trust in God, but tie your camel'."

"And I'm your camel?"

"In a way, Harry, in a way. I would not like to see our business venture disappear with you to the fog and frost of London. It would not be a correct thing to do. You understand?"

"Never even crossed my mind, Foo Tang. I have too much respect for my own life. I know that your retribution is just, fast and final. You are also well informed. I might even say omniscient."

"Ah." For the first time, Tang unbent, turning his skull face toward Byrd and smiling. "Not omnipotent also? I think you wrongly equate me with Mr. Sax Rohmer's diabolical Dr. Fu Manchu."

Even in the darkness of the moving car, Byrd's surprise must have been evident. "You are fascinated, amazed, that I know of the iniquitous Fu Manchu?"

"A little. I guess I thought of you as a reader of the poems and philosophies of your own country."

"Indeed, but the monkey tricks of certain writings are often more diverting than the elephantine musings of great literary talent."

"Who said that?"

"Alas, myself." The word was almost a laugh, strange coming from the usually sombre skull. "But I am flattered if you think it an original proverb. I read many works of fiction written in your mother tongue, Harry. They are shipped over for me, or I have them brought in by the American Bookshop. Fu Manchu amuses me, as does the whole conception of a criminal mastermind – Carl Peterson, Moriarty – I have read and enjoyed many stories of mystery, adventure and villainy, though I admit to enjoying the great perpetrators of crime more than their adversaries. But then the conception of a devil is more interesting than God."

Byrd put his head back, resting it on the padded leather seat. During Tang's last monologue the familiar ache, nausea and pain in the eye had returned, slightly at first, then more harshly, like the onset of a fever.

"Are you ill?" Tang had moved, looking at him seriously.

Byrd said the blow on his head the previous day was still giving him discomfort.

Tang did not seem concerned. "Then you tell me you are not plotting to gain a British passport, nor sell off our investment?"

Byrd said no, again. When Tang seemed to believe him he added that the future of the Flamingo had been discussed with Bingham.

"He has an interest?"

"In a way. It is his theory that the Black Dragon Shoshi will make things most unpleasant. He has asked me to do certain favours for him."

Tang remained silent.

"He is a skilled diplomat: like yourself. You wish to hear what he says?"

"It is always useful to have other opinions."

"He suggests that you might pretend to do some kind of a

deal with the Japanese. Lull them into believing they are going to gain control of the café, with me still in charge. In that way we would gain their confidence."

"So they would doze and we could despatch them in their sleep?"

"Something like that." Byrd was pleased with the lie and the interpretation he had managed to put on Bingham's plan.

"It bears thinking about. They can be creatures of great violence, and I wish to avoid a blood bath at this time. I have some particularly exacting work in hand concerning the Americans who came yesterday. I may yet need you to assist with that."

The pain decreased a fraction; a tactical withdrawal. In the rear of his mind, Byrd thought it would be best if he could see a doctor before long. When he got back to the café he would arrange it.

"You want me to assist in the – " stopping just in time. Christ, he thought, I'm slipping: on the edge of mentioning the arms for opium arrangement.

"Only in a small capacity. Possibly the storage of certain items. In a few months. December or January."

"If we're going to lull the Japanese, it's got to be before then."

Tang's death-head snapped up, the thin lips pursed in displeasure. "I am well aware of that."

"Then if the Black Dragon try to stop me again, what do I do? Send them over to you with half-promises?"

"My people will always be near at hand, but, yes, I think we must speak with their leaders." The displeasure went as quickly as it had appeared. "Negotiations often take some time. Much conversation can be like smoke. What a man cannot see will not worry him. I shall do what I can. There are two men. . ."

"Takahome and Hitchimata?"

"Precisely. I shall make contact with them and keep you informed." He leaned forward and spoke to the driver. The car began to accelerate.

Byrd felt them making a left turn and then a right. They

slowed again: back in heavy traffic. He could hear the noises beyond the covered windows. Tang said they would be back at the café quite soon. It was gone six o'clock so he would be late for his meeting with Geddes. The diamond business could be cleared out of the way, and maybe he could even get some reassurance from a doctor before the evening's work began in earnest. Byrd's only regret was that he did not feel well enough to kick Geddes out into the street, sending him back to Cat with a few bruises.

The café appeared very quiet; but the doors were usually locked until around six thirty. Byrd, not wishing to disturb Max or any of the others, walked to the side entrance, glancing back to see Tang's big blue Hotchkiss getting lost in the traffic.

He did not go into his own apartment, but turned right down the corridor, heading for the office, already fumbling for his keys. A second later the keys were forgotten and Byrd's hand was going for his hip pocket and the pistol, for the office door stood half open.

Shaking his head, like a boxer trying to summon up reserves of energy, he kicked the door open and entered quickly, glancing to left and right, then centring on the figure he saw sitting with his back to him, in the chair facing his desk. Automatically he walked the two paces towards the man and spoke, placing a hand on his shoulder as he did so.

"Who let you in, Geddes?"

Tom Geddes did not reply. He simply sagged and slumped forward, his head hitting the corner of Byrd's desk, turning him in the fall so that he ended face upwards sprawled in an odd position on the floor, knees drawn up and arms splayed awkwardly.

One side of the front part of his head was missing, just above the eyes. You could see that it was Geddes, but that was just about all.

Byrd felt very sick. A bullet; Geddes had probably turned his head just as the shot was fired otherwise he would have taken it right in the forehead. He could see the whole thing happening, everything except the person handling the weapon. Cat? Would Cat. . . ? He did not hear the slight movement behind him, only the thumping in his head which was turning into a blinding pain which then ceased as the floor came up to meet him, and blackness inked in consciousness.

"Monsieur 'Arry," the voice was saying.

"I think he's coming round." Another voice, with an unfamiliar accent. 'Theenk' instead of 'think'.

"Oh Harry, who do this?" A girl, also with an unidentifiable accent.

Then another couple of voices, one heavy with German gutturals, the other more obscure, but foreign.

He couldn't understand why there were no straightforward, honest-to-God American accents. Where in Christ's name was he? opening his eyes to see a ceiling and something turning, some kind of fan. Unfamiliar faces peered over him, and for a second he wondered if he was going out of his mind: it was as though he was a tiny baby again, in his pram being coochie-cooed.

"Take it easy, boss." A small man with a pencil moustache had an arm around him, lifting him.

"Oh, Harry. What do we do? What happened? That . . . that . . . man." The girl was oriental, Chinese, he thought. He had never seen her before. Only Cat called him Harry: come to that, where the hell was Cat? He remembered leaving the office. The rain and the January cold. Yes: hadn't seen her for a few days. Dinner. Dinner tonight with Cat and then the meeting at the Statler. They were coming in from all over. Christ, how had he got mixed up in all that?

"Where the hell am I? What happened?" His voice seemed different, croaky.

"Come on, Monsieur 'Arry. We get you sitting up." This one was in a chef's hat and apron. What the hell? He couldn't remember.

"Cat," he croaked. "Must call her," repeating her number at the *Globe*.

"Where am I?" Now in a sitting position, he looked

around at the strange room and unknown faces. He was bruised. Head, front and rear. Bruised but nothing more. Perhaps a little shaky. Then he saw the body. "Jesus." Was he being set up? He didn't recognise what was left of the guy, one side of his forehead blown away. Who the hell would have done that? They had always kept him clear of their blood and violence. That had been part of the understanding. No involvement. Whose style was this? A bullet in the head? Johnny the Barb? Freddie Carpione? No. Maes probably. A quick bullet through the head could be Val Maes. But how had he got here? He looked at his watch. The date with Cat. Seven o'clock at the Trattoria Macinare.

Of one thing he was certain. He had to put a lot of distance between the body on the floor, these strange people, and himself. Fast. There was no time to talk or argue or discover why. He could call one of the contacts from the Trattoria. Go. Go now.

Stumbling to his feet he swept the small group of people to one side and tried to make for the door. Someone shouted "Harry". Another grabbed at his arm, but he snatched it away and pushed hard into the man's stomach – a short, fat, roly-poly man, toppling backwards with a face that showed shock and concern.

He made it to the door: through, and into a passage with no idea of where he was. Cat in his head, and their date at the Trattoria. Which way? Left or right? Right. Now where? Left. Stairs. If he could make the street and a cab. Then a phone.

Henry Beech – known as Harry Byrd to his Shanghai friends and associates – took the down run on the stairs, three at a time, wrenched at the door and stepped out into the unexpected warmth of the night street: into a world he did not, could not, recognise or believe in.

Harry Byrd, who did not know himself under that name, had expected cold and pelting rain, people muffled like parcels, fighting the winds on the broad sidewalks. He had expected cabs and heavy traffic, high buildings and bland modern street lights.

Instead, the lights were vivid, multi-coloured; the noise was unique, an amalgam of chatter, shouts, music – odd, strange music – clapping sounds and cries like liturgical responses. A tram rattled by. There were automobiles, but there were also little buggies being hauled by men: Chinese people.

Beech thought – how did I end up in Chinatown? He had not been in Chinatown for years, it was way off to the north of the city, and quite a small area: not as large and bustling as the Chinatown of, say, San Francisco.

A dream. It could only be a dream, for this couldn't be Chinatown. Not in a million years. When he left the office it had been mid-winter, bitter cold, and the rain like the coming of the Flood. Now the air was moist but balmy with hardly any breeze. He was still running when he reached some kind of intersection, crowded; an air of gaiety, the whole throng washed with the atmosphere of people out to have a good time.

Rickshaws, trams, automobiles. He needed a cab. When you need a cab you shout. Harry Byrd, knowing himself only as Henry Beech, shouted towards a passing automobile which drove straight on, though three rickshaws came rolling up, their pullers padding and motioning him to get in.

"I want a cab." He could not recognise his voice.

"Taxicab?" One of the pullers laughed and chattered to the others, one of whom turned suddenly and pointed at a squat black vehicle, sleek enough in finish, but carrying a sign in Chinese characters. The motor veered across the road and came to a standstill. The driver was Chinese with a grin revealing an abundance of gold teeth, giving his mouth the appearance of a macabre bracelet.

"You want hire car?" the driver asked, and Harry was in the back without even replying.

"Where you want go?" The Chinese driver seemed uncertain of his passenger.

"Get me to the Trattoria Macinare. Eighth and Lake."

The driver laughed. "You go where?"

"I told you. Eighth and Lake. Italian restaurant. Trattoria Macinare."

"No place." The driver turned around to look him over, glinting eyes sizing up his fare. Then, as if making a decision, "I take you to Cathay. You ask doorman there. He know everything." He settled behind the wheel and drew the car away on to the brilliant gaudy street.

Harry glanced back to see the Chinese girl and two of the other men emerging from the doorway, shouting and gesticulating. "Go," he said to the driver who merely nodded and chuckled.

Looking from the window of the moving car, Harry was aware of the strange mixture – Chinese and Europeans, on the sidewalks. Cafés and bars. Music and more music. Strange discord. A man in black silk pyjamas wrestled with a chicken, holding the bird by the legs while it flapped wings in terror, lifting its body, jerking in the man's hand.

He closed his eyes, still not comprehending anything. Drugs? He had heard from some of the boys that there were drugs which distorted your senses, produced hallucinations. A nightmare? Was it possible to be conscious of being in the middle of a nightmare while you dreamed it? He became conscious of something else. Himself. He did not feel right. His body was somehow different. Opening his eyes he looked first at his hands to see they were not the usual pale pink; harder, as if browned by sun and work, the skin more wrinkled since he left the office; when? an hour ago? He lifted a hand to his hair. That also felt unfamiliar: an unaccustomed styling. Then his clothes. He was not wearing the usual business suit, but slacks and a shirt, with a lightweight jacket. Wallet? He could feel it in the breast pocket; and something else, heavy, unusual, in the hip pocket of his slacks. His hand went back and he brought out a small automatic pistol. Jesus, he never carried . . . then he became more concerned, illogically, because he was not wearing a tie. The wallet? Replacing the pistol he withdrew the wallet. Leather, but almost new. Certainly not his.

Harry began to open the flap when the cab lurched, and he glanced up to see they were turning onto a wide street.

They drove along a kind of waterfront, but it bore no resemblance to the seediness of the city's waterfront. Here there were high, white and elaborate buildings, flowers and trees; not the grey walls, brick, iron-roofed warehouses. And the sea itself, muddy, with a long slick of land visible in the distance, warships nestling beside freighters and liners, small oriental boats. He stared, not the smallest spark of recognition coming to him.

Lightheaded, anxiety tingling his nerve ends and rolling around his stomach, Harry was now in total confusion. He tried to open the wallet, but his hands trembled like a man suffering from *delirium tremens*. He fumbled; then got it open. There was money, but not American dollars; this was strange-looking paper stuff. Some kind of an identity card with a photograph that looked vaguely like him, only the face was thinner: a paradox, older yet younger, an older pair of eyes in a younger face. The name, neatly typed on to the card, said 'Harry Byrd' and the occupation given was 'Café Owner'. He shut his eyes again, squeezing them as if to make this incredible hallucination disappear. All he experienced was a slight twinge of pain in the right eye and, on opening them again, he still stared at the card. This time he noticed the heading – 'Resident of Shanghai. Nationality: Citizen of the United States of America'.

The cab was pulling over, coming to a stop outside a large white building with three arched doorways.

"Cathay Hotel." The driver grinned, holding his hand out. "One dollar."

Harry could hardly move, his legs leaden and his brain an accelerating whirlpool. Automatically he pulled some notes from the wallet, and without really looking, stuffed them into the man's hand. He was experiencing what he thought was probably claustrophobia, a sensation in which he was dwindling, while the inside of the cab became larger: menacing. Fear grabbed at his throat; mouth dry, limbs heavy.

As he stumbled from the cab, a vertiginous series of images crossed his mind – exact, detailed, almost photographic: Cat sitting opposite him at the Trattoria; windshield wipers; rain, and shapes against blurred lights; a courtroom; another room – some kind of club, seen from high up, a man at the piano, and arches lining the walls; Chinese girls; a tropical bird with a long tail and a Chinese man with a face like a skull; music – the swooping cadences of a romantic song he had never heard; the Chinese girl who had been leaning over him, now under him, calling him Harry. Only Cat called him Harry. The dead man on the floor; four stones, diamonds, lying on a piece of velvet; a large man with the face of a bulldog; a ranch with a pool and patio; a black limo moving away over a desert track, its tail lights bouncing. Then the whole lot crammed in around him. A vortex of images and voices from which he could decipher no sense, shape or pattern.

He stumbled on the pavement, and a uniformed Chinese stepped forward to take his arm.

"You okay, Mr. Byrd? You look not well."

"Yea. Yea, I'm okay." Brow creasing. *Mr. Byrd.* The residence card in his wallet. 'Harry Byrd'.

"Harry."

He nearly fell again as he turned. Cat was coming towards him. The whole image of life distorted, whirling him off into something much more than a dark, feverish nightmare.

BOOK TWO

Byrd in a Cage

— (1)

It had started, of course, with the original crack on his head
and eye, but Harry Byrd was not conscious of that. The last
blow, from behind, as he looked down on Tom Geddes'
body, did the final damage – something affecting the func-
tion of the brain; to his bank of memory. Harry Byrd had,
in that moment, sidestepped time, returning, in a very real
mental sense, to the day, almost four years ago now, when
he still lived under his original name, Henry Arthur Beech:
to all outward appearances a reliable and respectable member of his late father's old accountancy firm of Beech,
Murray & O'Connor, in the city where he had been born
and raised. Back in the US of A.

In his mind, the day to which he had returned was the day
that had changed his life, eventually bringing him to the
great port of Shanghai with the new, and perfectly legal,
name of Harry Byrd. But how, it may well be asked, could
a man with the respectable position and professional re-
sponsibility of Henry Beech suffer such a drastic change in
fortune?

Respectable? Well, yes, eventually. As a teenager and
young man, Beech had always been something of a hell-
raiser. Even when he finally settled down, agreed to finish
his accountancy exams and join his father's old firm, his
friends – and others in the city – thought of him as a bit of a
ladies' man. He clung to his smart bachelor apartment, and
even after he had been with the firm for quite a while people
would often see him with a pretty girl – always different – in
the more racy restaurants and clubs of the city. The senior
partners tried hard to get him to spend more time at the
exclusive Country Club, or the staid City and Professional
Men's Club. But Henry Beech, brilliant accountant though
he was, belonged to a new generation and went his own
sweet way. The city's matrons, with daughters bred of

good stock, tutted to themselves. Henry Beech should settle down with the right class of girl: meaning one of their own particular daughters. For goodness' sake, even the man's name was linked with the old 'aristocracy' of the city, and wasn't it a name which flavoured solidarity and sobriety? – Beech: strong, hard, close-grained and tough. But Henry showed no inclination to settle down. Within his profession he was beyond reproach, but his reputation for good living and girls was another matter.

That was until he met Kate Morrow.

Their first meeting had been at an official city shindig for a visiting celebrity in 1927. Henry Beech was at the reception with a proper invitation and his usual roving eye. His father, having been one of the great worthies of the city's establishment, had left a mantle to fall on his son regarding official functions, so his name was always 'on the list' at City Hall.

Kate Morrow went on a Press Pass, covering the event as a young girl reporter, still learning her trade with the city's number-one newspaper, the *Globe*. Later, she told him that she nearly missed her deadline because they had talked for so long. She wore a filmy black dress and used her hands a lot when she spoke. She also had trouble dealing with her notepad, drink, and the canapés at the same time; got a shade tipsy and was very flattered that Henry Beech spent so much time with her.

To Beech, her lips, as she spoke – animated and enthusiastic about everything – seemed almost too inviting; and, when she eventually walked away, the curves of her body under the thin dress fired his imagination. In bed that night he thought of her naked, and clearly remembered her laugh – easy and light, a chuckle which could turn so easily into infectious, uninhibited delight. He also thought about her eyes a great deal, and what her lips would be like to kiss, and if she wore underwear or not (at the time, there was a craze for not doing so among some of the city girls, who thought it very chic).

He made all the usual enquiries, and called Kate a couple of evenings later: they talked a lot on the telephone in those

132

first days. Then lunch. Then an abrupt silence. She wondered about the silence (Kate told him all her feelings during the following months); hoped he would call again, then wondered why he did not; then decided there was someone else, or that he did not, after all, like her. She was not to know that, at the time, Henry was becoming more and more enmeshed in the events which were to lead to the dramatic, and near-catastrophic, change in his fortune.

Of course, eventually he called her, and they had lunch again; then dinner; then dinner again. After the sixth dinner she went back to his apartment. He was not her first lover, but he was certainly the first man in her life who made any sense.

They had the best part of a year together; mostly intense happiness, though Kate, who had already seen so much impermanence in her life, still had lingering bouts of uncertainty and depression. In fact it was only a few weeks after they started seeing each other that circumstances forced her to tell Henry the truth about herself. First, that her name had not always been Kate Morrow – though, by now, it had legally become so.

Her original name had been Kathleen Kelly. She had two elder brothers, and her father was a grade one, hundred per cent bastard police sergeant, brutal in his bullying of her mother, deep into graft and corruption, yet keeping up a front as a good, hard-working, honest Catholic cop. His drinking did not help, but most of this was done within the privacy of their home, so Kate's mother bore the brunt. When she died, after neglected illness, Kate came to a decision. Long determined to escape the hell which awaited her, living as unpaid housekeeper for her father – with all its attendant dangers – and surrogate mother to her downtrodden brothers, she made the final split. Immediately after the funeral, she did not return to the family home but left town and worked, for six months, as Girl Friday on a small Mid-Western weekly newspaper, before returning to the city to land a cub reporter job with the *Globe*.

Later, she often wondered if she would have told Harry (she now called him Harry, the only person to do so; while he, after their visit to the zoo, called her Cat) all this so soon if her father had not himself forced it.

Six weeks or so after they had become lovers, the police sergeant – discovering belatedly that she was back in the city, under a legally-changed name – made one final effort to entice her home to care for him and his sons. It was not a subtle attempt, for he was a man who believed in force rather than guile, and it was made with threats and the unofficial use of two large plainclothes men.

Fortunately Harry was present and sent the plainclothes officers packing with a few threats of his own, and a stiff letter later, on Cat's behalf, from a lawyer friend. That was when Cat told Harry the truth. But it left the girl a wreck for days, having dredged up so much of the unhappiness of those early years at home.

There were other doubts in Cat's mind, but for both of them it was a time which in later years became distilled into a montage of happiness: scenes of remembered enjoyment, ranging from warm conversations over dinner tables, to walks in the country, small treasured gifts, weekends of abundant pleasure, nights of physical delight which neither imagined could ever be repeated.

Time together was often snatched between his work – which was not always confined to office hours – and her assignments, which were at odd, often inconvenient, shifts. Yet the bud of love grew between them, grew into full blossom. "It's as though everything's been invented especially for us," Cat once said.

Henry Beech – and Harry Byrd, as he was to become – had one special memory, which stayed with him even through the years of bitterness, seldom altering: Cat and himself eating spaghetti in their favourite Italian place; drinking chianti that was a little too raw, because only the cheapest rough wines were shipped in during those prohibition years – and sold at exorbitant prices.

They had gone to that same, well-loved, Italian restaurant on the final night of sanity; the night when Henry's life reached a watershed that was to lead him to the new name of Harry Byrd and the port of Shanghai.

When he had dashed from the Flamingo, his mind fractured and his grip on time destroyed, it was to that night Harry Byrd had returned: to that night, the city back home in the States, and to his old name – as though the night and all that followed had not yet happened. Over three years of life were blocked out, as though he was destined to live the same night, and the following days, over and over again, like a terrible punishment from legend or myth.

The night had been cold, wet and windy, as though the elements were already marshalling forces against him; and, though he had never admitted the truth to Cat, it was the culmination of months of mental agony, despair, stretched nerves and a seemingly insoluble problem.

A bleak night, then. A night also when – by luck, coincidence, or the meddlesome fates – a rookie policeman, not in on the conspiracy, had put in a report to headquarters about a large number of men arriving late, suspiciously, and under dubious circumstances, at the city's Statler Hotel.

But that was later. After midnight. Harry and Cat had met at seven; happy. They had not seen one another for five days, and tonight was special – dinner at the Trattoria Macinare: old Macinare himself, beaming and bowing, white moustache waxed and preened; the fat wife and plain, shy, daughter hovering nearby as Harry ordered their meal.

It was over the *passatelli* that Harry asked if Cat had ever thought of giving up the newspaper. "Why should I? God, it's given me a freedom I thought I'd never get." She had a characteristic little gesture when lost for words: a shrug; a kind of ripple of the shoulders, first one, then the other. "Why?"

"So I can make an honest woman of you." It was the nearest he could come to a proposal. "I guess I've never met anyone I wanted to marry until you. It can't be quite yet, honey, but as soon as I've got things straightened out. . ."

"What things? The Harridan?" she asked with a wry little smile.

He said, yes, the Harridan.

In the first months, Cat had really suspected that he was running another woman; but, wisely, checked her jealousy.

Held it in even in the face of guarded telephone calls, sudden trips out of town, last-minute meetings. She was goaded further by the knowledge that, in his past, Harry had walked in and out of other women's lives, as a man will wander through the rooms of a gallery, seeking the right picture for his home. But once he had convinced her, in those early days, that he had taken on extra work of a particularly exacting nature, she made a joke of it and her first fears – calling that area of his professional life the Harridan. Had she known the truth, Cat would not have joked. Certainly the work was exacting, but only Harry was aware that over the months it had also become unexpectedly, and terrifyingly, dangerous.

They went straight from the trattoria to his apartment (they had never lived together wholly), and made love, impulsively; then gently, for a long time, leaving them, finally, exhausted in the rumpled bed around which their clothes lay like scattered rocks in a carpet sea. They dropped slowly, entwined, into sleep, only to be wakened by the ringing of a telephone. It was one o'clock in the morning.

Harry had already warned her that, as there was a meeting he must attend later in the early hours of the morning, it was impossible for her to stay the whole night. Cat had protested, but knew, from his look and tone, there was no option. She had even suggested staying there to make breakfast on his return. He merely shook his head. You didn't argue with Henry Beech's business appointments. He was to have dropped her off at her apartment in his automobile before going on to wherever the meeting was scheduled to take place.

It turned out that the telephone call was a reminder; to check if he had left for the meeting; and, while he was not yet late, Harry was cutting it fine. "This is really important, Cat, honey; being late's going to screw me up."

There was a change of plan. He was going to the Statler Hotel and he had his doubts about leaving his car in the charge of the commissionaire. She would drive him, then take the car back to her place; he would pick it up later – in the morning. (In fact he had remembered how noticeable his car was and had no wish to advertise his presence at the hotel.) They were out of the apartment in fifteen minutes, delayed by a stocking mislaid under the edge of the bed. Cat was uncomfortable driving the big Stutz Victoria in teeming rain which made even the well-lit streets dark and difficult. She was afraid of not seeing someone step from the sidewalk, or of another car splashing suddenly from a side road. So she drove slowly, with great care, leaning forward, peering through the wet and darkness.

They turned on to Main and saw the lights ahead, grouped around the front of the Statler. There was no doubt in Harry's mind that the lights were the police, though they were supposed to have been fixed (he heard about the rookie cop's tactless report to headquarters later, though never found out what happened to him). There were dazzling white lights from the cars, mixed up with flashing reds and blues, distorted into odd shapes by the streaming rain on the windshield.

Cat wanted to stop; check it out for the paper; but, for the first time ever, Harry was abrupt with her, shouting that she should drive straight on. Through the drench, they saw the paddy waggons lined up, the rear doors open, and police – some with unholstered guns – shepherding men out of the hotel entrance. A couple of the men being taken out had their jackets over their heads, shielding themselves from the downpour, or the eyes of anyone foolish enough to be watching the show. Cat made some comment about hoping her father, the police sergeant, was there and getting soaked.

Harry's reaction told her a great deal even then, in the car. If they had not fallen asleep in his apartment, she thought, and if she had not lost her stocking, and if she had driven faster, then her Harry would have been one of those men being taken from the Statler. Theirs was the meeting on his schedule. She saw it in his face; heard it in his voice.

When they got back to the relative safety of the apartment, he was drained, white-faced, shaking, sick with fear, locking himself in the bedroom to spend the best part of an hour on the telephone. Cat waited, biding her time, using common sense, knowing now that the Statler business had much to do with all that extra work. The Harridan. That this was a crisis was in no doubt. The depth and seriousness of the emergency had yet to be revealed to her. Eventually, he returned to tell her of the immediate situation.

There had been thirty arrests. Over a third of the men picked up were armed; most carried large sums of money; but – "It's being taken care of," he told her, just as they had told him. "Being taken care of" he kept repeating like a litany. "That's how much pull they have. Being taken care of." Calmer now, for they had said they did not suspect him for his lateness. It was *they* or *them* for quite a while that night – before he really got down to naming names.

In fact, very little was heard about those arrests. It *had* been taken care of, and they did not even make the papers none of those pulled in even faced charges. Most were out of police headquarters within the hour; even though many were people for whom the Feds would have given their badges and pensions.

So Cat began to coax the whole story from him, until at last the gates were opened and the muddy waters which had so troubled him poured out. Almost immediately it was apparent to Cat, who knew him so well, that the whole thing went against the basic nature of a man like Harry. Hell-raiser he may have been when younger, but not a criminal.

It began only a few weeks before they had first met. Two old friends (*I'd known them for years, honey. They didn't understand the dangers any more than I did.*) had approached him. They all used private clubs and speakeasies, since the Volstead Act had put the final seal on prohibition. "I suppose we were naïve; dumb. Of course we were breaking the law, but it's such a stupid law. We knew the guys who provided the stuff were breaking the law as well, but the kind of people we met weren't hoods – leastways we didn't think so. Some of the most respected families in town used the joints we went to."

Harry's friends told him that the owner of a club they all visited from time to time was having trouble. He was not a man used to figures, and had made a lot of hard currency from illegal booze. Could Henry Beech have a word with him and assist with his tax difficulties? Of course. Nothing easier.

"It started out as innocently as that." Harry sat and sipped black coffee, chain-lighting cigarettes. "Helping a guy. Mind you, I discovered fast enough that it wasn't just the hooch – and I should have known that. There was illegal gambling as well."

Cat shook her head. They had argued many times about gambling. Her father gambled, and she had seen her mother deprived of money for essentials because of it – even with the graft he pulled in on the side.

Harry said he believed people had a right to spend their money just how they wanted. It was up to them to exercise restraint. "We're supposed to be the land of the free. I see no harm in having a drink or two; betting on the ponies or a card. I'm against such repressive laws; they're unconstitutional."

The club owner's name was Jimmy Veal. A nice, well-educated man, but a bit of a drifter. Harry sorted the finances and took a couple of risks in doing so. "You know. The kind of thing any accountant might do for a friend. Just within the law, but dubious. Nasty if they really probed." The prepared accounts, and some other documents, had Henry Beech's name on them. It was not until this was done that he discovered Jimmy Veal was only a front.

Harry was not innocent enough to be unaware of the rackets, and the kind of men who ran them; but it came as a shock to discover he had, in fact, been working for one of the biggest gangsters in the city – Johnny Barbera, known to his friends, and the newspapers, as Johnny the Barb.

The Barb had hooked Henry Beech. Fear, Harry supposed, had been the next motivation. The money that was put his way was incredible, but Harry had always been used to money, and it was fear that forced him on. Barbera made it clear, in plain, gentle terms, that he was very pleased with how Mr. Beech had handled matters. He wanted Mr. Beech to meet some of his friends. They needed a man like him. "The way he finally put it was, that, if I didn't go along with them, they'd blow me. If that didn't work there was the ultimate," running a finger across his throat. "The river. I was terrified. I'm still terrified. You don't fool around – not with people like that."

He paced the room while she made more coffee: black, the smell comforting, reminding him of his mother's kitchen. "Cat, I'm not the sort of fella who gets mixed up with graft, or killings: murder, corruption, theft. There are rules in my profession. You can bend them slightly and people shrug. No sweat. But this? It . . . it just got out of hand. Jesus, I should have realised . . ."

Of course he should have realised, because in a matter of weeks he was working almost full time for the largest and most powerful gangland figures in the city – Barbera; the Maes brothers; Freddie (Freddie the Carp) Carpionne; 'Big Mike' Donnelly; Isaac Krantz, and Joe (Joe the Fist) Fistulare.

The meeting at the Statler on that night had been very important: a kind of conclave of gang leaders from all parts of the country. Some of them had come in from the East and West Coasts especially. "Really big guys. Men with power you'd never credit. Christ, it's being taken care of; and I'm up to the hairline and over; because I'm probably the only one with access to the real records in black and white."

Then he told her that he knew where every financial body was buried – who owned bank accounts, and under what fictitious names; how much liquor came into the city; who was paid what to keep quiet; who ran the rackets and who fronted; how much money went where. "And I'm out of my league. I want out, but there's no way: except in a pine box."

But there was a way, and Cat saw it immediately. Hadn't he said the Feds would give their badges and pensions for some of the names? Harry could deliver them up to the Feds, complete with all documentation. It would put them away for a long time.

"Oh sure," Harry laughed, like a tooth grinding at a nerve. "And what happens to me? I'll either be inside with them, or shot to pieces. Doing what you're suggesting would mean getting up in court – in the open – and telling all I know: showing all I have on them. To use a cliché, I'd be signing my own death warrant."

Cat said not necessarily. She knew how the Feds worked. Look at his situation now. He was scared stiff anyway, and his world was finished: his professional life tainted. What would be the outcome? In the end, if the police didn't get him, the Mob would. If he was in that deep – knew so much and had it in writing – he could never last. But the Feds were a different proposition. If he really wanted out, she would act as a go-between. He could offer himself up, with all the documents. The Feds would nail the people they wanted, but there had to be a deal. Himself, in court with the evidence, in return for complete protection, before and during the trial. Afterwards, a new identity – new name, background, papers, everything. Money, a passport, and safe custody to somewhere out of the country. Hadn't he said, many times, that the accountancy business bored him? That he wanted something with more glamour? That, while he was good with figures and tax problems, he didn't like them? Well, the Feds could give him that. If he really had the dope on these guys, and the Feds wanted them so much, they would deal.

"What about you?" At that moment, Harry sounded completely uninterested in the idea.

"Me?" Cat wound her arms around his neck. "Harry darling, I love you. I'll see you through. Mind you, if I set things up with the Feds, I think we should stay apart until it's all over. But after that, I'll come with you. Wherever you want to go, I'll be with you."

Even as she said it, Cat had an inkling, for the first time, that it might not work out quite that way. Something else clicked into her mind. She loved Harry . . . but she loved her career as well. "Mind you, there'll be strings to that, Harry," she grinned. "I don't mean nasty, blackmail strings. Just a small, professional thing. Part of the deal – between the Feds, and between you and me – will be that I get exclusive rights on your story: from you. If it all works out; as soon as the trial's over and they've finished with you – before we leave – we'll get together and go through it all. I write the pieces and then we leave. After all, it'll be more money in the bank for us."

It took several days to convince him that this was the only possible way. In the end Harry agreed. Cat set the whole thing up for him and, within a week, the deal was on. And meanwhile she silenced her conscience. Whatever might happen in the end, she told herself, she was still saving Harry's life.

The Feds got what they wanted – except for Vincent and Valentine Maes, who somehow managed, more by luck than good judgement, to keep one step ahead of them. After the deal was done, and they had spirited Beech away, late one evening, they sealed off the city. First, under cover of darkness, they pulled in a lot of people – around twenty senior police officers, out of headquarters and precinct houses; thirty men and women who worked in City Hall; two judges, and at least half-a-dozen highly-respected citizens.

These people were not arrested, but simply taken out of circulation – to a couple of houses the Feds had prepared: men to one, women to the other. No charges were ever brought against them – they were merely removed to shorten the odds against the big fish being tipped. Beech had provided all the names on that particular cast list.

Then, at dawn, the Feds returned in large numbers. A lot of well-known folk were arrested this time, and the operation dramatically closed the city's major illegal activities for a long while.

Charges were brought against nearly one hundred small, and medium-time, criminals: but the big break-through was that five very big fish went into the net: Barbera; Krantz; Fistulare; 'Big Mike' Donnelly, and Freddie Carpionne.

The Maes brothers, who were at the top of both Beech's and the Feds' lists, were tipped – in spite of the precautions –

and disappeared as if by magic. Houdini could not have done it better.

The trial was, naturally, a showpiece; nationwide; coast-to-coast. Henry Arthur Beech, with his papers, ledgers and documents, was the star, and the Feds kept their word. They used every dodge: dummy cars, tails, different routes to the court house, six officers always with him (they played a lot of gin and poker), a different house or apartment every evening, after he had given evidence – sometimes way out in the country, outside city limits.

After the second afternoon of the hearing, one of the decoy cars was fired on – tommy-guns from a fast black automobile that was never traced. Towards the end, four hoods managed to get as far as the lobby of the apartment building where Harry was holed up. There was a gunfight which straggled out onto the street. One Fed agent died and one was badly wounded. Two of the hoods got their heads blown off.

Cat was in court, all through the trial, making notes and staying close to the other newspaper people. She even went through the charade expected of her as a reporter, trying to get near to Harry at the end of the day, or in the recesses. Occasionally they caught each other's eyes, but never for long. She always quickly looked away.

On the night Harry completed his evidence, and it was established that he would not be recalled, they took him off into the next State and flew him to an airstrip out in the desert, around fifty miles from San Francisco; then by car to the ranch, which was much nearer the city – set back from the main road, about a mile, and accessible only along a dirt track, hard and bumpy. It was open country – still desert really, and the Feds could have spotted a jack-rabbit trying to get within a mile of the place from any direction.

It took three days for the trial to finish, and in that time a Fed called Crowley coached Harry in his new identity. Crowley would be coming with him to Shanghai. "With us," Harry corrected.

On the fourth day they brought Cat. They had a week. Harry was not to know this was their last week, for much needed doing – working on the articles with Cat during the day; swimming naked in the pool with her as the sun went down, the air still hot, dry as baked sand; sitting on the patio eating dinner with her while the cicadas chirped descants; enjoying each other through the nights.

On the first day, he wanted to tell her all the plans. Shanghai, enough money and contacts to start up his own café, and how he was going to make it the biggest and best draw in the whole place. But she put a hand to his mouth. "No, Harry. Let it be a surprise. I don't want to know anything – where we're going, what we're going to do. You've got the tickets and passports? The money?"

"Yes."

"Then surprise me. Once this is over I want it to be like Thanksgiving, Christmas and New Year's all rolled into one. Keep it a secret. Wrap it in gold paper and tie it with a red ribbon, then open it on the boat or wherever."

He did as he was told, to please her; and she completed the articles on time – the day before they were due to leave. Arrangements had been made for her editor to come down to San Francisco, and she was to meet him at the Mark Hopkins that night. "I'll only be away for around three hours – hour there, an hour with the man, and an hour back." Cat said. "That's all it'll take. Geez, there's going to be a bundle of money in this." She patted the folder which held her manuscript. Kissed him, long and hard, and left the ranch.

Harry had loved her as no woman before or since: certainly loved her with the greatest happiness he had ever known on that last night, when he watched the Feds' black limo, its tail lights bouncing and jinking over the hard dirt track, until they disappeared from view into the traffic on the main highway.

It seemed they had the world by the ears, and the whole of their lives together stretched as far as the mind could see.

The limo was back in less than two hours. Only the pair of Feds who had gone with her. No Cat. One of the Feds brought the letter to Harry, written in her round, careful hand:

Darling Harry,

I love you. Never doubt that. I guess I'll always love you. You know better than anyone that I'm not a person for wrapping things up. I'd like to beat around the bush and wrap this up now, but I have to tell you straight. God knows, I hate the thought, but I'm not coming with you as we planned. Okay, yes, I've deceived you, but, believe me, only during this past week. Even on the trip out here I had not made up my mind. I finally did just before I arrived. I suppose that's why I asked you not to tell me where you're going, because that immediately removes the temptation to join you. I still don't know if I'm doing the right thing. Lord help me. I love you so and I'm letting you slip through my fingers. Maybe I'll live to regret it.

By now you will be calling me all the bitches ever born. I can't stop that, anymore than I can ask you to understand – particularly as I keep telling you the truth: that I love you. Please, please try to forgive me.

Believe me, I wanted to be with you in court, and believe me I know what courage it took for you to do what you have done. I was so very proud of you each day. There's no doubt that you're the bravest man I know.

And here's the irony. You are getting out, and I helped you. Because of that I've got the scoop of a lifetime, and a whole new world has opened up. I have the pick of the country's newspapers and magazines from which to choose; and I can write my own ticket. All because of you. Thank you, my darling Harry. Remember my dreadful ambition, which is the driving force. Forgive if you can. Love me a bit if you can. Understand if you can. Besides, I want to be there when the cop gets his.

Ever Your
Cat

The bands played on the quay, and they threw streamers from the decks as the ship left, on the following noon tide, with Harry aboard. One Fed for company. No Cat. It was a British ship. A large amount of booze during the voyage.

"Harry, I was worried. What the hell's happened? There's trouble at the café. I didn't know what to do. The police're there." So Cat greeted Byrd outside the Cathay, when he was deep within the nightmare of knowing only that he was Beech, and in America years ago.

"Café?" His voice floated back to him as a distant echo.

"The Flamingo. You okay, Harry? You look . . . Did you see Tom?"

"Tom?" He answered, brow creased. "Tom? We had a date, Cat. Remember? Macinare's at seven. What's happened? It was cold and wet. Where the blazes . . . ?"

She put an arm around his shoulders, her face showing concern, the tiny forked lines between her brows. "You're in shock or something, Harry. Come inside."

He was shaking. Maybe he was going crazy. The strain on him had increased recently, he knew that – the weight of work, threats, the keeping of criminal secrets for too long, and his conscience nagging for a whole year. The thing had become repugnant to him – to his moral judgement – so this was probably the retribution: some kind of nervous breakdown.

As Cat guided him through the glass doors into the large plush lobby, he experienced a sudden flash of recall, inexplicably seeing a man lying on the floor, knees bent and arms unusually postured, part of his head blown away. He asked who Tom was.

"I'll get you up to my room," Cat said.

They took four steps into the lobby. Suddenly he was aware of someone else, coming from the right, moving fast towards him. Two men. Cat breathed in horror – "Oh, my Christ," and he recognised the men. Could he ever fail to recognise them? Vincent Maes whom he knew well; and the other, the legend he had often seen, though never met – Boris Oblosky.

146

But he was perplexed, both by the look of loathing on Maes' face, and by the wide friendly grin offered by Boris.

Vincent Maes stepped close, and Harry felt the hardness of metal digging into his ribs through Maes' pocket.

"Henry Beech, of all people," Maes hissed. "I thought we'd never catch up with you."

"Catch up with me?" With his memory firmly entrenched as Beech, Harry had no way of understanding either the situation or the danger.

The pistol barrel dug even further into his ribs, and Maes moved closer. Boris, however, tried to intervene.

"This is my friend. The one from the place where we had the meet last night," said Boris.

"Yeah?" sneered Maes. "Well, buddy, I'm catching a train outa here. You know who this really is, Boris?"

"Sure, boss. It's Mr. Flamingo."

"Wrong, Boris."

"Percy."

"Wrong, Percy. This is the infamous Mr. Beech, well-known stoolie."

"The what . . . ?" Byrd started to say. Nothing made sense.

Maes went on talking. "The guy who put Johnny and Freddie, and the others, away."

Boris no longer smiled.

"What's with the gun? And what in hell're you talking about?" As he said it, Harry remembered that he also was carrying a weapon, something he never did. He looked around. Cat had disappeared. The lobby of this strange, ornamented building was crowded with people. He saw Chinese and Europeans. The confusion deepened within him. A monstrously fat man with heavy bulldog jowls sat to one side, reading a newspaper, a drink on the table in front of him. He kept glancing up from his paper at Harry as though he knew him, and was making some kind of sign.

"You crazy, Beech?" Vincent Maes said quietly. Then, to Boris, "Keep him here, by the door, while I call up to the suite and get Val down. Then you can take care of him properly. I gotta catch that train."

Boris' huge hand closed around Harry's arm and twisted. "I thought ya was my friend," he spoke with great deliberation. "Now I find you're just a lousy stoolie. Well, ya'll get what's coming."

Over at the reception desk, Vincent Maes spoke quietly into a house phone; and Harry again caught sight of the large man with the face like a bulldog, looking at him with a thoughtful expression.

"Yeah," Boris twisted harder. "Ya really got it coming. I think ya even tried to put away Vince and Val – my bosses."

Harry again remembered the body on the floor with part of its head missing. It made no sense, except in connection with the Maes brothers. He had seen them in unpleasant, and violent, action before. In a warehouse, with a little guy who was running a numbers racket and got sticky fingers. They had smashed his hands to pieces. Later he heard the man was found in the river.

Vincent waited across the vast lobby by the elevators. A car came down, and Harry recognised the man who emerged as the other Maes brother – Valentine. They walked, slowly it seemed, talking quietly, towards where Boris held him.

"There's been some mistake . . ."

"Shut up," cracked Vincent.

"I been waiting a long, long time for this," Valentine almost whispered. "Get the limo round, Percy, we're taking Vince to the railroad depot. Then Beech here is going for a ride."

Harry dragged back, trying to free himself from Boris, as the three men jostled him through the glass doors. He was going mad. He did not even recognise the scene which faced him across the road – water glinting, behind the foreground grass, trees and flowers; while ships rode at anchor, reflecting lines of portholes, rows of circular dots lifting with the water, superstructures blazing, contrasting with the dark shapes of sail craft; and tiny boats carrying only small specks of light: white, red and green. Glittering night streets. The air like a steam bath. He was going mad.

"What the hell's going on?" he shouted; almost screamed.

"Cut the crap, Beech. We've had guys searching for you since three years now. There's been a paper out on you a long time." Vincent's usually placid voice was filled with loathing.

Valentine jostled against him. "Freddie the Carp, and the Barb, together with the others, all want you *not here*. There's a nice collection in it for us."

The confusion reached its peak then, as if he were being sucked into a whirlpool. Complete disorientation. They pressed close around him, edging him to the sidewalk, to where a long black automobile waited – he thought it was probably a big British Daimler: its Chinese driver, impassive at the wheel.

"A little ride," Vincent Maes whispered again. "Me, they drop off at the South Central Station. You they take for a ride, Beech." The rear door of the auto was open now, and Vincent looked back towards his brother and Boris. "You see he has a lot of pain before you dump him. Get his teeth for proof, okay?"

A blue and red electric sign flashed from a nearby building, on and off in constant motion, the colours touching Boris' face, giving it a strange, macabre cast: a portrait of evil. The big man's mouth split into a gaping grin. Red, then blue.

"Don't you worry, boss. I thought he was my friend. Now I know different, I'll do the job proper."

"I want to hear the screams from the train, ten miles away." Vincent Maes climbed into the car first. Valentine was obviously going to sit next to the Chinese driver. Boris twisted Harry's arm even harder, and they were within a pace of the door when, out of the traffic – to their right – came the commotion of a car approaching at speed, lights full on and horn blaring.

There were shouts from the sidewalk, and Harry was aware of the oncoming car, slewing over the road in a squeal of rubber, sliding almost sideways towards the kerb, doors opening as it did so.

Someone – he thought it was Valentine – called out that the cops were there. As he yelled, so Boris relaxed his grip. Harry pushed hard, remembering the gun, wrenching his arm from Boris' arm.

His reactions were automatic, deft, surprising him – the right hand going for the hip pocket, and the little pistol, very firm in his palm, fingers curling: there in a fraction of time.

"Back off," he said, sounding as if he meant it. A tougher, harder man than Henry Beech had ever been. Equally, without his conscious direction, his thumb was working the safety catch on the weapon.

For a moment, the tableau by the Daimler was frozen: Vincent Maes leaning forward from the inside of the vehicle; Valentine by the front section, and big Boris starting to flex his knees, as if about to spring. Then all their attention became focused once more on the police car. Men leaped from the car almost before it came to rest: three or four policemen in unfamiliar khaki uniforms. They were followed by a sag-bellied individual, in a state of crumpled disarray, who bawled, in an unmistakably British accent: "Stop. Stop that man. Stop, Byrd. Stop or I fire."

Byrd. The name on the identity card he found in his wallet. The man still shouted: while all of the police seemed to be running towards him – "Byrd . . . Byrd . . . Byrd . . ."

Harry lifted his hand, angling the pistol upwards and nervously pressing the trigger. He felt the kick-back, heard the explosion and experienced a twinge of satisfaction at the result of his action. The police, Maes brothers, and Boris – not to mention people on the sidewalk – diving and rolling for cover.

He heard another small explosion, saw a flash from the direction of the bloated-looking man as he twisted across the ground towards the Daimler. Something zipped past Harry's head.

He turned and began to run, dodging and zig-zagging through the traffic. This was a good way to commit suicide, he thought, as he swerved to avoid cars and rickshaws. The shouting continued, and another sound grew in volume around him, like waves crashing over his body and head – waves, surf, beaches. Run. Run like hell. The noise and pounding went on. Cat in his head: with him on the beach; a hot weekend, and the little wooden hut behind them, with the door open. California. The hot sand on his feet, and Cat in her bathing dress, arms wrapped around him, while the breakers crashed and boomed far off, and the creamed surf came running in, making ever-changing outlines on the sand.

He stuck the pistol out of sight in his waistband, could still hear the shouts from across the road, and kept running, trotting and then plunging himself into the crowds which moved, four or five deep, along the sidewalk nearest the sea.

Weaving into the crush of people, who sauntered and pushed, elbowed and shouldered, moving against each other, Harry slowed his pace. Within the mass of humanity he felt safer from the immediate threat, though the sense of disorientation still enveloped him. To his left was water: ships, oriental vessels, small boats. On the right, through the throng, he could see large cars and rickshaws, tall buildings, lush green and flowered trees.

He seemed to have left his pursuers behind. The larger, bright, white buildings now started to give way to smaller constructions, and the Chinese signs were interspersed with ones displayed in French instead of English. Although he did not know it, he was passing through the French section of the Bund, heading now into the exclusively Chinese section beyond.

There was little sense of time. He appeared to drift through the people, some in the white linen suits and flowered dresses of the West; others in more traditional Chinese garb. Young Chinese girls smiled at him. A pair of very young girls, school age he thought, approached with an older woman, a bent little Chinese who unleashed them like dogs, so that they ran after him, clamouring and leaving him in no doubt as to the services they offered.

The sounds were constant: the eternal noise of any dockside or harbour, backed by the strange calls and clappings of street traders; while music, the thin wail of Chinese instruments, and the more raucous noise of brass bands, seemed, at times, far away; and then very close.

He still walked by the water, though the sidewalk narrowed, and the water on the left now lapped directly below him. The lights were not so bright, nor was there, now, a wide thoroughfare. The traffic thinned out, the main transport becoming the occasional padding and rattling rickshaws.

The flowers had also vanished, and the buildings were now makeshift affairs. Occasionally a large, well-built block appeared, but in the main the brick façades were cracked and flaking, only rising a few storeys; while the shop fronts and cafés were mean and shabby. Light came from all of them, and the bars seemed full: traders sold from the small stalls placed in front of unglazed openings.

Harry felt great fatigue. There was a small guard rail, rickety, between the sidewalk and a long drop to the sea. He leaned against it – to rest, puzzle out his predicament, take stock. He did not know how long it was before the unmistakable voice, slow and heavy, came from behind him.

"Mr. Flamingo."

Boris stood three or four paces away, balanced massively on the balls of his feet.

"I told Vince and Val I'd find you. I saw the way ya went, Flamingo, into the crowd." He took a step forward. "Ya found my Polly for me. Just like my Wanda. Pity ya can't be my friend, 'cause you're a lousy bastard. Ya sold out a long time ago. I gotta do what they tell me."

He started forward again, faster now, and Harry, driven by three years' Shanghai conditioning, reached for his hip pocket, then remembered the pistol in his waistband. By the time his fingers curled around the butt, the giant was on him.

He ducked, as the huge ham hands lifted towards his throat. Boris was not a man of finesse. But the weave away was just enough. Boris' hands missed, then clasped together, swung, and came thudding down on to the side of Harry's head. There was a numbing flash as the two-handed blow connected. He had the impression that Boris was taking a step back, to balance himself and come in for the kill. But the smash to the side of his head had thrown Harry back with the force of a sledge hammer, so that his ribs seemed to crack against the metal guard rail.

The world turned upside down and he was drifting, the figure of Boris receding slowly, then disappearing as he hit the water.

Dark wetness took over, enclosing him warmly, returning him to a black soft womb, the ocean rocking him gently so that he did not fight back as it drew him down.

All pain and anxiety trickled away. Floating. Drifting. Now there appeared to be conscious thoughts in his head. Water. Drowning. It was said that a man's life passed through his mind when that happened, but Harry experienced no such biography, only one or two strange memories which did not seem complete, or even real. Cat, and a Chinese girl called Jeannie, whom he could not quite place. There was also a sense of the folly he had shown in getting mixed up with the rackets; though this appeared to be dulled by a distinct feeling that, in some way, he had managed to atone for that particular series of sins. Then conscious memory retreated with a kind of roar, like a subway train leaving a station and delving into a tunnel, receding until even the tiny dot of light faded.

Consciousness returned again, but there was no point of reference for him – either in time or place. Just the sense of drifting, cold now with a soaking wetness. Somebody talking. Pain returning in his ribs and head. Somebody pulling at him. Then the lap of water, and the bobbing sensation as the waves lifted him along on their undulating swell. Darkness again.

Time passed. Light in his eyes. Someone forcing liquid on to his lips. The rise and fall of his body still continued. There was no fear. For a second or two he thought he could see a face – some old, old Chinese woman, toothless and grinning, leaning over him. There was an unpleasant smell of fish. Then the subway train pulled away again, diminished down the labyrinth, and disappeared into the darkness.

Beech. Henry Beech. That was him. He dipped in and out of knowing and unknowing. There was a point when the smell of fish seemed to pull him from the tunnel of comfortable incomprehension. The woman was there again, though he could hear the water, and feel its movement. The woman forced food into his mouth; and liquid. The smell of fish was very strong, so that he retched, feeling a pain in his side. Harry Byrd. Who the hell was Harry Byrd? He was Harry Byrd. Only his name was Henry Beech. He did not understand, and it was easier to retreat again. This time there was a great roaring in his ears, and he was on board the subway train so that it was the lights of the station that were diminishing.

The dream came – a ferocious jumble of incidents, like the courtroom and the ranch house, with its patio and the pool out back; the endless desert; the lights of the black limo bumping away from him; the feeling of deep depression; diamonds and a dead body; some kind of fight; falling; pain.

He half woke, and the rocking of the water had gone. He was warm, and a sheet covered him, his head on a pillow. Was this death? The calm comforter? He knew it was not, because of the pain in his ribs and head. Briefly he opened his eyes, but the light hurt. Nobody bent over him this time.

There were other moments of knowledge. The light again. Very conscious of the light behind his closed lids. Occasional lucid times, lasting only for a moment or two, when he was conscious of people around him; moving him; speaking to him. On one of these occasions he was certain that there had been some kind of an accident as he had driven from the office in the city to meet Cat at the Trattoria; on another there was a clear picture of a café called the Flamingo.

There was motion and noise. Bumping, as though someone was carrying him. Then the noise of a lot of people moving around; clangs, bangs and scrapes. Then the slight rise and fall of the sea again, lifting, then dropping, so that he lay, quiet and relaxed. Now there seemed to be a constant thrumming noise: a regular, heavy pulse beating – but that was inside his body.

The dawn of his understanding came up like thunder. He did not know if it was across the bay, but he did know, quite clearly, that he had been Henry Beech, and was now Harry Byrd, and he was in China. Like a trigger in his head: sudden, fast as a bullet or lightning flash, the whole picture of events clear and precise. Now, not at the point of drowning, the whole of his life passed through his head – from childhood right to the point of his secret world, working for the Mob; Cat, the deal with the Feds; Cat's treachery; Shanghai and the Flamingo; the return of Cat; the Maes brothers; Waldo Bingham; the pressure from the Black Dragon; the attacks. . . His life as Henry Beech, and then Harry Byrd. All the things which had led up to the finding of Geddes' body.

Eyes closed tightly, Byrd began to sweat. He had arrived in front of the Cathay and had met Cat, still imagining that he was Beech, and back in the States. He must be running a fever because he began to shake as he recalled what had happened from that point onwards. He had met Cat, and then the Maes brothers had found him. Jesus. His head in the lion's mouth; and had the lions got him here? He lay quite motionless, listening, eyes still closed. The recall, the putting together of the Beech and Byrd jigsaw, had done nothing to ease his anxiety. There was a whole blank area, from when he had hit the water, held in his mind only as a muddled dream of raw dried fish and subway trains and an old Chinese woman.

Slowly, Harry opened his eyes. A fan whirred above his head, and below him the ground shook with a rhythmic beating, which he recognised as the sound and feel of marine engines. He lay on a bunk. So? A ship? The gut anxiety clutched at him again as the name *Bel Canto* connected with his other thoughts. The *Bel Canto*, the Maes' arms ship. It was all so obvious. They had him – Vincent, Valentine and Boris. Ready to dispose of him in the water from which they had fished him, after Boris sent him hurtling into the darkness. (*Get his teeth for proof, okay?* Vincent had said.)

He wondered almost objectively which would be worse – facing whatever the Maes brothers had in store, with death inevitable; or meeting with Pearly Fisher, upon whom he had undoubtedly fired outside the Cathay Hotel. He plumped for Fisher.

Footsteps on metal. People approaching. Byrd tried to raise himself up in the bunk, as the cabin door swung open and the two familiar figures came slowly in.

BOOK THREE

Byrd on the Wing

— (1)

"Are you back with us, Harry Byrd, my friend?" The bulldog jowls of Waldo Bingham quivered above him.

"Harry?" Cat, who had come in with Bingham (two familiar figures indeed), sat at the foot of the bunk.

"What the hell happened?" Byrd swallowed. His throat was dry and he knew there were bandages around his head and ribs. Relief brought a smile to his mouth. "You get the number of the truck?" he asked.

"Oh God, he's still hallucinating," Cat's hand to her mouth.

"I think not. You know who you are, don't you, Harry?" Bingham's growl was touched by a slight note of concern.

Byrd nodded, surprised that it did not hurt. "Harry Byrd." He could recognise his own voice now. Looking straight at Cat, he added, "Once upon a time I was Henry Beech. The lady is Kathleen Ann Morrow, but that's not her real name either. You're Waldo Bingham, by the way. Jesus, I'm thirsty."

Cat leaned over and put a glass to his lips. Lime juice. She cautioned him not to swallow it all at once. "Just sip it, Harry."

"What I want to know is what the hell happened, and where in God's name am I?"

"On a ship." Bingham sat down heavily on the side of the bunk.

Byrd sighed. "I know that. But what ship? Going where?"

Bingham told him that it was a long story. "You're on the ferry to Dairen. We're a day out from Shanghai and just about to dock at Tsingtao. By tomorrow night we'll be in Dairen. After that it's a long trip through Manchuria. I have first-class accommodation arranged. Moscow, Berlin, Paris, London."

Although he had never travelled it, coming from America's west coast, Byrd knew the route. The ship from Shanghai took two days. The train journey was about twelve days to Moscow, via Mukden and Harbin before they got out of Manchuria.

The implications were slow to hit him. But when they did – "I can't leave Shanghai. The café! The Flamingo! My life's there."

Bingham gave a small shrug. "You have no option but to leave. That is why I took the liberty of getting you away. It's called for a great deal of subterfuge. Miss Morrow was not safe either. A lot's happened, Harry Byrd. The police want you for murder; there are some most unpleasant thugs of American origin after you – they would like to get you before the police, and they wouldn't leave much of you to be found. As for your café – the Flamingo. Well, it would seem that your partner has sold out to the Japanese. You recall your partner . . . ?"

Byrd said his name and Bingham nodded. "Foo Tang," he repeated. "Your precious Mr. Foo Tang has given the Black Dragon boys a controlling interest."

Byrd opened his mouth to speak and thought better of it. He clearly remembered the scheme he had discussed with Foo Tang about lulling the Black Dragon people into a false sense of security, carefully leaving out Bingham's hoped-for involvement, but something told him to say nothing now.

"In all, you are in a difficult situation. By all the rules I should have left you to it . . ."

"Then why the hell didn't you?"

"Because I have a conscience, and you came highly recommended. My people will find work for you." Bingham gave a deep, embarrassed grunt. "I'm a pragmatist at heart. But I do have my more sentimental moments."

Byrd remained puzzled. Cat smiled as he tried to straighten his thoughts. He asked how long he had been unconscious, and ill.

"Around three weeks." Bingham's calmness only served to make Byrd's shock more acute.

"*Three* –?" he began.

"You went missing, under somewhat dramatic circumstances, on the evening of Tuesday, 25 August. Today is Wednesday, 17 September."

What in heaven had happened to him during those three missing weeks? Byrd wrestled, for a while, with a kaleidoscope of fears. Then he grinned. "Better get up. Get my sea legs. Well . . . middle of September, eh? Well. *Pai-lu* – season of the White Dew, eh?"

Bingham grunted again: "'No Spring, nor Summer beauty hath such grace, As I have seen in one Autumnal face' – John Donne." He coughed apologetically. "Made us learn it by the ream when I did me schooling."

The ship's engines changed note, and Cat got up. Moving over to the porthole, she announced that they seemed to be coming into Tsingtao harbour.

Bingham glanced at his watch and muttered something about being well on time. "Be in Dairen tomorrow evening. On the Express tomorrow night. Be glad when you're out of China, my dear chap. In the meantime, we'd better start getting you moving. You'll be as weak as the proverbial kitten."

Byrd shifted, raising himself in the bunk. "Three weeks," he repeated. "What the devil happened to me in three weeks?"

"A long story. I've arranged for food down here tonight. The three of us. Cramped, yes, but at least we'll have some privacy. Tell you the whole tale then. Involved. You were damned groggy, Byrd."

Once his feet were on the cabin deck, Byrd acknowledged that he was still groggy. Cat went aloft while Bingham helped him into clothes, then left also. His own clothes. He made a mental note to ask how they had got some of his own wardrobe from the café to the boat. Come to that, how Bingham had found him at all. Recurring in his mind was the moment when Boris struck his head and he had gone whirling down into the darkness of the water.

After about an hour of gently standing, sitting for a while, and then taking a few paces around the cabin, Byrd began to feel that, while weak, he could manage. There was bruising on the side of his head, but the pain had gone from the forehead, and his eyes appeared to focus properly. No needles in the eye. Apart from that, the right side of his ribs ached, and, as he had thought, were strapped up.

He went up on deck, laboriously mounting the companionway, and joined Cat and Bingham who were watching the preparations already being made to leave the small harbour. Already the ship had made its way, hugging the coast, up the Hwang-Hai – the Yellow Sea. Now they would cross between a scattering of islands into the Strait of Pohai, and on to Dairen which lay on the tip of the Peninsula which jutted down from Manchuria.

Byrd stayed on deck for about fifteen minutes. The sea air was fresh and felt good on his face and in his lungs; but he tired quickly: kitten-weak when they got him back to the cabin and lying on his bunk.

At around seven that evening, a cheerful steward brought food – rice, meat balls, noodles, various sauces and the eternal tea. Byrd sat on his bunk with Cat – who had remained reserved and preoccupied, since his return to near normality, perched at the foot. Waldo Bingham crammed his girth into the small chair, and they balanced the various dishes on the little let-down shelf, on the floor, even on the bunk itself.

Between mouthfuls of food, Waldo Bingham, good as his word, went through the story. "You remember what happened on the Chinese Bund?"

Byrd nodded, saying that was when he copped out into the ocean, with the help of Boris.

"And the little affray outside the Cathay?"

"When I fired over the heads of Fisher and his merry men?"

"Not quite the way he tells it, but it'll do." Bingham chewed and swallowed. "Right, I'll tell you what happened after that."

Over supper in Byrd's cabin that night Bingham told him
that he had realised something was very wrong as soon as he
saw Byrd enter the Cathay with Cat. He was, in fact, about
to approach them when the trouble started with Vincent
Maes. From that point he had been placed in the role of a
helpless observer. Had he intervened, he said, there was a
fair chance that Vincent would have shot Byrd out of hand.

After the shooting outside, he had tried to follow Byrd
into the crowds, knowing that Boris had lumbered after
him with surprising agility, way ahead of the police, but,
losing both of them quickly, he returned to the hotel. His
links with the British Secret Service had brought him plenty
of contacts in Shanghai, mainly Chinese, and he could
quickly put out a warning for them to set watch for Byrd;
but, on arriving back at the hotel, he gathered that Cat was
being interrogated by Fisher, who was not in the best of
moods.

The Maes brothers had naturally taken advantage of the
confusion after Byrd's escape and disappeared, and Fisher
did not reportedly seem anxious to search for them. Bingham discreetly gleaned that Cat's photographer–fiancé,
Geddes, had been shot to death at the Flamingo; none of
the staff was talking; and there was a warrant out for Byrd's
arrest on a charge of murder.

Bingham immediately got word out on to the street, and
in the bars, that he wanted to make contact privately with
Harry Byrd. Several days passed without any news. By
that time Valentine Maes and Boris had reappeared and
were living, without any harassment, together with Dr.
Zuchestra in their suites at the Cathay. The situation was,
to say the least, not hopeful.

At this point, Bingham made contact with Cat who,
eventually—with some avuncular persuasion—poured out her

story. The police had released Geddes' body, and she had made all the funeral arrangements. Now she was planning to return to America, but was unwilling to leave Shanghai quickly, sensing another, and possibly bigger, story in the air. There were increasing rumblings at that time about yet another build-up of Japanese forces in and around Manchuria. She also admitted that she wanted to know what had happened to Harry Byrd.

On the fourth day news came to Bingham. Apparently an old Chinese fisherwoman from Woosung had picked a white man out of the water. She had just started the return journey to Woosung, needed to make a good catch, and so had taken the white man with her, putting her work first. She was now back in Woosung, the informant said. Nobody had been told – meaning neither police nor local authorities. The man was still alive but in a poor way.

Bingham and Cat set out immediately, in a hired junk, and were in the fortified village of Woosung before nightfall. Byrd was unconscious in the old woman's sampan, hidden there because she was afraid of the police who had already issued a description of him which had been sent as far as the rickety earth-floored dwellings of the small fishing community. Bingham was soon able to reassure and obtain general silence by small sums of cumshaw.

The woman said she had kept the taipan alive by sharing her own meagre rice with him, together with some dried fish and water. He was in very bad condition. Cat said she thought he was dying, while Bingham had taken a more optimistic line. As someone with secret authority, he was able to return to Shanghai, use his contacts, and what private pull he had with the British Foreign Service people, to organise proper care for the sick man, and a more satisfactory hiding place.

The villagers at Woosung remained silent and, two days later, Byrd was moved, by night, back into Shanghai: this time to a comfortable and safe apartment kept for the special use of Bingham's own service. A British doctor was at hand, and diagnosed three cracked ribs, severe bruising on the jaw and head (*A mercy nothing's broken*, he said), exposure and dehydration. Cat described the earlier symptoms of mental derangement, and the doctor thought it possible that Byrd had suffered some kind of blackout, telling them they would have to watch him carefully when he regained consciousness – which could be tomorrow or next year. He was alive, comfortable and not seriously injured. Nor was there any sign of skull fracture. *Watch him if he gets severe headaches once he's back in the land of the living.*

"Head all right?" Bingham now asked, and Byrd, leaning back on his bunk, said it felt better than it had done for a long time.

The fat man regarded him quizzically. "Incidentally, old chap, you didn't actually take it upon yourself to do in young Geddes by any chance, did you?"

"Me? kill Geddes?" Byrd frowned. "What the hell for? Didn't I have enough trouble without that, for God's sake?"

Bingham nodded, his jowls bouncing complacently. "I thought as much. But one has to ask these things, you understand."

Cat, who remained watchfully at the bottom of the bunk, relaxed. Bingham cleared his throat and continued his story.

The next item was for Byrd the most serious yet. The *North-China Daily News* announced, in its entertainment columns, that the fashionable Flamingo Café, formerly owned and run by Mr. Harry Byrd – now disappeared and wanted for murder – would be taken over by Byrd's former partner, the well-known philanthropic Mr. Foo Tang of Jessfield Park. Mr. Foo Tang would be taking others into partnership. So far he had been Mr. Byrd's sleeping partner only. Now the café would be controlled, and run, by a consortium consisting of Foo Tang together with Mr. Takahome and Mr. Hitchimata, both well-known and prosperous Japanese businessmen. The day to day running of the café would be in the hands of a Mr. Toshiro Sessaku.

Bingham also told him that Valentine Maes and Zuch-estra had been seeing Foo Tang at regular intervals, and that they all appeared to be on very friendly terms. Among the other gossip, the police were of the opinion that Byrd had disappeared and would, perhaps, turn up dead; but the Maes faction were still making enquiries.

"It was at that point I felt discretion was the better part of valour, as we used to say." Bingham took an enormous mouthful of tea, savoured it and swallowed. "We decided it best to remove you from Shanghai."

Byrd asked about his staff at the Flamingo and was told they had all been kept on.

"They're not happy," Cat said. "I went there one evening and the place has changed. They seem repressed somehow. Repressed and depressed."

Byrd nodded. He had his own ideas about what would finally happen at the Flamingo.

Bingham revealed he held all Byrd's old identity documents, but they had him booked on the ferry under a British passport, and in the name of Henry Booth. "We even had you taken into the Shanghai General Hospital as a street-accident case the night before we embarked," he chuckled. "Had our own tame quack hanging around, of course; and Miss Morrow stayed out of the way. Private English nurse came abroad with you. She slipped off before we sailed. Miss Morrow's taken her place. Once we're over the Chinese border we'll be home and dry."

Harry Byrd said nothing. He was weak, and needed time to think; to clear his head. Cat's relative silence worried him, for she appeared withdrawn, communicating with him only by smiles and an occasional squeeze of the hand. Maybe she was starting to regret her actions of three years earlier, but he had little doubt that her main reason for being with them was for the story she might finally put together.

His gratitude to the fat Waldo Bingham went without saying, but experience had taught him to beware of anyone bearing gifts: even the gift of life and survival. What was really in it for Waldo? He wondered. Above everything, Byrd knew his personal polarities – to get fit quickly and return to Shanghai; clear himself of the murder charge; fix the Maes brothers for once and all; spike the deal between them and Foo Tang; and reclaim his rights to the Flamingo

Café. And clearly none of this fitted in with Waldo's planned journey for him to London.

They all retired early, Byrd falling quickly into a doze, then into deep sleep. The autumn storms, which sometimes come up unexpectedly in that part of the sea, stayed away overnight and through the following day, which they spent taking exercise. Byrd could now walk without discomfort, and stay on his feet for an hour at a time. Food, and a new sense of security and purpose, were making him stronger by the minute and, when they docked in Dairen, he walked unaided from the ship.

An hour later they were on the train, gently pulling out, heading towards the Manchurian capital of Mukden. Byrd went along because, for the moment, he had no alternative. Bingham had arranged matters so that they had a double compartment, with an adjoining door into a single. The first-class sleeping accommodation was comfortable and the large British agent assured them that the service was excellent. "Done the trip many times. Tiring but not unpleasant. Not over-hot at this time of year either."

Byrd felt pangs of anxiety as the train gathered speed, beginning to take them through the flat terrain as night fell; the pink last rays of the sun staining the damp paddy fields, turning them into a rich, watery gold. The further he travelled from Shanghai, the more laborious would be his eventual return.

It was the evening of September 18th. None of them knew then that it was an historic date: the night of the Japanese take-over of Manchuria.

三 (3)

They had steamed out of the station at the port of Dairen just after seven, and the two hundred-and-fifty mile journey on the South Manchurian Railway track to Mukden would take just under four hours. Bingham said there would be an inevitable hour or so wait in the Manchurian capital before the train went on to Harbin, and from there to the Russian frontier.

The compartments were luxurious, though somehow out of place in this austere part of the world. They would have seemed more at home in Central Europe with their plush velvet, hanging chandeliers and brass accoutrements. If Bingham's word was anything to go by, the second class was, by comparison, spartan; while third was not even fit for rats.

Cat went in to the single compartment for a wash and change; then after a while, Bingham suggested that he should go and reconnoitre the dining car and book dinner.

He had been gone only a few minutes when Cat tapped at the adjoining door and came through, looking as neat as ever in a tailored cream pleated dress. Byrd lay on his bunk, which had already been made up for the night by a small, obsequious steward. He lit another cigarette – his fifth since they left Dairen – and dragged smoke in through his teeth.

"You'll pardon me not getting up," looking Cat straight in the eyes. This was the first time they had been alone since he had regained consciousness on the ferry.

"You need the rest, Harry. Stay where you are." She smiled, sitting herself on his bunk, the lower part of her back touching his legs. Against his wiser nature Byrd sensed an unmistakable thrill at being close to her again. He pushed the thought away.

"You still hanging on to the diamonds?"

168

She gave her characteristic shrug: the ripple effect, first one shoulder, then the other. "Of course. I don't know how to thank you for that."

"You already did it. Helping Waldo get me out."

She dropped her eyes, as though embarrassed. "I rather let you down in the Cathay, didn't I? Walking out when you saw Vincent Maes."

"I'm used to people walking out." The bitter edge back in his voice.

"Harry, I tried to stop you. You were confused: wouldn't listen. If I hadn't got out then I wouldn't have been around to help old Waldo." She smiled, a dazzle. He wondered sourly if she was trying to twist him round her finger.

"True. I haven't said how sorry I was about Geddes."

Her face froze. "Harry," she reached over and took his hand. "You can tell me. I know you were pretty sore about Tom – about Tom and me; then the business with the diamonds . . ."

He did not need time to let it sink in. "You're not suggesting –"

"I know what you said to Bingham. But . . . Harry, if you did it, you can tell me."

Anger boiled, and then went cold. "Don't be stupid, Cat. Work it out, kid, I didn't have time. Anyway, all I wanted was to kick his butt out of my café, then send him back to you with his tail between his legs. Jesus, you had more time than I did. Don't ever accuse me of that kind of thing again."

"I'm sorry, but . . ."

"But nothing. Get it straight now, Cat. Whatever we had, however I felt, I'm not such a fool as to kill for you – or anyone else, except perhaps myself if it came to a matter of survival. If you want to know, I'm not happy about any of this deal. I'd rather be back in Shanghai talking to 'Pearly' Fisher, clearing my name and dealing with the Maes boys once and for all." He took a deep drag on his cigarette. "What did Fisher have to say to you, by the way? Waldo said he interrogated you."

"It wasn't easy . . ."

"It never is with Pearly, he's a drunken bum."

"No, I mean I was upset. Right there in the lobby of the Cathay he told me about Tom."

"That's my boy's style. A man of tact and talent. I suppose he gave you five minutes to cheer up and then started in with the lights and rubber hoses."

"He apologised. Said I had to understand. It was his job to ask questions quickly."

"So?"

"He asked if I'd seen the shooting outside the hotel."

Byrd remained silent. The train had picked up speed, driving on through the now pitch-black night. The moon had yet to rise.

"I told him, yes, and he went on about you: did I know you? All that sort of stuff. It was only routine."

"How much routine? After all, you know about routine."

She knew about routine: what routine was, and what lay above the call of routine duty. She had to: the bastard Pat Kelly, police sergeant extraordinary, back home in the city, was her father.

She gave a long sigh. "He asked if I knew you. Had known you."

"And you told him."

She nodded, biting her lip.

"Everything?"

"I said I'd known you in the States a long time ago."

"That we were lovers?"

She had not said that, but Fisher jumped to the conclusion. Bloated drunk though he was, Fisher had an eye and an ear — at least vestiges of that intuition which was a requirement for a good detective. He would note her eyes and manner, then jump to conclusions. Once he had put them into words, and watched her reaction, he would soon be able to unearth the truth about her past.

"You tell him my name from those days?" Byrd tried to sound casual, but inside the worry worms gnawed away.

She gave a quick negative shake of the head.

"It'll please him to know he could pin a motive on me. Fisher's after my guts."

"Then you're better off out of it."

He stubbed out the cigarette and told her no: no, he wasn't better off out of it. His asset in Shanghai was the café. There was a lot of money tied up in it: money he'd worked for. "My old age needs it."

Bingham came back with the news that there was a table ready. They could go and eat now.

Over the meal, Byrd stayed off the subject of Cat's interview with Fisher. They indulged in small-talk, with Cat mainly asking Waldo Bingham about the general situation in Manchuria. They had already spoken, on the ship, about the possible threat to Shanghai.

Bingham was a mine of information. He spoke first about the capital, Mukden, through which they would pass that night. "Pity we can't stay over. Interesting historically. Walled city. Cradle of the old Manchu dynasty."

Was it true that the Japanese were massing forces in and around Manchuria? Certainly, Waldo always warmed to the doom-laden prophecy of Shanghai's final annihilation by the Japanese. His view was unchanging. It would start in Manchuria where the Japanese held very high trading rights, factories, businesses. Even the railways were run with Japanese money and assistance.

"They keep armed forces here to protect their interests and rights. My information is that, over the past months, the Japanese army has increased its military presence here. To anyone who can analyse political and military information that means only one thing. Japan sees itself as the pearl of the Orient. It wishes to grow into the richest and most powerful of pearls. The larger the Japanese army grows in Manchuria, the more likely armed conflict will come. In the end, Japan will make a bid for China, and first they will seize Shanghai."

They returned to their compartments just before ten. Talked for a short time, then Cat moved towards her door. Perhaps they could sleep through the wait in Mukden.

At a little before ten-fifteen there was a sudden lurch, the train slowing dramatically, with the coaches swaying violently. They could hear the brakes being applied and the squeal of the metal wheels on the rails. With a sliding, grinding bump, the train came to a stop.

Byrd was still fully dressed, lying on his bunk with Waldo opposite, talking to him quietly, rehearsing him in the role he might have to play if his passport was queried. The compartment door burst open and Cat stumbled into their quarters. She looked white and frightened, her voice pitched high, and she had thrown a pink quilted robe over her nightgown.

"What's happening? Have you looked out of the window?"

Bingham went over and lifted the blinds. The moon was high, and there were bright lights moving, about a mile away Byrd judged as he pulled himself from the bunk, looking over Bingham's shoulder. Star shells curved upwards, throwing extra light over the paddy fields and clumpy bushes.

Bingham dragged the window down, and at first all they could hear was the hiss of steam from the engine. Gradually, however, other, more sinister noises came to them across the countryside. Sporadic gunfire: rifles and automatic weapons. The star shells rose continually.

"We're on the outskirts of Mukden," Bingham growled. "You can even see it up ahead. I'd guess the Japanese take-over's on, and we could be in trouble." As he said it, he reached up for his case and placed it on the bunk. Before opening it he took his old big revolver from the rear copious pocket of his trousers. He checked it carefully and replaced it, then opened the case, dug inside and produced a smaller weapon – a Colt .38 US Army revolver – which he handed to Byrd, together with a small box of shells and the admonition that he should use it only under extreme provocation.

There were noises approaching in the corridor outside and the handguns were quickly put out of sight. A railway guard was tapping at each compartment, and Waldo slid back the door before he reached them. Behind the guard, in his navy-blue uniform, were a pair of Japanese soldiers.

A few words were exchanged in Chinese between Bingham and the guard, while the soldiers looked on, showing neither interest nor emotion. Then the little party moved on to the next compartment and Bingham closed the door.

Bingham cleared his throat. "That was the official view. I have my doubts."

"Well?" Cat was impatient.

"If I were you, dear lady, I should get yourself into some clothes."

"What's the official story?"

"Something stinks." Waldo gave an unperturbed smile. "We are asked to believe that the gunfire we can hear is nothing more than military manoeuvres. The Japanese Army has been carrying out exercises in the Mukden area for the last couple of nights. There is, they say, nothing to be concerned about."

"But you think. . .?" started Cat.

"However," Bingham held up a hand, "there has been some kind of unfortunate accident. Somewhere, they did not stipulate where, part of the railway track has been damaged. An explosion was mentioned. We will be held up here for a while; then the train will move into Mukden as scheduled. It is unlikely that we will be able to proceed from there on time."

"Okay, how do you read it?" Byrd asked.

"I read it in the worst possible light. You saw the military. Come to that, though I did not draw your attention to them, there were more Japanese soldiers than one would have expected back in Dairen. I'd bet my pension on some kind of coup. All we can do is be prepared, as they say in the Boy Scouts. Powder dry – all that kind of thing; and pray that the delay will not be too long. They may well still allow the train through, though I fear my timing has been bad. Clothes, Miss Morrow. Warm and comfortable clothes that you can wear for some considerable time if necessary. Stout shoes, none of your high heels. Same goes for you, Byrd."

"I try not to wear high heels."

Bingham gave a growl.

After an hour, Bingham opened the sliding door and peered out into the corridor. They heard a voice bark in a commanding tone, and the big man dodged quickly back with the news that there was a Japanese soldier posted at each end of the carriage, and nobody was to leave their compartment. Outside, the gun-fire had grown more intense, and seemed nearer. From this Bingham concluded that there was fighting dead ahead. In Mukden itself.

At one in the morning, waiters brought tea, but it was not until nearly four that the train gave a slight jolt and began to move slowly forward. The movement woke Byrd who had been dozing, wrapped in a comfortable dream of being warmly in bed above the Flamingo. He was confused as to who was sharing the bed with him. Sometimes it seemed to be Cat, sometimes Jeannie Chin.

"Alert," Bingham whispered. "They're taking us into Mukden. Now we'll get the full strength of the thing."

The station was fully lighted. It was also lined with Japanese troops, bandoliers slung around their shoulders and rifles at the ready. As the train stopped, more soldiers stepped forward. Byrd looked out of the window on the other side, and saw there were troops swarming from the far platform, taking up positions around the train.

At once Bingham tried to get into the corridor to speak with the soldiers from the window, but was peremptorily ordered back into the compartment.

By this time Cat had become agitated, smoking compulsively and twisting her hands, asking again and again what would happen to them.

Both Bingham and Byrd tried to calm her. "You've got an American passport," Byrd soothed. "They can't touch you. Me, I have other worries. I'm travelling on a British passport which I hope isn't a forgery." He looked with some mistrust at Waldo Bingham, who responded by puffing his cheeks and asking, rhetorically, if Byrd thought the British Secret Service would stoop so low as to provide him with forged documents.

"You've got my real ones. What if they do a thorough

search? It was you who told me the Black Dragon was really part of the Japanese military intelligence set-up. If they find my real passport it shouldn't take long for them to make the connection."

Bingham, disconcertingly, did not answer.

More tea, and a little food, was brought. Then, at about nine, there was activity on the platform – the sudden arrival of a number of Japanese officers with some railway officials. Two officers passed down the corridor, knocking on doors. They could hear them making statements, curt and short, in different languages, as they drew near.

They had other armed soldiers with them – a pair of alert infantrymen – and they saluted politely, bowing to Cat, then to the other two men in turn, their eyes constantly moving, taking in the occupants of the compartment with a piercing shrewdness, making their minds up very quickly. English? American? they asked in English which they spoke well. Bingham answered, indicating Cat as an American citizen, and Byrd and himself as British.

"We apologise for delay," one of the officers smiled. "There has been much trouble. Unrest. Imperial Japanese forces in Manchuria have had to take drastic action to protect treaty rights. Purely defensive measures. You will be allowed to continue journey as soon as it is safe. In meantime you will prepare yourselves for perfectly normal passport and identity check. This in your interest as well as ours. There could be subversive elements on board the train. You may be certain they will be removed if found, so you can continue journey in peace." He saluted, bowed again, and the two men withdrew.

Neither Byrd nor Bingham liked the sound of it. Cat was in a panic. She was no longer the gay, laughing and happy girl Byrd had known in his other life; nor even the self-possessed journalist who had arrived in Shanghai.

"You wanted a story, honey, now you've really got one. By the way, if you're carrying that ice, I'd put it in a really safe place where the little yellow gentlemen can't get at it."

"Ice?" Bingham asked, looking wary.

"He's joking. Old joke," Cat replied quickly, but Byrd was not to be stopped.

"New joke and no joke. She's carrying around five grand's worth of diamonds, Waldo."

"Oh my God." He paused and then brightened. "Could be handy, Miss Morrow. But, as Byrd says, get it really well hidden. I don't trust this business of a perfectly normal passport and identity check."

It was almost two in the afternoon before the Japanese began their systematic search. Waldo Bingham had been right not to trust them. They came on to the train in the familiar groups of four: two officers and a pair of private soldiers or NCOs, taking either single coaches or blocks of two carriages at a time. Within five minutes, Byrd glimpsed several people being led out of the station at gun point – mainly Chinese, but there were at least two Europeans.

"Lady. Gentlemen." The officers assigned to their carriage were older, very experienced-looking men. Most correct, and unsmiling. "You will please present documents."

They handed over their passports. "I am an American journalist," Cat said as she passed the papers to them. They showed no sign of even hearing; one of them merely looked up and asked if she was travelling with the two gentlemen. Byrd started to say that she was not, but Cat answered yes before he could stop her.

They spent a long time looking at Waldo Bingham's papers; even longer examining Byrd's. "You are this Henry Booth, British citizen?" one of them finally asked.

"That's what it says."

The Japanese officer repeated the question and Byrd told him yes, firmly.

The two men conferred, looking through a file which they carried. Then, unexpectedly, the senior officer gave a quick order to the soldiers who moved into the compartment with speed, one towards Byrd, the other in front of Bingham. Before they had any chance to act, both men were undergoing a body search which revealed both Bingham's large revolver and the Colt he had given to Byrd.

The officers took the guns, neither of which was seen again.

"So," one of the officers pointed to the baggage. "Now you will open all cases."

The luggage was searched and produced nothing incriminating – not even, to Byrd's surprise and relief, the diamonds. The more senior officer again addressed himself to Byrd.

"You still claim to be Henry Booth, a British citizen?"

Byrd said of course he was.

"And the three of you are travel together?"

They nodded.

"You will take your luggage and follow us."

"I have rights," Cat's voice was very high. "I am an American citizen and an accredited journalist."

"If you are what you say, then you need not fear."

"I must also protest," Bingham drew himself up to his full height. "Mr. Booth and myself have rights also. We are British citizens and our passports are in order."

"Then you have nothing to fear. Come." The Japanese gave a curt wave of his hand and the two soldiers stood back, rifles covering all three of them.

Bingham grunted that they had better do as they were told.

Byrd half smiled at the irony of the situation. Having escaped the mobsters, police and Black Dragon hoodlums, they were now in the hands of the Japanese Army, and the common rumour, in Shanghai, was that Imperial Japanese troops had a tendency to shoot first and do their interrogations through their departed ancestors.

They were taken into a large wooden waiting room, bare but for benches set around the walls, a door at the far end with Chinese characters painted on it. There were two armed guards by the door, and half-a-dozen Chinese, sat, looking very unhappy, on the benches.

The senior officer told them to sit and place their luggage on the floor. He also warned that, because of the emergency situation, the guards had orders to shoot anyone who tried to leave the waiting room. He then went over to the door in the end wall, knocked and entered. Byrd would have liked to ask Cat about the diamonds but did not dare, in case they were overheard. The senior officer was away for about ten minutes, then the door opened and he called an order. The other officers, who had been with him on the train, followed by two soldiers, advanced upon Byrd, Bingham and Cat. They were told to follow the senior officer into the room; to make the instructions clear, the two soldiers raised their rifles and started to prod at them.

The room had obviously been the station master's office, but now its desk was occupied by a small, tubby Japanese officer with a thick drooping moustache. He wore elaborate insignia of rank and his moon face was relaxed in a disconcerting smile. His skin had a pitted, oily, texture.

"Lady. Gentlemen," he acknowledged in English. "Please to sit down."

Three chairs stood in front of his desk, and Byrd glimpsed their passports and documents set before the officer, together with some other official looking papers.

The Japanese leaned forward, scanning their faces one at a time before speaking.

"I'm Colonel Yukuzawa, in charge of security here at Mukden," he began, running the first finger of his right hand inside his collar, inserting it up to the knuckle. It was a habit often repeated before speaking – like a nervous tic. Byrd saw his neck was red and sore from the action.

"The Imperial Japanese Army is in control of Manchuria's capital?" Bingham queried, making it sound as if he was surprised.

"Imperial Japanese Army has taken certain defensive steps in this country, yes. To safeguard our treaty interests here, you understand. There was serious incident last night which resulted in small battle here in Mukden. Fighting is now over, and we have military and police control. The ports of Dairen and Antung are also under our control. Troop ships are on their way at this moment from Japan. General Honjo has arrived here and set up his headquarters. All major towns have been taken after some fighting, though there is still battle raging – up the line – at Kirin. We do not expect this to last long. Senior Chinese officers are under arrest. I wish you to know this so you will appreciate your situation."

"We are bona fide travellers; going to Europe," Bingham spoke firmly, with conviction.

The colonel smiled. "That you intend to travel to Europe I have no doubt. I am, however, worried about your identities."

Bingham was a good actor, he began to protest, but Colonel Yukuzawa held up a hand. "Oh, I have no doubt about your identity," he paused and smiled. "Nor your occupation. Mr. Waldo Bingham: a member of the British Foreign Service, I believe. The *Secret* Service. We know about you, Mr. Bingham. Just as we know about Miss Morrow here, a beautiful and talented lady journalist." He tapped his fingers together. "My problem is that you are travelling with this gentleman," he indicated Byrd, "who claims that he is a Mr. Henry Booth of London: a British citizen. You see this is my dilemma. You are travelling with this gentleman, and are, therefore, suspect; because he is suspect. I believe he is not Mr. Henry Booth of London: a British citizen. I believe that he is a Mr. Harry Byrd, of American origin, currently a resident of Shanghai where he is, among other things, wanted by the police for the murder of Miss Morrow's fiancé. It is strange that you should all be on this train, going to Europe together."

"My name is Henry Booth," Byrd said firmly.

"Your name is Harry Byrd, though that too is possibly an alias." The smile had now disappeared from the colonel's lips. "I said you were wanted for murder in Shanghai. Murder among other things. The other things concern acts against members of one of the Japanese Foreign Services. By association, all three of you must now be regarded as subversives. I have to tell you that you will be confined here in Mukden until it is decided what is to be done with you."

Bingham violently demanded to see the British Consul, only to be told that the British Consul had left Mukden on the previous evening. It was said blandly, the colonel giving the impression that he knew he was not being believed, and did not care.

"What will you do with us?" Cat sounded a fraction calmer now.

Colonel Yukuzawa spread his hands wide apart. "We could deport you as undesirables." He smiled, charmingly. "Or we could, perhaps, shoot you."

四 (4)

Colonel Yukuzawa dismissed them with a wave of the hand, immediately after making his quiet threat of death or deportation. They were marched outside and prodded into a small open army truck, with slatted side boards. Six armed soldiers sat with them in the back of the vehicle: hustled them, butted them with rifles and bayonets, and cursed at them in shrill Japanese.

So they were driven through the streets, where it was evident that the Japanese take-over of Mukden was total. Troops jeered as they passed, while the few Chinese who were aboard turned and looked the other way.

Occasionally they saw bodies along the wide tree-lined streets, together with other signs of fighting – broken windows, bullet scars on walls, every now and then a shop, or dwelling, wrecked and burned out.

The bodies were being dumped together in piles at street corners or intersections: Japanese troops giving orders; overseeing while local Chinese performed the grisly operation.

Their destination proved to be the North China Barracks, though Byrd and Cat only knew this because Waldo Bingham, familiar with the city, grunted the fact as they neared the area. The Japanese NCO in charge of their guards immediately ordered silence, and the soldier sitting next to him raised a rifle with some menace.

On approaching the high white barrack walls, with the

squat impersonal buildings behind them, it was apparent that this was where the main battle for Mukden had taken place. The Chinese troops quartered here had obviously put up stiff resistance. Sections of the wall had been blown apart, some of the buildings within were wrecked, and the place stank of death. In fact, over three hundred Chinese troops had died at the barracks.

Already the Japanese had organised a Chinese labour force who were busy repairing damage, but, once inside the compound, the full stench hit them. Again the Japanese were using cowed Chinese to dispose of the corpses, or what was left of them, piling mounds beside trucks that would be used eventually to cart the remains away and dump them into mass graves. The most repellent stink came from several small bonfires smouldering on what had been the parade ground.

At first, Byrd could not identify these little mounds, until, with horror, he saw one being put together, a Japanese soldier pouring gasoline over it, ready for ignition, laughing as he did so. Cat put a hand up to her mouth as they passed near. The pile was made of severed parts of human bodies – arms and legs that had been blown from their trunks, hands, and, on top of this particular mound, a bloodied and battered head.

Cat retched as the soldier cheerfully put a flame to the stacked remains; Bingham swore, and Byrd turned away, sickened by such callous disregard for basic human dignity.

They were frog-marched into one of the buildings that was still intact, then down a long passage, through a metal door, down steps and into another passage from which small cells led off on either side. This had undoubtedly been the detention area, and another smell now struck at their nostrils, catching at the back of their throats – the odour of sweat, dirt and excrement: the fetid reek of humanity crammed together without proper sanitation.

Most of the cells were closed, occupied – by the senior Chinese officers, Byrd presumed. Colonel Yukuzawa had casually mentioned as having been arrested. At this point they expected to be separated, so it came as a surprise when the guards halted them at the end of the passage, and opened a slightly larger metal door which led into a chamber some thirty of forty feet square.

The floor and walls were of bare stone, the ceiling was roughly plastered; three rush mats lay in the centre, and a barred window, high on the furthest wall, let in a dim oblong of light. Later they discovered the window was unglazed, covered by iron bars, and, behind it, a kind of chimney led up through the ground to the outside of the building. It was their main source of light and air: a cement-lined tunnel measuring about five feet by three.

For once the Japanese, usually so punctilious in these matters, apparently regarded the question of segregating the sexes to be of little importance. They departed abruptly, leaving their prisoners in dank half-darkness. Cat had retched almost constantly since they reached the barracks: she now looked ghastly white, shaking from head to foot. Byrd felt at a low ebb also. Only the bulky Waldo Bingham remained outwardly calm.

"It would seem that I have made a gross error both of judgement and timing." He paced across the cell, peering up through the barred opening, then back to examine the door, which was of studded metal with no handle on the inside. It had clanged, echoing depressingly, once they were inside.

"They're keeping all three of us in here?" Cat's voice was weak and close to breaking.

"Even better story for your glossy mag." Byrd tried to raise their spirits. Tired and depressed, he busied himself in shaking out the rush mats, placing them far apart in different corners of the cell. "At least there's a little space. I wonder if they have bathrooms. I distinctly ordered a treble room and bath."

"I would not count on it, my dear Byrd." Bingham still peered up at the window. "I do not take kindly to the management here. Room service may prove interesting."

Cat began to speak, then swallowed, the words sticking

in her throat. She started again. "Waldo, what do you think? Will they really. . . ?"

"Shoot us? I doubt it. Too many international repercussions. I do *not* doubt, however, that there has been a military take-over here in Manchuria. Neither do I doubt that we will be kept here, in quiet seclusion, for some time. But there will be a lot of diplomatic activity going on."

"Escape?" Byrd asked without any real enthusiasm.

"Suicide at the moment. Wait a day or so. See if they're going to feed us. Get our strength up and rest, eh? Primitive conditions, I know, but we'll do our best to provide some privacy for Miss Morrow. You'll have noticed I didn't let on about speaking a bit of their lingo. Method there: better they shouldn't know. However, I trust you'll accept me as your spokesman." He paused, flapping his big hands. "That is – we must be realistic – if they even bother to come near us."

They came. About an hour later a pair of soldiers arrived with three blankets and some food in metal bowls – unpalatable rice mixed with a little fish which tasted stale. They had water to drink.

As the light began to fade, the soldiers arrived again and ordered Cat to go with them. She said nothing; just followed them out like a zombie. They returned her in fifteen minutes, and motioned Bingham to come this time.

"Bathroom," Cat explained, with a disgusted look. "It's pretty filthy, but I think that's it for the night."

Bingham returned, and they took Byrd last.

"They stand over you?" he asked Cat when they brought him back.

She said no, they had left her alone; but Bingham had suffered the same indignity as Byrd – a pair of soldiers standing over him as he used the latrine and tried to sluice his hands and face in what amounted to a saucer-full of water.

The following day saw the start of what was to become a regular routine. They were allowed three trips to the lavatory and wash room each day – after the three meals, which never seemed to vary: the same rice and fish, occasionally a little meat mixed with it; only water to drink.

The first month was the worst – at least for Byrd. On the train he had bought three packs of cigarettes, and even with a drastic cut-down in his consumption, he was through them in ten days. Then he began to suffer the worst symptoms of nicotine withdrawal – the sweats, anxieties, and nervous twitches which all heavy smokers know so well when forced to discard the habit. His generally weak state of health, following the memory loss and exposure, did not help.

Each afternoon – late, around five – they were taken through the passages and up the stairs, with a guard normally consisting of six soldiers, and marched solemnly around the parade ground for twenty minutes of exercise.

Every time the guards came with food, Bingham made a protest in English, asking to see the British and American Consuls; or at least to speak with the officer in command. His demands were ignored.

After several days an officer arrived, with the usual escort, and removed Bingham. Byrd and Cat hardly spoke for the time he was away: both, not unnaturally, thinking the worst. During the nights they had dozed, on and off, but were often wakened by noises from along the passages – cries, shouts, screams, the steady sound of marching boots. Twice they had heard the sound of men marching along the corridor and, a little later, from above them, down through the funnel, the unmistakable crash of a rifle volley. During their exercise period they had noticed large wooden stakes driven into the ground in front of one of the walls. The wall was heavily pitted and there were dark stains on the stakes. Even more terrifying, nearby stood a pair of wooden blocks, the ground around which was even more heavily stained. They did not speak of these things, any more than Byrd and Cat spoke while Bingham was absent.

After about an hour the soldiers returned Bingham to the cell. Outwardly he seemed as calm as ever, putting his finger to his lips as they asked him what had happened, and waiting until the door had closed, and the sound of the soldiers' boots retreated down the passage. Then he sat down on his rush mat, using his blanket to ease the hardness of the wall behind him.

"I have had an interview with our old friend Colonel Yukuzawa, who, to be honest, is not being helpful." Yukuzawa had apparently given him the official line. The Chinese government in Nanking was in disarray, and appealing both to America and to Great Britain. Bingham contorted his plump face, performing a fair imitation of the colonel – "We have announced two thing. First, the Japanese military occupation of Manchuria is temporary only; until our treaty rights are secured and law has been enforced. Second, outside interference is not solicited." He meant, Bingham continued, that the Americans and British were to mind their own bloody business. He claimed that both the consuls had left Mukden. He also claimed that they were being held as spies of the Americans and the British. "I cannot deny being a shade worried. There have already been some executions – Chinese officers, and one or two other people they've been holding either as spies or hostages. Yukuzawa asked me for certain information about my service, and British plans in this part of the world. Shanghai in particular. When I was unable to oblige he didn't press me. This time. . ."

He had managed to squint at some Japanese documents on the colonel's desk, and with his knowledge of the language – which Byrd had always felt was more extensive than Bingham allowed – he had discovered that already some decisive plan to overrun Shanghai was in operation.

"So they'll probably take us into that yard and shoot us?" Byrd put the probability into words without emotion.

"It could happen, but I still think not. The colonel," Bingham jabbed his finger into his collar and ran it around his neck in mimicry of Yukuzawa's habit, "said some things which indicated we would be sent back."

"Back?" Cat looked alarmed. "Back to Shanghai?"

Bingham nodded.

"But that would mean Harry would . . ."

"Precisely."

Bingham gave a wary smile, and Byrd laughed: "Figures.

I'm the real pawn. The good old Black Dragon want to even things up, and they'll want to do it themselves, not leave it to the military."

"That is how I see it. There's also the diplomatic situation. While the Japanese rattle sabres at America and Britain they know they must not go too far. After all, Britain helps them with their Navy, and the International Settlement treaties in places like Shanghai are sacrosanct. No. I think we have a fair chance of remaining alive – at least until we get to Shanghai. Then . . ." his words trailed off and he looked thoughtfully at Byrd.

"Then," Byrd clenched his teeth, "I shall have to keep myself fit and make plans of my own." He had wanted to return to Shanghai, but in his own time and in his own way. Frankly, if his hand were forced, he didn't think much of his chances.

As they settled for sleep that night – though sleep was a luxury they did not enjoy much, what with the noises and the cold – Bingham said they should really start thinking of escape. It would be a good idea for them to take in as much information as possible regarding the sentries, gates and barrack lay-out, every time they were taken up to the parade ground. He had become their natural leader, this unlikely, fat, sometimes pompous, and intolerant man. But, in their dire extremity, neither Cat nor Byrd questioned Bingham's experience or competence. In some ways he had become a father figure to both of them.

Then another routine began. Bingham was taken up to see the colonel on an average of about once every two days. "Sort of interrogation," the big man explained. "Few threats thrown in. Gives me a chance to get a look-see at the papers on his desk," he winked broadly, "I'm feeding them bits and pieces. Rubbish, of course, but it gives us more time."

And time was passing; slowly but surely. One of the things Waldo insisted on, immediately after their arrival, had been some kind of calendar. With a chip of stone they had marked off days on the wall ("Château D'Iff stuff," Bingham laughed. "Count of Monte Cristo and all that.

Know your Dumas, do you, Byrd?"). September passed into October. They were now entering the beginning of November, which worried Byrd. What he knew of the climate told him it would soon become really cold. Even if they were to escape they would not survive long in what the Chinese called a 'four-coat winter'.

As time passed they also became conscious of each other's looks. The washing facilities were kept to a minimum. It was impossible to keep clean and, with no changes of clothing, things could only get worse. Cat had managed to keep a comb, which they all used, but it did not stop the ragged growth of their hair and, for the men, beards. Nor did it help with the lice.

November neared December. During the periods when Bingham was being interrogated by the colonel, Cat and Byrd slowly began talking again. Mainly about the past. It started when Cat asked about his first days in Shanghai, and progressed to her telling him the story of her own rise in the newspaper and magazine field.

"Did the old man ever get his comeuppance?" Byrd asked her, casually, one day. He spoke of her father, the cop.

She smiled, a secret and almost closed face, nodding vigorously, then recounting how after the trial – after Byrd had gone – she had contributed to a newspaper campaign to stamp out corruption in the city's police. "There was a lot of pressure on him to resign from the force; but you know what a hard-headed son-of-a-bitch he was. Just refused. Stuck it out. I was working for a couple of magazines and had some clout. I fed back information to the old *Globe*. They ran a couple of stories." She gave a small bitter laugh. "The mob was back in action again by then, of course – not as bad as before, but they were around. The old man got drunk one night and had a row with some shyster who was fronting for a gaming operation. The old man said he'd been taken by them. The next night they flew in a couple of guys from out of town. They put several ounces of lead into the old man." She laughed again. "Right on the steps of City Hall."

Byrd stayed awake longer than usual that night, wondering what really made Cat tick – a girl who hated her father so much that she even showed pleasure in the fact of him being gunned down: a girl who had surely loved Byrd himself, yet had broken their pact with unflinching ruthlessness – after advising him and helping him through the most troubled period of his life.

As their conversations continued, however, he began dimly to see that leaving him had not been an easy act of treachery. When she had finally separated from her family, managing to escape from her father, Cat was obsessed by the need to prove herself. "I so wanted to be with you, Harry," she told him warmly. "But I don't think we'd have stood a chance together. I'd have always been looking back: wondering if I'd have ever really made it on my own. It was the hardest decision of my life, and I don't blame you for hating me. Just remember there was never anyone else – until Tom. And that wouldn't have worked either." She gave her odd two-shouldered shrug.

They talked a lot about the past after that, remembering times together, and many small details: like entire menus in favourite eating places; jokes shared; people liked or loathed.

One morning at the end of November, while Bingham was away on one of his sessions with the colonel, they made love, with total giving and forgiving, on Cat's rush matting, using her blanket, with Byrd's rolled up as a pillow. The grime of their bodies did not seem to matter. For a while they were almost back where they started, in the city well over three years before.

It was just after this that Waldo Bingham returned to say he felt things were getting worse. Yukuzawa had flown into a rage at him that morning. "I think they've cottoned on to one of my pieces of rubbish. They've caught me out, and he's making more threats. Could be he means it."

They had already made some preliminary plans; though neither of the two men had liked the idea of an escape. If they even managed to get out of the barracks, the odds were not in favour of three Caucasians making it in mid-winter over the two hundred and fifty miles south to Dairen – or even the hundred and fifty to the port of Antung – and then stealing a boat for the difficult journey back to Shanghai: let alone travelling north across country and getting over the now heavily-guarded border with Russia.

Byrd was determined that, if they had to go, he would head for Shanghai. He had business there, and spent a lot of his waking time planning his actions once he got back. Though he told neither Bingham nor Cat, he was also watching the calendar. Time was running out. He wanted to be in Shanghai before the middle of January, in time to deal with the proposed arms-for-opium exchange between Tang and the Maes brothers.

They had all lost weight, most noticeable in Bingham, and had calculated that it might just be possible for the three of them to edge their way up the chimney funnel on the other side of the barred opening. Experiments, consisting of Byrd (who spent much time building up his muscles and exercising in the cell) climbing on Bingham's shoulders and examining the bars, proved the cement was badly cracked. With care, Byrd reckoned he could loosen the bars, and have them out, in a matter of half an hour.

They had also checked where the chimney surfaced: close to the building, beneath a grating flush with the earth and almost in line with the main gates to the barracks across the parade ground. There were armed sentries day and night, pacing back and forth – with lights brilliant around the gates throughout the period of darkness.

Bingham was well trained, though, and taught Harry Byrd the cleanest way to take a sentry from behind: moving silently behind him, using the forearm of the right arm, with the hand on the triceps of the left, around the man's neck; the left hand behind his head to give leverage. Bingham said you could snap a man's neck like a twig if you did it fast enough. The only thing you had to watch for was catching his rifle as he fell.

"And, with the way you two smell, keeping up-wind of them," Cat added.

After that it would be a case of making it through the

lights and stealing transport; maybe spreading a false trail, which might cost precious days; and relying on friendly Chinese. It was a gamble, the odds of which they had all considered many times over the last few weeks. But Bingham's latest news, added to his assessment – and its gravity – made up their minds. And they had to make their move now, for Bingham figured that, unless something dramatic happened, there was a strong possibility that all three of them would be tied to those stakes in front of the wall before nightfall on the following day.

"Or kneeling by one of those chopping blocks." Cat spoke calmly, surprising the men, who had carefully avoided mentioning the purpose of those sinister pieces of wood.

"If they're going to kill us anyway, we might as well put up some kind of fight." Harry Byrd said it for all of them.

The evening routine followed its usual pattern. The food arrived and then, one at a time, they were escorted to the latrine.

They let an hour go by, and then began work. After so much time in the dim light of the cell, their eyes had quickly adjusted to the near-darkness of night.

Bingham braced himself against the wall, and Byrd mounted his shoulders. The grille was well above Bingham's head level, and beyond it the cavity tunnelled horizontally for a few feet before angling upwards. The cement was even more cracked than he had imagined, for the bars came away easily, cement and brickwork spattering down on to Bingham, making him sway and cry out so that Byrd almost toppled from his shoulders. After the first three he climbed from the larger man's shoulders and they both rested against the wall.

"Nobody's checked those things in years." Byrd rubbed his hand where he had scraped it on the ledge. Bingham was flicking flakes of cement and stone from his face and eyes. "Probably too much sand in the cement."

There were six bars in all; each one coming away without difficulty. Grasping a bar, he put pressure forward, then pulled back gently to avoid a sudden fall if it came away quickly. He then rotated the bar and finally, as the dry brick and cement gave way, eased it out.

It took less than the planned half an hour to extract all six bars.

Because Byrd was certainly the most muscular of the two, he would be the first to enter the cavity, then assist Waldo to scale the wall, holding the big man's hands as he himself braced his legs securely in the angle of the chimney. He would then steady Bingham while he, in turn, stretched down to pull Cat into the opening. If, at any point, one of them failed to get up, the others would descend – either to try again or abandon the attempt.

They took a ten-minute breather, then Byrd climbed on to Bingham's shoulders for the final effort. Thrusting his arms inside, pressing outwards, he pulled his shoulders into the hole, squirming forward, feeling his feet leave Bingham's body, knowing that he was now on his own.

There was room to spare, and Byrd was able to lever himself in by using his hands stretched out, palms flat against the sides of the shaft. They were sore and scraped by the time his whole body was inside, but, again, by twisting, he had room to turn his body. Within a few minutes he lay, with his head and shoulders half out of the cavity, looking down into the darkness of the cell.

The shape of Bingham's head and hands were barely visible below him. He whispered, asking if Bingham could see his hands well enough to grasp them and make the upward jump. Affirmative.

Quietly he counted to three, aloud, then added "Go". A second later he felt as though his arms were being ripped from his shoulders as Waldo Bingham's palms connected with his, slipped, then jerked upwards and grasped firmly.

Byrd's whole body started to slide forward. Bingham had lost weight, but was still heavy, and Byrd forced his legs hard against the sides of the tunnel to stop both men cascading back into the cell. He whispered urgently for Waldo to get his feet against the wall, to relieve some of the weight, while Cat pushed as well as she could from beneath.

Then, slowly, Byrd began to wriggle backwards, the

strain on his legs increasing as he retreated in a series of jumps, one leg at a time, so that he could eventually pull Bingham up as far as the opening.

At last, Bingham's face and shoulders were close to his own, and the man edged himself into the hole. Byrd still held on, until the larger man had the bulk of his chest inside, and could wriggle the remainder of his body into the tunnel. Then he shuffled backwards, until Bingham had enough room to turn, and repeat the process with Cat.

Now Byrd squirmed, braced his legs against the sides once again, and took a tight grip on his partner's ankles.

Getting Cat up was easier. Light enough before their arrest, the prison diet had rolled all traces of fat from her, and Bingham quickly had the girl up into the cavity. The only difficulty was that, with two men already in the confined space, it took longer for them to writhe back and give Cat the room she needed to haul her whole body into the tunnel.

From start to finish, the operation must have taken the best part of an hour. They gave themselves a few minutes' rest, then Byrd began to twist his body, speaking softly to the others; telling them to follow at a slight distance, in case the grille at the other end proved difficult to shift.

The chimney seemed to go on for ever, and Byrd found it necessary to stop and rest every few yards. His knees, palms, and elbows must, he thought, by now be completely skinned, for the angle of the upward slope was more acute than any of them had imagined.

The small light patch in the distance drew nearer. Finally he reached the bars and stopped for a moment, listening to the scraping and panting as the other two followed him.

The grating at the far end was a single unit. He pushed and felt it give. He heaved again: one side of it lifted, teetering up to the vertical and falling back on to the beaten earth. The sound was deafening. He cringed back: nothing happened.

Bingham was up close now, telling him that Miss Morrow was just behind, touching his heel. Byrd whispered that they seemed to be in the clear. "I'll go to the left,

Waldo. You to the right. Flat on our stomachs once we're out, then we can pull Cat over to my side."

He took hold of the earth outside, lifting his body into a sitting position, head and shoulders protruding from the opening. The air hit him – cold and refreshing on his face – but after a second or two, all sense of elation was gone in the freezing air and only the cold remained. Slowly, Byrd levered himself out of the ground and rolled to the left. He could see clearly across the parade ground, to the gateway where the sentries patrolled back and forth, in slow strides under the lights. They had no visible shadows.

Bingham came out, rolling to the right, then they both reached down, pulling the panting Cat into the open. She lay, for a moment exhausted, next to Byrd on the hard cold earth.

"We made it." She swallowed, gasping as though clutching for breath.

"So far." Byrd took another deep inhalation of air. Already the three of them were shivering violently. Then night suddenly became day. Searchlights flared into life; figures rose from the ground, circling them with rifles, bayonets fixed.

"A most ingenious and brave attempt," said Colonel Yukuzawa, waddling towards them. "We have watched with much interest after arriving at your cell. Lady had just manage to get through window when we came to give you news. Your fate, lady and gentlemen, has now been decided. You have had wasted effort. Pity."

五 (5)

There was a large iron stove in Colonel Yukuzawa's office: it burned logs and the fire could be seen through a little grille in its black pot-belly. The office was very warm; this and the sight of the busy flames were the only cheering aspects of their situation.

There was no doubt in Byrd's mind that they would have been lucky to last the night out in the open; the weather was much colder than any of them had anticipated. As bad as conditions were in the cell – they had failed to appreciate the freezing atmosphere in the open air above.

All three were shivering and dejected, though they noticed that the soldiers who led them back into the barracks did not push, jostle, or prod them with their weapons. Byrd could not make up his mind about this. Were they being solicitous towards the condemned, or did their actions augur good news?

Yukuzawa's face betrayed nothing, and he kept them standing before his desk as he shuffled papers around, not looking at them. Byrd recalled the old story that returning juries in murder trials did not look towards the prisoner if they had found him guilty. He concentrated on the warmth coming from the stove instead, willing the cold from his body, so fixing his attention that he almost ceased to care about the coming verdict. Yukuzawa cleared his throat and began to speak. It was a sudden picture of Cat which filled Byrd's head – a volley of bullets smashing into her body as she slumped forward on the stake in front of the wall.

The picture was so vivid that he almost lost the colonel's first words.

Yukuzawa inserted his finger behind his collar and ran it around his neck. "I have official declaration here," he started, "released in last few days. This I have to read to you first." He coughed again, full of self-importance, like some

194

petty bureaucrat reading a statement to the press, peering forward at the parchment document, raising it short-sightedly to his face as he started to read. "Perceiving in the people of Manchuria an unmistakable desire to have an Emperor of their own, the restoration of the ancient dynasty has been decided upon, and Pu-yi, the heavenly cousin of his Imperial Japanese Majesty the Emperor Hirohito, will be placed on the throne of Manchukuo." He paused, looking up at them. "Manchukuo is Japanese name for what you have called Manchuria."

Bingham grunted. "Manchuria belongs to Japan then."

"Precisely, Mr. Bingham." Yukuzawa allowed a smile. "I also have a communication from the Commanding Officer of the Imperial Japanese Army in Manchukuo, Lieutenant-General Honjo, who has been to speak with the heavenly cousin of our Emperor of Enlightened Peace. He has, in fact, pleaded for your case. We wish no harm to befall any foreign traveller in this land. This is why you have been kept safely here at the barracks in Mukden: for your own safety."

"Balls." Byrd did not bother to speak softly.

"On instructions of General Honjo, all three of you will be escorted, in the next few days, to Dairen. From there you will go back to Shanghai, on the normal ferry service which is now running without any hindrance. For your safety, two officers of our police will make the journey to watch over you, and make certain no ill befalls you. Also to be sure you *all* arrive safely in Shanghai." He looked directly at Byrd and smiled again.

So, Byrd thought, the Black Dragon have had their way. He was being taken back to Shanghai so that Mr. Takahome and Mr. Hitchimata could put their ronin on to him. Possibly if they had got to hear of his connection with Bingham, he would suffer prolonged interrogation. Either way, he was certain that they would hurt him a great deal before finally killing him – that was unless the Maes brothers, with their tame idiot Boris, got to him first. So that for once, incredibly, 'Pearly' Fisher seemed his best hope. He asked when exactly they were scheduled to leave.

The colonel remained as unhelpful as ever, simply repeating to him what he had already said – within the next few days.

"We would not like people to think you have been ill-treated." He smiled yet again. "There must be time for you to be well rested." He made a signal to the NCO in charge of the troops by the door. "First a doctor will see you."

The armed troops still remained with them, but, for the first time since their arrival at Mukden barracks, they were now separated. They were not to meet again until the day of their departure.

Two orderlies, with an armed soldier in tow, led Byrd to a warm bath house. The orderlies lifted him gently into the bath after stripping him of his filthy clothing, soaping and washing him with great care. The soap smelled strongly of disinfectant. Then a doctor arrived. Byrd was examined, sprayed with delousing powder, and had the many cuts and scrapes treated and dressed. He felt clean and comfortable – save for the stinging of his skinned and cut areas – for the first time in weeks.

One of the orderlies went away and reappeared with underclothes, trousers, shirt and jacket from Byrd's luggage, which miraculously still seemed to be unplundered. He dressed as far as the waist, and they sat him in a chair to shave him, and cut his hair – short and close to the scalp.

When he was completely dressed, the doctor came in again – he was obviously working between all three prisoners – and re-examined him, nodding and grinning as if to say that the American was in the best of health.

The small room to which they led him contained a bed, fresh blankets and sheets, a table and a chair. It was warm, and even though the window was barred, this time there was glass in it, and a blind above it which the orderlies pulled down before bringing a tray of food – rice; succulent meat balls; tea.

On the bed lay Byrd's original case which had been taken from him on the train. On top of the case was his own passport, in the name 'Harry Byrd', together with his Shanghai papers. Since Byrd's true documentation had been well hidden in the lining of Bingham's case, they had obviously been very thorough, going through all Waldo's luggage with the proverbial tooth-comb. Which augured ill for the fate of Cat's diamonds.

It was now early morning, and when the orderly came to remove the tray, he brought with him a glass of water and two tablets. "Make sleep," he said, and Byrd took the tablets without a thought. They could have been poison for all he cared; the fatigue of the past hours, combined with the stresses of the last months and weeks, had left him mentally suspended. He undressed and climbed into the bed: so luxurious that for a time he merely allowed his hands to wander over the sheets and blankets, relishing the softness of the mattress below him.

As he drifted into sleep, Byrd's mind began to picture everything he had left behind in Shanghai. If he could find ways of evading Yukuzawa's police, who were to watch them during the return journey, then escape the attention of the Shoshi society, the Maes brothers, and Fisher, he would try to make contact with Tang. At least Tang would want the Flamingo returned to its former status; and he had the added leverage of the information – regarding the Maes' proposed double-cross – he could pass on to the Chinese gangster.

In this state of semi-euphoria he edged into sleep, pictures of his old staff at the Flamingo crossing and recrossing his brain – little loyal Max; Herman at the piano; Casimir, excitable and always bustling; the temperamental Descales: and Jeannie Chin. Jeannie, the delectable Chinese girl, who made love so softly and gently, yet mounted to such noisy passion.

Cat's image crossed the picture of Jeannie. In spite of what had taken place in the cell, he really did not know how he truly felt about Cat. During the last days they had spoken as though the years apart had never been; but there was still an understandable element of distrust in his heart. Cat was ambitious and unpredictable. Jeannie on the other hand, had not a single original thought in her head and she served him well. It was Jeannie who stayed in his mind, as he finally

197

allowed sleep to take hold and drag him into its dark, comfortable world of nothingness.

Byrd slept for almost forty-eight hours. He woke feeling light-headed, for a second not knowing where he was; then stretching and easing his painful muscles. Slowly the memories returned, and he climbed from the bed, and tried the door handle. It was locked, inevitably, and he would have put a lot of money on there being a guard outside.

Pulling up the window blind he saw that it was first light; a new day just beginning. He returned to the bed and lay there, wide awake and very alert – the final thoughts before sleep coming straight into his mind.

He went over the past. Particularly those last two days before his memory went haywire in Shanghai. Now he fully realised that the blow to the right side of his head, and the pain in his eye, caused by the first ronin's attack, were certainly responsible for the final loss of memory. He began to work forward from the morning when the Delage exploded, giving the initial hint of trouble. Most of the details remained clear, but it was only when he got to the point where he returned to the café to find Geddes' body, that something eluded him: something he could not quite touch. He remembered going into the office and finding Geddes: watching him keel over, his head hitting the desk, the body tumbling and ending in that strange position on the floor: the face with one side of the forehead shot away.

Then the world had gone mad. Something had hit him, hard on the back of the head. And just before that came the sense, the feeling, the movement – something familiar buried deep in his memory, refusing to come into the open.

The orderly arrived, and, finding him awake, brought food. Byrd could see he had been right about the guard, for he glimpsed an armed soldier outside. Later the doctor reappeared, examined him and had the dressings changed on his torn skin.

In slow English, Byrd asked if his friends were all right. The doctor understood, nodding vigorously, saying, "Friends. Lady and big man very good. Resting like you. You go home soon."

Home? Home to Mr. Takahome and Mr. Hitchimata with their desire for retribution; home to 'Pearly' Fisher who would want to see him topped for Geddes' murder (again a half-flash of memory, almost grasping the buried key to something, then losing it again); home to the Maes brothers, and Boris ready to break every bone in his body, and then some. Home to the Flamingo Café: to Tang and his information. Back to *freedom* – he started to think positively: it was essential for him to slip the others and get to Tang, for Tang alone could provide him with sanctuary and the means to regain all that he had lost.

In the ten days that passed before he was reunited with Cat and Bingham, Byrd was given treatment, rest, exercise and plenty of good food. He also had a lot of time to think – about the past and the future. The nightmare of the time spent in the cell below the barracks did not fade quickly, but he only thought of it occasionally – the noises, cold, uncertainty, stench, discomfort and foulness. The unavoidable embarrassments to Cat, having to share this stone hole in the ground with two males.

The bulk of his mind, however, was filled with plans for evasion, and righting the future. All through this time he drilled away at the missing memory of what had happened in the few seconds before he had been sapped, after finding Geddes. It was like trying to trap a small, brightly-coloured insect by the hand. The memory lay on the brink of his recall a hundred times, and a hundred times it disappeared leaving no trace.

One evening after he had eaten, the orderly came back for his tray, followed by Colonel Yukuzawa, who motioned Byrd to sit down. He had not risen to his feet to greet the colonel; merely to stretch his legs. Now he sat on the bed while the little Japanese officer took the one chair.

Yukuzawa smiled, peering at Byrd: the safe smile of a benign uncle. "So, tomorrow you and your companions will return to the safety of Shanghai," he began, running a finger around his collar.

Byrd gave a small laugh which he meant to sound mocking.

"There are many friends in Shanghai who wish to see you, yes?" The colonel leaned forward still peering, the smile oily and constant. "Friends of yours, and friends of the Imperial Japanese Army, I think."

"Okay, I know the score, Yukuzawa. I'm not an idiot. You should just shoot me here, and have done with it."

"For one who has offended so mightily, the way to death must not be made easy. And, before you die, perhaps there are things you will wish to tell. Yes, our friends in Shanghai will be waiting. I wanted you to have no doubts about that."

"There were never any doubts."

"As long as we understand one another. Great changes are coming in this part of the world, and people must be made to see who holds the true power. Yes, Mr. Harry Byrd, you are being sent back to Shanghai to face the ultimate truth, at the hands of those whom you have offended. They have claimed the right. I merely wanted to be sure that you understood."

Byrd understood.

Cat and Waldo Bingham looked more like their old selves when they all met on the following morning, December 24. They were provided with winter coats, for they had left Shanghai in fine warm weather, carrying only light rain-wear apart from the small amount of normal clothing. The weather, with the approach of Christmas, had turned to almost zero temperatures in Mukden.

Bingham's weight was returning – "Fed me like a pig" – and Cat looked trim and neatly made up. She revealed that she had recovered the diamonds untouched from her lug-gage. The Japanese, she said, blushing slightly, had clearly not cared to investigate too closely the more feminine toilet items in her case. Bingham praised her foresight: Mr. Nip, he said, had a positive horror of such things. And diamonds themselves might very well now come in useful.

They were driven to the station just in time to catch the train to Dairen. An armed soldier sat with the driver of an army staff car, and their police shadows were waiting at the station – two small men, sharp-eyed and muscular, wearing heavy clothing, both speaking English with a confident fluency which suggested that they knew their job.

Throughout the four-hour train journey the two Japanese sat in the same compartment as Bingham, Cat and Byrd. Conversation, therefore, was restricted – their guards frequently spoke to each other in Japanese, occasionally nodded at their three charges, but did not once address them directly.

"What a way to spend Christmas Eve," Bingham remarked at last as they chugged through the flat steppes, bleak and wintry in the evening light. Cat suggested some kind of party on board ship, and Byrd agreed. Silence settled over them again. They dozed fitfully.

The Japanese guards followed them aboard the ferry at Dairen, staying near the cabin doors, and keeping close until they were at sea.

Bingham and Byrd shared a cabin; Cat had a berth next door.

"They'll relax now we're at sea," Bingham prophesied of the Japanese plainclothes men. The three of them got hold of some gin and whisky, and met in the men's cabin after the evening meal. It was too cold to go up on deck, and the swell made them fear that it was going to be a rough trip. "They think you're a good looker, Miss Morrow. Maybe we can use you as a decoy. Listened to their conversation on the train. They'll stick close when we dock for the hour or so at Tsingtao, and then stay very tight for the Shanghai docking."

They spoke frankly of Byrd's dilemma.

"There'll certainly be a reception committee waiting for you." Bingham wrinkled his plump brow. "With those devils, I'd give you about half an hour ashore. If that."

"If Fisher or the brothers Maes haven't been informed. Fisher'll probably come on board and lift me." Byrd was becoming more depressed at the idea. "And I don't fancy my chances, even in a police jail, with the Shoshi after me."

"There is no chance that the Japanese are going to let the news of your arrival out of the bag." Bingham was adamant. "Only their people will know; and they obviously want you to themselves."

"Which means," Cat said softly, "they mustn't find you, darling."

She was being most affectionate, had held his hand on the train, and his arm when boarding the boat. It made Byrd edgy, his emotions still uncertain. Even their love-making had not completely wiped away the reserve he felt about her past actions. And when he thought of Cat, he often felt the elusive memories stirring: the moment when he had found Geddes, just before someone had caught up with him. More and more he thought it had something to do with Cat. The diamonds, perhaps? Had they really been hers in the first place?

"They just must not find you," she repeated now, with quiet intensity.

"Which means," Bingham sipped thoughtfully at his whisky, "we either have to hide you on board, or get you off the ship before passengers are disembarked. Let me cogitate awhile."

They drank until late. Wished each other a merry Christmas. Kissed, and, finally, went to bed. Cat had whispered briefly to Waldo during the evening, and, without comment when the time came for turning in, Bingham departed, taking Cat's single cabin.

She turned, unbuttoning her dress to reveal her nakedness beneath. "You deserve a special Christmas present, Harry. I think *I* do as well."

They had sailed on the night ferry, which meant their arrival in Shanghai would be on the early evening of Boxing Day. The sea, while choppy, did not run high, and they arrived at Tsingtao on time. Bingham had been right. The Japanese plainclothes men stuck to them closely throughout the whole of their time in harbour, only disappearing when they were sure the trio were still safe on board, and they were an hour out to sea.

It was about then that Waldo Bingham went missing for a couple of hours. When he reappeared he called what he, somewhat melodramatically, referred to as 'a council of

202

war', in the larger cabin. His first question was addressed, without preamble, to Cat.

"For Byrd's sake, Miss Morrow, would you be prepared to part with one of those precious diamonds?"

She hesitated, wanting to know more, and Byrd reflected on the past – fair-weather lover? Bingham told them in simple terms. His experience of this part of the world, combined with the kind of work he had been doing for years, had taught him much about human nature. It had also made him many friends.

"Our Chinese captain has a second cousin who owes me a favour," he said blandly. For another favour – like one of the diamonds – the captain would not only get Byrd off the ship, but provide him with a weapon, and arrange some kind of transport.

After further explanation, Cat agreed. No more hesitation; eagerness and excitement taking hold of her.

"Then what has to be done must be arranged with speed." Bingham took the diamond and left the cabin quickly.

"Where will you go?" Cat put her arms around Byrd's neck.

"To Foo Tang to put some pressure on him," Byrd said, carefully not telling her exactly what that pressure might be. When all was safe he would make contact with her. He presumed she would be at the Cathay.

"Unless I'm otherwise occupied, explaining your absence to friend Fisher, or any of the others."

"Stick to Waldo. He'll see you okay. What I have in mind should only take a few days."

When Bingham came back to the cabin he was smiling. The deal was on. All ships, even the ferries, had to stop in the river's mouth for a moment to pick up the pilot at Bell Buoy. The pilot's job was to navigate the ship up the Yangtze, through the last forty miles to Woosung, and then the final fourteen miles up the Whangpo to Shanghai.

"The diamond has bought you a passage on the pilot boat," Bingham said. "You'll go down with a greatcoat and peaked cap, looking very nautical. Then they'll transfer you to a sampan which'll take you up to Woosung. They promise me there'll be overland transport waiting for you – and a gun. After that, you'll be on your own.''

Cat and Bingham were going to distract the pair of Japanese cops while the transfer was made. ''We'll separate – lead 'em a bit of a dance. Chase-me-Charley round the boat deck. They can't be in three places at once, and the chances are they'll stick with us.''

The pilot would be due on board at about five, just as it was getting towards dusk. If all went well, Byrd could be in Woosung by nine or ten. By midnight, if the transport was reliable, he would be in Jessfield Park and, with some climbing and ingenuity, at home with Foo Tang.

The weather, mercifully, was considerably warmer by the time they first hit the thick yellow mud that presages the Yangtze, some twenty miles from the mouth of that great river. Not the stifling heat of summer, but nowhere near the freezing temperatures they had experienced in Manchuria.

The ferry was on time – at Bell Buoy a shade early, around quarter to five. Byrd, muffled in a seaman's coat, a peaked cap jammed on his head, waited in the larger cabin, while Cat and Bingham went on deck, to draw off the opposition if it proved necessary. Waldo instructed him to wait until one of the deckhands came down to tell him the coast was clear.

''Don't worry,'' Bingham said. ''That diamond's famous now. Wonderful thing about radio messages, even from old tubs like this. One diamond; one word from the captain, whose second cousin owes me a favour, and we've bought action; and silence you only get in the grave.''

Byrd hoped it would not turn out to be his grave. He lit a cigarette and paced the cabin, but had only dragged his way through two lungfuls of smoke when a soft tap at the door heralded the arrival of the deckhand: a finger to his lips, motioning Byrd to follow him.

They went up and down companionways, along narrow passages, and through stretches of the small ship that Byrd had never seen. At last they reached the deck, and the misty dusk which surrounded the vessel. There was no sign of the two Japanese guards. The ship was already lit up, but his guide brought him out into a dark area only a few feet from where one light was being held among a group of deck-hands and officers by the rail. There, a rope ladder was secured, snaking down to the small pilot launch, rising and falling against the ship's side below.

At that moment the pilot was climbing over the rail, and the deckhand led Byrd quickly to the group. One officer saluted, the pilot nodded, and Byrd, head lowered, climbed over the rail and began a wavering descent down the swaying ladder.

Hands grasped him as he reached the small boat, helping him aboard. Within seconds the launch had pushed off and was heading away, the cold spray catching Byrd's breath as he looked up to see the ferry disappear into the mist and dusk. The two men controlling the pilot boat gave him smiles and nods, but nobody spoke.

Within half-an-hour he was transferred to a sampan, fitted with a small outboard motor. His companion was a young Chinese who, like the men on the pilot boat, did not speak. This one did not smile either. Byrd wrapped the coat around himself and settled in the prow for the long journey through the mouth of the Yangtze and into the Whangpo.

They came in sight of Woosung a little after nine – the lights of the moored sampans flaring on the water, and the flicker of burning brands throwing moving shadows on the bamboo jetty. By nine thirty they were gliding in, and the young Chinese raised his hand, pointing to a battered and decrepit little car, like a box on wheels – Byrd thought it was an old British Austin. Scrambling from the Sampan, Byrd walked quickly to the car and opened the door.

Another young Chinese was at the wheel. He nodded, pointing at the passenger seat on which lay a small Mauser pistol. Byrd picked it up and checked the action, reaching forward to pocket the small box of ammunition which lay beside it. They could have done him prouder than this elementary piece of weaponry, he thought, but it was better than nothing: straightforward and little to go wrong with the blowback mechanism, even though he would have preferred something heavier than a 6.35 calibre.

Having cocked the pistol he pushed it, to join the ammunition, into his pocket, then pulled himself into the passenger seat, closing the door as quietly as possible.

"Where you want go?" The driver was the first person to speak to him since Bingham had grunted his farewell, and Cat had kissed him, clinging for a second in the cabin.

Byrd told him Jessfield Park, Shanghai. He would decide exactly where to go when they got there. The driver, having apparently exhausted his supply of conversation, remained impenetrably silent for the rest of the journey. *Silence you only get in the grave.* Bingham had been right. If Byrd was not already in his grave, he was probably heading rapidly towards it.

It would be unwise to approach Tang's villa head on. Byrd was out of touch; no idea about what reception he would get from the usual armed guards at the gate. The property was walled – about twenty feet high, as he remembered it – but easily climbable, with no wire or glass on the top. Tang did random checks with guards, but they were usually haphazard affairs: unless the Black Dragon moves had made him tighten his security.

He gave the driver instructions, guiding him to a secluded spot he remembered, about five minutes' easy walk to the rear of the Tang property. The driver simply followed the instructions, still without a word.

Byrd stood by the roadside watching the lights of the old car move away. In his head he again saw the lights of the black limo as it bounced off over the hard road from the ranchhouse with Cat in the back. Leaving only silence.

His eyes adjusted to the dark, and he began to walk. The wall, when he came to it, was easy – built from uneven chunks of stone, giving good footholds. Once up, he lay along the top for a few seconds, listening for the sound of any of Tang's hoods patrolling the grounds. Lights showed from the villa. He saw he was positioned directly behind the aviary. The gardens within the wall appeared deserted.

The springy, well-watered ground under his feet made no sound as he dropped from the wall then moved off, low and fast, skirting the aviary – strangely quiet at night – and making for the rear steps and stone walk running the length of the villa's rear. There were lights in the room behind the curtained French windows where he had last talked with Tang on the visit after the Delage had blown, but Byrd turned away cautiously, moved around the wall, and peered out towards the front of the house. Through the bushes lining the driveway, he could see the main gates, lit by overhanging lanterns; the soft voices of the men on duty floated back on the night air. A long black car which he did not recognise was pulled up in front of the house – he could just make out the driver behind the wheel: waiting for someone.

Retracing his steps, Byrd quietly approached the French windows, placing his palm firmly on the handle, moving it downwards. The windows were not locked; the handle made no sound.

Voices came from inside, beyond the curtains. Tang's voice, speaking in English, obviously seeing someone to the door.

"You have done well, my dear," he heard Tang's voice, reedy, enunciating carefully. "It was right you should give me the news that Harry Byrd is back in Shanghai. Do not worry about him. I hope he is sensible enough to come straight to me. I have one most important job for him: his last, I suspect; for once it's done there is no more use for him. He will work well for me; he cannot refuse. But after that, well, let us say he will disappear, like a firefly burning out."

Byrd realised the far door to the room had closed, leaving it empty. He felt cold and sick, but at least he knew he was in danger of being played for a sucker. This fact put paid to any hope of buying Foo Tang's co-operation by tipping him off on the Maes' double-cross.

Anxious to discover the identity of Tang's visitor, he ran close to the wall, and peered out at the front of the house again, trying to glimpse the figures who now stood by the car. But he was too late. Tang was already closing the rear door, and he could only make out the shape of someone – he was certain it was a woman – sitting well back, as the car pulled away.

Again the memory of what had occurred just after he had found Geddes' body came floating very close to the surface of his mind. Then, as ever, it was gone.

Taking a grip on the pistol he stole back along the wall, and this time pushed the French windows open, shouldering through the curtains.

He was hardly inside the room when the door opened and Foo Tang, his face more skull-like than ever, came in. He hesitated, as though not recognising Byrd at first, then closed the door firmly behind him.

"Ahhh," the Chinese let the sound out in a long gasp. "Harry Byrd. How fortunate. You have risen from the tomb to which our good friend Inspector Fisher has wishfully consigned you. You are not, after all, dead. That is good. You arrive at a most opportune moment."

Byrd slowly raised the pistol, but Foo Tang gave a wave of his hand. "Harry Byrd, none of that. We are partners, remember? You will be safe here. Safe, and in good time for us to make plans together. I am just about ready for us to reclaim our inheritance – our beloved Café Flamingo which is lost without you. Come, you must be tired." He stretched out his arms in a welcoming gesture, then froze.

"What *have* you done to your hair, Harry?" The skull face broke into a bizarre grimace of amused disapproval.

BOOK FOUR

Byrd to Roost

— (1)

Byrd kept the Mauser pointing at Tang's stomach. "No jokes, Uncle Tang. Not even about my hair: I've been through too much and don't trust anyone."

The grimace lingered on Tang's face as he started to walk carefully towards the wall, down which a silken bell rope hung like a yellow snake.

"I mean it. Touch the bell and I kill you." Byrd's voice sounded tired, as though he was beyond caring what happened to anyone.

The languid delivery must have got to Foo Tang, for he stopped, turning back toward Byrd. His expression, however, was impassive once more. "You are my guest, Harry Byrd. You come to me, I presume, for your safety. Let me assure you that, as long as you are in my house, you are protected. You may rest here – I expected you."

"You've sold out to the Black Dragon. They have the Flamingo."

Tang raised his hands in a gesture of pity. "My friend, was it not your own idea? We were to lull them into false confidence."

"With me still in charge."

"You were not here. The police want you; the Black Dragon want you." He sighed: coming from the skull it sounded like a death rattle. "Even my American friends want you. You should have told me that your past was linked to theirs." His hand came up lazily, and Byrd twitched the pistol barrel to make certain it did not reach the bell pull. "The Americans have not told me everything, but you must have done something very bad to them. Not that I blame you," he added quickly. "They are not our kind of people, Harry." He sounded more like a Wimbledon matron than a wealthy Chinese gangster. "I give you my word that you will be safe here."

"I don't feel safe anywhere."

"That is understandable. But there is work to do. The Flamingo has to be returned to its rightful owner – yourself. Handing it to the Shoshi was expedient; but has meant a loss for us all."

"You mean they've reduced your take."

"I would not put it so crudely. Harry Byrd, please remove that weapon. It makes me nervous."

"And you've always made me nervous. What's to stop you calling your boy Lee Yung to take me apart, or hand me over to Fisher?"

"What indeed? But is that likely? I need you to assist me in the Flamingo business. It is time Harry Byrd came home to roost. There is much anti-Japanese feeling among all the Communists now, since the business in Manchuria."

Byrd said that he could imagine, and Tang asked if there was any truth in the charges which Fisher had levelled against him.

"Geddes? No, but Fisher's not likely to believe that. And the courts of law grind very slowly." He paused. "Listen, Tang, I have friends . . ."

"The Mr. Bingham and Miss Morrow?"

"They're two. Messages have been sent to others," he lied. "It is known I am coming here, and I've said that if I'm found dead in the river, or some rice field, they're to come looking for you. If you really mean I'm safe here, I'll put the gun away."

"You are perfectly safe." Foo Tang spoke with conviction, and Byrd was too tired to let the charade continue. He put away the Mauser. Then the Chinese betrayed something of his real need. "You see, we must get the Flamingo back under your management soon. I need its use by the middle of next month."

Byrd recalled an earlier conversation: Tang saying something about the Flamingo being used for storage. He had spoken of it on that last motor journey from the Cathay. Storage in December or January, which could only mean that he needed space at the Flamingo for the opium while it was in transit. Suddenly all was clear. It may well have been temporarily expedient for Tang to let the Black Dragon boys have their way with the café; but time was now pressing hard. This would be his one job – and his last – for Tang. The Chinese need have no outward part in it. Byrd, the avenging owner of the Flamingo, returns for justice: with feeling running high against the Japanese he would triumph. Then Tang could step in, and Byrd would be fed to the highest bidder – Fisher or the Maes brothers. From Tang's viewpoint Byrd was the loser. From Byrd's viewpoint he was the loser.

"Okay, I'll trust you." At least it would give him time in which to make plans of his own.

Tang pulled the silk bell rope. "We really have to do something with your hair, Harry. You look as though you've just been released from prison."

Byrd told him he had. He presumed that Tang in fact already knew this, but just then Lee Yung entered, sparing the old man any further pretences. Yung's eyes only showed minute surprise at the sight of Byrd: one hand tensed, the fingers coming together, palm flat, so that he could, if given the opportunity, use it as a chopping weapon.

"Mr. Byrd is our guest." Foo Tang ordered that Byrd was to be treated with respect; fed, given the guest apartments, and not disturbed until fully rested. Lee Yung bowed, his eyes not leaving Byrd, showing alert suspicion. Tang ended with a small joke – "If you would like a food taster, to make sure I am not going to drug you and have you taken away for white slavery, perhaps my faithful Lee Yung will oblige?"

Like hell, Byrd thought. He'd stuff the muck down my throat and laugh while did it.

The guest apartments were as stylish as the rest of the house: a large room with a marble floor, huge bed and furnishings; the centrepiece of the adjoining quarters was a sunken bath in cool aquamarine tiles. The bath was large enough for Byrd to take a morning swim.

Lee Yung brought a white-coated boy with him to the room, and asked what kind of food he required. Byrd, who had been deprived of his favourite dish for a long time, chose a plate of ham and eggs. It arrived within half an hour, together with coffee, and he wolfed it down. There were cigarettes also. He had hardly smoked in months, and lit one eagerly; he felt dizzy after the first few puffs, but then the old familiar soothing of life's new edges returned.

Lee Yung told him – still using the pidgin English he affected in Byrd's hearing – that there were keys and bolts on the inside of both the door and windows. When he needed anything, all he had to do was pull the tasselled bell cord. His mind still laced with mistrust, Byrd locked everything before retiring, placed the loaded Mauser under his pillow and, helped by the amount of food he had eaten, dropped into a deep sleep, dreamless and untroubled.

It was three o'clock in the afternoon when he woke: eyes flicking open suddenly, all senses alert, hand moving for the gun. On the crest of waking he had remembered what troubled him in the moment after finding Geddes' body; but now, fully awake, the memory had again flown.

Byrd lay silent for a time; listening. From away beyond the window came raucous cries from the exotic birds in Tang's aviary. He thought over the events of the previous night – Tang's conversation with the woman, whoever she was, and then his need to use Byrd to regain the café. Slowly a plan of action began to develop in his mind. Since Tang was still anxious to use the Flamingo as a storehouse for the opium prior to its transfer, it seemed unlikely that the Chinese had an inkling of the double-cross planned by the Maes brothers and Dr. Zuchestra. And, for the moment, Byrd did not intend to enlighten him. That piece of information was to be saved for later . . . emergencies.

With Tang's support, regaining control of the café should present few problems. The real action would start once he was reinstated. Fisher and the rest would know within hours, if not minutes, and the trap would close. Vincent Maes was, presumably, at sea by now on the *Bel Canto*. Even so, that left Valentine, Boris, Fisher and the Shoshi. And even if Fisher won the race, he had little doubt that someone would get to him before there was any trial. Unless? . . . He started to reason the whole thing out. Once the Flamingo was back under his command, there was one thing he could do: must do. It all depended on Fisher reaching him first. 'Pearly' Fisher, of all people, would be his salvation.

Byrd pulled at the bell cord, easing himself from the bed and going to the door, pulling at the bolts and turning the key in the lock.

Tang had been very busy and exceptionally efficient. When the boys brought him food and drink, Byrd found they also carried an assortment of suits, jackets, trousers, silk shirts, underclothes, shoes and other necessities.

"Tailors work from moment you go sleep." Lee Yung actually grinned. "He have all your size."

Fattening up the turkey, Byrd thought: lulling him to make him feel safe and contented. He looked at himself in the mirror, preparing to shave. There was little he could do about his hair, which had now started to grow spiky from its close crop at the hands of the Japanese orderlies in Mukden. His face looked haggard, and he was still in poor physical condition. He needed a week at least before they made any moves. If he was to take over the café from its present incumbents, and survive thereafter, he needed to be in the best possible shape, both physically and mentally.

He said as much to Tang when they met at sundown.

"Time is important," the Chinese sipped a dish of tea. "I need you back in the café by, at the latest, the eighteenth day of January."

Byrd asked an ingenuous why, and Foo Tang appeared to consider the question carefully. At last he nodded, saying there were reasons.

"Your enemies, the Americans, have asked for my help in a small matter. I am carrying out a business transaction with them." He raised a placating hand, "Do not worry, I shall see that you are not troubled: not involved personally. You will be well protected. They will not come near you. I shall see to it personally."

"So what do you require?"

"Behind your kitchens at the Flamingo there is a large store room."

Byrd nodded. He had intended to utilise the area at some time – an extra gaming room, perhaps; it was certainly large enough, and stairs could have been put in. As it was, the warehouse could only be reached from the rear, doors giving access from an alley running at right angles from Nanking Road. The last time he had been there it was empty, but for a few tea chests and boxes.

"Part of my business with the Americans concerns goods which have to be ready for transfer to one of their ships around the eighteenth of the month – maybe twentieth, twenty-first, depending on arrival. I need them in a place of safety, near to the harbour." He gestured as if the matter was really of little consequence. "It would be best if they were kept from prying eyes."

"Of course." Byrd nodded understandingly. He told Tang that, because he needed to recuperate following his long imprisonment, he would like as much time as possible before taking over the café. "I presume it'll mean some pretty rough stuff. I shall be expected to fight for what is mine?"

Tang gave a nod of polite regret. "That is so. The men I did business with have placed one of their most trusted people in charge at the Flamingo. Toshiro Sessaku: very strong man; hard man; small but hard like iron."

Byrd asked if his own people were still employed at the café.

"Most certainly," Tang looked surprised at the question. "They are good. Work hard. It may seem disloyal, perhaps, but they need the jobs. Hunger is a constant barrier to a man's finer feelings."

Sessaku had put some of his own people – Black Dragon people – into the café as well? Byrd asked; and was told: naturally. "About fifteen, sixteen. The waiters are mainly Dragon men – yours are still there also, but do more menial tasks; there are two or three in the kitchen; some in the gaming room: about five there, I think."

"And the clients? Have they changed? More Japanese?"

Tang spread his hands, again regretful. The clientele had changed a fraction. "Men like Mr. Takahome and Mr. Hitchimata take their wives to the café about one time a week. The wives like the Chinese girl who sings there – Jeannie Chin."

Byrd looked up sharply, asking who the husbands liked.

"Ahhhh," the long, drawn-out sigh of sympathetic understanding. Outside, from the garden, came the sound of a cheng, reed pipe, being played; its plaintive, strange melody rising and falling. "The men like best the girl called Polly Sing." Tang paused. "And of course, the Russian girl, Arina. They are both popular."

Byrd experienced a stab of jealousy. He hoped that, perhaps, Messrs. Takahome and Hitchimata would be there on the night he took over. Once more he told Tang that he would need all the time he could get. "I would like to leave it to the eighteenth if that is agreeable." He was pushing his luck, but the longer he stayed under Tang's protection, the easier it would be to carry out the plan he now had mapped in his head.

Tang did not like it; but, having already made light of his use of the warehouse, did not wish to lose face over dates. He would start moving his goods on the seventeenth. If Byrd could reclaim the café on the evening of the eighteenth, which was a Monday – "A quiet night, I understand" – Tang might even get his goods under cover later on the same night; during the hours of darkness. "Yes, it would be well to give you the time. You need more strength. Also the feeling against the Japanese increases all the time, in every area. Yes," he convinced himself that it was best to make it the eighteenth.

Byrd then asked about support. Presumably Tang did not expect him to do this single-handed?

There would be help: "Nobody who is known to be associated with me, you understand. Except, possibly, Lee Yung keeping his eye on matters. You will be given twenty good men."

"Armed?"

"I think only clubs and knives. You have a gun, Harry. One gun should be enough."

"And we just march in and kick the Japanese out?"

"It would seem most practical. I could then have my own people guarding the café from every entrance: plenty of my people."

Byrd asked what the police would be doing all this time. Tang smiled again and said he thought a small diversion could be arranged for the police. He would see. "You just take exercise; rest, build your body; eat and sleep. Prepare yourself in mind and body."

Later, Byrd casually brought Cat and Bingham into the conversation. "Mr. Tang, you know all things that go on in Shanghai. Is there news of those who were imprisoned with me in Manchuria?"

Tang was as well informed as ever. "The man Bingham has taken refuge in the British Consulate. The American girl is with him. I am told arrangements are being made for them to leave in one, two, months. Sometime in February."

That made sense. Doubtless they were lying low, waiting for word from him. Byrd decided not to attempt any contact with either of them until the right moment arrived on the eighteenth of January, or just before. They would worry, but that couldn't be helped. When the time came he would have to move with great speed. And until then, the fewer risks he took the better.

There were almost three weeks for him to prepare, and he followed Tang's advice: eating and sleeping well, getting a lot of exercise in the mornings, and again during the late afternoons.

To all appearances, he was free to go wherever he chose: to wander around Tang's house and the spacious and scented gardens as though they were his own. He was conscious, however, of those who watched him – sometimes one of the boys, but usually Lee Yung himself, who often appeared, suddenly and with no warning, near him in the house or gardens.

The inside of the mansion was a revelation to Byrd.

Having, at first sight, the appearance of great opulence, it was strange to discover that most of the rooms – unlike the one in which he had always met Foo Tang – were very simply furnished.

Yet, in the midst of this simplicity, Byrd would come across the most exquisite treasures and works of art. For a gangster, Foo Tang had great taste. In one corridor there were no less than four priceless scroll paintings, obviously dating back to the fourteenth century at least: birds and flowers; trees; with the largest being a group of women, fragile figures against a marshy landscape, hazy and ethereal. Also there was Tang's remarkable collection of jade.

Byrd did not know a great deal about Chinese art; enough, though, to identify some Sung vases and bowls in one room, and a particularly old gilt bronze Buddha of rare and quiet beauty, alone in a small and otherwise bare room.

One evening – some three or four days after his arrival – as he stubbed out a cigarette in preparation for his bath, Byrd heard a soft tap on the door, heralding the arrival of Lee Yung, accompanied this time by a pair of beautiful young Chinese girls, with skins like porcelain and caps of black hair, so smooth and silky that it looked almost painted on.

They stood behind the sinister Chinese boy, smiling and patient: no cosmetics; dressed only in loose white shifts.

"My master say, perhaps you like company for your bath time," Lee Yung spoke boredly, giving no hint of lasciviousness. Byrd, now that he felt stronger, would scarcely have been human to spurn such an offer. He nodded, and Lee Yung gestured to the girls, who bowed and moved meekly into the room, their eyes lowered.

As the door closed on Yung the girls relaxed, looked up, their eyes now openly inviting. One of them made another little bow, this time towards the bathroom with its sunken tub. The other girl slipped past them and began to run the water.

Wearing a towel around his waist, Byrd entered the bathroom. The girl with him caught hold of this last piece of protection and, with a playful giggle, pulled it from him. Her mouth widened in mock honour at what was exposed.

Now the girls both allowed the white shifts to fall from their naked bodies, revealing themselves as unashamed, slim-waisted creatures, with high, firm breasts; pink-nippled.

As the bath filled, so the one who had entered with Byrd turned him towards her, put her long hands up to his neck, resting just behind the ears, placing her lips close to his. Their mouths did not quite touch, and he smelled the scent of her body, oiled with some erotic fragrance. Her skin was slightly slippery to the touch as he tried to draw her near to him; but she resisted, easing her tongue into his mouth, still without either lips or body touching him.

Her tongue was long, probing and flicking, its tip searching his lips, gums, and then the inside of his mouth. He was conscious of the bathwater running, and his own animal arousal; so it was with pleasure, and not surprise, that he felt the other girl behind him, sliding a hand up the inside of his thigh, then taking him between her fingers, pressing her body, moulded, against his back.

Byrd decided they were obviously sisters. They also knew exactly what they were doing. He marvelled that two such young women were so deft and experienced in their craft.

The lipless kiss continued, the first girl occasionally drawing back to breathe into his open mouth, the other stroking him, then taking her hand away, then returning with both hands, well oiled with the same scented lotion which covered their bodies: massaging him, then finally curling her fingers hard around his shoulders and forcing him down on to his back.

The first girl withdrew her tongue and began to kiss his body softly: neck, chest, belly, down until she reached her goal; while the other girl slid her thighs around his shoulders, moving so that he could feel the soft conjunction of her legs hard against the back of his neck.

Eventually, the trio toppled into the now full bath, where

the girls washed him first, before taking him – he was certainly the seduced – in turns, until all three found satisfaction. They washed him again, pulled him from the water, dried him off and, after each had kissed him – the first on the lips, then, as a kind of farewell, elsewhere – left him, body-weak with pleasure.

Nobody had spoken throughout: the only sounds being that of their quiet, urgent noises, mingling with the slap and plash of water.

After that, the girls visited him again, on an average of once every two days.

This sensual stimulation – which had many variants – appeared to be rewarding in many ways. His sleep was sounder than ever, and he felt his body responding with a sense of vital awareness, aggressive, with superb control and a formidable ability to survive. There was a new clarity in his mind also – centred on recapturing the Flamingo.

Foo Tang, he recognised, was no fool. He was not only being fattened: his determination was being honed to a fighting edge. By the end of the second week in January, he was even smoking less. He planned constantly for the future. The attack on the café had to be fast; retribution would come as a bolt of lightning. Each evening he sat down with a sheet of paper and a pen, drawing diagrams of the Flamingo; working on his strategy.

A week before the due date, he asked Tang when he would meet the men who would help in his task. Tang did not tell him until the day before the actual assault. "While I am away, arranging the movement of my goods. The men will be brought here, and Lee Yung is to interpret anything you have to tell them. They will come to this place under cover of clearing the garden. We have left it so – untidy – for that purpose."

On the arranged day, the twenty men arrived, coming in pairs or singly and, in fact, working on the garden during the morning. Tang left early. They had arranged that the attack would take place at eleven in the evening, and Tang would have his goods – Byrd did not give a hint that he knew their exact nature – brought to the warehouse just after midnight. A watcher would be posted to let his drivers know if all had been successful.

Lee Yung issued each of the men with a stout club like a sawn-off baseball bat, that could be hidden easily beneath the men's clothing. Byrd then showed his drawings of the café, and gave the instructions. Fifteen of the men were to force their way in through the front of the café, separate the Japanese, drag them out, well beaten, and throw them into the street. The remaining five would go in with Byrd through the street side entrance, up to the living quarters, the private room and the office, to flush out any Black Dragon men who happened to be there; also to cut off the retreat of anyone trying to make his escape. Byrd hoped sincerely that the hard Mr. Toshiro Sessaku could be found in the office. He wanted to deal with him personally, and issued an order to the men that if the manager was found, he had to be left unharmed for Byrd's personal attention. When Lee Yung translated this, the men chuckled and nodded understandingly.

There was nothing more to do but wait until the following evening. The men were sent away with instructions to be at precise points along Nanking and Bubbling Well Roads at definite times, so they could converge on the café at eleven – the time when, according to Tang, Arina Verislovskaya now made her first appearance, with Herman at the piano.

By the evening, Byrd looked forward with positive pleasure to the action. Lee Yung seemed to soften slightly towards him, but watched wherever he went. That night, Byrd had wanted to make a telephone call to the British Consulate; but, no matter how he tried, he could not evade him.

In the end he reluctantly gave up, deciding to rely on luck, and great speed, the following night.

Monday, 18 January 1932 dawned dry and cold. Byrd woke with excitement already tickling his stomach. Nothing could be changed now. Within days, he knew, he would either be dead, in police custody, or a free man, back where he started. With the right kind of surprise, it was unlikely the first part of the plan would go wrong.

He expected no hitches; but he had not bargained on the Black Dragon Society.

He lay in bed late, and it was Lee Yung who brought him the news.

二 (2)

This time, Lee Yung even forgot his pidgin English.

"There has been much trouble," he began, half-way through the door. "I only just hear. It could be good for you – make things easier – but there is talk of curfew which would be bad."

Byrd asked him to repeat what he had heard.

The trouble had long been expected, for much enmity was now being openly shown between the Chinese and Japanese communities. There was even a boycott on Japanese goods in the shops of Shanghai. Now it had come to a head – today, the one day Byrd needed no violence in the streets, with all the police activity that implied. He needed the police, but not until after his take-over was complete.

As he listened, however, he calmed, for the incident had taken place to the north, just outside the settlement areas in Chapei – the heavily populated Chinese area bordering on the main International Settlement, and the Japanese Hong-kew district.

That morning, five Japanese monks – known members of the Black Dragon Society – had gone from Hongkew, carrying their musical instruments, and taken up a position outside a Chinese factory in Chapei.

There they had started a protest by sitting in front of the

gates and singing patriotic Japanese songs – mainly concerned with the way in which the glorious Imperial Japanese Army had wiped the verminous Chinese under their heels in Manchuria.

The Chinese workers took little notice, until the monks stopped singing and began to shout abusive and offensive remarks through the flimsy factory gates and walls.

This proved too much for Chinese self-control, and there had been a major riot. All five monks had been severely beaten long before the police could intervene. It was said that one was already dead. As always in Shanghai there was much rumour and speculation. What was certain was that the Black Dragon Society would not let matters end with the riot, especially if one of the monks was dead. General reprisals could be expected, and Byrd had no doubt that the Municipal Police Force would be out on the streets in larger numbers than usual – even if a curfew were not after all called.

The one thing Byrd wished to avoid was a clash with the police – or the arrival of 'Pearly' Fisher – until he had secured the café, and made certain his own steps had been taken to consolidate his situation.

Lee Yung brought reports during the day – mainly rumours of clashes between individuals, or relatively small groups of Chinese and Japanese. No curfew orders had been issued; but there were many police about.

At a little before nine that evening, Lee Yung came with a message from Foo Tang. A decoy had been arranged – a fight, to be staged on the Bund, at the bottom of Nanking Road, just before eleven. That should give Byrd his chance. In some ways the incident in Chapei was what he needed. Nobody was going to think it too odd that the café, recently taken under Japanese management, should be the centre of a minor fracas. And by the time anybody noticed that the fracas was in fact *not* minor, he would be in control.

A car had been arranged for Byrd, due to leave at just after ten thirty, so that he could arrive at the rendezvous exactly on time. At nine thirty he changed: evening trousers, white silk shirt and jacket, evening tie – his uniform for nights at the Flamingo. He eyed himself in the mirror: Foo Tang's tailor had served him well.

He had smoked heavily during the day as the tension mounted, and now lit yet another cigarette as he checked the Mauser and spare ammunition. The car arrived on the stroke of ten thirty, the driver nodding, acknowledging that he knew what to do and where to go. To Byrd's surprise, Lee Yung joined him in the back of the car. "I keep well out of the way," the Chinese smiled. "I come to watch."

The driver was obviously well rehearsed, using side streets, avoiding the Bund completely. At one minute to eleven, the motor purred down Bubbling Well Road. There were few police about and Byrd, craning forward, could clearly see activity going on at the far end of Nanking Road, on the Bund itself – Tang's arranged fight.

They pulled up just short of the Flamingo's entrance, and as Byrd stepped from the car, so his twenty assistants materialised from doorways, or hurried across the road. Lee Yung disappeared into the shadows. Byrd's five picked men crowded near him, while he nodded to the others, using what little Chinese he knew to order them in. The clubs came from their hiding places, and, as he led his party to the street door, Byrd heard the fifteen raiders going in through the front – the crash of glass, and yells which sounded like an ancient battle cry.

Putting his shoulder to the street door, Byrd found it locked tight, so motioned to his party to stand aside while he put two shots into the lock from the Mauser, cursing as he did so at the loss of surprise.

The lock blew out in splinters of wood and metal; he kicked the door open and began the dash up the stairs, finding to his amazement that he was joining in the war cries of the men behind him. Somewhere from above he could hear Arina still trying to sing, to Herman's ever-louder accompaniment.

At the top of the stairs he motioned two of the men to take the private quarters, and one to stay at the landing to cut off any stragglers. The other two he directed to the private room, remembering the meeting there between Tang, Vincent and Valentine Maes; and the disturbed night of love for Boris and Polly Sing. Then he himself lifted a leg and smashed in the door of his office.

A stocky, leather-faced Japanese, dressed in evening clothes, was reaching for the desk, opening a drawer.

"Mr. Sessaku, I presume," Byrd said quickly.

The Japanese was so off guard that he even answered with a half bow, still pulling at the drawer which, Byrd concluded, must contain a gun.

He did not wait to find out. The Mauser came back in his hand and swung on to one side of Sessaku's head. As the Japanese reeled, so Byrd brought his hand back and hit him hard, giving him a matching blow on the other side of his head.

Sessaku staggered again, but still did not go down. The drawer was open now, and he was reaching within it. Byrd brought his gun arm back and gave him the butt of the pistol straight in the face.

This time, Sessaku's body thumped against the desk and he fell forward on to the ground, straight, like a wooden plank going down. One of the Chinese, who had now followed Byrd into the room, stepped forward and delivered a swift shattering kick to the prone man's head. Then he smiled, and indicated that the room across the passage was empty.

It was only then that Byrd was aware of the noise – the sound of shrieks and crashes, splintering woodwork and heavy thuds. He motioned the two Chinese to watch the stairs leading down to the café itself, and, as soon as they were out of the room, made a dive for the external telephone.

The operator seemed to take an age to answer. In fact it was only a few seconds, but in that time, Byrd was able to squint down through his two-way mirror and view the carnage taking place below him.

The main assault party appeared to have little respect for any of the fittings of the place; already there were broken chairs and tables dominating the scene. Smashed dishes and plates, together with food, littered the floor.

The few people who had been dining or listening to Arina either cringed in corners, against the walls, or had succumbed to panic, rushing and jamming the main entrance in an attempt to get out. He thought it was lucky there were not many customers that night – the combined result of it being Monday, and the general instability in the city.

Herman crouched, close to Arina, behind the piano; and the girls huddled, faces frozen in fear, hunched together at the far end of the bar, upon which Max stood, in his element. The little Mexican had his coat off and brandished a broken bottle, shouting wildly and directing Tang's hoods towards any of the Japanese trying to make good their escape.

A pair of the attacking Chinese force had already stationed themselves in Casimir's territory, occasionally catching beaten, or unconscious, Japanese, who they continued to club before dragging them towards the street doors and booting them outside.

The centre of the room was one great seething mêlée: the Chinese, with their clubs flailing, cornering every, and any, Japanese they could spot.

But they had not had it all their own way. At least one of the attacking force lay by the steps leading down to the main room; another nursed a head, dripping with blood, bent double and vomiting, nearby. Casimir leaned over the one who had fallen near the steps, the little roly-poly man turning his anxious face constantly towards the main group struggling in the centre of the room.

Chairs and tables were still flying, and one Japanese waiter was using a chair to defend himself – to no avail, for, as he was about to smash it towards his attacker, another of Tang's men was behind him, delivering a series of shuddering blows to the head, so that the waiter fell, was caught, and slung out of the throng towards one of the assault party standing by the steps.

As he turned away, Byrd smiled, for three Japanese had come catapulting through the kitchen swing doors, closely followed by Descales, the chef, armed with a huge iron frying pan and uttering loud gallic war cries. Byrd winced as he saw the pan make contact with one of the Japanese heads, causing the man to drop to his knees, throwing his hands over his head in a vain attempt to ward off the next, inevitable, blow from the enraged Descales. Cat had been right when she reported to Harry that his staff at the Flamingo were not happy with the new management.

Out of the corner of his eye, Byrd also thought he glimpsed a fleeting figure moving, sinister, behind the pillars near Casimir's entrance hall. Lee Yung.

Then the operator answered.

Byrd asked for the British Consulate. It took them only a few seconds to get Waldo Bingham to the telephone. He wasted a small amount of time explaining, jovially that he was having a nightcap with the Consul; but he knew exactly what to do when Byrd cut in on him and gave him quick instructions. "Be there in a jiff," was all Bingham said, hanging up instantly.

Below, the fighting was furious, but it was obvious that the attacking force, in spite of a number of injured, had not only flushed out all the Japanese, but also neatly disposed of most of them. A couple of isolated man-to-man fights were still in progress, but the Black Dragon people had been trounced and were, to all intents and purposes, finished. It flashed through Byrd's mind that it might not be long before Mr. Takahome and Mr. Hitchimata – from their palatial hideouts in the smarter section of Hongkew – would organise a return match; but, with anti-Japanese feeling so strong in the rest of the city, that was unlikely during this night.

It was nearly all over. Again, he was just turning away when he froze, appalled at what he saw at the other end of the room.

Casimir lay spreadeagled, on the steps down which he had so often led customers. His shirt front was drenched with blood, face grey in the unmistakable pallor of death; and Byrd once more caught sight of Lee Yung lurking at the head of the stairs. So far, it was the only real horror of the night, but a shock so gross that Byrd could have wept. Casimir, for all his faults, had been very dear to him.

Why? Had Tang instructed Lee Yung to watch, and take the opportunity to dispose of as many of the regular Flamingo staff as possible during the confusion? It was the only answer that made sense. After all, Byrd was acutely aware of the fact that Foo Tang had no intention of allowing him to continue running the Flamingo. His death sentence had already been passed. Hadn't he heard it from the outside of Tang's own window? This was to be Byrd's final task for the old man.

Max hurried over to the stricken Casimir, while Byrd's old stalwart Chinese staff had already emerged, and were starting the business of tidying up the debris. The fighting was over. Most of the assault force had discreetly disappeared; only one or two lingered – apart from those who had been injured.

Depressed and sickened though he was at not having been down there to help Casimir, Byrd saw the need to have his moment of symbolic glory. There was no question of arrogance, this was a necessary part of consolidation. There had to be a drawing together of his personal forces. He went to the door, beckoning in one of the smiling Chinese thugs, telling him, mainly by signs, that he was to watch over the prostrate Mr. Sessaku; leaving the man in no doubt as to what he should do if Byrd's Black Dragon locum recovered consciousness.

In the passage, he jerked his thumb at the other Chinese, indicating that he was to tell Tang's other watchers that they had conquered and taken over. He then brushed himself off, smoothed back his hair and took out another cigarette, ready to light it on his leisurely way down the curving staircase.

Max was the first to see him. The emotional little Mexican was weeping over Casimir's body, but the sight of Byrd cheered him so that he managed a tearful shout of welcome. Then Herman, who had been tidying up by the piano, spotted him and immediately sat down at the keyboard –

Birds do it,
Bees do it,
Even educated fleas do it. . .

The girls rushed from their huddle, crowding around the bottom of the staircase, Jeannie Chin throwing herself forward from the others, wrapping her arms around his neck; clinging tightly, sobbing, "Oh Harry . . . Casimir. . . They killed Casim. . . Harry, you're back . . . but Casimir. . ."

"I know," he said, gently. Just then the fact that he knew who had done the killing seemed unimportant.

Max ran across, his voice still uncertain, strange in this tough little man – "So good to see you back, boss . . . We thought. . . But Casimir. . ."

"Yes. Knifed?"

Max nodded. "Dead."

"See to him, Max. I'm back in charge now." He was pleased at the amount of authority in his voice. "You organise the girls. For the time being you'll have to put one of the senior boys – Hang, if he's really okay, perhaps – in Casimir's job. We'll see about a full-time man later; get the place tidied up, and all those roughs out. I want us back in business as usual."

Descales – who had been at the far end of the room, helping to move Casimir's body, suddenly turned, shouting over his shoulder – "*Les flics*. Monsieur 'Arry. The police are 'ere."

Byrd gave three abrupt orders. The girls faded, moving back towards the bar. Arina, drying her eyes, almost ran to the piano, as Herman went into her number, and Byrd took the curving stairs, two at a time, followed by Max.

The Chinese hood still stood over the motionless form of Mr. Toshiro Sessaku. Byrd gave him the quick get-out sign, and spoke rapidly to Max, who crouched low, behind the desk, out of sight. He was to be Byrd's insurance, a witness in case things got rough. Byrd chain-lit another cigarette, leaning back, his buttocks against the desk just as Inspector 'Pearly' Fisher came in, gun in hand.

Fisher's jaw dropped as he saw Byrd. Then, recovering himself quickly, he tilted his head sarcastically. "Well, well, Harry Byrd. Got you bang to rights, as they say back home. Been waiting for you."

"Thought you'd put me down as dead." Byrd sucked smoke in through his teeth and grinned, very sure of himself.

"File's not closed, Byrd. Can't tell you how glad I am that you dropped in. You're under arrest. Murder of one Thomas James Geddes – but, then, you know all about that, don't you?"

"I know nothing about Geddes' death, Pearly, and I want to do a bit of horse trading."

"No deals, Byrd. You are, as the song says, my heart's delight."

"Hear me out."

"You're booked. It breaks my heart to do this, but I have to tell you that you need not say anything, but that anything you say will be taken down and –"

"Hear me out," Byrd shouted. "I had nothing to do with Geddes' death. That's straight and, if you give me a couple of days, a week at the most, I'll prove it."

"You're joking, of course."

"No. You'll get the biggest pinch of your rotten career if you go along with me. I'll give it to you now, and you'd better take it, sweetheart."

"What could you possibly give me? I've told you; you're booked."

Byrd took a deep breath. "Within the hour, your old friend Mr. Foo Tang – who you have, yourself, told me you wanted badly – will be loading five hundred thousand pounds, weight, of raw opium into the warehouse behind the kitchens of this café. Sometime during the next few days – and you only have to watch it closely – that raw opium will be transferred onto a ship called the *Bel Canto*, sailing under Paraguayan flag, where it'll be exchanged for arms and ammunition. You'll cop the lot; and then, if I can't clear myself, I'll surrender to you."

Fisher's mouth opened, not, as Byrd hoped, in amazement, but in a guffaw of laughter – "Yes, Harry Byrd. Yes, I'm sure you will. I never said it, but I'd be in a right mess if I stuck around for all that to happen. Valentine Maes, my good old buddy, might pop a rivet or two. He's paid me rather a handsome sum to make certain the opium goes aboard the *Bel Canto* with no problems. But, I've just told you, I never said that. Let's go."

三 (3)

Byrd had thought everything was taken into account – even Fisher's personal animosity and resolve to get him on the murder charge. He had not reckoned on the possibility of Fisher's venality leading to an alliance with Valentine Maes.

The call to Waldo Bingham had simply been to provide some sort of buffer with authority. It seemed, now, to have been a waste of time.

"Come on, then, Byrd." Fisher's hand was very steady, the revolver held near to his body. "We haven't got all night – I haven't anyway – and I'm taking you in."

In his mind, Byrd had a picture of a craps table, the dice hitting the green wall and the caller shouting "Snake Eyes." He seemed to have reached the end of the line. Certainly he had Max as a witness, but the Mexican's evidence would take time to organise and one thing he did not have was time. Six hours was the most he thought he would survive in jail before the Black Dragon got to him.

"Move." Fisher started forward.

Then the door behind him swung open. "Nobody's going anywhere for a moment."

Waldo Bingham was fully restored to his impressive girth, and the Enfield Service revolver (obviously a replacement) looked small in his massive fist. He smiled at Byrd, jerking his head back at the pair of Sikh constables behind him. "Had the sense to come up the back stairs. Softly, softly, and all that. And just in time, I gather."

Fisher backed off towards the desk. "Who the hell –"

"Bingham's the name. And I'm afraid you've cooked your goose, Inspector. The Commissioner's going to be very interested when we tell him about your arrangement with Mr. Maes."

Fisher, face bloated and scarlet with rage, pushed his own service revolver out towards Bingham's paunchy gut. "I don't know what you're talking about. What arrangement? You've no proof."

"Only your own words, Inspector." Bingham, unperturbed, did not move. "That door's quite thin you know. I might as well have been in the room. . . Come on, Fisher, let's not have any gunplay here. You're in enough trouble without that."

"You're wrong there, Bingham." The gun moved a fraction in the inspector's hand. "This is Shanghai. You come here, impeding a lawful arrest – I can shoot you and your two chums, and –"

"Like hell you can." Max, who now clutched Byrd's emergency bottle of Teachers from the drawer of the desk, sprang out like a jack-in-the-box, bringing the bottle down on Fisher's weapon with enough force both to knock the revolver flying, and shatter the bottle. Whisky spilled over the policeman's hand like blood, dripping to the carpet.

Max shrugged, an apologetic look at Byrd. "Sorry, boss. A waste of the good stuff, I think."

Byrd smiled at the familiar 'I theenk'.

The two constables moved into the room from behind Bingham as Fisher mouthed obscenities, laced with protests – they'd never get him on any charge. Nobody would believe verbal evidence. Bingham cut him short.

"Maybe not. No, I don't think it'll come to an enquiry, or evidence being brought, Inspector Fisher. But *we* all know, don't we? You'll probably simply get a nice free passage back to England. Hate to pull rank," he flashed a small

233

identity card close up to Fisher's face. "*Colonel* Bingham. His Majesty's Foreign Service."

"You're bloody Secret Service. I know you." The hatred came from Fisher in almost tangible waves. Bingham merely gave an enormous shrug.

By now, Max was bending over Mr. Toshiro Sessaku. "This one still alive. Should be moved, I think."

"Quite right," Bingham nodded, then turned to the pair of constables, speaking to them in their native tongue before addressing Fisher, who was leaning against the desk, clutching his hand which had been cut by the bottle. Blood now dripped to the carpet, mingled with the whisky. He looked dangerous, like a wounded animal, but Bingham spoke to him calmly, saying that he was going to be taken away quietly. The constables were armed and had orders to shoot if necessary. "There's a car by the back entrance, and you'll go as if you're still in charge of things. It's in your own best interest. You hardly want prying eyes reporting that you've been dragged off in chains – I presume there are prying eyes?" He turned to Byrd, who nodded silently. "Right. Another police officer should have taken command downstairs by now. He'll deal with this." He stabbed lightly with his toe at Mr. Sessaku, who moved his head and moaned.

Fisher, still mouthing wild threats and accusations, left with the two constables.

Byrd relaxed. "Thanks for coming so quickly." He lit another cigarette. "Lucky you got to the door in time. You knew about Fisher's liaison with Maes?"

"No. That was a bonus," Bingham grinned amiably. "Had some lesser ammunition I could have used, though. That's why I picked up the constables and got the Consulate people to send another officer. I haven't remained entirely idle."

"Look as if you've eaten well."

"Goes without saying, my dear fellow. No, let me tell you: the authorities – as we all know – tolerate a small amount of corruption, but they've been getting a little tired of Fisher. There've been a lot of complaints: been giving corruption a really bad name; so, when I got your message I took precautions. Apparently Fisher's been haunting the Flamingo ever since you disappeared and the Black Dragon boys took over. On the cards that he'd be first at the scene. His superiors suspected he was taking cumshaw from the Japanese. As I said, the Maes business is a bonus. Got to keep it quiet, though. Scandals like that do the Administration no good at all. Besides, those with an eye to justice would like to see the despicable Maes brothers and your friend Tang nabbed in the act."

Max had been looking down through the two-way mirror at the café below, clearly anxious to get back to his half-ruined bar. Byrd put a hand on his shoulder. "Thanks for what you've done, Max. You didn't hear any of that, okay?"

"Any of what?" Max shrugged in genuine puzzlement and left the room, muttering something about breakages, and getting the café back to normal.

"Fine," Bingham tucked away his revolver, as another pair of constables came in to remove the moaning Sessaku. He waited until they had carried the Japanese from the room before continuing. "Best thing you can do, Byrd, is to carry on here as if nothing had happened. I'll talk to the right people, and they'll be keeping a discreet eye on things."

Byrd said he sincerely hoped they would, adding that there seemed to be enough people watching the place as it was. He then went on to give Bingham an outline of what he had heard at Tang's window. "For some reason of his own – I suspect greed and needing a free hand with the Flamingo – Tang wants me buried. Fisher's not going to get me now; so it'll be the Maes boys, the Black Dragon, or Tang. Even with Fisher removed, the odds are still against me."

Bingham grunted. He thought the Black Dragon Society would probably have its hands full for the moment – "Though they do have this nasty tendency to seek retribution with speed. But you realise there's going to be one hell of a mess here in Shanghai for the next few days – Nip versus the Chinaman. Nothing's going to stop that. So obviously for the moment your main threat comes from the Maes brothers, and your Mr. Tang. Take great care." He rubbed a forefinger thoughtfully along the side of his nose. "The ship? You did say it was the *Bel Canto* when we talked at the Cathay? Seems a lifetime ago."

Byrd confirmed the ship's name, asking if there was any news of it.

"Been delayed. Lot of Japanese sea traffic around. Doubt if the *Bel Canto*'s going to make Shanghai for a week or so; and God knows what the situation's going to be by then. Things look bad, so all you can do is go about the business of keeping this place running; getting it on its feet again. And watch out for Tang and the Americanos."

"And Geddes?"

"The murder charge? Still being followed up. No way to hide it, Byrd, you're still a prime suspect. Wouldn't be surprised if you had detectives on your doorstep in a day or so – but they're going to be busy as well. May take a while to get round to you. Play for time."

Lastly, Byrd asked about Cat.

"Worried about you. Sends her love and all that kind of thing. You'll see her again before long. I'll fix that."

Byrd was about to say that he did not know if he really wanted to see her just yet, but stopped himself in time. Of course he wanted to see her: the confusion over their reunion, and his own deep suspicions of her motives, might play tricks with his mind, but his folly was the folly of most men, as far as women were concerned. He let it go.

"Tell her I'm looking forward to seeing her." He smiled. "And thanks, Waldo. Thanks for everything."

Bingham gave an embarrassed growl. "Don't thank me until we're completely in the clear. If the Japanese are intent on making trouble in Shanghai, it'll eventually lead to a full-scale invasion. You might have to take to the boats again, Byrd. Don't forget, there's still a job with my people in London." He got to the door, then suddenly turned, snapping unexpectedly, "If you didn't kill the Geddes fella, then who the hell did?"

Byrd reached for his cigarettes. "That worries me as well, Waldo. Worries me to blazes."

If Foo Tang was surprised to see Harry Byrd still at liberty he did not show it. But then, possibly Fisher's little arrangement had been with Valentine Maes alone. Tang got into the café at around one in the morning. Byrd had joined the others after Bingham left, and they were all working flat out in the Flamingo's main rooms, clearing the debris and starting to refurbish as quickly as possible.

Even with the continuing troubles in the streets, Koo and Hang – who had long returned from hospital after his brush with death in the exploding Delage – were despatched to haul carpenters and decorators out of their homes, and beds, so that the café would at least take on an air of normality by the next day.

Byrd was aware that Tang's trucks had arrived, and the storing of the opium was going on behind the walls of the gaming room: the noises filtered through from the storehouse, in spite of the activity in the café. He had posted guards at all the entrances and himself kept a watchful eye out for intruders.

The mood in the Flamingo was bubbling with the tremendous sense of relief everyone felt now that the Black Dragon interregnum was over. The men, even the waiters and kitchen staff, nodded and smiled at Byrd, as if to reassure themselves that he was back in command. The girls paid special attention to him; putting their arms around him, grasping his hand, and kissing his cheek at the slightest opportunity. This, as ever, enraged Jeannie Chin, who seemed intent on staying close to Byrd, even to the detriment of the work. She whispered endearments, pushed her soft body against his; seductively described what she would do for him when they finally got to bed.

"I miss you a lot, Harry. Need you much. Cried for you often."

"What about the Japanese gentlemen: Mr. Takahome and Mr. Hitchimata?"

She made a sound of disgust. "Pigs. Arina they forced; and Polly Sing. I told them get fucked."

"And did they?"

Tang himself arrived at that moment – Koo bringing the news that the Chinese was up topside, in the office. Byrd checked the gun in his back pocket and went up to him, taking Koo by way of insurance.

"Ahh, so your birthright is now returned to you." Tang was accompanied by Lee Yung, who stayed outside the office door. Koo also remained in the passage: the two men glaring at one another. Byrd remembered the murdered Casimir, and bided his time.

"Went as smooth as clockwork. The men you provided did well."

Tang inclined his head: a gesture of acknowledgment and thanks. "I have done well also. The goods are safely in your storehouse, and my men are watching everywhere. I shall hope to move these goods as soon as word reaches me from the Americans."

"As long as they don't arrive here in person."

"Have no fears. I take special precautions. If they come near, you will be warned in good time." Then, as though an afterthought, he asked if there had been any trouble with the police. It was too casual and studied for Byrd's peace of mind.

The police had been, he told Tang; but they seemed to approve of the Japanese rout.

"The most despised Inspector Fisher was here. My men saw him: what of you?" The question clinched it as far as Byrd was concerned. However untroubled he might appear, Tang believed that Byrd had been perfectly set up for Fisher, and should now be at the Shanghai Municipal Police Headquarters, down on Hankow Road, charged with the murder of Tom Geddes.

"I kept out of the way." He played it as lightly as possible. "Saw none of the police; it seemed better that way."

"You were wise. What of your fat friend – the Bingham man? He paid you a short visit."

"Naturally. He heard there was trouble here. They get most information quickly at the Consulate." He paused for effect. "We became comrades in arms during the Manchurian business. It was reasonable that he should come, but I sent him away."

"Yes," Tang appeared lost in thought for a time. "To be safe, I should prepare yourself for a visit from the police. Informants tell me that Fisher is anxious to talk with you about the shooting which happened here: anxious to charge you with the murder."

Byrd stayed relaxed, making a casual gesture and saying that Fisher was at liberty to ask as many questions as he pleased. "I had nothing to do with that shooting, Tang; you had better be clear about that; and Fisher must know it also." In the back of his mind, a voice murmured insistently, telling him to trust nobody. It repeated *nobody* – so clearly that he thought he could be hallucinating.

Tang's face assumed the passive inscrutability for which his race is famous. "Take care of yourself, Harry Byrd, and also I shall take care of you." It may have been the knowledge gained at Tang's window, but to Byrd the words seemed to carry a threat.

"You'll warn me when you wish to move your goods?" He switched the subject.

"Of course. It may be at short notice, but you will know in advance." Once more he told Byrd to take especial care, adding that the troubles in the north of the city could easily spread. "Black Dragon are behind much of these disturbances, so they are very busy people at this time. However, you can never tell with them: it is still possible that they will quickly come again, in the night, to steal our investment. If that should happen, my men will move to help you." He was tired, he said. He was an old man, and today had been long and hard: now he must return to Jessfield Park and rest.

Byrd stood in the passageway, watching Tang depart, with the muscular Lee Yung at his heels. Lee Yung had returned to his familiar role, looking at Byrd with the hunger of a predatory animal. The voice in Byrd's head once more told him to trust nobody, and he fingered the butt of the Mauser automatic in his hip pocket. Who knew what had gone on, here in the Flamingo, while the Japanese were in control? Even his most loyal staff could have been manipulated: by fear, blackmail, even the promise of great rewards. He also silently vowed that it would only be a matter of time before Casimir's death would be traded for Lee Yung's, and, almost certainly, Tang's also.

It was five in the morning by the time they decided to call it a night. The craftsmen who had been brought in would carry on with the work, and Max, with some of the boys, elected to stay up and see the job through.

As the night had worn on, Jeannie's constant importuning gradually drove Byrd wild with need for her: his mind and body warming to the memory of how expert Jeannie could be as a seductress. At first, thinking of Cat, he resisted her. But Jeannie was so obviously delighted at the mutual chemistry they produced, that Byrd's guilt quickly disappeared and the old magic took over.

Jeannie was a sorceress of the erotic. Once they were in bed her fingers, moving like those of a virtuoso instrumentalist, plucked out a passionate melody on his body, while her every move – from the subtle turns and twists of her own frame, to the deft snaking and lapping of her tongue – combined to produce a pleasure only dimly recalled from their past. The memory of pain does not stay clear in the mind. Byrd realised the same applied to ecstasy such as this.

She took advantage of his desire, whispering teasing instructions close to his ear – "There, Harry; no, not there. There. Come, feel this; and this. Oh Harry, it's so good to have you with me again. See how ready I am for you. . . No, not yet. This; this first. Now, feel this . . . feel. . . No . . . wait . . . see how ready. . . Smell. . . Touch. . . Now, now, now. . ." and on, until he entered her and reality contracted, becoming simply the two of them, lost to everything but the experience of now; then diminishing even more, as all senses became centred upon their conjoined loins, upon all that was vital, tender, enchanting.

She was as exuberant as ever, and, in the early hours of

that morning, it was as though Cat had never returned: their love-making stretching out, seemingly to the edge of time and space. Even the skill of the girls at Tang's mansion was as nothing to this.

When they were finally exhausted, with Byrd dropping into the preliminary shallows of sleep, she whispered again that she loved him, making him promise as he had promised a thousand times before – lying as ever – never to leave her.

"Harry? The horrible Inspector Fisher? Did he talk about the night we found you with the body in the office?"

He struggled up through the first cobwebs of sleep, the small voice still active with its silent warnings in his head. "He mentioned it, Jeannie. Sleep now: yes?"

"He ask many questions while you were away. He said you were a murderer."

"Yes, but he knows – and you know – that I'm not. Sleep, uhu?"

"I did not see him leave tonight."

"He went by the street door. Probably be back in a day or two. He was called away to the troubles in the north. Sleep, Jeannie."

She snuggled close, and they plunged together into the velvet darkness.

Hang wakened them, early – only noon. He brought coffee. Max wished to speak with the boss, he said; the situation of the city was getting worse. Jeannie grumbled, as she always did on waking – particularly before late afternoon – but Byrd's senses were oddly alert: his nerves had been tried to new limits in past months, and he was more than usually aware of the dangers: both those personally besetting him, and the wider perils facing Shanghai and its international communities.

Max waited in the main living room. As Bingham had predicted, the situation was deteriorating by the hour. First, the Black Dragon membership had refused to rest over the Chinese reaction to the monks' protest, and there had been a savage reprisal. The factory, where it had started in Chapei, had been attacked and burned down: it was thought at the instigation of Black Dragon leaders.

In the street-fighting around the factory, at least one member of the Shanghai Municipal Police Force had lost his life. Many people were injured.

As Max was breaking this news, Hang came through again to say that Mr. Bingham had telephoned: would Mr. Harry like to take the call in his office.

Waldo sounded far from his usual buoyant self. "Real trouble, Harry. The Consul has just been asked to attend an emergency meeting of the Shanghai Municipal Council," (the true governing body of Shanghai, with an elected membership including members of all racial groups living inside the city and the Settlements). "The Japanese members refuse to attend. They've had their own meeting – over a thousand of them – and they've sent an urgent request to their government, to take drastic action against what they call the severe anti-Japanese measures in Shanghai. The Consul also says that the Imperial Japanese Government has delivered an ultimatum to the Chinese Government in Nanking."

"Ships?" Byrd asked, meaning, in particular, the *Bel Canto*.

Bingham replied that, if he meant the Americans, he thought it would develop into a race. "The Jap navy's on the move. I reckon they'll be here in a matter of days. Maybe even before your friend. My advice is to pack a suitcase."

"Hold on," Byrd told him. If there was any chance of Shanghai's survival, and of getting the Maes brothers and Tang out of the way once and for all, he had no option but to stay.

Cat wanted a word with him, but Byrd was in no mood to speak with her. In any case it would have been embarrassing, for Jeannie had now walked into the office, sleek in a silk wrap-around, and every movement she made reflecting the pleasures they had shared a few hours before.

He told Bingham it was difficult: he would call back later.

"Careful, Harry. We're still watching you, but so are others. The Flamingo seems to have become a tourist attraction for some very odd folk." Bingham closed the line without even saying goodbye.

No curfew was announced, but later in the day a warning was circulated saying that people within the various Settlements should stay where they were. Areas in the north of the city could be entered only in emergency as they were dangerous.

The police obviously had their hands full, for nobody called to question Byrd about the Geddes' shooting. Tang did not telephone, but that night the Flamingo was crowded. Byrd recalled stories of dancing, as the *Titanic* went down, and the bands playing. Many local Europeans were talking of leaving, and the general atmosphere was one of live-for-today – tomorrow would wait. Many people got drunk; Arina was at her best; and the girls did a roaring after-hours trade with the young taipan bachelors. In the gaming room they turned over the largest profit Byrd had known since he opened the café. He himself now went nowhere without Koo as his personal bodyguard.

It was the same on the next night: even though, during the day, the tension had mounted in the streets. You could feel it, like an electric charge, even safe within the walls of Byrd's office. At odd moments he still experienced glimpses of the forgotten memory from just before finding Geddes' body: not quite grasping the elusive factor, though becoming more and more convinced it had something to do with Cat. Had she, perhaps, followed Geddes to the Flamingo with the sole intention of settling matters with him? Had Geddes already been lying dead in his office when he bumped into Cat in the Cathay's lobby – before she poured out the story of the diamonds to him? Had it been Cat who followed him back to the Flamingo and sapped him, setting him up as the patsy?

During the evening, he asked Max what he could remember of that day. Had there been much police activity afterwards? Any strange incidents? For instance, had they found a weapon?

"Sure, boss, you must've seen it. Lying on the floor by your desk. They found a .25 Pieper auto, like yours. Fisher said it *was* yours, but I knew different. Made a statement. Looked like a plant to me, I think."

Quite a number of people knew the kind of weapon he used to carry. It would not have been hard for Cat to find out. But then there was the timing. She would have to get professional advice very quickly, and be as ruthless as Satan. Could he believe that of her now? The ruthlessness of leaving him for her career was one thing: setting him up on a murder charge, and disposing of her lover to do it, was a different can of worms. Apart from anything else, what motive could she have? There was still something, though: tucked away, hidden, refusing to surface.

Still no word from Tang about moving the contents of the store room.

Occasional calls from Bingham at the Consulate kept Byrd informed of the worsening crisis – "London and Washington have backed off," the Secret Service man said over the weekend. "I'm expecting to be recalled any day, and I shall take Miss Morrow with me. Got your case packed?"

Byrd said he did not need a case. If it came to the push, he would leave as he was.

Business had begun to drop off. After the initial spree, people were coming to their senses. Statements were issued, saying that the Japanese Government pledged there would be no action against the International Settlement areas; but they demanded apologies from the Chinese, together with new rights in territories to the north of the city.

By midweek, Bingham was certain of his facts. The *Bel Canto* was about a day ahead of a Japanese fleet. One cruiser and twelve destroyers were steaming in from Sasebo, the third naval station of the Japanese Empire. Already there had been some landings of Japanese bluejackets up the coast.

A State of Emergency was declared on the Thursday. Still no word from Tang. The café was empty that night, and even the waiters were drinking. Herman sat at the piano playing nostalgic German songs, as though suddenly homesick for his fatherland; and Byrd was depressed to discover that both Descales and Herman had suitcases stashed away around the premises. It was little comfort to know that these men had at one time or another been through the experience of leaving cities, and even countries, at a moment's notice.

Only Max remained calm, and, like Byrd, had no suitcase packed. "So, if they come, they come. They'll want cafés, and girls, and drinks."

"They'll also want my skin, pegged out to dry," Byrd answered.

"Oh, I think you sweet-talk them out of that, boss. You were always a good talker."

"And a good lover." Jeannie Chin came up to them at that moment, a glass in her hand, like everyone else. "No business tonight, Harry. Let's go and have fun. We've got a lot of time to make up."

It was the earliest they had been to bed since his return. Just after midnight. They were making love at the moment the gun-fire rumbled out from the north.

"They're here," Byrd did not pause as he spoke.

"So am I." Not stopping either.

Byrd had always suspected Jeannie could sleep through anything. Tonight she proved it. After curling into a ball, when the loving was through, she did not stir, even though the sounds of fighting became worse. Byrd lay on his back, smoking, until dawn came up. When it was light enough, he decided to get up and see if there was anything to view from the windows. As he gently pushed the bedclothes back, two things happened almost simultaneously. First, he heard a distinct, distant creak in the passage outside the main door to the apartment – they had left the bedroom door open, and he could see straight through the living room to the far door.

He reached for the Mauser, and, as he did so, the faint muskiness of Jeannie Chin's body drifted to his nostrils, as it had done a hundred times before. But this time, combined with the distant creak, it was different: like a piece of jigsaw the whole elusive memory clicked into place. He was standing looking at Geddes' body as it toppled from the chair to fall into that odd shape on the floor. Then, just before the lights fused in his head, he had smelled that same, sexy, musky, erotic scent of Jeannie Chin. She had been in his office when the blow fell. He turned, still sitting on the bed, the Mauser in his hand, staring down at the Chinese girl's face, innocent in sleep, his mouth silently framing the query 'Why?'

Then he heard further movement, and launched himself from the bed, striding into the main room, grabbing his bathrobe as he went. A key was turning in the locked door. He realised, too late, that he had forgotten to fix the retaining chain. A second later the door swung back to reveal Lee Yung.

"Stay where you are, Yung." The Mauser came up ready.

"Not again, Harry Byrd. It is becoming boring." Tang, his teeth bared in anger, making the skull face even more hideous, pushed past Yung. "You can hear, there is fighting in the north; coming near the city. This is no time for playing games."

Byrd still kept the pistol up as Lee Yung closed the door.

"The fighting," Tang continued, "is around Chapei, where the trouble started; and, as you know, the Chapei area is bordered by the Settlement boundaries and Hong-kew. It is inland, but there are troop movements along the coast. I have just received word that the Americans will be ready to take delivery of my goods tonight. Unfortunately it will not be possible for them to bring their ship down river as far as the harbour. There is Japanese naval activity in the mouth of the Yangtze, and up the Whangpo – down past Woosung. My goods will have to go by truck up the coast, at great risk, and be taken off from quite near to where the fighting is going on. There is no other way."

Byrd could hardly concentrate on Tang, his mind still in a state of confusion over Jeannie Chin, and the mystery of her presence before he had been set up with Geddes' body.

Lamely, he said, "Then you'd best make your arrangements."

"It is what I have come to do. My trucks will be arriving in an hour or so. It will take much time to load them, and we must keep a careful watch. Also we must leave as soon as darkness falls. You, Harry Byrd, will be coming with us. I need somebody nearby whom I can trust.''

"You said I wouldn't get mixed up with the Americans." He would not go. He too needed someone, somewhere, whom he could trust.

"By the time we get there, it will be dark. There will be confusion, for the fighting will distract everyone even at a distance. I see no chance of you being recognised." He paused, his eyes gliding to a point behind Byrd's shoulder. "Ah, my dear Jeannie Chin. You look as lovely as ever, if a little tired."

Byrd glanced back. Jeannie, bleary and pulling her wrap around her, stumbled from the bedroom.

"Good to see you also, Mr. Tang. Welcome to Harry Byrd's home." She also spoke in English.

For a second, Byrd was outside the French windows, in the dark, at the back of Tang's house.

He felt around for his cigarettes with his left hand, still pointing the gun. "Never heard you two talk before," forcing an easy casual manner. "You don't speak in Chinese? Could that be out of deference to me?"

Tang gave a throaty sound that was meant to be a laugh. "I wish I could say so, but it is a difficulty of mine. Talking with Jeannie Chin can be slow and complicated. I have problems with her dialect. We always converse in English. . ." He stopped, sensing the impact on Byrd in what he had said. Byrd could almost see his mind working out the possibility that he had overheard them speaking when he should not have. "Ahhh." The long, drawn-out sound of full comprehension; then an almost imperceptible movement of his head.

Byrd hardly saw Lee Yung move, he was so quick: just a blur. Then the stabbing pain as the Mauser was chopped from his hand, and Lee Yung spun him into an arm lock from which there was no escape.

"When, my dear Harry Byrd, did you overhear us speaking?"

"Get lost." He would have said more, but his words were

247

drowned in his cry of pain as Lee Yung applied pressure to his arm.

"Come, Harry."

Jeannie walked over to stand by Tang's side, her face expressionless.

Lee Yung put on more pressure, bending him forward.

"Okay. The night I got back into Shanghai; after the Manchurian business. I was at the windows. She was there, yes?"

"Yes, she was there. So you heard many things?"

"I heard that you would sacrifice me. After I had performed one more service for you."

Tang sighed. "Did you hear why?"

"No."

"There is one good reason, Byrd; and many smaller ones. It is, I fear, inevitable."

Byrd craned his head upwards in an attempt to look Jeannie in the eyes, but it only caused more pain for Lee Yung's arm lock bent his body almost double.

"And you," ignoring the pain as best he could, trying to spit the words at her in his fury. "You tried to set me up with Fisher. Did you actually kill the taipan, Geddes?"

The girl turned away, unable to look at him. Tang answered for her.

"She did no killing. There are things you do not know about your sweet little Jeannie Chin. Myself, I only discovered them with the passage of time. For instance, you would not know that she is half Japanese and that her brother – whom she refers to as a Communist – is, in fact, a member of the Black Dragon. I only detected it by chance, Harry Byrd, and you have said many times that I know all things that happen in Shanghai."

Tang sighed again. "You would not know either, that your sweet Jeannie Chin came to you at an opportune time on the express orders of the Black Dragon Society. For a year she has been a spy for them in the Flamingo. She has informed on many things, and it was on her information they decided the Flamingo would be a good investment for them – a base near the Bund. It was Jeannie Chin who

248

provided them with plans of the building, of ways to – is the word infiltrate?"

He paused, sucking in air. He was an old man, and so many words were a burden to him. "I have no doubt that she knew of the bomb placed in your car; and also passed information to the society about the relationship between us. Certainly she saw to it that the little thug was secreted in your apartment to murder you; and I believe she played the actress when they sent Mr. Katachi and his men to deal with you.

"All those attempts failed, so the ultimate treachery followed. I now know she suggested the more subtle way to dispose of you. She had overheard of your appointment with the man Geddes, and was quite prepared to delay you herself, had you been on time. As it turned out you were late anyway, which helped the plot. Geddes was already there, waiting for you, when she admitted the killer provided by the Black Dragon. He shot Geddes and then, when you arrived –" Tang's right fist closed into a ball and he brought it down, hard, on the palm of his left hand. "So you were put to sleep. Unhappily it went wrong for her." He tried his grim smile again. "It went wrong in many ways. You became confused and escaped, while I managed to capture her brother, and also sent men to bring her parents from Woosung. They are kept in good condition, and I took her to see them – after you had disappeared and I had discovered the truth. They remain alive only as long as she does as I say. Jeannie Chin is a good girl and loves her parents much. She works for me with great diligence. She has been my spy during the Black Dragon occupation of the Flamingo."

"You don't know everything, though." Byrd heard his own voice coming out as a croak. Now that he understood the full extent of Jeannie's treachery, and the guile Tang had used to turn her situation to his own advantage, he was both angry and saddened. He realised, too, that only one hope remained.

"No? I do not know everything? Such as?"

Byrd had one last card and knew it. There was no possible chance of withholding it any longer. "Okay, Tang. You have me in a noose. I'll do one more bargain, and this time it's for my life. I have some very special information about the business you're supposed to be transacting tonight. I – I discovered it only this morning." He could hardly admit that he'd been keeping it to himself for months. "I've been trying to get in touch with you all day."

Tang's eyebrows lifted slightly. He nodded to Lee Yung, who took some of the pressure off Byrd's arm, allowing him to straighten a little.

"There is not much you can tell me about that piece of impertinence, Byrd; but I am fair. You can try."

"I want Yung to release me first. And I want my gun back. I'm getting out, Tang. Leaving Shanghai. And I promise you that the information I have will mean more to you than the satisfaction of killing me."

Tang's lips curved. "First also, Harry Byrd, before I agree to anything, let me ask you something. You are not going to tell me what I know already, are you? That the Maes brothers, and their slimy Dr. Zuchestra, were planning to pass me inadequate weapons for good opium?"

Byrd felt the bile rise into his throat, and heard in his mind the craps caller cry 'Snake Eyes': the losing throw. He retched, tried by will power to halt the humiliation; failed as the retch grew, and the terrible nausea turned his stomach. Horribly and violently, Harry Byrd vomited.

四 (4)

Lee Yung put more pressure on Byrd's arm, so that he bent double again, repelled by the stench of the vomit at his feet.

He heard Jeannie crying out, "Harry, I loved you. That part is true. I loved you. The rest was not my fault. I tried. . ." There was the flat, wincing sound of a slap, and, as Lee Yung eased off his arm again, Byrd was able to raise his head and see Jeannie, one hand to her cheek, with Tang just recovering his poise after delivering the blow.

"You disgust me, Byrd." Tang came closer, then backed off because of the unpleasant stink. "You try to buy your life with information a child could have guessed. You are frightened, now; and with reason." He looked around for a suitable chair, pulled it away from Byrd, and sat down. "You disgust me," he repeated. "You come here to this country; this city which has been bought up – piece by piece – and rented like some brothel girl, to plundering Caucasians; and you expect the people who really own it to crawl for you. You want cheap labour and servants; you dishonour our women, and abuse our land; you spread your puny sophistication over a culture so old that, should your societies last for a thousand years, you white men will never match it."

"Listen, you two-bit gangster –" Byrd began, but the bile still in his mouth made it impossible for him to continue.

"Listen?" Tang mocked. "*I* listen to you? No, Harry Byrd. You are like all the others. You come and want to make the quick dollar; make it the easy way. You prey on the Chinese, and on your own race."

"You're not clean either, Foo Tang." Byrd overcame his queasiness.

"Indeed no. But have you known me go against my own, Harry Byrd? Never, because we know what loyalty should be: what it should mean. Gangster you call me; but I am a gangster only because the gang I lead is my family – people I have taken in and nurtured over the years. A family that needs protection, clothing, feeding. They are like children – wilful sometimes, yes; easily led, and a prey to the white rubbish who come here and play the Mandarin over them. Now, Byrd, have you any other special information for me, concerning my transaction with the contemptible Maes brothers and their entourage?"

Byrd shook his head. "No. You seem to have it already."

"Yes. That I was to provide high-grade raw opium for weapons which had been rejected, damaged, were incomplete and bought cheaply by the disreputable criminal

Zuchestra? Useless weapons, and ammunition that was old and unstable. That was all you were going to tell me?"

Byrd nodded, as Tang turned to Jeannie Chin. His English altered, became more carefully enunciated. "Clean up his feet and the floor. Bring his clothes. Later we will require food."

Jeannie bowed and left silently. Hope flared in Byrd's heart. Tang would hardly ask for his clothes if he were going to have him killed immediately.

"When you are tidy and clean, I shall tell you the secrets of negotiation with people like the Maes brothers."

Temporarily reprieved, Byrd found it difficult to direct his mind on to the many new problems which had erupted. He had to listen carefully; gather as much information as possible; and at the same time try to find some lasting way out of his predicament. Now that he had recovered from the first shock, his nerves were calmed by the knowledge that Bingham and the police were watching the Flamingo, and knew the exchange was to take place. Bingham said the authorities wanted to *see 'em nabbed in the act*. If Byrd could survive that long, the police and customs would undoubtedly make their move at some point, always provided that the battle raging down river in Chapei did not stop them.

Even from this apartment, the sound of gun-fire could be clearly heard across the city: the heavy thump of artillery and, occasionally, the fainter crackle of rifle and machine-gun fire. When, he wondered, would the authorities act against Tang? To make a certain case they might wait until the exchange had been made. If that was so, the police would pounce as Tang's people brought the weapons back into Shanghai; and the customs authorities would probably detain the ship – maybe at Woosung, or near the entrance where the Whangpo river entered the mouth of the Yangtze. But that only applied if Tang were still to make the exchange, which surely he would not, now that he knew the full extent of the Maes' intended duplicity.

Jeannie returned with a bowl of warm water, a cloth and his clothes – a pair of slacks, shirt, pullover and jacket; shoes and other necessities – and began to wash the vomit from his feet, cleaning up the floor. Lee Yung still held a tight grip on his arm, and Tang rose from his chair for a moment, to retrieve the Mauser pistol.

"My people?" Byrd asked. "What have you done with my staff?"

Tang frowned. "There – it is still *my* staff; *my* people. You have two Europeans and a Mexican left. I suppose they could be called *your* staff. The girls, apart from the phony Russian princess, are Chinese; as are your boys and waiters. *My* staff, you say." He allowed himself a thin smile, the lips not parting. "They are safe, and will remain so until the transaction is finally settled. I have them locked away in your gaming room, guarded by my own people – two of them, and well armed. The café, for the moment, is closed." He signalled to Yung, indicating he should release Byrd's arm and let him dress, gesturing towards his man with the Mauser, which Yung took from him – hefting it in his hand, checking it was loaded, and then holding it loosely towards Byrd as he dressed.

Jeannie had taken the bowl away and now returned with tea, which she poured, passing dishes to Tang and Byrd. Lee Yung she ignored.

A tap on the door heralded the arrival of another Tang lieutenant, whom Byrd had not seen before; and there was a quick exchange in Chinese.

"The first of my trucks has arrived," Tang told them when the man left. "They are starting to load it now. As the trucks are filled, each will be driven to a rendezvous down river, still just inside the Settlement – near the waterworks and the Woosung railway line. I have doubts if the Japanese forces would dare cross the railway line into the Settlement area; though I am told their warships are moving into the Yangtze. They could easily bombard the Chapei district from up river, past Woosung."

Byrd tried to picture the situation in his mind. The Whangpo river snaked in a tight S-bend, which turned roughly east from the Bund before it settled into a fairly straight run down the twelve miles to Woosung village where it emptied into the Yangtze – then the forty-mile trip to the sea. On the left hand side of the S-bend, moving down river, were the northern and eastern parts of the International Settlement. If Japanese warships anchored off the Shanghai waterworks which were within the eastern part of the Settlement, their guns would easily carry shells over the mile and a half into the Chapei district, to their west. But a few miles down river the buildings began to thin out and there were plenty of places where cutters could ferry to and fro from a ship anchored in the river – always assuming that Foo Tang was in fact still serious about carrying out the exchange.

The sounds of fighting seemed more intense now; above the gun-fire they could plainly hear the buzzing of airplanes. Tang crossed to the window, and a second later louder crumps rattled the building.

"The Japanese appear to have resorted to an aerial bombardment," Tang observed calmly, as though watching some kind of game. "Perhaps they will prefer this to the dangers of bringing warships into the river."

He returned to his seat, and Lee Yung dragged another chair over for Byrd, motioning him to sit. Byrd sipped his tea, deciding that for the time being, docility was to his advantage. The more he could learn now, the easier it would be to work out some kind of strategy.

"You look puzzled, Byrd. All we have to do is stay here in peace until dusk. Then we begin a hard night's labour. Your last night, I should imagine."

"Of course I'm puzzled. If you know about the wretched Maes and their deceit, how can you think of going ahead with this exchange?"

"Ahh," Tang's skull head nodded like that of a porcelain mandarin. "Of course, you do not know why you are to be sacrificed." He took another sip of tea. "Incidentally, you lied when you said you only discovered this morning that the Maes brothers were intent on a dishonest exchange."

Byrd shrugged. He admitted it, saying that he had very nearly come to Foo Tang with the information back in

254

November, but it was a foolish man who did not try to keep something in reserve for emergencies.

Tang appeared to be amused at the irony. "If you had, I doubt the situation would have changed. You see, you obtained the information from the drunken Boris and so, indirectly, did I."

Apparently after Byrd disappeared and Tang had secured Jeannie Chin for his own purposes within the Flamingo, she had told him the facts. Boris had spoken to Byrd in front of Polly Sing, who had repeated the conversation to Jeannie.

"By this time, I knew that Vincent and Valentine Maes were out for your blood, Byrd: that they wanted you with a great desperation. In fact, Valentine Maes gave me his version of what you had done to their criminal organisation in America. I do not wonder they wish to dispose of you in the most painful and prolonged manner."

Tang had seen Valentine Maes, and flatly informed him that the deal was off; that he knew what they were trying to do. Valentine, with Zuchestra, had come clean. They both maintained, however, that the circumstances could be altered. Zuchestra had other, sound weapons at his disposal. They would be slightly more expensive, however. For the right amount of opium and some additional inducement, they would make contact with Vincent in America, and Zuchestra could see to it that the brand new weapons and ammunition were loaded as cargo instead of the rubbish.

"And you trusted them?"

"Not completely. I have proposed certain safeguards. They will see the opium – examine it – but I shall have the weapons examined also. Lee Yung, here, will help me to make certain only the prime materials of war come ashore to me. As each load is taken off, so a consignment of opium will go aboard. And finally the extra cargo. We are to use two motor cutters. I don't think they will try to play me false this time."

"You are giving them more opium?" Byrd asked.

"No, Mr. Byrd. I am giving them you."

A series of heavy explosions rocked the building. The buzzing of Japanese aircraft became louder, then began to dwindle. The sounds of fighting diminished – the distant rattle of occasional weaponry, far away; and only the odd thump of more solid artillery shells. It was as though the battle was orchestrating, counterpointing, the news that Byrd was to be handed over to the Americans.

"But how . . . ?" he began. He had disappeared from Shanghai while all this was taking place. Bingham had spirited him away in total secrecy. Even the police had been of the opinion that he was dead. "How could any of you be so sure that I would return?"

"How? Byrd, give a little thought to my position here. My contacts are many, and spread far across China. It did not take long to discover that you were being held a prisoner of the Japanese at Mukden in Manchuria. Through the same channels I was certain that you would be released. I relied on your ingenuity to slip away from the Black Dragon. Precautions were taken. The logic of the situation was clear to me. You would come to me, and I would deliver you up to the Maes brothers, after allowing you to secure the Flamingo once more. For my future use, you understand. I told the Americans that. They were informed as soon as you returned to Shanghai, and, naturally, they agreed."

Byrd asked what he would have done if things had not worked out? If the Japanese had not released him, or the Black Dragon hoods, or police, had got him first?

Tang said he would have gone ahead anyway. "I would have played them false. I shall still do that." He made a dismissive gesture, as if to show that the talking had finished. All had been said, and there was no point in continuing the discussion. What was left would be action –

that night: a dangerous drive to some arranged point between Shanghai and the village of Woosung; an arduous checking of the items which were to be exchanged, and then, once the work was done, the final handing over of Tang's most prized bargain – Byrd himself.

Byrd asked for cigarettes, which he was given; and Jeannie, instructed by Tang, left the apartment to get food, returning an hour or so later and preparing simple dishes. Occasionally, one of Tang's men would come to the door and report progress in loading the trucks. And all the time Tang's words echoed in Byrd's ears: *I would have played them false. I shall still do that.* Did they mean that there was hope for him after all? He doubted it.

The only time Tang spoke to his captive was to relate news of the battle for Chapei: bulletins were brought by Tang's men when they came to inform him about the opium.

In the late afternoon, the Chinese reported that some of the Japanese warships were anchored off the mouth of the Yangtze. Others had been despatched up the river, presumably to bombard Nanking. The first Japanese Marines had been repulsed in the Chapei district, but more troops had now been landed, and the Chinese 19th Route Army was under severe pressure. Refugees were flooding into the International Settlement zones; there was sniping everywhere to the north, and along the eastern river banks – where they would be going that night – while some Japanese military units were already camped in Hongkew Park.

Byrd was allowed to go to the window and crane out, in the hope of glimpsing some of the action. But below, in Nanking and Bubbling Well Roads, life appeared to be normal. The trams and motors, rickshaws and pedestrians, went about their business, though without their usual speed and good humour, possibly aware that Japanese troops could be sniping their way down these very streets in a day or so.

The sky was heavily overcast and a fine drizzle occasionally swept down from the low cloud. Smoke drifted over the northern and eastern parts of the city, and the crack of Chinese Mauser rifles was carried on the breeze like the breaking of dry twigs. These shots were punctuated by the more solid far-off bump of Japanese Arisakas.

As he watched, Byrd heard the drone of aircraft, and caught sight of Japanese monoplanes – with lumpy radial engines – undercarriage legs sprouting from their squat bodies – turning over the city, snarling in and out of the low cloud. They passed from his view, and a few seconds later there was a ragged thud of Chinese anti-aircraft fire, followed by the ground-shaking detonation of bombs.

Byrd had no desire to see more. He lit another cigarette, and went back to his chair, his mind clinging to the hope that Bingham, the police or customs men, would come to his rescue sooner rather than later.

Tang's men brought the news that the last of the four trucks had been loaded and was on its way to the rendezvous. Within the hour a messenger should return to say the small convoy was ready.

The low clouds, combined with the smoke blown back over the city, made the onset of dusk come earlier than usual. The messenger finally arrived, and Tang announced they soon would be leaving. Jeannie brought them last bowls of tea, and, as she handed Byrd his bowl, she pressed the palm of his hand, indicating the bottom of the vessel. Bending his fingers, he felt a small piece of paper stuck against the china. Accepting the bowl with his left hand, he balled the paper in the palm of his right, and, after a suitable lapse of time, asked if he might visit the bathroom.

They had allowed him this at intervals during the day, Lee Yung having first been despatched to clear it of anything which Byrd might use against himself or his captors. With malevolent thoroughness, Lee Yung had smashed all the mirrors, making Jeannie sweep the shards of glass from the room. Even the light bulb had been taken away. There was nothing Byrd could convert to his advantage, though the visits did allow a few moments' privacy.

There was just enough light coming under the door for him to read the badly-formed pencil scrawl on the crumpled paper – writing in English had not been Jeannie's strong point, but he had taught her the rudiments, and was able to make sense of the note: obviously Jeannie was trying to atone for the damage she had caused.

SORY BOM GO ON SHIP IN LAST LOD OPIUM.

Tang's final retribution. Byrd was mildly surprised. Sacrificing him along with the crew of the *Bel Canto* would never worry Tang, but it seemed he was willing also to see five hundred thousand pounds of raw opium go up in flame and smoke, in order to despatch the Maes brothers, Zuchestra and Boris. There was no alternative, the Chinese clearly considered, if their attempted double-dealing was adequately to be repaid. It was typical of Foo Tang. Byrd might have known already that he was quite capable of such an action, in pursuit of what he would see as just punishment for any who dealt ill with himself or his 'family'.

He flushed the paper away, unlocked the door, and was taken back into the main room where Tang, now on his feet, paced slowly up and down.

"I regret," he looked at Byrd without malice, "that your hands will have to be secured during the journey."

Byrd said there was no need: that he would go quietly; but Tang insisted, and Lee Yung roughly tied his wrists with a short length of cord – but in front of his body rather than behind as he had at first feared.

The cord bit painfully into his wrists. Needing to know the worst, Byrd asked Foo Tang if he had thought of the possibility of police or customs action and, if so, what he planned to do about it.

Tang gave him a look of pity. "You think I have not already taken care of this? It is the one thing I was able to trust Valentine Maes with. I even had a man hidden in the room where it was done; and I suspect that is why you have heard nothing more from the pig-like Fisher. Mr. Valentine Maes bribed Inspector Fisher, with much money, to be certain nobody interfered with the exchange."

At least – Byrd was happily relieved – Tang did not know that Fisher was out of action. Maybe there was still a chance that he would squeeze through.

As the night was cold, coats were brought. Byrd showed surprise that Jeannie Chin also prepared to leave with them. Tang must have seen the look, for he quietly said that he felt she would be safer with them. This was not a night for a girl to be alone in Shanghai. "When we return, it will be Jeannie who will run the Flamingo on my behalf. Your Europeans will be allowed to keep their jobs if they wish to stay."

"If the Japanese don't take it all away from you."

Foo Tang shook his head. "With what I am collecting tonight, we will be able to harass any Japanese for a long time to come. If they do come, however, they will be allowed to use the café, and certain other facilities I can offer them." He came close to Byrd, who could smell the slight odour of incense on the man. "I grow old, Harry Byrd. But my people will live on: generation by generation; they will be flexible, cling to their faith, and finally show the world that, while usurpers and conquerors may come and go, the Chinese will remain and overcome." He flicked his hands towards the door which Lee Yung opened. Then, with Tang leading the way and Lee Yung following Byrd, still lifting the Mauser, they went down the passage, Jeannie Chin bringing up the rear. Past the private room and the office, then descending the curving stairs into the café, darkened and with no sign of life, but for one of Tang's men at the doors on the far side of the entrance lobby.

Tang's large Hotchkiss Chantilly saloon waited in the street outside, and Byrd saw there was a notice attached to the doors of the café proclaiming, in Chinese and English, that *Owing To The State Of Emergency Ordered By The Shanghai Municipal Council, The Flamingo Café Will Be Closed Until The Restrictions Are Lifted.*

The man on guard closed and locked the doors carefully, then ran forward to open the car for Tang. The driver was already inside, and Jeannie sat in front with him. Byrd was placed between Tang and Lee Yung, in the back. Tang leaned back and closed his eyes, as though either very tired, or making a conscious effort to suppress his rising excitement.

Slowly the car pulled away from the kerb, and began its

journey through the darkened streets. Though some of the bars were still open, most of the cafés, restaurants and dance halls were closed, their gaudy electric signs switched off. The effect was depressing – the once-crowded and bustling streets were shorn of their glamour, and appeared merely gim-crack and tawdry.

Within minutes they were driving north-east, towards the river and the Shanghai Municipal Waterworks, down narrow streets, almost devoid of traffic and out of the good-time district which was the whole of Shanghai for the fun-loving residents and visitors. Now the roadways were flanked by crammed dwelling houses and apartment buildings. Lights could be seen through closed shutters, and few people were on the pavements.

"What if there're road blocks? The army?" Byrd asked.

Tang replied without opening his eyes. "Then you will keep silent, or Lee Yung will hurt you badly. You have your knife, Lee Yung?"

The hoodlum nodded in the dim light.

"He will make your last hours most painful. So you will remain silent."

"I meant, how will you get through the road blocks?"

"If there are any. Wait and see. I have all the necessary means."

They turned down into an alleyway in which four dark-painted trucks stood nose-to-tail. They were open vehicles, similar to the one in which Byrd had been taken, with Cat and Bingham, to the barracks at Mukden. Only these had their backs covered with large tarpaulins.

Tang's driver flashed his lights, and the Chantilly edged past the small convoy, the trucks' engines starting up as they went. As they reached the first truck, Byrd saw the driver signal, and the saloon took the lead, with the trucks following close.

They continued to head through built-up streets, moving closer to the river, on the road which ran along beside it, near to the railway line leading downstream to Woosung. Already, long before they reached the open country, they became acutely aware of the fighting. From the left came the flicker and glow of large fires; spreading; tongues of flame visible even at the distance of a mile or so; leaping into the air as though trying to lick at the lowering clouds.

Explosions came from within the heart of the fires: heavy thuds which could be felt through the car itself; while, even over the engine noise, shots, much clearer now, made them cringe down into the heavily-armoured Hotchkiss.

Twice, as they started to edge into open country, there was the whistling whine of some projectile above them. The burning buildings inland, still to their left but almost behind them now, formed a wide torch which, reflected down from the clouds, lit the surrounding fields, and the waters of the river on their right, like day.

A mile into open country, the driver gave a shout and Tang leaned forward. Ahead of them, a barrier had been thrown across the road, and Chinese troops – a dozen or so – stood with rifles pointed towards them.

"This is where you remain very silent, Mr. Byrd," Tang said; and Byrd felt the sharp blade of a knife on his thigh.

Tang had the rear window down long before they were at a standstill. An officer came running up, with a pair of soldiers in attendance. They looked very young, and even the officer appeared nervous: he was shouting and waving them back as he came towards them.

Completely at ease Tang produced an official-looking pile of papers, clipped together in the top left-hand corner. He spoke to the officer slowly and quietly, without a trace of alarm in his voice.

The officer was uncertain, and went forward to examine the papers under the car's headlights, leaving the young soldiers standing by the car; jumpy, their rifles held awkwardly as though they did not really know how to use them, and would not wish to do so anyway.

Byrd had to clamp his teeth together to stop shouting a warning, for Lee Yung had the knife pressed home now, and he could feel its point between his legs. He was sure that Lee Yung was not bluffing. Tang's henchman had waited a long time for a moment such as this.

The officer came back, handed the papers to Tang, spoke

a few words, and then stepped away, waving the other soldiers to lift the barricade. As he did so, something screamed through the air, seemingly above them. The young soldiers flinched, one throwing himself to the ground. Far behind them came the muffled crunch as the shell found its mark. Byrd glanced back, and the fires appeared to have increased, the conflagration bursting upwards over a larger area. From the direction of the flames there was a sudden flurry of firing, carried on the night air so that it seemed near at hand: the mocking – almost cachinnatory – rattle of a machine-gun, ripping in short bursts.

The officer spoke briefly, then waved the convoy on, and they drove away, Tang winding up his window once more.

"You see?" he said, his grim features hideous in the dancing firelight from Chapei.

"Tell me." Byrd felt sick again, suddenly very tired. He had gone through enough. And there must, inevitably, be worse to come.

The documents, Tang told him, were official permits allowing him to take four truck-loads of medical supplies down to Woosung. "The officer told me I was a good man." He smiled coldly. "He also warned me that we should take care – there is much sniping going on along the road."

Byrd felt Lee Yung's knife move from his thigh. He slumped further into his seat, pushing his hands down far between his legs, starting to work on the knotted cord.

They went about a mile along the road, the reflection from the fires growing less, becoming a bloodied glow in the sky behind them.

"Keep a watch out now." Tang spoke to the driver, and Byrd glanced to his right, seeing the river glinting through the grass on its low bank. "Any minute now. Slow down, they'll be on the right here, and the ship should be some three hundred yards in midstream."

Byrd cursed to himself. They had arrived too soon. He had managed to loosen one knot, and was working hard on the next. He looked up quickly as Tang and the driver both exclaimed. In front, and to the right, a light winked out

263

from the river. Then another beside the road; dead ahead.

The car slowed, pulled over – the trucks following – and three figures emerged from the shadows. Tang wound down the window. The muffled sound of gun-fire back towards the city rose and fell. Byrd froze as familiar faces appeared at the open window.

"Gentlemen," Tang spoke in his softest voice. "Your opium is in the trucks: and here is the bonus I promised."

"Good to see you, Henry Beech." Vincent Maes, the eternal cigarette between his lips, was just discernible in the darkness.

"Hope Mr. Tang's been looking after you real good, Henry, because we've got important plans for you, Vince and me." Valentine Maes withdrew his head and spat.

"You got away from me last time, stoolie." Boris Oblosky's face filled the window. "Val chewed me up bad for that. And I don't make the same mistake twice. Vince and Val've given me orders. You're gonna get hurt, Flamingo. Then you're goin' for a nice long swim."

六 (6)

"Nobody gets hurt until we are all satisfied with the exchange of goods." Tang's voice turned sharp, cutting through everything else: the tone of authority.

"Come on now, Mr. Tang," Valentine Maes drawled, leaning arrogantly against the car door. "Be realistic. If we had the mind, we could take the lot of you this minute."

"I think not. Look around yourself, Mr. Maes."

Byrd glanced to right and left, then out of the rear window. Valentine Maes stepped back a pace. More shadows had emerged from the far side of the road, standing like dark statues. Back – from towards Chapei – came a rumble, and the great fire flared brighter for a second, lighting the river bank as Tang violently threw his door open, sending Valentine Maes stumbling back against the side of the car.

Tang called out in Chinese, and there was an answering cry from the shadows across the road. "You see," he swept his arm in a wide arc. "I have men here for the last two days: long before you arrived. We need weapons, yes, but I have to warn you there are two quite good Maxims trained on you. Now, what arrangements have you made?"

Boris looked from Byrd to Vincent Maes, as if expecting some order, but Vincent shook his head. "You won't be disappointed, Mr. Tang. Everything's in order. You'll find the weapons in first-class condition, and Carlo Zuchestra's here to help you check them out."

They moved away, but Byrd could hear the whole conversation clearly. They had got hold of two large converted sampans, which had been stripped of all extraneous gear and fitted with a powerful outboard motor.

They had brought in the first batch of weapons, which were piled in their crates, still in the sampan. The other craft was ready to receive its initial load of opium. There were also a dozen deckhands, from the *Bel Canto*, waiting to help with the lifting and carrying.

"If I might check the opium as it comes out of the trucks, I'll have my men bring the crates up for your examination here." Valentine glanced across the road.

Byrd followed his look. The shapes had disappeared, presumably sinking into the long wet grass. He reflected uneasily that, if any trouble started, he would be caught between the two factions.

Tang shouted orders, and the drivers of his lorries climbed out of their cabs. As he walked towards the first lorry, with Vincent Maes in tow, the driver started the engine of the Chantilly, took it a few yards down the road and turned, so that it came back, parked facing the first truck.

Byrd could see activity going on at the back of this truck – the examinations already taking place under the headlights of the second vehicle. As he watched, the deckhands from the *Bel Canto* started to heft the large crates up from the riverside, placing them in front of the car.

Zuchestra was there, and Tang, giving orders with quick imperious waves of the hand, began to scrutinise the contents of the first crate. All seemed to be in order, for it was soon closed and dragged alongside the first lorry. At the same time, men began to manhandle the heavy drum-like bales of opium – inspected by the Maes brothers – down the bank to the other sampan.

As one crate came up to be examined and checked, so a couple of the large bales of opium were removed to their points of departure; and, as each crate of arms was cleared, so it was moved alongside the truck. When the first truck was finally unloaded, the crates would be heaved into the empty rear, in a well-co-ordinated exercise.

It took around half an hour for the empty sampan to be filled with opium bales, and Tang had still not completed checking the crates already brought over in the first vessel.

As the opium-loaded sampan was about to leave, Tang broke away from the crates and Dr. Zuchestra, returning to the car, speaking with Lee Yung in Chinese.

Lee Yung climbed from the car, said a few words to Jeannie Chin in the front, while Tang leaned through the window.

"Lee Yung is going out to the ship with the first batch of opium, and will supervise its transfer. The sampan will return with more weapons. Your old friend Jeannie Chin, and my driver, will be looking after you, Byrd. But do not get any exalted ideas. She will have a knife, and the driver is an excellent shot. You do anything stupid and I shall have you maimed and given over to Boris straight away."

Boris, who had stayed by the car, his eyes never leaving Byrd since the work began, split his face into a grin. "I'll look after him, Mr. Tang. Don't you worry about that. He's goin' to be mine anyway."

Tang spoke sharply, "Eventually. But keep your distance for the moment."

Boris clenched his huge fists angrily but moved back a pace or two, as the driver shifted his body, turning towards the rear of the car, and Byrd. He now held the Mauser, balanced firmly in his hand.

Jeannie Chin took Lee Yung's place in the rear. She did not speak to Byrd, but held a knife most expertly in her right hand. Boris stood a short distance from the car, watching patiently.

The examination of the crates continued, Byrd's mind working, sluggish, unable to see any way he could get clear without ending up either in Boris' arms or with a lead acupuncture. He tried to work on the cord around his wrists but, with Jeannie so close, it was difficult. Looking out towards the river he saw lights come on at the aft of the *Bel Canto*, showing the ship to be a freighter of some size. She was moored less than three hundred yards offshore, and he could clearly see a deck crane being hoisted out, the bales of opium lifted in a net and swung inboard. There were crates on the deck, and men swarmed around the crane.

In front of them, Tang continued to go through the boxes and weapons with Zuchestra. He smiled, pleased with what he found. Bales of opium were still being taken down to the river bank, for loading into the other sampan as it became empty of the crated arms.

On the ship, the working lights were eventually extinguished. The first sampan was presumably making its return run, ferrying the second consignment of weapons to shore.

The process was repeated. About every half-hour the deck lights would come on while the bales were hoisted aboard, and a new load of arms taken off – the sampans crossing and recrossing the dark stretch of water.

When the first truck was emptied of opium, the weapons were loaded, the tarpaulin replaced, the lorry turned, and driven off to the back of the convoy, placed facing the way it had come, ready for the return. Byrd could not see his watch, but figured that it had taken around an hour and a half to clear the first truck, then stow it with the boxes of weapons. It would be a long night, he thought. And the longer the better, for at its end he would be forced to leave

267

on the doomed *Bel Canto*. Even if, once he was on board, he tried to warn the Maes brothers about the bomb they would not believe him. They would think he was playing for time. And if they did believe him, there was little chance that they would get to the bomb before it exploded.

It must have been nine o'clock when the convoy had arrived at the riverside rendezvous. Four trucks, at an hour and a half's work each, would take them until at least three in the morning: call it four to be on the safe side. Four would just about be Tang's limit if he wanted to get back into Shanghai before dawn. Though there was little question of real darkness there, for the fires in Chapei still flared and grew. Occasionally Byrd could hear the thuds of explosions, and shock waves passed through the earth, shaking the car.

Byrd dozed, then woke with a start. From what he could make out, they had shifted the second truck, and were working on the third. The driver had hardly moved, the barrel of the Mauser pointing unwavering towards him. Jeannie Chin turned her head.

"Driver doesn't speak English," she said.

The driver rapped out something, and Jeannie spat back a couple of words as though she was telling him to mind his own business.

"So?" Byrd saw Tang in the lights ahead, nodding dispassionate approval as Zuchestra held up a Thompson submachine-gun for his inspection.

"I just wanted to say sorry, Harry."

"You said it."

"It is my family. Foo Tang forced me. He would kill them."

"The Americans will kill me. So you've done a good piece of work, Jeannie. Now shut up."

He remained awake after that, hands thrust low between his legs, occasionally shifting his body to cover the attempt to loosen the knots on the cord. He was not doing well, did not fancy his chances, but felt that at least he could put up some kind of fight if his hands were untied.

The pictures in his head ranged from Boris dealing with

the Black Dragon hoods in the bedroom, to Cat and himself back in the city, during their days of happiness. He thought about his success with the Flamingo, and the great times they had gone through when the place was full every night. Somehow he had foolishly imagined that these would go on for ever. He saw Jeannie with him, pleading with him never to leave her, never to stop loving her. Then Jeannie was overlapped by Cat saying similar things, and he again saw the tail lights of the black Fed limo rising and falling, jerking and bumping away from the ranch that had been his hideout after the trial. Lastly, he thought of the nice, happy, harassed Casimir, who would not have hurt a fly, lying soaked in blood where Lee Yung's knife had ripped at him. There must be justice of some kind. Retribution. But life, and death, were not always that easy.

They got to the last truck. Across the river the working lights were on, aft of the *Bel Canto*, the crane out and lowering a crammed net into the flat, waiting sampan.

Tang was resting, leaning against the bonnet of the Chantilly, waiting for the next batch of crates. He pushed himself away from the car and walked around to the rear, Jeannie winding the window down.

"It will not be long now, Byrd. I must thank you, for your presence has made this exchange much more easy for me." The skull face flashed a row of gold-filled teeth. "They put a high price on you. You notice the way the big one – Boris – has not assisted with any of the heavy work? They have assigned him solely to watch you, in case I might still wish to keep hold of you."

Byrd said he had seen. "And you don't want to keep me?"

"Unfortunately, you are too much of a liability. The Black Dragon . . . the police . . . you have too many enemies, Harry Byrd." Tang turned away as the deck-hands, watched by Zuchestra, lowered the heavy boxes into the car's lights.

They were coming very near to the end now. All Byrd could count on was a sudden swoop by the police and customs; with, possibly, Waldo Bingham in attendance.

But, as time passed, he had all but given up hope of even that last-minute reprieve. If it happened after they got him out to the ship it would be of little use anyway the chances of his surviving Tang's bomb were remote. Having had plenty of opportunity to view the Chinese gangster's methods, he knew it would cause a sizeable explosion. Tang needed the ship to be sunk with all hands. The blame, of course, could be put down to a stray shell. The Japanese action had come at a most opportune moment for Foo Tang.

In what seemed to be record time, they cleared out the last truck. Lee Yung reappeared from the river bank, and the final crates and boxes of arms and ammunition arrived. The work seemed to be more concentrated, Tang examining the last boxes in time to supervise the removal of the final bales of opium from the truck.

Yes, he would be there for that, Byrd thought. If only to check whatever explosives were hidden within the bales. He wondered how Tang had fused the device, or, more probably, devices. Some kind of timing mechanism, he supposed – which would account for the efficiency of the transfer and exchange. Tang needed to be well clear, for the margin had to be flexible. Unless of course he could set the mechanism as the final bales were being taken from the truck.

By this time the men were lifting the last bales down to the water, and Tang walked slowly back to the car, the action suggesting weariness. He was accompanied by both of the Maes brothers, and Byrd sensed a movement outside the car. He glanced through the window to see Boris closing in.

The doors opened on both sides. "It is time," Tang said. Then, turning to Vincent and Valentine Maes, "My bargain holds good. You have been honourable and kept your word. I keep mine. Take him."

"Okay," Valentine smirked. "You come with us, Henry. Out."

He began to shuffle his body towards the door, when, unexpectedly, Jeannie Chin leaned over him, wrapping an arm around his neck and putting her lips on his.

"Goodbye, Harry. Remember, whatever else, I did love you. I am sorry."

Tang rapped out that she was to stop this foolishness; but, before Jeannie pulled away, Byrd felt her knife move down between his wrists and slice through the cord. She had warned him of the bomb; now she was giving him at least a fighting chance before going to join the great café owner in the sky, he realised, with a flash of his old spirits.

He kept his wrists together, holding in the cord so that it would not slip away.

As Byrd's feet reached the ground, Boris loomed over him, placing a ham hand on his shoulder and squeezing. For a second, Byrd thought the shoulder would be crushed under his pressure, but Vincent Maes told Boris to go easy until they got on to the ship and under way. There was no hurry. Sea passages could be boring without something to pass the time.

Tang said nothing as the little party went away down the bank to the remaining empty sampan. Across the water, the working lights were on, and the final opium bales appeared to be half-way between the other sampan and the ships; being winched slowly, figures on the deck clustered together so they could unhook the net and get the bales out of sight with all speed.

As they pushed him towards the moored sampan Byrd attempted to assess who was carrying weapons. All of them, probably. Certainly Vincent Maes had an automatic pistol in his right hand. Byrd had seen him take it from the shoulder holster after shaking hands with Tang, and saying farewell.

They pushed him to the forward end of the boat, scrambling in after him, Boris staying close. The outboard engine gave a splutter and started. The deck swayed under them and, within seconds, the sampan was heading away from the river bank.

He could see the line of loaded trucks, now pointing back towards Shanghai; the glow of burning Chapei in the distance; and figures flitting between the headlights. Tang stood in view, in front of the Chantilly, Jeannie at his side.

As they reached the *Bel Canto*, he saw Jeannie Chin raise a hand, then drop it quickly to her side.

The working lights remained on, and the ship towered above them as the sampan slid gently up to the metal ladder running down its side. Faces peered from the deck rails, and Byrd thought he glimpsed one man with a tommy-gun.

"You go up first, Byrd." Vincent Maes sounded weary, the voice flat, almost uninterested.

Byrd said it would be difficult with his hands tied.

"Don't worry about it. Boris is going to see you up." As he spoke, so Boris caught hold of Byrd, lifting him bodily and placing his feet on the third rung of the ladder, positioning his own body directly behind Byrd.

"You just lean back on me, Flamingo. I'll be your arms. You just use the legs."

It was awkward and painful on the thigh muscles. Twice he felt himself slipping sideways as the large ship dipped in the water, but Boris' arm tightened around his hips, preventing him from falling, the great banana-bunch hands moving up in time with Byrd's ascending feet.

Boris gave a childish little giggle. "If I was made different, this could be sexy, Flamingo."

They were half-way up when Byrd realised that it was now or never. Whatever else happened, he was dead once on board the *Bel Canto*.

Now, Byrd thought. Now, as he's shifting his hands. He stopped climbing for a second, glanced down to see there was enough space to launch himself clear without crashing into the sampan. Vincent Maes was climbing slowly behind Boris, while Valentine still stood in the bobbing sampan, one arm on the ladder.

Byrd raised one foot, and then brought it back, hard, into Boris' face. At the same moment he pulled his wrists apart, grabbing with both hands on to the sides of the ladder, and kicked back at Boris' face for a second time – with both feet – hearing a gasp from below, followed by a cry. Boris' right hand had disappeared and, without hesitating, Byrd flung himself clear of the ladder, plunging well away from the sampan.

As he went down he was conscious of Boris clawing the air, falling backwards on top of Vincent Maes: and of the first shots starting to crash out.

七 (7)

Byrd's body seemed to shriek with pain as it hit the icy water. Then there was no feeling as he sank, the cold walled around him, breath knocked from his lungs. He had never felt such cold before, and only the will to live made him move his arms and legs, turning on his belly, straightening out, arms stretched, kicking up towards the surface.

He reached the air to find he was heading in the direction of the river bank, his instinct for survival making him dive deeply again as he heard a whine, and felt the water being plucked nearby; bullets ricochetting, pluming white scars on the water.

The numbness and cold were so great that he did not know if he had been hit by the burst, presuming it had missed simply because he could still move his arms and legs. He kicked and swam, letting the current take him so he might reach the river bank to the right of Tang's convoy. His lungs were protesting, and he thought his brain would burst: it seemed to be swelling inside his skull: pain behind the eyes, lungs finally giving out, and his head about to explode.

He broke surface for a second time, swivelling quickly in the water, conscious of his own chattering teeth, bemused at what he saw. No shots came his way, but there was the beat of engines, moving at speed. He was about a hundred yards from the bank, and, out towards the *Bel Canto*, fresh lights flared up across the water, moving fast.

Shaking the water from his eyes, Byrd tried to make out what was going on. Two fast cutters appeared to be bearing down on the *Bel Canto*, searchlights spearing from their bows, and a voice booming from some kind of megaphone. He could not hear it all, but the voice was shouting for the merchant ship *Bel Canto* to prepare to receive boarders. He also heard the words 'Customs Service'. It was the moment for which he had hoped. If the customs men were now taking action against the Maes brothers, and the *Bel Canto*, it should not be many seconds before the police closed in on Tang's convoy. He struck out towards the bank. A burst of firing came from behind him – away, probably directed at the customs launches. Forcing himself on through the water now; Byrd knew that, if he stopped even for a moment he would most probably give up altogether, for it was as though some surgeon had packed ice into every vein and artery. Then he remembered Tang's extra men and the Maxim guns.

Suddenly there was a heavy fusillade of rifle fire from the shore line. Byrd lifted his head, craning his neck from the water. The police, he thought. The people by Tang's trucks were running, frantically, and he clearly saw a figure; Jeannie Chin, throw up her arms and topple over, rolling down the bank towards the water. Then the Maxims started up.

The firing from the ship and customs launches had become intense, and, as he felt a muddy soft solidity under one foot, a flare rose high into the air behind him, throwing white magnesium light over the whole scene.

There was heavy firing still coming from around Tang's trucks – the solid stutter of the Maxims being returned from the stretch of ground running back from the river bank on to which he was now crawling. He snaked his body into the reeds, pushing his face down as a vicious hail of bullets chopped into the ground above the bank. He heard a grunt of pain from where the bullets had spattered, and another cry from further off. The Maxims were proving their worth.

Squirming through the reeds on to the soggy earth, Byrd pulled himself up the bank. The flare had reached its apogee, and began to sink rapidly, its light diminishing. Yet as Byrd peered over the bank, he could distinguish what was left of a man on the ground, slashed by bullets from one of the Maxims. He had expected to see someone in the uniform of the Shanghai Police Force. Instead, the corpse was in military uniform: a uniform he had known only too well from his experiences at Mukden. For a moment he thought it was an hallucination, the body was unmistakably that of a Japanese soldier.

Another chatter of shots came from behind, about fifty yards to his front, and he caught sight of three or four men, running, bent double, trying to get to the flank of Tang's people.

Crawling forward towards the dead soldier, his will overcoming the pain of returning sensation as the icy numbness of the water started to wear off, Byrd began to reason things out. It was guesswork, but he thought he had a rough explanation for the situation.

From the reports brought to Tang at the Flamingo during the day, he knew the Japanese were said to be landing more troops on the coast and just down river. This must be a small Japanese patrol, moving stealthily along the road, probing forward to report the quickest, most direct route into the fighting zone at Chapei. They had run straight into Tang's people and the pair of Maxims had done deadly work.

Reaching the dead soldier, Byrd shook the Arisaka rifle from the man's hand, his numb fingers fumbling with the bolt action. It appeared to be loaded. Groping inside one of the pouches on the soldier's belt, he pulled out a spare magazine, and managed to get it into his pocket, prising with fingertips which still had almost lost all sense of touch.

Byrd then retreated part of the way back down the river bank, peering into the darkness. There was a shout in Japanese; another burst of firing, followed by the soft pad of running feet. Two Japanese soldiers came panting by, heading back down river: presumably to make their report to the following forces.

The firing stopped. Up on the road he heard one of the trucks' engines start up. Tang was preparing to move back into Shanghai. Byrd slid down into the water and began to wade, as quickly and quietly as possible in the direction of the convoy. He beat his hands against his body, exchanging the rifle from one to the other, in an attempt to bring the blood flow back into his fingers; wading faster now, as another engine started up. There seemed to be problems with the third and fourth, the starters whining but the engines coughing and dying at each attempt.

He was getting near now, almost level with them, for he could hear Tang's voice, raised in fury, shouting at the drivers. Then he realised that, at some time during all this, the firefight had ceased out in the river. He glanced towards the *Bel Canto* to see that she was turning, and the two lines of white spray that were the customs launches, had moved level with the far river bank, searchlights extinguished, shadowing the freighter. There must have been too much firepower from the *Bel Canto* for the two lightly-armed launches to make a successful boarding. He reflected that, for their sakes, it was probably for the best.

Turning his attention back to the noises on the road above him, Byrd's foot caught something soft, heavy, but yielding. He dropped one knee into the icy water and reeds, just as another flare hit the sky directly above. Glancing up, he saw that it came from ahead, in front of the still stationary convoy. The police at last, he hoped.

The light revealed the object in the reeds. Jeannie Chin lay on her back, eyes closed, her face as calm in death as it had been when she slept so peacefully beside him back at the Flamingo. A small trickle of blood smudged the corner of her mouth, and the water around her was brown with the stain of the blood which had pumped from her chest.

Gripped by a combination of fatigue and emotion, Byrd put his arms around her, pulling the limp body to him. He felt the warmth of tears in his eyes, and heard his voice. But through his sobs, he realised that he was repeating, not Jeannie's name but, "Cat . . . Oh Cat . . . dear Cat . . . Why?"

Pitching the Japanese rifle up the bank, Byrd dragged himself forcibly from the tears, confusions, and unhappy memories, gently lowering Jeannie back into the reeds. Above, on the road, there was more shooting, and shouts. Another megaphone voice which he could hear clearly this time.

"Foo Tang, come out: Shanghai Municipal Police. The Japanese troops have gone, but they will probably be back. You are surrounded. We have both your Maxim gunners. Come out."

With relief, Byrd edged himself to the top of the bank. He retrieved the rifle. There were lights – from down the road towards Shanghai, and a few yards inland, almost encircling the convoy of Tang's trucks. The Hotchkiss Chantilly was directly in front of him, motor running, its driver hunched low over the wheel. Behind the vehicle, crouching and reaching up to the rear door, Foo Tang was making a last desperate bid to gain the safety of his car and run the police gauntlet.

A body lay between the river bank and the car: Lee Yung, his chest ripped open by Japanese fire. Tang had his hand on the door now, pulling down on the handle as the police megaphone started up again, the voice saying that time was up and they were closing in.

Byrd acted by instinct alone. The sides of the car were armoured – Foo Tang might well escape. Half rising from the bank he called softly – "Foo Tang. Here. Come quickly. It's your only way. Quickly."

Tang remained motionless, his hands still on the car; then, panicking for once, began to run, an old man's hobble, towards Byrd.

The icy trembling disappeared from Byrd's body, his whole concentration now on the running figure. He allowed Tang to get within a few paces, then straightened up fully, standing in front of the Chinese.

They were so close he could see the sudden look of shock, and naked terror on the skull face.

He did not need to take aim. The rifle butt was firmly tucked into his side, and he fired the first shot low.

Foo Tang went down like a skittle, his legs banged from under him. A claw-like hand came up, opening and closing, reaching towards Byrd, the mouth moving and pleading for mercy.

Byrd spoke quietly, knowing that, even through his pain, Foo Tang would hear him. "This is for Casimir and Jeannie, and all the other suckers." He fired twice, feeling no revulsion as 'Billion Dollar' Tang's terrified face disappeared in a fine spray of blood, tissue and bone. No revulsion; just a sense of relief that he had done what had to be done.

He threw the rifle to one side, yelling loudly – "Police – it's Harry Byrd . . . Over here." He felt his knees go, the cold swarming back through his body, and the ground coming up fast.

Arms lifted him, and as someone wrapped a blanket around him he heard the growl of Waldo Bingham's voice, calling his name.

"You were nearly too late, Waldo," Byrd opened his eyes, and saw the smile on the bulldog face. "I suppose you missed your train."

They helped him to his feet – police everywhere, spreading sheets over the bodies of Foo Tang and Lee Yung; rounding up the other members of Foo Tang's force. Some even worked on the stalled engines of the two trucks.

"There's another body down there," Byrd nodded to the river bank, and Bingham said he was sorry they had cut it so fine.

"Just moving in when the Japs arrived. Saved our bacon really. Didn't know Tang had the Maxims. Only problem is we couldn't stop the ship. Should have used more launches: more firepower."

"Tang's got the ship for you. I shouldn't worry." Byrd smiled to himself, looking back down river, where the *Bel Canto* was now steaming away at full speed. Bingham grunted. He was thinking of something else.

"I presume Tang was about to fire when you shot him?" His heavy eyebrows were raised in ironic query.

Byrd said, of course, and Bingham nodded.

"Better put this by the body, then." He walked over to the sheet which covered the remains of Foo Tang, and dropped an automatic pistol on to the ground beside it. It made a solid thud.

"Get you in the warm, old Byrd, best thing." The large Bingham put a fatherly arm around Byrd's shoulders, and started to lead him up the road to where the police had cars parked. "Ought to be moving fast anyway. The Japs'll presumably mount a heavy offensive along here. Gather they're badly needed at Chapei."

He was about to speak again, when a dull thud, followed by a great blast, rocked across the water. They both span around, to see the crimson bloom of fire and thick smoke shatter the *Bel Canto*. The shock wave hit them a second later, and, as the smoke cleared, the ship lurched to one side, debris still turning and rising in the air as another ball of fire swept through the vessel, its list becoming more pronounced as it finally toppled, turning turtle so that only its rusty keel showed above the surface of the water, like a long and misshapen abscess.

"Told you Tang'd get the ship for you," Byrd said, as the ground appeared to tilt under him, and the strain, numbness and exhaustion took hold, dragging him into unconsciousness yet again. Just before he passed out completely, he felt Bingham's hands reassuringly catch him under the armpits.

八 (8)

The fighting went on for another three weeks. When the Japanese eventually entered Chapei, the district was almost completely in ruins; the Shanghai North Station was gutted and thousands lay dead.

But Byrd knew little of this as he fought for his life, suffering from pneumonia and exhaustion in the Shanghai

General Hospital. Waldo Bingham and Cat told him everything when he was well enough to have visitors.

"I got the greatest story of my life," Cat said. "It seems
I'm a war correspondent now."

Byrd smiled. He said bleakly that he always seemed to
provide Cat with her best stories.

"They'll come again," Bingham declared. "I give Shanghai four years at the most. They've got it lined up. You'd
best sell the Flamingo and come to work for us, Byrd."

Byrd agreed that if things got really bad he would think
about it. Who was to know, then, that the Japanese would
not occupy the city completely until 1937?

Max, Descales and Herman were regular visitors; while
Koo, Hang and one or two of the other senior boys put in an
embarrassed appearance. The girls – particularly Polly Sing
and the beautiful Arina – caused great excitement when they
visited the hospital.

But the times which Byrd relished most were Cat's visits
– when she came on her own. They talked a great deal about
the possibility of starting again. At least they were close
once more, and could think of each other without memories
clouded in bitterness. She had to go back to the States soon,
she told him – if only to sort things out with the magazine
and other syndicates.

Max showed great excitement at the progress they had
made at the Flamingo, since the curfew and State of
Emergency ended. The redecoration was complete and
they all planned a massive party for the first night of Byrd's
return.

There was a point, when they had sent him away for a
couple of weeks' convalescence, when Byrd wondered if he
wanted to return to the Flamingo at all – the place held too
many bad memories mixed up with the good. Sometimes,
on bad nights, he dreamed of Jeannie Chin's body shattered
in the reeds and icy water of the Whangpo; waking and, for
a second, expecting her to be lying there, warm beside
him. His dreams were also haunted by Casimir – smiling,
bowing to clients, his shirt front covered in blood, the
chubby face ghastly in death.

Then there were other times when he would fantasise about the possibility of Cat being there: helping, working with him to build the Flamingo into something bigger. Yet in the realistic depths of his heart, Harry Byrd knew that running the Flamingo Café was not Cat's way.

As it turned out, his first night back at the Flamingo coincided with Cat's last night in Shanghai. Waldo Bingham was leaving also – by ship this time, to make a report to London.

"I shall ask them to put pressure on you, Byrd. Goin' to have you working for us yet."

Byrd only shrugged, and said he asked for one small favour. "Look 'Pearly' Fisher up and get him fixed, will you?" Fisher, they all knew, had been shipped out of Shanghai and returned to London within days of the final showdown.

So, on Byrd's first night back at work, the party took place as Max, Descales and Herman had planned – all three of them proud, and showing genuine joy at having their old boss back in the café. Descales had a brother he wanted Byrd to meet with a view to taking over Casimir's old job. "All Frenchmen have brothers," Bingham commented.

Descales had also provided a special menu, and a large number of the old regulars were present. When Byrd came down from the office – pausing on the curving stairs to light his cigarette – Herman struck up 'Let's Do It', and the applause went on for nearly five minutes.

Arina made a particular play for him throughout the evening; but Byrd really wanted a quiet night with his special friends. He sat at a table, dining and talking until late with Waldo Bingham and Cat.

He talked seriously with Cat, but they both avoided the true issues.

When it was time for them to leave, in the early hours, Bingham grunted his gruff farewells, saying that he would be back in a few months.

"Inevitable. London won't let me rest in Europe. Once a China hand always a bloody China hand." He then tactfully left Byrd alone, at the doors of the Flamingo, with Cat.

He kissed her tenderly, and held her close.

"Don't worry, Harry. I'll write and straighten things out. I'll be back. Please don't worry. I've found you again and we have to pick up the threads. I'll see the editors, then I'll be back so we can talk it all through."

"Sure," Byrd said, putting her into the waiting car.

As the motor disappeared into the early morning traffic of Nanking Road, he did not see the litter of lights, or the ships, dressed overall, down in front of the Bund. He saw the big black limo bouncing its way over the dirt road from the ranch, heading for San Francisco, with Cat's promises ringing in his ears.

Byrd let out a long sigh and turned, slowly walking back into the Flamingo Café to the strains of Herman playing 'Blue Moon'.

JOHN GARDNER

THE DANCING DODO

World War Two scattered the wreckage of countless
warplanes across the countryside of Europe. Thirty years
later, they are just half-buried, harmless hunks of scrap.
Except one. One is different. Hideously different . . .

A bunch of kids playing on Romney Marsh stumbled
across it. The Marauder's Badge was just visible below
the pilot's canopy –

The
Dancing
Dodo

But the DODO didn't fit the record books. And the mystery deepened when ghostly figures were seen near the
site of the wreckage. As David Dobson investigated,
evidence came from wartime archives of a top-secret
Nazi plan that never made the war histories. Evidence of
a nightmare from the past that could become a
holocaust for today . . .

A Royal Mail service in association with the Book Marketing Council & The Booksellers Association.

Post-A-Book is a Post Office trademark.

JOHN GARDNER

THE WEREWOLF TRACE

In the closing hours of the Third Reich Adolf Hitler emerged from his bunker and singled out for special decoration one of the uniformed boys who were the last defenders of Berlin . . .

In 1977 Hitler's 'last hope' is a respectable British businessman, suspected by British Intelligence of being the key to the Nazi revival. But the man code-named 'Werewolf' is haunted by his past. And by something far more terrifying . . .

Was a boy smuggled out of the Fuhrer's bunker? What did he grow into? What kind of political threat does he pose? *THE WEREWOLF TRACE is a stunning story of a nightmare that would never die.*

CORONET BOOKS

JOHN GARDNER

LICENCE RENEWED

James Bond, Ian Fleming's master spy, has returned, and he's better than ever. Miss Moneypenny thinks so and so soon will Lavender Peacock, the beautiful ward of the Laird of Mulcaldy. Bond is drinking a little less these days, and political restraints are squeezing the department – but M still turns first to his top agent when the country needs a trouble-shooter.

And one of these moments has arrived with an ominous meeting between an international terrorist and the top nuclear physicist, the Laird of Mulcaldy. Only James Bond, with his Ruger Super Blackhawk .44 Magnum, his new Saab 900 Turbo and an impressive selection of the latest gadgetry from Q Branch, can challenge a dangerously deranged opponent bent on the destruction of the Western World in a nuclear holocaust . . .

CORONET BOOKS

JOHN GARDNER

FOR SPECIAL SERVICES

With a new pair of Sykes-Fairbairn commando daggers and a new Heckler & Koch VP70 hand gun . . . and the turbo-charged silver Saab 900 ready . . .

With a new woman, even more desirable than Pussy Galore or Lavender Peacock, in his arms . . . and the arch-enemy Blofeld and Spectre back on his hands . . .

The master spy, the ultimate hero is once again ready to serve Her Majesty . . . and thrill his millions of readers with an all-new, brilliant novel of suspense . . .

CORONET BOOKS

JOHN GARDNER

ICEBREAKER

BOND IS BACK in the arms of more beautiful women and on the trail of one of his oldest enemies . . .

BOND IS BACK in a dangerous operation undertaken in collaboration with agents from the United States, the Soviet Union and Israel . . .

BOND IS BACK assigned by M to the freezing forests of northern Finland, near the border with Arctic Russia . . .

BOND IS BACK on his deadliest mission yet!

CORONET BOOKS

ALSO AVAILABLE FROM CORONET